GIUSEPPE · TOMASI DI · LAMPEDUSA

THE LEOPARD

The Sicilian prince, Don Fabrizio, hero of Lampedusa's great and only novel, is described as enormous in size, in intellect, and in sensuality. The book he inhabits shares his dimensions in its evocation of an aristocracy confronting democratic upheaval and the new force of nationalism. In the decades since its publication shortly after the author's death in 1957, THE LEOPARD has come to be regarded as the twentieth century's greatest historical fiction.

EVERYMAN,
I WILL GO WITH THEE,
AND BE THY GUIDE,
IN THY MOST NEED
TO GO BY THY SIDE

GIUSEPPE TOMASI DI LAMPEDUSA

The Leopard
with Two Stories and a Memory

Translated from the Italian by
Archibald Colquhoun

with an Introduction by David Gilmour

EVERYMAN'S   LIBRARY

Alfred A. Knopf New York London Toronto

23

THIS IS A BORZOI BOOK

PUBLISHED BY ALFRED A. KNOPF

First included in Everyman's Library, 1991
Copyright © 1960 by William Collins Sons & Co. Ltd. and Random
House, Inc. (*The Leopard*)
Copyright © 1962 by William Collins Sons & Co. Ltd. and Random
House, Inc. (*Two Stories and a Memory*)
Introduction, Bibliography and Chronology Copyright © 1998
by Everyman's Library
Typography by Peter B. Willberg
Seventh printing (US)

www.randomhouse.com/everymans

The Leopard originally published in Italy as *Il Gattopardo* by
Giangiacomo Feltrinelli Editore
Copyright © 1958 Giangiacomo Feltrinelli Editore
Two Stories and a Memory originally published in Italy as
Raconti by Giangiacomo Feltrinelli Editore
Copyright © 1961 by Giangiacomo Feltrinelli Editore

ISBN 978-0-679-40757-7
LC 91-52980

Library of Congress Cataloging-in-Publication Data
Tomasi di Lampedusa, Giuseppe, 1896–1957.
[Gattopardo.   English]
The leopard / Giuseppe Tomasi di Lampedusa.
p.   cm.—(Everyman's library)
Translation of: Il gattopardo.
Includes bibliographical references.
ISBN 978-0-679-40757-7
I. Title.
PQ4843.O53G313   1991   91-52980
853'.914–dc20   CIP

Book design by Barbara de Wilde and Carol Devine Carson
Typeset in the UK by AccComputing, North Barrow, Somerset
Printed and bound in Germany by GGP Media GmbH, Pössneck

THE LEOPARD

CONTENTS

INTRODUCTION

Noble families seldom suffer such rapid and annihilating decline as the Tomasi di Lampedusa. In two generations this princely Sicilian family passed from wealth to penury, from influence to impotence, from an abundance of male descendants to sheer physical extinction. The last Prince of Lampedusa died, childless and impoverished, in Rome in 1957. He left few possessions except the manuscript of a novel which had recently been rejected by two leading Italian publishers.

The Tomasi, who dubiously claimed descent from the Byzantine Emperor Tiberius, established a Sicilian feudal base in the sixteenth century at Palma di Montechiaro near Agrigento. Although they held the titles of Duke of Palma and Prince of Lampedusa, most of their family found their vocation in the Church rather than in warfare, public service or managing their estates. One heir renounced his inheritance in order to pursue a career that made him a cardinal and – nearly three hundred years later – a saint. In three generations the propensity of the boys to follow their sisters into the Church led the family to the brink of disappearance: on each occasion its survival depended on the health of a single male baby.

The Tomasi di Lampedusa were not one of the greatest landed families of Sicily, those clans with *latifondi* stretching across the interior that were seldom administered or even visited by their owners. But they possessed considerable wealth, augmented in the nineteenth century by the sale of the island of Lampedusa to the King of Naples, and retained it after the unification of Italy. Prince Giulio Fabrizio, the model for *The Leopard*'s protagonist, still held the feudal lands at Palma together with smaller estates in the north as well as villas and a palace in Palermo. He also presided over a large family which seemed to guarantee it against those dangers that had threatened earlier generations: his heir Giuseppe had eight brothers and sisters and was himself the father of five married sons. But the hereditary reluctance to breed reasserted itself among Giuseppe's siblings and his children. Those five sons produced only three children between them, two of whom died young.

The family's extinction was preceded by its economic ruin. In 1885 Giulio Fabrizio died without making a will, an act of carelessness which caused so much discord among his nine children (who now gained equal rights to the property) that the estate was put under judicial administration for sixty years, during which its value was seriously diminished. On his father's death in 1934, the last prince, another Giuseppe, inherited little more than the palace in Palermo, which was destroyed a few years later in air raids shortly before the Allied landings in Sicily. A half-century afterwards its ruins remained largely undisturbed in the centre of the city.

Giuseppe di Lampedusa was born in 1896 and grew up during the Belle Epoque when Palermo enjoyed a twilight revival as a resort frequented by European royalty. The chief influence on his childhood – and on most of the rest of his life – was that of his mother, Beatrice, who came from a more cultured and liberal aristocratic family than the Tomasi. A powerful and extroverted personality, she educated him, nurtured his love for books and almost smothered him with affection. But devastated by the death of her only daughter and frustrated by a tedious marriage, she became possessive and jealous of any other influence over her shy and solitary son. While she encouraged his intellectual interests, her treatment of him as an eternal child even after he reached adulthood was plainly detrimental to his emotional development.

Giuseppe had little in common with his father Don Giulio, a truculent society figure who was said to have an 'infallible eye' in matters of equestrianism. Irritated by his son's incessant reading, Giulio refused his request to study Literature at university and insisted that he read Law instead. It is unlikely that Giuseppe would have made a successful lawyer, but in any case his studies were interrupted by his military call-up in 1915. Two years later, during an Austrian offensive on the Trentino, he was wounded and captured; after a year's imprisonment he returned to the army and was demobilized early in 1920.

For the future author the post-war years were a period of nervous exhaustion and disillusionment. He declined to pursue his legal studies or to follow his uncle, the Marquess of Torretta, into the diplomatic service. Instead he spent much of his time in Palermo reading, acquiring so extensive a knowledge of history and literature that his Piccolo cousins dubbed him *il mostro*, the monster. At the age of thirty he decided to exhibit some of his learning in print, writing three long articles in an obscure Genoese journal on Paul Morand, W. B. Yeats and Julius Caesar. But so far as we know, he wrote nothing else with a view to publication for nearly thirty years.

During the 1920s this diffident young aristocrat travelled frequently to France and Britain. Both countries, their history and their literature, appealed strongly to him. But it was in London, where his uncle spent some years as ambassador, that he was at his happiest. The city on the Thames, he later recalled, was the only place where he could find the satisfaction of 'disappearing, of losing oneself in an ocean, of not being anyone'. He loved browsing among the book stalls of the Charing Cross Road and made literary pilgrimages to all corners of the country: one Sicilian friend teased him for having visited 'every' house in England where a writer had once lived. Years later he told his wife that he had an English temperament, and he was proud of his reserve, his self-control and his ironic sense of humour. He was impressed too by certain phrases and concepts such as 'fair play' and 'the underdog' which led him to make favourable comparisons with the Sicilians. But much as he loved England, he was too shy to make friendships and thus sought consolatory acquaintanceship with the characters of English fiction. For Giuseppe, Falstaff and Micawber were as real as Shakespeare and Dickens, quintessential Englishmen and vicarious friends. He would have sacrificed ten years of his life, he once remarked, for the privilege of spending an hour with Sir John Falstaff.

On a visit to London in 1925 Giuseppe met his uncle's step-daughter, Alessandra Wolff, known as Licy, whose father had been a Latvian baron and a Tsarist official at St Petersburg. That first evening they spent walking from the embassy to

Whitechapel talking about Shakespeare. Seven years later, after she had divorced her Estonian husband, they were married in Riga. But the marriage was not, at any rate to begin with, a great success. An intelligent and formidable woman whose chief interest was Freudian psychoanalysis, Licy clashed with her equally powerful mother-in-law almost immediately she arrived in Sicily. Within a year of the wedding she had returned to Latvia, travelling to Italy to see her husband at Christmas and receiving visits from him in the summer. Their marriage became what one commentator has called *un matrimonio epistolare*, based on a lengthy and rather banal correspondence in French. Only at the end of 1942, when her homeland was threatened a second time by the Russians, did she return to live with Giuseppe in Palermo. At no stage was their marriage a passionate relationship, but in middle age they settle into a contented companionship based on shared literary tastes and a devotion to their dogs.

Lampedusa and his wife lost their ancestral homes at almost the same time. Friends believed that the Prince never really recovered from the destruction of the great Palermo palace, that beloved world of his childhood. He salvaged some of the furniture and most of his books and installed them in a smaller house in a dilapidated quarter on the seafront. But although the new house had one great merit in his eyes – it had once belonged to his great-grandfather – he never really cared for it. In an effort to distract himself he acquired a job for the first time in his life, spending two years at the end of the war as President of the Red Cross in the province of Palermo. But after resigning from the post at the beginning of 1947, he settled back into an existence that revolved around reading in cafés, browsing in book shops and buying cakes and ingredients for his wife's eccentric cooking.

Literature remained, as always, essential to Lampedusa's life. It gave him most of his ideas and much of his happiness, and it also attenuated the heavy depressions to which he was increasingly prone. He never left his house, recalled Licy, 'without a copy of Shakespeare in his bag, with which he would console himself when he saw something disagreeable'; at his bedside he kept *The Pickwick Papers* to comfort him during sleepless nights. In the early 1950s Licy suggested he should give informal seminars to a couple of young students who visited him to talk about literature and history. Lampedusa was delighted with the idea, which gave him a pretext to re-read his favourite authors, and carefully prepared his lessons, filling a thousand pages of manuscript on English literature from Chaucer to Graham Greene. On completing the seminars, he embarked on a somewhat shorter course on French literature, concentrating on the sixteenth century and on Stendhal, whose *Charterhouse of Parma* he regarded as 'the summit of all world fiction'.

Lampedusa's closest friend was his cousin Lucio Piccolo, who lived with his highly eccentric family at Capo d'Orlando, east of Messina on Sicily's northern coast. Lucio was in a learned if amateur way an astronomer, mathematician, poet and musician whose knowledge of literature was almost comparable to his cousin's. The literary rapport between them was so strong and enduring that neither of them bothered to look for other intellectual friends. Visitors to Capo d'Orlando were amazed by their conversation at meals, the literary games, the allusions, the rhymes and intellectual jokes, the attempts to catch each other out. Both of them seemed satisfied with the other as almost sole audience and appreciator of their talent. But in 1954 Lucio sent some of his poems to the poet Eugenio Montale, who was so impressed by them that the unknown Sicilian was invited to a conference at San Pellegrino near Milan and awarded a prize. Lampedusa accompanied him for moral support and thus experienced his solitary contact with Italian writers. He was not greatly impressed by the way they wandered around like marshals of France, and their self-importance prompted the feeling that it was time for him to embark upon a literary career. So did the success of Lucio, whom he had been teasing and trying to deflate for decades. 'Being mathematically certain,' he told a friend the following year, 'that I was no more a fool [than Lucio], I sat down at my desk and wrote a novel.'

The explanation is true but over-simplified. For about twenty years Lampedusa had contemplated writing a novel that would record the vanishing world of his class and the decadence and extinction of his family. More recently his wife had been encouraging him to write in order to mitigate the desolation suffered from the loss of his home and to 'neutralize his nostalgia'. But laziness and diffidence had held him back. He needed incentives, and the year 1954 provided them. As Gioacchino Lanza, the student friend whom he adopted as his son in 1956, observed later, it was the combination of Lucio's prize, the San Pellegrino conference and the literary seminars in Palermo that impelled him to pick up his pen.

There was also a more desperate incentive. Although Lampedusa was only fifty-seven at the time, his poor health gave him the appearance of a man in his seventies. Unaware of the illness that would eventually kill him, he nevertheless realized that he was not well; he was having increasing difficulty with his breathing and was told he had emphysema. If he was ever to redeem through writing what he recognized had been a largely wasted life, he knew he had to begin soon.

The Prince started writing with diffidence. *'Je fais ça pour m'amuser'*, he told Licy, and when his uncle asked what he was doing, scribbling away, he replied, 'Enjoying myself'. Yet this nonchalance was a pretence. Once he had taken the decision to write, he committed himself to his newly-found vocation: during the last thirty months of his life he worked almost every day on his novel and stories, writing in blue biro at a café table or in his library at home.

His first idea was to base the novel on the character of his great-grandfather, Prince Giulio Fabrizio, and to confine the action to the day of Garibaldi's invasion of Sicily in 1860. But finding the time limit too constricting, he decided to divide the novel between 1860, 1885 (the death of his great-grandfather) and 1910, when the fiftieth anniversary of Italian unification would reveal both the shortcomings of the Risorgimento and the decadence of the protagonist's family. In fact the work developed in haphazard form and other years crept in; intended to be a novel of three or four chapters, it was eventually published with eight.

Lampedusa lingered for four months over the opening chapter, writing and re-writing, altering names and changing characters. Writing in Italian was for him an unfamiliar occupation, confined in the past mainly to business letters and his notes on literature; in some ways he was more comfortable in French, which he had used for hundreds of letters to Licy over the previous two decades. Partly as a result of his slow progress, Lampedusa paused after completing the first chapter in order to write the early sections of an autobiography he never finished. Describing the places of his childhood facilitated the composition of future chapters of the novel, particularly the evocation of his maternal family's house at Santa Margherita, which he enlarged and recreated as Donnafugata in *The Leopard*. Further inspiration came from a first visit to his family's old territorial base at Palma, where the princes of Lampedusa had retained the right as 'patron' to enter a former Tomasi palace that an ancestor had turned into an enclosed convent. Afterwards he summed up the visit in his diary with a single word – *commosso* ('moved') – and used it in the second chapter of his novel.

In the autumn of 1955 Lampedusa returned to *The Leopard* and completed a first draft the following March. Its four chapters were rather impetuously despatched to the publisher Mondadori in May under the title *Il Gattopardo*.* During the summer its author decided that the novel was incomplete and added two futher chapters. But even the expanded version failed to please Mondadori's consultant, Elio Vittorini, the Sicilian writer who was a prophet of neo-realism and experiment and who saw himself as a moulder of post-war Italian literature.

The rejection, which reached Lampedusa in December 1956, did not cause him to give up. Indeed the next few months, before learning he had lung cancer in May, were the

---

*A *gattopardo* is not in fact a leopard but a serval or ocelot. However, the inhabitants of one Tomasi estate used to refer to the leopard on the family's coat of arms as a '*gattupardu*', and the title presumably derives from this circumstance. Lampedusa certainly envisaged his protagonist as a proud and massive leopard rather than one of the more meagre cats, but seems to have thought *Il Gattopardo* sounded better than *Il Leopardo*. In foreign editions the animal has enjoyed several metamorphoses, including *Le Guépard* (a cheetah) in French and *De Tijger Kat* (a margay or tiger-cat) in Dutch.

most productive of his life. Apart from adding two more chapters and writing a further draft of the whole book, he composed two short stories and the opening chapter of another novel.

These three fictional fragments are quite unlike each other. The first, *La gioia e la legge* ('Joy and the Law'), is a compassionate tale about a poor clerk and his family in Palermo, a short and unambitious story which nevertheless manages to evoke the corrosive tentacles of Sicilian life and the absurd code of honour under which people have to live. The last is the beginning of an unfinished novel called *I gattini ciechi* ('The Blind Kittens') in which Lampedusa intended to trace the rise and fall of a family of prototype mafiosi. While neither of these pieces is of the same calibre as *The Leopard*, the middle story, *La Sirena* ('The Siren'), reaches the literary standard of the longer masterpiece. The novel has themes that are grand enough, the decay of a noble family, the destruction of its society and the corruption of the Risorgimento ideals. But 'The Siren', an elegy for archaic Sicily, expands them to encompass the ruin of the Mediterranean and the classical world over the subsequent millennia.

At the end of May 1957 Lampedusa learnt that he was suffering from lung cancer. He went to Rome for treatment and spent the last weeks of his life correcting his manuscripts. A few days before his death he received a second rejection from Vittorini, this time in his capacity as a director of Einaudi, who complained that *The Leopard* was 'essayish', unbalanced and 'rather old-fashioned'. The Prince died on 23 July leaving an instruction for his adopted son: 'I would be pleased if the novel were published, but not at my expense'. He knew *The Leopard* deserved publication but he would not countenance the humiliation of having to pay for it.

Early the following year a copy of Lampedusa's manuscript (with six chapters) found its way into the hands of Giorgio Bassani, the young Ferrarese writer, who realized that it was a masterpiece. He travelled to Palermo, received the two further chapters from Licy and Gioacchino, and persuaded Feltrinelli to publish his edited version of the text in November 1958. In his preface Bassani declared *The Leopard* to be an exceptional novel, one of those works which require a lifetime's preparation. A fortnight after publication an enthusiatic review in *La Stampa* set the book along its path of unprecedented popularity. In July of the next year it won the Strega Prize, Italy's leading award for fiction; by the following March, it had gone through fifty-two editions.

No novel in Italian literature has aroused so much passion or caused so much argument. After enthusiastic early reviews from Montale and other leading literati, *The Leopard* came under attack from several directions: from fervent Catholics who disliked its pessimism; from the literary Left which thought novels ought to be avant-garde and 'committed'; from Marxists who attacked its view of history and apparent denial of progress; and from Sicilian apologists who were outraged by its portrayal of Sicily and who argued that Sicilians were no more violent and irrational than other people.

A debate so intense that it spawned more than four hundred articles in Italian cannot adequately be dealt with here. It remains indisputable, however, that by the time all the polemics had died down, Lampedusa's reputation had risen. The radical intelligentsia, which had acquired a virtual monopoly of Italy's literary output since the Second World War, was horrified by a novel which was easy to read, with well-drawn characters and conventional syntax, written by someone who made no concessions to experimentalism or socialist realism. Novelists such as Moravia, Pratolini and an embarrassed Vittorini lined up to denounce it. They were disconcerted, however, when the French writer Louis Aragon, one of the leading Marxist intellectuals of Europe, declared *The Leopard* to be 'one of the great novels of the century, one of the great novels of all time, and perhaps ... the only Italian novel'. It was 'absolutely senseless', he observed, to call it right-wing because Lampedusa's criticism of his class had been not only 'merciless' but even left-wing. After dismissing Moravia's grumbles, Aragon mocked other intellectuals who complained that the book ignored modern techniques, that it owed nothing to Joyce or Proust and that, most heretical of all, it was not 'committed literature'.

Some reviewers claimed that two pages of *The Leopard* could explain more about Sicily than volumes of learned works. But others denied that its author's version of his island had any validity whatever; a Cardinal of Palermo regarded the novel as one of the three factors which contributed to the dishonour of Sicily (the others being the Mafia and the social reformer Danilo Dolci). But the passage of time has done little to confute the Prince's pessimistic and fatalistic views of his birthplace. Leonardo Sciascia, the finest Sicilian writer since Lampedusa, first attacked *The Leopard* for its lack of historical understanding but later admitted that the Prince 'was unfortunately right and we were wrong' about Sicilian history. No one could claim that industrialization and greater prosperity had eradicated the violence, political corruption and other evils of modern Sicily.

Those critics who dismissed *The Leopard* as an historical novel read it carelessly. As E. M. Forster perceptively observed, this 'noble book' was not a historical novel but 'a novel which happens to take place in history'. Of course it says much about Sicily and Italian history, but it is primarily a contemporary novel about the problems and anxieties of a twentieth-century figure, a man in search of spiritual anchors who can no longer find them in the Church. The old certainties have gone, replaced by nothing substantial he can hold on to. Under the skin of his great-grandfather Lampedusa inserted his own anxieties – and those of many of his contemporaries. He thus transformed an account of Garibaldi's impact on Sicily into a work of timeless quality that has already outlived its detractors. The book is more than the memorable evocation of a certain place in a certain epoch. It is a work of art that will survive, long after the last sad palaces of Palermo have gone, because it deals with the central problems of the human experience.

David Gilmour

SELECT BIBLIOGRAPHY

CARDONA, CATERINA, *Lettere a Licy*, Sellerio, Palermo, 1987. A portrait of Lampedusa's marriage which includes much of the couple's correspondence in French.

GILMOUR, DAVID, *The Last Leopard; A Life of Giuseppe di Lampedusa*, Harvill, London, 1996. A biography of the author based on Lampedusa's private papers in Sicily.

ORLANDO, FRANCESCO, *Ricordo di Lampedusa*, Vanni Scheiwiller, Milan, 1963. A memoir of the prince by one of his unofficial students in Palmero.

SAMONA, G.P., *Il Gattopardo, i racconti, Lampedusa*, La Nuova Italia, Florence, 1974. An analysis of Lampedusa's work and the critics' response to it.

TOMASI DI LAMPEDUSA, GIUSEPPE, *Il Gattopardo*, Feltrinelli, Milan, 1960. The Italian edition of *The Leopard*.

TOMASI DI LAMPEDUSA, GIUSEPPE, *Letteratura inglese* (2 vols), Mondadori, Milan, 1990–91. The full text of Lampedusa's 'seminars' on English literature.

TOMASI DI LAMPEDUSA, GIUSEPPE, *Lezioni su Stendhal*, Palermo, 1987. Lampedusa's views on one of his favourite writers.

TOMASI DI LAMPEDUSA, GIUSEPPE, *The Siren & Selected Writings*, Harvill, London, 1995. A collection of three short stories, a childhood autobiography and a selection of Lampedusa's writings on literature.

C H R O N O L O G Y

———

DATE	AUTHOR'S LIFE	LITERARY CONTEXT
1896	Birth of Giuseppe Tomasi in Palermo to Sicilian aristocratic parents, Giulio Tomasi, Duke of Palma (son of the Prince of Lampedusa) and Beatrice Mastrogiovanni Tasca Filangeri di Cutò. Educated privately and then at the Liceo-Ginnasio Garibaldi in Palermo.	Conrad: *An Outcast of the Islands.* Fogazzaro: *The Little World of the Past.*
1897		James: *What Maisie Knew.* Wells: *The Invisible Man.*
1898		James: *The Turn of the Screw.* Svevo: *As a Man Grows Older.* Tolstoy: *What is Art?*
1899		James: *The Awkward Age.* Tolstoy: *Resurrection.*
1900		Conrad: *Lord Jim.* Freud: *The Interpretation of Dreams.*
1901		Capuana: *The Marquis of Roccaverdina.* Mann: *Buddenbrooks.* Serao: *Sister Giovanna of the Cross.*
1902		
1903		Butler: *The Way of All Flesh.* Shaw: *Man and Superman.*
1904		Chekhov: *The Cherry Orchard.* Conrad: *Nostromo.* D'Annunzio: *Alcyone.* Pirandello: *The Late Mattia Pascal.*
1905		
1907		
1908		Forster: *A Room with a View.* Oriani: *The Ideal Revolt.* Pirandello: *On Humour.*
1909		Marinetti publishes first Futurist manifesto.

Italians defeated by Abyssinians at battle of Adowa. Italy recognizes French protectorate over Tunisia.

The Curies discover radium. First performance of Puccini's *Tosca* in Rome.

Boer War (to 1902).

King Umberto I is shot dead by an anarchist; Victor Emmanuel III succeeds. First Zeppelin airship. Planck's 'Quantum Theory'.

Death of Queen Victoria. Death of Giuseppe Verdi. Marconi sends first radio message across Atlantic.

Triple alliance of Germany, Austria and Italy renewed for six years. The campanile of St Mark's cathedral in Venice collapses.
First Wright brothers' flight. Death of Pope Leo XIII in Rome; succeeded by Pope Pius X.
Puccini's *Madam Butterfly* premières in Milan.

'Bloody Sunday' in St Petersburg.
Italian bishops urged to suppress Modernist teaching in schools and press.
Messina earthquake.

Blériot flies English Channel. Henry Ford produces first 'Model T' automobile.

DATE	AUTHOR'S LIFE	LITERARY CONTEXT
1910		Fogazzaro: *Leila*. Forster: *Howards End*.
1911		Gozzano: *Conversations*.
1912		Mann: *Death in Venice*. Papini: *The Failure*.
1913		Lawrence: *Sons and Lovers*. Proust: *Remembrance of Things Past* (to 1927).
1914	Briefly studies Law at Genoa and Rome universities (to 1915).	Campana: *Orphic Songs*. Joyce: *Dubliners*.
1915	Called up for military service.	Ford: *The Good Soldier*. Lawrence: *The Rainbow*.
1916		Chiarelli: *The Mask and the Face*. Joyce: *A Portrait of the Artist as a Young Man*.
1917	Wounded and captured by Austrian troops near Asiago.	Pirandello: *It Is So! (If You Think It Is)*.
1918		Antonelli: *The Man who Met Himself*.
1919		Birth of Primo Levi. Ungaretti: *The Joy of Shipwrecks*.
1920	Demobilized.	Lawrence: *Women in Love*. Tozzi: *Three Crosses*; *Diary of a Clerk*.
1921		Pirandello: *Six Characters in Search of an Author*. Tozzi: *The Farm*.
1922		Birth of Pasolini. Eliot: *The Waste Land*. Joyce: *Ulysses*. Pirandello: *Henry IV*.
1923		Birth of Italo Calvino. Svevo: *The Confessions of Zeno*.
1924		Ford: *Parade's End* (to 1928). Hemingway: *In Our Time*. Mann: The Magic Mountain. Pirandello: *Each in His own Way*.

CHRONOLOGY

DATE	AUTHOR'S LIFE	LITERARY CONTEXT
1925		Bulgakov: *The White Guard.* Eliot: *Poems 1905–1925.* Fitzgerald: *The Great Gatsby.* Kafka: *The Trial.* Montale: *Cuttlefish Bones.* Woolf: *Mrs Dalloway.*
1926–7	Writes three articles for the Genoese journal, *Le Opere e i Giorni.*	Kafka: *The Castle.*
1927		Cather: *Death Comes for the Archbishop.* Hesse: *Steppenwolf.* Woolf: *To the Lighthouse.*
1928		Bulgakov: *The Master and Margarita* (to 1940). Lawrence: *Lady Chatterley's Lover.*
1929		Hemingway: *A Farewell to Arms.* Moravia: *The Time of Indifference.*
1930		Alvaro: *Revolt in Aspromonte.* Musil: *The Man Without Qualities* (vol. 1). Pirandello: *Tonight We Improvise.* Quasimodo: *Water and Land.*
1932	Marries Alessandra Wolff in Riga.	Céline: *Journey to the End of the Night.* Quasimodo: *Sunken Oboe.* Roth: *The Radetzky March.*
1933		Ungaretti: *The Feeling of Time.*
1934	Succeeds his father as Prince of Lampedusa.	Palazzeschi: *The Sisters Materassi.* Waugh: *A Handful of Dust.*
1935		Canetti: *Auto da Fé.*
1936		Céline: *Death on Credit.* Pavese: *Hard Labour.*
1937		Hemingway: *To Have and Have Not.* Silone: *Bread and Wine.*
1938		Bacchelli: *The Mill on the Po* (to 1940). Greene: *Brighton Rock.* Sartre: *Nausea.*

CHRONOLOGY

First television broadcast. General Strike in Britain.

Lindbergh flies Atlantic.

The Grand Fascist Council becomes the supreme legislative body in Italy; Electoral Law reduces electorate from 10 million to 3 million.

Wall Street Crash; beginning of the Depression. Lateran Treaty establishes independent Vatican City.

Election of Roosevelt in USA. Nazis become largest party in German Reichstag.

Hitler becomes Chancellor of Germany; declaration of the Third Reich. Britain, France, Italy and Germany sign non-aggression pact.

France, Britain and Italy agree to form united front against German rearmament. Italian Fascist troops march into Abyssinia.
Civil War in Spain (to 1939). Mussolini anounces anti-Communist Axis with Germany, urging Britain and France to join.
Japan joins Italy and Germany in anti-Communist pact. Japan invades China.

Germany annexes Austria and invades Czechoslovakia. Mussolini abolishes Chamber of Deputies.

DATE	AUTHOR'S LIFE	LITERARY CONTEXT
1939		Joyce: *Finnegans Wake.* Montale: *Occasions.*
1940	Called up but discharged from Italian army for health reasons without seeing active service (1942).	Buzzati: *The Tartar Steppe.* Greene: *The Power and the Glory.* Hemingway: *For Whom the Bell Tolls.*
1941		Pavese: *The Harvesters.* Vittorini: *In Sicily.*
1942		Camus: *The Stranger.* Quasimodo: *And it's Suddenly Evening.*
1943	Palazzo Lampedusa in Palermo largely destroyed in Allied bombing raid.	Montale: *The Storm and Others* (to 1954). Saint-Exupéry: *The Little Prince.*
1944	Works as president of the Palermo provincial committee of the Italian Red Cross (to 1947).	
1945		Borges: *Fictions.* Carlo Levi: *Christ Stopped at Eboli.* Sartre: *The Age of Reason.* Waugh: *Brideshead Revisited.*
1946		De Filippo: *Filumena Marturano.*
1947		Calvino: *The Path to the Nest of Spiders.* Camus: *The Plague.* Gramsci: *Letters from Prison.* Mann: *Doctor Faustus.* Moravia: *The Women of Rome.* Pavese: *Dialogues with Leucò.* Pratolini: *A Tale of Poor Lovers.* Quasimodo: *Day After Day.* Ungaretti: *Life of a Man.* Vittorini: *The Twilight of the Elephant.*
1948		Gramsci: *Notebooks* (to 1951). Ionesco: *The Bald Prima Donna.* Vittorini: *The Red Carnation.*

CHRONOLOGY

DATE	AUTHOR'S LIFE	LITERARY CONTEXT
1949		de Beauvoir: *The Second Sex*. Calvino: *Adam, One Afternoon, and Other Stories*. Orwell: *Nineteen Eighty-Four*. Quasimodo: *Life is Not Dream*. Vittorini: *Women of Messina*.
1950		Pavese: *The Moon and the Bonfires*; death of Pavese. Ungaretti: *The Promised Land*.
1951		Moravia: *The Conformist*.
1952		Beckett: *Waiting for Godot*. Calvino: *The Cloven Viscount*. Cassola: *Fausto and Anna*.
1953	Begins informal seminars on English literature with Francesco Orlando and Gioacchino Lanza.	
1954		Cassola: *Timber Cutting*. Soldati: *The Capri Letters*.
1955	Starts writing *The Leopard*.	Nabokov: *Lolita*. Pasolini: *The Ragazzi*. Pratolini: *Metello*.
1956	Completes first draft of *The Leopard*, which is rejected by Mondadori; writes the short stories.	Sciascia: *Salt in the Wound*.
1957	Writes further draft of *The Leopard*, which is rejected by Einaudi; dies of lung cancer in Rome on 23 July.	Barthes: *Mythologies*. Gadda: *That Awful Mess on the Via Merulana*. Moravia: *Two Women*; *Roman Tales*. Pasolini: *The Ashes of Gramsci*. Pasternak: *Doctor Zhivago* receives first publication in Milan.
1958	*The Leopard* is published by Mondadori in Milan.	Calvino: *Short Stories*. Primo Levi: *If This is a Man*. Pasolini: *A Violent Life*. Sciascia: *Sicilian Uncles*.
1959	*The Leopard* wins the Strega Prize.	
1982	Death of Lampedusa's wife.	

CHRONOLOGY

Foundation of NATO (Italy is one of founding members).

India declares herself independent republic. Korean War (to 1953).

Discovery of DNA. Death of Stalin.

Suez Crisis.

Treaty of Rome sets up European Economic Community: France, Italy, West Germany, Belgium, Holland and Luxembourg.

THE LEOPARD

Contents

I
Introduction to the Prince

'*Nunc et in hora mortis nostrae. Amen.*'

The daily recital of the Rosary was over. For half an hour the steady voice of the Prince had recalled the Sorrowful and the Glorious Mysteries; for half an hour other voices had interwoven a lilting hum from which, now and again, would chime some unlikely word; love, virginity, death; and during that hum the whole aspect of the rococo drawing-room seemed to change; even the parrots spreading iridescent wings over the silken walls appeared abashed; even the Magdalen between the two windows looked a penitent and not just a handsome blonde lost in some dubious daydream as she usually was.

Now, as the voices fell silent, everything dropped back into its usual order or disorder. Bendicò, the Great Dane, grieved at exclusion, came wagging its tail through the door by which the servants had left. The women rose slowly to their feet, their oscillating skirts as they withdrew baring bit by bit the naked figures from mythology painted all over the milky depths of the tiles. Only an Andromeda remained covered by the soutane of Father Pirrone, still deep in extra prayer, and it was some time before she could sight the silvery Perseus swooping down to her aid and her kiss.

The divinities frescoed on the ceiling awoke. The troops of Tritons and Dryads, hurtling across from hill and sea amid clouds of cyclamen pink towards a transfigured Conca d'Oro and bent on glorifying the House of Salina, seemed suddenly so overwhelmed with exaltation as to discard the most elementary rules of perspective; meanwhile the major Gods and Goddesses, the Princes among Gods, thunderous Jove and frowning Mars and languid Venus, had already preceded the mob of minor deities and were amiably supporting the blue armorial shield of the Leopard. They knew that for the next twenty-three and a half hours they would be lords of the villa once again. On the walls the monkeys went back to pulling faces at the cockatoos.

Beneath this Palermitan Olympus the mortals of the Salina family were also dropping speedily from mystic spheres. The girls resettled the folds in their dresses, exchanged blue-eyed glances and snatches of school-girl slang; for over a month, ever since the outbreaks of the Fourth of April, they had been home for safety's sake from their convent, and regretting the canopied dormitories and collective cosiness of the Holy Redeemer. The boys were already scuffling with each other for possession of a medal of San Francesco di Paola; the eldest, the heir, the young Duke Paolo, longing to smoke and afraid of doing so in his parents' presence, was squeezing through his pocket the braided straw of his cigar-case. His gaunt face was veiled in brooding melancholy; it had been a bad day; Guiscard, his Irish sorrel, had seemed off form, and Fanny had apparently been unable (or unwilling) to send him her usual lilac-tinted billet-doux. Of what avail then, to him, was the Incarnation of his Saviour?

Restless and domineering, the Princess dropped her rosary brusquely into her jet-fringed bag, while her fine crazy eyes glanced round at her slaves of children and her tyrant of a husband, over whom her diminutive body yearned vainly for loving dominion.

Meanwhile he himself, the Prince, had risen to his feet; the sudden movement of his huge frame made the floor tremble, and a glint of pride flashed in his light-blue eyes at this fleeting confirmation of his lordship over both humans and their works.

Now he was settling the huge scarlet missal on the chair which had been put in front of him during his recitation of the Rosary, putting back the handkerchief on which he had been kneeling, and a touch of irritation clouded his brow as his eye fell on a tiny coffee stain which had had the presumption, since that morning, to fleck the vast white expanse of his waistcoat.

Not that he was fat; just very large and very strong; in houses inhabited by common mortals his head would touch the lowest rosette on the chandeliers; his fingers could twist a ducat coin as if it were mere paper; and there was constant coming and going between Villa Salina and a silversmith's for the straightening of forks and spoons which, in some fit of controlled rage at table, he had coiled into a hoop. But those fingers could also stroke and knead with the most exquisite delicacy, as his wife Maria Stella knew to her cost; while up in his private observatory at the top of the house the gleaming screws, caps and studs of telescopes, lenses and 'comet-finders' seemed inviolate beneath his gentle manipulations.

The rays of the westering sun, still high on that May afternoon, lit up the Prince's rosy hue and honey-coloured skin; these betrayed the German origin of his mother, the Princess Carolina whose haughtiness had frozen the easy-going court of the Two Sicilies thirty years before. But in his blood also fermented other German strains particularly disturbing to a Sicilian aristocrat in the year 1860, however attractive his fair skin and hair amid all that olive and black; an authoritarian temperament, a certain rigidity of morals, and a propensity for abstract ideas; these, in the relaxing atmosphere of Palermo society, had changed respectively into capricious arrogance, recurring moral scruples and contempt for his own relatives and friends, all of whom seemed to him mere driftwood in the languid meandering stream of Sicilian pragmatism.

In a family which for centuries had been incapable even of adding up their own expenditure and subtracting their own debts he was the first (and last) to have a genuine bent for mathematics; this he had applied to astronomy, and by his work gained a certain official recognition and a great deal of personal pleasure. In his mind, now, pride and mathematical analysis were so linked as to give him an illusion that the stars obeyed his calculations too (as, in fact, they seemed to be doing) and that the two small planets which he had discovered (Salina and Speedy he had called them, after his main estate and a shooting-dog he had been particularly fond of) would spread the fame of his family throughout the empty spaces between Mars and Jupiter, thus transforming the frescoes in the villa from the adulatory to the prophetic.

Between the pride and intellectuality of his mother and the sensuality and irresponsibility of his father, poor Prince Fabrizio lived in perpetual discontent under his Jove-like frown, watching the ruin of his own class and his own inheritance without ever making, still less wanting to make, any move towards saving it.

That half hour between Rosary and dinner was one of the least irritating moments of his day, and for hours beforehand he would savour its rather uncertain calm.

With a wildly excited Bendicò bounding ahead of him he went down the short flight of steps into the garden. Enclosed between three walls and a side of the house, its seclusion gave it the air of a cemetery, accentuated by the parallel little mounds bounding the irrigation canals and looking like the graves of very tall, very thin giants. Plants were growing in thick disorder on the reddish clay; flowers sprouted in all directions: and the myrtle hedges seemed put there to prevent movement rather than guide it. At the end a statue of Flora speckled with yellow-black lichen exhibited her centuries-old charms with an air of resignation; on each side were benches holding quilted cushions, also of grey marble; and in a corner the gold of an acacia tree introduced a sudden note of gaiety. Every sod seemed to exude a yearning for beauty soon muted by languor.

But the garden, hemmed and almost squashed between these barriers, was exhaling scents that were cloying, fleshy and slightly putrid, like the aromatic liquids distilled from the relics of certain saints; the carnations superimposed their pungence on the formal fragrance of roses and the oily emanations of magnolias drooping in corners; and somewhere beneath it all was a faint smell of mint mingling with a nursery whiff of acacia and a jammy one of myrtle; from a grove beyond the wall came an erotic waft of early orange-blossom.

It was a garden for the blind: a constant offence to the eyes, a pleasure strong if somewhat crude to the nose. The *Paul Neyron* roses, whose cuttings he had himself bought in Paris, had degenerated; first stimulated and then enfeebled by the strong if languid pull of Sicilian earth, burnt by apocalyptic Julys, they had changed into objects like flesh-coloured cabbages, obscene and distilling a dense almost indecent scent which no French horticulturist would have dared hope for. The Prince put one under his nose and seemed to be sniffing the thigh of a dancer from the

Opera. Bendicò, to whom it was also proffered, drew back in disgust and hurried off in search of healthier sensations amid dead lizards and manure.

But the heavy scents of the garden brought on a gloomy train of thought for the Prince: 'It smells all right here now; but a month ago . . .'

He remembered the nausea diffused throughout the entire villa by certain sweetish odours before their cause was traced: the corpse of a young soldier of the Fifth Regiment of Sharp-shooters who had been wounded in the skirmish with the rebels at San Lorenzo and come up there to die, all alone, under a lemon tree. They had found him lying face downwards in the thick clover, his face covered in blood and vomit, crawling with ants, his nails dug into the soil; a pile of purplish intestines had formed a puddle under his bandoleer. Russo the agent had discovered this object, turned it over, covered its face with his red handkerchief, thrust the guts back into the gaping stomach with some twigs, and then covered the wound with the blue flaps of the cloak; spitting continuously with disgust, mean-while, not right on, but very near the body. And all this with meticulous care. 'Those swine stink even when they're dead.' It had been the only epitaph to that derelict death.

After bemused fellow-soldiers had taken the body away (and yes, dragged it along by the shoulders to a cart so that the pup-pet's stuffing fell out again), a *De Profundis* for the soul of the unknown youth was added to the evening Rosary; and now that the conscience of the ladies in the house seemed placated, the subject was never mentioned again.

The Prince went and scratched a little lichen off the feet of the Flora and then began to stroll up and down; the lowering sun threw an immense shadow of him over the grave-like flowerbeds.

No, the dead man had not been mentioned again; and anyway soldiers presumably become soldiers for exactly that, to die in defence of their king. But the image of that gutted corpse often recurred, as if asking to be given peace in the only possible way the Prince could give it; by justifying that last agony on grounds of general necessity. And then around would rise other even less attractive ghosts. Dying for somebody or for something, that was perfectly normal, of course: but the person dying should know, or at least feel sure, that someone knows for whom or for what he is dying; the disfigured face was asking just that; and that was where the haze began.

'He died for the King, of course, my dear Fabrizio, obviously,' would have been the answer of his brother-in-law Màlvica had the Prince asked him, and Màlvica was always the chosen spokesman of most of their friends. 'For the King, who stands for order, continuity, decency, honour, right; for the King, who is sole defender of the Church, sole bulwark against the dispersal of property, the "Sect's" eventual aim.' Fine words, these, pointing to all that lay dearest and deepest in the Prince's heart. But there was, even so, something that didn't quite ring true. The King, all right. He knew the King well or rather the one who had just died; the present one was only a seminarist dressed up as a general. And the old King had really not been worth much. 'But you're not reasoning, my dear Fabrizio,' Màlvica would reply, 'one particular sovereign may not be up to it, yet the idea of monarchy is still the same.'

That was true, too; but kings who personify an idea should not, cannot, fall below a certain level for generations; if they do, my dear brother-in-law, the idea suffers too.

He was sitting on a bench, inertly watching the devastation wrought by Bendicò in the flowerbeds; every now and again the dog would turn innocent eyes towards him as if asking for praise at labour done: fourteen carnations broken off, half a hedge torn apart, an irrigation channel blocked. How human! 'Good Bendicò, come here.' And the animal hurried up and put its earthy nostrils into his hand, anxious to show it had forgiven this silly interruption of a fine job of work.

Those audiences! All those audiences granted him by King Ferdinand at Caserta, at Capodimonte, at Portici, Naples, any-where at all.

Beside the chamberlain on duty, chatting as he guided with a cocked hat under an arm and the latest Neapolitan slang on his lips, they would move through innumerable rooms of superb architecture and revolting décor (just like the Bourbon monarchy itself), plunge into dirty passages and up ill-kept stairs, and finally emerge into an ante-chamber filled with waiting people; closed faces of police spies, avid faces of petitioners. The chamberlain apologised, pushed through this mob, and led him towards another ante-chamber reserved for members of the Court; a little blue and silver room of the period of Charles III. After a short wait a lackey tapped at the door and they were admitted into the August Presence.

The private study was small and consciously simple; on the white-washed walls hung a portrait of King Francis I and one, with an acid ill-tempered expression, of the reigning Queen; above the mantelpiece was a Madonna by Andrea del Sarto look-ing astounded at finding herself in the company of coloured lithographs representing obscure Neapolitan saints and sanctu-aries; on a side table stood a wax statuette of the Child Jesus with a votive light before it; and the modest desk was heaped with papers, white, yellow and blue; the whole administration of the kingdom here attained its final phase, that of signature by His Majesty (D.G.).

Behind this paper barricade was the King. He was already standing so as not to be seen getting up; the King with his pallid heavy face between fairish side-whiskers, with his rough cloth military jacket under which burst a purple cataract of trousers. He gave a step forward with his right hand out and bent for the hand-kiss which he would then refuse.

'Well, Salina, blessings on you!' His Neapolitan accent was far stronger than the chamberlain's.

'I must beg Your Majesty to excuse me for not wearing court dress; I am only just passing through Naples; but I did not wish to forgo paying my respects to Your Revered Person.'

'Nonsense, Salina, nonsense: you know you're always at home here at Caserta.'

'At home, of course,' he repeated, sitting down behind the desk and waiting a second before indicating to his guest to sit down too.

'And how are the little girls?' The Prince realised that now was the moment to produce a play on words both salacious and edifying.

'Little girls, Your Majesty? At my age and under the sacred bonds of matrimony?'

The King's mouth laughed as his hands primly settled the papers before him. 'Those I'd never let myself refer to, Salina. I was asking about your little daughters, your little princesses. Concetta, now, that dear godchild of ours, she must be getting quite big, isn't she, almost grown up?'

From family he passed to science. 'Salina, you're an honour not only to yourself but to the whole kingdom! A fine thing, science, unless it takes to attacking religion!' After this, however, the mask of the Friend was put aside, and in its place assumed that of the Severe Sovereign. 'Tell me, Salina, what do they think of Castelcicala down in Sicily?'

Salina had never heard a good word for the Lieutenant-General of Sicily from either Royalists or Liberals, but not wanting to let a friend down he parried and kept to generalities. 'A great gentleman, a true hero, maybe a little old for the fatigues of the Lieutenant-Generalcy ...'

The King's face darkened; Salina was refusing to act the spy. So Salina was no use to him. Leaning both hands on his desk he prepared the dismissal: 'I've so much work! the whole Kingdom rests on these shoulders of mine.' Now for a bit of sweetening: out of the drawer came the friendly mask again. 'When you pass through Naples next, Salina, come and show your Concetta to the Queen. She's too young to be presented, I know, but there's nothing against our arranging a little dinner for her, is there? Sweets to the sweet, as they say. Well, Salina, 'bye and be good!'

On one occasion, though, the dismissal had not been so amiable. The Prince had made his second bow while backing out when the King called after him, 'Hey, Salina, listen. They tell me you've some odd friends in Palermo. That nephew of yours, Falconeri ... Why don't you knock some sense into him?'

'But, Your Majesty, Tancredi thinks of nothing but women and cards.'

The King lost patience; 'Take care, Salina, take care. You're responsible, remember, you're his guardian. Tell him to look after that neck of his. You may withdraw.'

Repassing now through the sumptuously second-rate rooms

on his way to sign the Queen's book, he felt suddenly discouraged. That plebeian cordiality had depressed him as much as the polite grins. Lucky those who could interpret such familiarity as friendship, such threats as royal might. He could not. And as he exchanged gossip with the impeccable chamberlain he was asking himself what was destined to succeed this monarchy which bore the marks of death upon its face. The Piedmontese, the so-called *Galantuomo* who was getting himself so talked of from that little out-of-the-way capital of his? Wouldn't things be just the same? Just Torinese instead of Neapolitan dialect; that's all.

He had reached the book. He signed: Fabrizio Corbera, Prince of Salina.

Or maybe the Republic of Don Peppino Mazzini? 'No thanks. I'd just be plain Signor Corbera.'

And the long jog back to Naples did not soothe him. Nor even the thought of an appointment with Cora Danolo.

This being the case, then, what should he do? Just cling to the status quo and avoid leaps in the dark? Then he would have to put up with more rattle of firing-squads like that which had resounded a short time before through a squalid square in Palermo; and what use were they, anyway? 'One never achieves anything by going bang! bang! Does one, Bendicò?'

'Ding! Ding! Ding!' rang the bell for dinner. Bendicò rushed ahead with mouth watering in anticipation. 'Just like a Piedmontese!' thought Salina as he moved back up the steps.

Dinner at Villa Salina was served with the slightly shabby grandeur then customary in the Kingdom of the Two Sicilies. The number of those taking part (fourteen in all, with the master and mistress of the house, children, governesses and tutors) was itself enough to give the dining-table an imposing air. Covered with a fine but mended lace cloth, it glittered under a powerful carcel-lamp hung precariously under the Murano chandelier. Daylight was still streaming through the windows, but the white figures in painted bas-relief against the dark backgrounds of the door-mantels were already lost in shadow. The silver was massive and the glass splendid, bearing on smooth medallions amid cut

Bohemian ware the initials F.D. (*Ferdinandus dedit*) in memory
of royal munificence; but the plates, each signed by an illustrious
artist, were mere survivors of many a scullion's massacre and
originated from different services. The biggest, vaguely Capodimonte, their wide almond-green borders engraved with little
gilt anchors, were reserved for the Prince, who liked everything
round him to be on his own scale except his wife.

When he entered the dining-room the whole party was
already assembled, only the Princess sitting, the rest standing
behind their chairs. Opposite his own chair, flanked by a pile of
plates, swelled the silver flanks of the enormous soup tureen
with its cover surmounted by a prancing Leopard. The Prince
ladled out the *minestra* himself, a pleasant chore, symbol of his
proud duties as paterfamilias. That evening, though, there came
a sound that had not been heard for some time, a threatening
tinkle of the ladle against a side of the tureen; sign of great
though still controlled anger, one of the most terrifying sounds
in the world, as one of his sons used to call it even forty years
later. The Prince had noticed that the sixteen-year-old Francesco Paolo was not in his place. The lad entered at once
('Excuse me, Papa') and sat down. He was not reproved, but
Father Pirrone, whose duties were more or less those of sheep-
dog, bent his head and muttered a prayer. The bomb did not
explode, but the gust from its passage had swept the table and
ruined the dinner all the same. As they ate in silence the Prince's
blue eyes, narrowed behind half-closed lids, stared at his children
one by one and numbed them with fear.

But, 'A fine family,' he was thinking. The girls plump, glowing, with gay little dimples, and between the forehead and nose
that frown which was the hereditary mark of the Salina; the
males slim but wiry, wearing an expression of fashionable melancholy as they wielded knives and forks with subdued violence.
One of them had been away for two years: Giovanni, the second
son, the most loved, the most difficult. One fine day he had
vanished from home and there had been no news of him for two
months. Then a cold but respectful letter arrived from London
with apologies for any anxiety he had caused, reassurances about
his health, and the strange statement that he preferred a modest

life as clerk in a coal depot to a pampered (read: 'fettered') existence in the ease of Palermo. Often a twinge of anxiety for the errant youth in that foggy and heretical city would prick the Prince's heart and torture him. His face grew darker than ever.

It grew so dark that the Princess, sitting next to him, put out her childlike hand and stroked the powerful paw reposing on the tablecloth. A thoughtless gesture, which loosed a whole chain of reactions in him; irritation at being pitied, then a surge of sensuality, not however directed towards her who had aroused it. Into the Prince's mind flashed a picture of Mariannina with her head deep in a pillow. He raised a dry voice: 'Domenico,' he said to a lackey, 'go and tell Don Antonio to harness the bays in the brougham; I'll be going down to Palermo immediately after dinner.' A glance into his wife's eyes, which had gone glassy, made him regret his order: but as it was quite out of the question to withdraw instructions already given, he persevered and even added a jeer to his cruelty; 'Father Pirrone, you will come with me; we'll be back by eleven; you can spend a couple of hours at your Mother-house with your friends.'

There could obviously be no valid reason for visiting Palermo at night in those disordered times, except some low love-adventure; and taking the family chaplain as companion was sheer offensive arrogance. So at least Father Pirrone felt, and was offended, though of course he acquiesced.

The last medlar had scarcely been eaten when the carriage wheels were heard crunching under the porch; in the hall, as a lackey handed the Prince his top hat and the Jesuit his tricorne, the Princess, now on the verge of tears, made a last attempt to hold him – vain as ever: 'But Fabrizio, in times like these ... with the streets full of soldiers, of hooligans ... why, anything might happen.'

'Nonsense,' he snapped, 'nonsense, Stella; what could happen? Everyone knows me; there aren't many men as tall in Palermo. I'll see you later.' And he placed a hurried kiss on her still unfurrowed brow which was level with his chin. But, whether the smell of the Princess's skin had called up tender memories, or whether the penitential steps of Father Pirrone behind him evoked pious warnings, on reaching the carriage door he very nearly did countermand the trip. At that moment, just as he was opening his mouth to order the carriage back to the stables, a loud shriek of 'Fabrizio, my Fabrizio!' followed by a scream, reached him from the window above. The Princess was having one of her fits of hysteria. 'Drive on,' said he to the coachman on the box holding a whip diagonally across his paunch. 'Drive on, down to Palermo and leave Father at his Mother-house,' and he banged the carriage door before the lackey could shut it.

It was not dark yet and the road meandered on, very white, deep between high walls. As they came out of the Salina property they passed on the left the half-ruined Falconeri villa, owned by Tancredi, his nephew and ward. A spendthrift father, married to the Prince's sister, had squandered his whole fortune and then died. It was one of those total ruins which engulfed even the silver braid on liveries; and when the widow died the King had conferred the guardianship of her son, then aged fourteen, on his uncle Salina. The lad, scarcely known before, had become very dear to the irascible Prince, who perceived in him a riotous zest for life and a frivolous temperament contradicted by sudden serious moods. Though the Prince never admitted it to himself, he would have preferred the lad as his heir to that booby Paolo. Now, at twenty-one, Tancredi was enjoying life on the money which his uncle never grudged him, even from his own pocket. 'I wonder what the silly boy is up to now?' thought the Prince as they drove past Villa Falconeri, whose huge bougainvillaea cascaded over the gates like swags of episcopal silk, lending a deceptive air of gaiety to the dark.

'What is he up to now?' For King Ferdinand, in speaking of the young man's undesirable acquaintances, had been wrong to mention the matter but right in his facts. Swept up in a circle of gamblers and so-called 'light' ladies, all dominated by his slim charm, Tancredi had actually got to the point of sympathising with the 'Sect' and getting in touch with the secret National Committee; maybe he drew money from them as well as from the Royal coffers. It had taken the Prince a great deal of labour and trouble, visits to a sceptical Castelcicala and an over-polite

Maniscalco, to prevent the youth getting into real trouble after the 4th of April 'riots'. That hadn't been too good; on the other hand Tancredi could never do wrong in his uncle's eyes: so the real fault lay with the times, these confused times in which a young man of good family wasn't even free to play a game of faro without involving himself with compromising acquaintanceships. Bad times.

'Bad times, Your Excellency.' The voice of Father Pirrone sounded like an echo of his thoughts. Squeezed into a corner of the brougham, hemmed in by the massive Prince, subject to that same Prince's bullying, the Jesuit was suffering in body and conscience, and, being a man of parts himself, was now transposing his own ephemeral discomfort into the perennial realms of history. 'Look, Excellency,' and he pointed to the mountain heights around the Conca d'Oro still visible in the last dusk. On their slopes and peaks glimmered dozens of flickering lights, bonfires lit every night by the rebel bands, silent threats to the city of palaces and convents. They looked like lights that burn in sick-rooms during the final nights.

'I can see, Father, I can see,' and it occurred to him that perhaps Tancredi was beside one of those ill-omened fires, his aristocratic hands stoking on twigs being burnt to damage just such hands as his. 'A fine guardian I am, with my ward up to any nonsense that passes through his head.'

The road was now beginning to slope gently downhill and Palermo could be seen very close, plunged in total darkness, its low shuttered houses weighed down by the huge edifices of convents and monasteries. There were dozens of these, all vast, often grouped in twos or threes, for women and for men, for rich and poor, nobles and plebeians, for Jesuits, Benedictines, Franciscans, Capuchins, Carmelites, Liguorians, Augustinians ... Here and there squat domes rose higher, in flaccid curves like breasts emptied of milk; but it was the religious houses which gave the city its grimness and its character, its sedateness and also the sense of death which not even the vibrant Sicilian light could ever manage to disperse. And at that hour, at night, they were despots of the scene. It was against them really that the bonfires were lit on the hills, stoked by men who were themselves very like those living in the monasteries below, as fanatical, as self-absorbed, as avid for power or rather for the idleness which was, for them, the purpose of power.

This was what the Prince was thinking as the bays trotted down the slope; thoughts in contrast to his real self, caused by anxiety about Tancredi and by the sensual urge which turned him against the restrictions embodied by religious houses.

Now the road was crossing orange groves in flower, and the nuptial scent of the blossoms absorbed the rest as a full moon does a landscape; the smell of sweating horses, the smell of leather from the carriage upholstery, the smell of Prince and the smell of Jesuit, were all cancelled out by that Islamic perfume evoking houris and fleshly joys beyond the grave.

It even touched Father Pirrone. 'How lovely this would be, Excellency, if . . .'

'If there weren't so many Jesuits,' thought the Prince, his delicious anticipations interrupted by the priest's voice. At once he regretted this rudeness of thought, and his big hand tapped his old friend's tricorne.

Where the suburbs began, at Villa Airoldi, the carriage was stopped by a patrol. Voices from Apulia, voices from Naples, called a halt, bayonets glittered under a wavering lantern; but a sergeant soon recognised the Prince sitting there with his top hat on his knees. 'Excuse us, Excellency, pass on.' And a soldier was even told to get up on to the box so that the carriage would have no more trouble at other block posts. The loaded carriage moved on more slowly, round Villa Ranchibile, through Torrerosse and the orchards of Villafranca, and entered the city by Porta Maqueda. Outside the Caffè Romeres at the *Quattro Canti di Campagna* officers from units on guard were sitting laughing and eating huge ices. But that was the only sign of life in the entire city; the deserted streets echoed only to the rhythmic march of pickets on their rounds, passing with white bandoleers crossed over their chests. On each side were continuous monastery walls, the Monastery of the Mountain, of the Stigmata, of the Cross-Bearers, of the Theatines, massive, black as pitch, immersed in a sleep that seemed like the end of all things.

'I'll fetch you in a couple of hours, Father. Pray well.'

And poor Pirrone knocked confusedly at the door of the Jesuit Mother-house, Casa Professa, as the brougham wheeled off down a side street.

Leaving the carriage at his palace, the Prince set off for his destination on foot. It was a short walk, but through a quarter of ill repute. Soldiers in full equipment, who had obviously just slipped away from the patrols bivouacked in the squares, were issuing with shining eyes from little houses on whose balconies pots of basil explained their ease of entry. Sinister-looking youths in wide trousers were quarrelling in the guttural grunts Sicilians use in anger. In the distance echoed shots from nervous sentries. Once past this district his route skirted the Cala; in the old fishing port decaying boats bobbed up and down, desolate as mangy dogs.

'I'm a sinner, I know, doubly a sinner, by Divine Law and by Stella's human love. There's no doubt of that, and tomorrow I'll go and confess to Father Pirrone.' He smiled to himself at the thought that it might be superfluous, so certain must the Jesuit be of his sins of today. And then a spirit of quibble came over him again. 'I'm sinning, it's true, but I'm sinning so as not to sin worse, to stop this sensual nagging, to tear this thorn out of my flesh and avoid worse trouble. That the Lord knows.' Suddenly he was swept by a gust of tenderness towards himself. 'I'm just a poor, weak creature,' he thought as his heavy steps crunched the dirty gravel. 'I'm weak and without support. Stella! oh, well, the Lord knows how much I've loved her; but I was married at twenty. And now she's too bossy, as well as too old.' His moment of weakness passed. 'But I've still got my vigour; and how can I find satisfaction with a woman who makes the sign of the Cross in bed before every embrace and then at the critical moment just cries, *"Gesummaria!"* When we married and she was sixteen I found that rather exalting; but now ... seven children I've had with her, seven; and never once have I seen her navel. Is that right?' Now he was almost shouting, whipped by this odd anguish, 'Is it right? I ask you all!' And he turned to the portico of the Catena. 'Why, she's the real sinner!'

Comforted by this reassuring discovery he gave a firm knock at Mariannina's door.

Two hours later he was in his brougham on the way home with Father Pirrone beside him. The latter was worried; his colleagues had been telling him about the political situation which was, it seemed, much tenser than it looked from the detached calm of Villa Salina. There was fear of a landing by the Piedmontese in the south of the island, near Sciacca; the authorities had noticed a silent ferment among the people; at the first sign of weakening control the city rabble would take to looting and rape. The Jesuit Fathers were thoroughly alarmed and three of them, the oldest, had left for Naples by the afternoon packet-boat, taking their archives with them. 'May the Lord protect us and spare this holy Kingdom!'

The Prince scarcely listened. He was immersed in sated ease tinged with disgust. Mariannina had looked at him with her big opaque peasant's eyes, had refused him nothing, and been humble and compliant in every way. A kind of Bendicò in a silk petticoat. In a moment of particularly intense pleasure he had heard her exclaim 'My Prince!' He smiled again with satisfaction at the thought. Much better than '*mon chat*' or '*mon singe blond*' produced in equivalent moments by Sarah, the Parisian slut he had frequented three years ago when the Astronomical Congress gave him a gold medal at the Sorbonne. Better than '*mon chat*', no doubt of that; much better than '*Gesummaria!*'; no sacrilege at least. A good girl, Mariannina; next time he visited he'd bring her three lengths of crimson silk.

But how sad too: that manhandled, youthful flesh, that resigned lubricity; and what about him, what was he? A pig, just a pig! Suddenly there occurred to him a verse read by chance in a Paris bookshop while glancing at a volume by someone whose name he had forgotten, one of those poets the French incubate and forget next week. He could see once more the lemon-yellow pile of unsold copies, the page, an uneven page, and heard again the verses ending a jumble of a poem:

> . . . *donnez-moi la force et le courage*
> *de contempler mon coeur et mon corps sans dégoût.*

And as Father Pirrone went worrying on about a person called La Farina and another called Crispi, the Prince dozed off into a kind of tense euphoria, lulled by the trotting of the bays on whose plump flanks quivered the light from the carriage lamps. He woke up at the turning by Villa Falconeri. 'Oh, he's a fine one too, tending bonfires that'll destroy him!'

In the matrimonial bedroom, glancing at poor Stella with her hair well tucked into her nightcap, sighing as she slept in the great brass bed, he felt touched. 'Seven children she's given me and she's been mine alone.' A faint whiff of valerian drifted through the room, last vestige of her crisis of hysterics. 'Poor little Stella,' he murmured pityingly as he climbed into bed. The hours passed and he could not sleep; a powerful hand was stoking three fires in his mind; Mariannina's caresses, those French verses, the threatening pyres on the hills.

Towards dawn, however, the Princess had occasion to make the sign of the Cross.

Next morning the sun lit on a refreshed Prince. He had taken his coffee and was shaving in front of the mirror in a red and black flowered dressing-gown. Bendicò was leaning a heavy head on one of his slippers. As he shaved his right cheek he noticed in the mirror a face behind his own, the face of a young man, thin and elegant with a shy, quizzical look. He did not turn round and went on shaving. 'Well, Tancredi, where were you last night?'

'Good morning, Nuncle. Where was I? Oh, just out with friends. An innocent night. Not like a certain person I know who went down to Palermo for some fun!'

The Prince concentrated on shaving the difficult bit between lips and chin. His nephew's slightly nasal voice had such a youthful zest that it was impossible to be angry; but he might allow himself a touch of surprise. He turned and with his towel under his chin looked his nephew up and down. The young man was in shooting kit, a long tight jacket, high leggings. 'And who was this person, may I ask?'

'Yourself, Nuncle, yourself. I saw you with my own eyes, at the Villa Airoldi block-post, as you were talking to the sergeant. A fine thing at your age! With a priest too! Old rips!'

Really this was a little too insolent. Tancredi thought he could allow himself anything. Dark blue eyes, the eyes of his mother,

his own eyes, gazed laughingly at him through half-closed lids.
The Prince was offended; the boy didn't know where to stop;
but he could not bring himself to reprove him: and anyway he
was quite right. 'Why are you dressed up like that, though?
What's on? A fancy-dress ball in the morning?'

The youth went serious; his triangular face took on an unexpectedly manly look. 'I'm leaving, Uncle, leaving in an hour.
I came to say good-bye.'

Poor Salina felt his heart tighten. 'A duel?'

'A big duel, Uncle. A duel with Francis-by-the-Grace-of-
God . . . I'm off into the hills at Ficuzza; don't tell a soul, specially
Paolo. Great things are in the offing and I don't want to stay at
home. Anyway I'd be arrested at once if I did.'

The Prince had one of his visions: a savage guerrilla skirmish,
shots in the woods, and Tancredi, his Tancredi, lying on the
ground with his guts hanging out like that poor soldier. 'You're
mad, my boy, to go with those people! They're all *mafia* men,
all crooks. A Falconeri should be with us, for the King.'

The eyes began smiling again. 'For the King, yes, of course.
But which King?' The lad had one of those sudden serious
moods which made him so mysterious and so endearing. 'Unless
we ourselves take a hand now, they'll foist a republic on us. If
we want things to stay as they are, things will have to change.
D'you understand?' Rather moved, he embraced his uncle.
'Well, good-bye, for now. I'll be back with the tricolour.' The
rhetoric of those friends of his had touched Tancredi a little too;
and yet, no, there was a tone in that nasal voice which undercut
the emphasis.

What a boy! Talking rubbish and contradicting it at the same
time. And all that Paolo of his had on his mind probably at that
moment was Guiscard's digestion! This was his real son! The
Prince jumped up, pulled the towel from his neck and rum-
maged in a drawer. 'Tancredi, Tancredi, wait!' He ran after his
nephew, slipped a roll of gold pieces into his pocket, and
squeezed his shoulder.

The other laughed. 'You're subsidising the Revolution now!
Thank you, Nuncle, see you soon; and my respects to my aunt.'
And off he rushed down the stairs.

Bendicò was called from following his friend with joyous barks through the villa, the Prince's shave was over, his face washed. The valet came to help him into shoes and clothes. 'The tricolour! Tricolour indeed! They fill their mouths with these words, the scamps. What's it got, that geometric emblem, that aping of the French, compared to our white banner with its golden lily in the centre? What hope can those clashing colours bring 'em?' It was now the moment for the monumental black satin cravat to be wound round his neck: a difficult operation during which political worries were best suspended. One turn, two turns, three turns. The big delicate hands smoothed out the folds, settled the overlaps, pinned into the silk the little head of Medusa with ruby eyes. 'A clean waistcoat. Can't you see this one's dirty?' The valet stood up on tiptoe to help him into a frockcoat of brown cloth; he proffered a handkerchief with three drops of bergamot. Keys, watch and chain, money, the Prince put in a pocket himself. Then he glanced in a mirror; no doubt about it, he was still a fine-looking man. 'Old play-boy indeed! A bad joke, that one of Tancredi's! I'd like to see him at my age, all skin and bone as he is!'

His vigorous steps made the windows tinkle in the rooms he crossed. The house was calm, luminous, ornate; above all it was his own. On his way downstairs he suddenly understood that remark of Tancredi 'if we want things to stay as they are ...' Tancredi would go a long way: he'd always thought so.

The estate office was still empty, lit silently by the sun through closed shutters. Although the scene of more frivolity than any-where else in the villa, its appearance was of calm austerity. On white-washed walls, reflected in wax-polished tiles, hung enormous pictures representing the various Salina estates; there, in bright colours contrasting with the gold and black frame, was Salina, the island of the twin mountains, surrounded by a sea of white-flecked waves on which pranced beflagged galleons; Querceta, its low houses grouped round the rustic church on which were converging groups of bluish-coloured pilgrims; Ragattisi tucked under mountain gorges: Argivocale, tiny in contrast to the vast plains of corn dotted with hard-working

peasants; Donnafugata with its baroque palace, goal of coaches
in scarlet and green and gilt, loaded with women, wine and
violins; and many others, all protected by a taut reassuring sky
and by the Leopard grinning between long whiskers. Each picture was jocund – each illustrating the enlightened rule, direct
or delegated, of the House of Salina. Ingenuous masterpieces of
rustic art from the previous century; useless though at showing
boundaries, or detailing tenures or tenancies; such matters
remained obscure. The wealth of centuries had been transmuted
into ornament, luxury, pleasure; no more; the abolition of feudal
rights had swept away duties with privileges; wealth, like old
wine, had let the dregs of greed, even of care and prudence, fall
to the bottom of the barrel, preserving only verve and colour.
And thus eventually it cancelled itself out; this wealth which had
achieved its own object was now composed only of essential oils
– and like essential oils soon evaporated. Already some of the
estates which looked so gay in those pictures had taken wing,
leaving behind only bright-coloured paintings and names.
Others seemed like those September swallows which though
still present are already grouped stridently on trees, ready for
departure. But there were so many; endless, they seemed.

In spite of this the sensation felt by the Prince on entering his
own office was, as always, an unpleasant one. In the centre of
the room towered a huge desk, with dozens of drawers, niches,
sockets, hollows and folding shelves; its mass of yellow wood
and black inlay was carved and decorated like a stage set, full of
unexpected, uneven surfaces, of secret drawers which no one
knew now how to work except thieves. It was covered with
papers and, although the Prince had taken care that most of
these referred to the starry regions of astronomy, there were
quite enough of others to fill his princely heart with dismay.
Suddenly he was reminded of King Ferdinand's desk at Caserta,
also covered with papers needing decisions by which the King
illuded himself to be influencing the course of fate, actually
flowing on its own in another valley.

Salina thought of a medicine recently discovered in the
United States of America which could prevent suffering even
during the most serious operations and produce serenity amid

disaster. Morphia was the name given to this crude substitute for the stoicism of the ancients and for Christian fortitude. With the late King, poor man, phantom administration had taken the place of morphia; he, Salina, had a more refined recipe: astronomy. And thrusting away the memory of lost Ragattisi and precarious Argivocale, he plunged into reading the latest number of the *Journal des Savants*. '*Les dernières observations de l'Observatoire de Greenwich présentent un intérêt tout particulier . . .*'

But he was soon exiled from these stellar realms. In came Don Ciccio Ferrara, the accountant. He was a scraggy little man who hid the deluded and rapacious mind of a Liberal behind reassuring spectacles and immaculate cravats. That morning he looked brisker than usual; obviously the same news which had depressed Father Pirrone had acted as a tonic on him. 'Sad times, Excellency,' he said, after the usual ritual greetings. 'Big troubles ahead, but after a bit of bother and a shot or two things will turn out for the best: then glorious new days will dawn for this Sicily of ours; if it weren't that so many fine lads are sure to get killed, we should be really pleased.'

The Prince grunted and expressed no opinion. 'Don Ciccio,' he said then, 'the Querceta rents need looking into: we haven't had a thing from them for two years.'

'The books are ready, Your Excellency.' It was the magic phrase. 'I only have to write to Don Angela Maza to send out collectors: I will prepare the letter for your signature this very day.'

He went to turn over the huge registers. In them, with two years' delay, were inscribed in minute writing all the Salina accounts, except for the really important ones. When he was alone again the Prince waited a little before soaring back through the clouds. He felt irritated not so much by the events themselves as by the stupidity of Don Ciccio, whom he sensed at once to represent the class which would now be gaining power. 'What the fellow says is the very contrary of the truth. Regretting the fine lads who're sure to die! there'll be very few of those, if I'm any judge of the two adversaries; not a single casualty more than is strictly necessary for a victory bulletin, whether compiled at Naples or Turin. But he does believe in "glorious new days for this Sicily of ours" as he puts it; these have been promised us on every single one of the thousand invasions we've had, by Nicias onwards, and they've never come. And why should they come, anyway? What will happen next? Oh, well. Just negotiations punctuated by a little harmless shooting, then all will be the same though all will be changed.' Into his mind had come Tancredi's ambiguous words, which he now found himself really understanding. Reassured, he ceased turning over the pages of the scientific review and looked up at the scorched slopes of Monte Pellegrino, scarred like the face of misery by eternal ravines.

Soon afterwards appeared Russo, whom the Prince found the most significant of his dependants. Clever, dressed rather smartly in a striped velvet jacket, with greedy eyes below a remorseless forehead, the Prince found him a perfect specimen of a class on its way up. He was obsequious too, and even sincerely friendly in a way, for his cheating was done in the certainty of exercising a right. 'I can imagine how Your Excellency must be worried by Signorino Tancredi's departure; but he won't be away long, I'm sure, and all will end well.' Again the Prince found himself facing one of the enigmas of Sicily; in this secret island, where houses are barred and peasants refuse to admit they even know the way to their own village in clear view on a hillock within a few minutes' walk, here, in spite of the ostentatious show of mystery, reserve is a myth.

He signed to Russo to sit down and stared him in the eyes. 'Pietro, let's talk to each other man to man. You're involved in all this too, aren't you?' No, came the answer, not actually; he had a family and such risks were for young men like Signorino Tancredi. 'I'd never hide anything from Your Excellency, who's like a father to me.' (Yet three months before he had hidden in his cellar three hundred baskets of lemons belonging to the Prince, and he knew that the Prince knew.) 'But I must say that my heart is with them, those bold lads.' He got up to let in Bendicò, who was making the door shake under his friendly impetus. Then he sat down again. 'Your Excellency knows we can stand no more; searches, questions, nagging about every little thing, a police-spy at every corner of the street; an honest man can't even look after his own affairs. Afterwards, though, we'll have liberty, security, lighter taxes, ease, trade. Everything will be better; the only ones to lose will be the priests. But the Lord protects poor folk like me, not them.'

The Prince smiled. He knew that he, Russo, was at that moment trying through intermediaries to buy the estate of Argivocale. 'There will be a day or two of shooting and trouble, but Villa Salina will be safe as a rock; Your Excellency is our father, I have many friends here. The Piedmontese will come cap in hand to pay Your Excellencies their respects. And then you are also the uncle, the guardian of Don Tancredi!'

The Prince felt humiliated, reduced to the rank of one protected by Russo's friends; his only merit, as far as he could see, was being uncle to that urchin Tancredi. 'In a week's time I'll find my life's only safe because I keep Bendicò.' He squeezed one of the dog's ears so hard that the poor creature whined, honoured doubtless but in pain.

Shortly afterwards a remark of Russo's relieved the Prince. 'Everything will be better, believe me, Excellency. Honest and able men will have a chance to get ahead, that's all. The rest will be as it was before.' All that these people, these petty local Liberals wanted, was to find ways of making more money themselves. No more. The swallows would take wing a little sooner, that was all. Anyway there were still plenty in the nest.

'You may be right. Who knows?' Now he had penetrated all the hidden meanings; the enigmatic words of Tancredi, the rhetorical ones of Ferrara, the false but revealing ones of Russo, had yielded their reassuring secret. Much would happen, but all would be play-acting; a noisy, romantic play with a few spots of blood on the comic costumes. This was a country of arrangements, with none of that frenzy of the French; and anyway, had anything really serious happened in France, except for June of '48? He felt like saying to Russo, but his innate courtesy held him back, 'I understand now; you don't want to destroy us, who are your "fathers". You just want to take our places. Gently, nicely, maybe even putting a few thousand ducats in our pockets. And what then? Your nephew, my dear Russo, will sincerely believe himself a baron; maybe you, because of your name, will become descendant of a grand duke of Muscovy instead of some red-skinned peasant, which is what that name of yours means. And long before that your daughter will have married one of us, perhaps Tancredi himself, with his blue eyes and his willowy hands. She's good-looking, anyway, and once she's learned to wash . . . For all will be the same, just as it is now: except for an imperceptible change round of classes. My Court Chamberlain's gilt keys, my cherry-coloured cordon of St Januarius will stay in a drawer and end up in some glass case of Paolo's son. But the Salina will remain the Salina; they may even get some sort of compensation; a seat in the Sardinian Senate, that pistachio ribbon of St Maurice. Both have tassels, after all.'

He got up. 'Pietro, talk to your friends, will you? There are girls here. They mustn't be alarmed.'

'I felt that, Excellency, and have already spoken of it – Villa Salina will be quiet as a convent,' and he smiled with amiable irony.

Don Fabrizio went out followed by Bendicò; he wanted to go up and see Father Pirrone, but the dog's yearning look forced him out into the garden; for Bendicò had thrilling memories of the fine work he'd put in the night before, and wanted to finish it off like a good artist. The garden was even more odorous than the day before, and under the morning sun the gold of the acacia tree clashed less. 'What about our King and Queen, though, what about them? And what about the principle of legitimacy?' The thought disturbed him a moment, he could not avoid it. For a second he felt like Màlvica. Those Ferdinands, those Francises that had been so despised, seemed for a moment like elder brothers, trusting, just, affectionate, true kings. But the defence forces of his inner calm always on the alert in the Prince were already hurrying to his aid, with the musketry of law, the artillery of history. 'What about France? Isn't Napoleon III illegitimate? And aren't the French quite happy under that enlightened Emperor, who will surely lead them to the highest of destinies? Anyway, let's face it. Was our Charles III so defin-itely within his right? Was his Battle of Bitonto so unlike that of Bisacquino or Corleone or any of these battles in which the Piedmontese are now sweeping our troops before them? One of those battles fought so that all should remain as it was? And anyway, even Jupiter was not legitimate King of Olympus.'

At this, of course, Jupiter's *coup d'état* against Saturn was bound to bring his mind back to the stars.

Leaving Bendicò panting from his own dynamism, he climbed the stairs again, crossed rooms in which his daughters sat chatting to friends from the Holy Redeemer (at his passage the silken skirts rustled as the girls rose), went up a long ladder and came into the bright blue light of the observatory. Father Pirrone, with the serene air of a priest who has said Mass and drunk black coffee with Monreale biscuits, was sitting immersed in algebraical formulae. The two telescopes and three lenses were lying there quietly, dazed by the sun, with black pads over the eyepieces, like well-trained animals who knew their meal was only given them at night.

The sight of the Prince drew the priest from his calculations and reminded him of his humiliation of the night before. He got up, and then, as he bowed politely, found himself saying, 'Is Your Excellency coming to confession?' The Prince, whose sleep that night and conversations that morning had driven the episode of the previous night from his mind, looked amazed. 'Confession? It's not Saturday.' Then he remembered and smiled, 'Really, Father, there wouldn't even be need, would there? You know it all already.'

This insistence on his enforced complicity irritated the Jesuit. 'Excellency, the efficacy of confession not only consists in telling our sins, but in being sorry for them. And until you do so and show me you do so, you will remain in mortal sin, whether I know what your sins are or not.' He blew a meticulous whiff at a bit of fluff on his sleeve and plunged back into his abstractions.

Such was the calm produced in the Prince's mind by the political discoveries of that morning that he smiled at what would at other times have seemed to him gross impertinence. He opened one of the windows of the little tower. The country-side spread below in all its beauty. Under the leaven of the strong sun everything seemed weightless; the sea in the background was a dash of pure colour, the mountains which had seemed so

alarmingly full of hidden men during the night now looked like
masses of vapour on the point of dissolving, and grim Palermo
itself lay crouching quietly around its monasteries like a flock of
sheep around their shepherds. Even the foreign warships
anchored in the harbour in case of trouble spread no sense of
fear in the majestic calm. The sun, still far from its blazing zenith
on that morning of the 13th of May, was showing itself the true
ruler of Sicily; the crude brash sun, the drugging sun, which
annulled every will, kept all things in servile immobility, cradled
in violence and arbitrary dreams.

'It'll take any number of Victor Emmanuels to change this
magic potion for ever being poured for us.'

Father Pirrone had got up, adjusted his sash and moved
towards the Prince with a hand out. 'Excellency, I was too
brusque. Let me not trespass on your kindness, but do please
listen and come to confession.'

The ice was broken. And the Prince could tell Father Pirrone
of his own political intuitions. But the Jesuit was far from sharing
his relief and even became acid again. 'Briefly, then, you nobles
will come to an agreement with the Liberals, and yes, even with
the Masons, at our expense, at the expense of the Church. Then,
of course, our property, which is the patrimony of the poor, will
be seized and carved up among the most brazen of their leaders;
and who will then feed all the destitute sustained and guided
by the Church today?' The Prince was silent. 'How will those
desperate masses be placated? I'll tell you at once, Excellency.
They will be flung first a portion, then another portion and
eventually all the rest of your estates. And so God will have done
His justice, even by means of the Masons. Our Lord healed the
blind in body; but what will be the fate of the blind in spirit?'

The unhappy priest was breathing hard; sincere horror at the
foreseen dispersal of Church property was linked with regret at
his having lost control of himself again, with fear of offending
the Prince, whom he genuinely liked and whose blustering rages
as well as disinterested kindness he knew well. So he sat down
warily, glancing every now and again at Don Fabrizio, who had
taken up a little brush and was cleaning the knobs of a telescope,
apparently absorbed. A little later he got up and cleaned his

hands thoroughly with a rag; his face was quite expressionless, his light eyes seemed intent only on finding any remaining stain of oil in the cuticles of his nails. Down below, around the villa, all was luminous and grandiose silence, emphasised rather than disturbed by the distant barking of Bendicò baiting the gardener's dog at the far end of the lemon-grove, and by the dull rhythmic beat from the kitchen of a cook's knife chopping meat for the approaching meal. The sun had absorbed the turbulence of men as well as the harshness of earth. The Prince moved towards the priest's table, sat down and began drawing pointed little Bourbon lilies with a carefully sharpened pencil which the Jesuit had left behind in his anger. He looked serious but so serene that Father Pirrone no longer felt on tenterhooks.

'We're not blind, my dear Father, we're just human beings. We live in a changing reality to which we try to adapt ourselves like seaweed bending under the pressure of water. Holy Church has been granted an explicit promise of immortality; we, as a social class, have not. Any palliative which may give us another hundred years of life is like eternity to us. We may worry about our children and perhaps our grandchildren; but beyond what we can hope to stroke with these hands of ours we have no obligations. I cannot worry myself about what will happen to any possible descendants in the year 1960. The Church, yes, She must worry for She is destined not to die. Solace is implicit in Her desperation. Don't you think that if now or in the future She could save herself by sacrificing us She wouldn't do so? Of course She would, and rightly.'

Father Pirrone was so pleased at not having offended the Prince that he did not take offence either. Of course that word 'desperation' applied to the Church was quite inadmissible, but long habit as confessor had made him capable of appreciating Don Fabrizio's disillusioned mood. He must not let the other triumph, though. 'Now, Excellency, you have a couple of sins to confess to me on Saturday; one of the flesh yesterday, one of the spirit to-day. Remember!'

Both soothed, they began discussing a report which they would soon be sending to a foreign observatory, at Arcetri. Supported, guided, it seemed, by calculations which were invisible at that hour yet ever present, the stars cleft the ether in those exact trajectories of theirs. The comets would be appearing as usual, punctual to the fraction of a second, in sight of whoever was observing them. They were not messengers of catastrophe as Stella thought; on the contrary, their appearance at the time foreseen was a triumph of the human mind's capacity to project itself and to participate in the sublime routine of the skies. 'Let's leave the Bendicòs down there running after rustic prey, and the cooks' knives chopping the flesh of innocent beasts. From up in this observatory the bluster of the one and the blood on the other merge into tranquil harmony. The real problem is how to go on living this life of the spirit in its most sublimated moments, those moments that are most like death.'

So reasoned the Prince, forgetting his own recurrent whims, his own cavortings of the night before. During those moments of abstraction he seemed more intimately absolved, in the sense of being linked anew with the universe, than by any blessing of Father Pirrone. For half an hour that morning the gods of the ceilings and the monkeys on the walls were again put to silence. But in the drawing-room no one noticed.

When the bell for luncheon called them downstairs, both had regained their serenity, due to understanding the political scene and to setting that understanding aside. An atmosphere of unusual relaxation had spread over the house. The midday meal was the chief one of the day, and went, God be thanked, quite smoothly. This in spite of one of the ringlets framing the face of the twenty-year-old Carolina, the eldest daughter, dropping into her soup plate because apparently of an ill-secured pin. Another day the incident might have had dreadful consequences, but now it only heightened the gaiety; and when her brother, sitting next to her, took the lock of hair and pinned it on his neckerchief where it hung like a scapular, even the Prince allowed himself a smile. Tancredi's departure, destination and reasons were now known to all, and everyone talked of them, except Paolo who went on eating in silence. No one was really worrying about him, in fact, but the Prince, who showed no signs of the anxiety he still felt deep down, and Concetta who was the only one with a shadow on her pretty forehead. 'The girl must have her eye on the young scamp. They'd make a fine couple. But I fear Tancredi will have to aim higher, by which of course I mean lower.'

To-day, as political calm had cleared the mists generally veiling it, the Prince's fundamental good nature showed on the surface. To reassure his daughter he began explaining what useless muskets the royal army had; the barrels of those enormous pieces had no rifling, he said, so bullets coming from them would have very little penetration; technical comments thought up on the spur of the moment, understood by few and convincing none but consoling all, including Concetta, as they managed to transform war into a neat little diagram of fire-trajectories from the very squalid chaos that it really was.

At the end of the meal appeared a rum jelly. This was the Prince's favourite pudding, and the Princess had been careful to order it early that morning in gratitude for favours granted. It was rather threatening at first sight, shaped like a tower with bastions and battlements and smooth slippery walls impossible to scale, garrisoned by red and green cherries and pistachio nuts; but into its transparent and quivering flanks a spoon plunged with astounding ease. By the time the amber-coloured fortress reached Francesco Paolo, the sixteen-year-old son who was served last, it consisted only of shattered walls and hunks of wobbly rubble. Exhilarated by the aroma of rum and the delicate flavour of the multi-coloured garrison, the Prince enjoyed watching the rapid demolishing of the fortress beneath the assault of his family's appetite. One of his glasses was still half-full of Marsala. He raised it, glanced round the family, gazed for a second into Concetta's blue eyes, then said: 'To the health of our Tancredi.' He drained his wine in a single gulp. The initials F.D., which before had stood out clearly on the golden colour of the full glass, were no longer visible.

In the estate office, to which he returned after luncheon, the sunlight was oblique, and the pictures of his estates, now shadowed, sent no messages of reproof. 'Blessings on Your Excellency,' muttered Pastorello and Lo Nigro, the two tenants of Ragattisi who had brought the portion of their rent they paid in kind. They were standing very straight with stunned-looking eyes in faces carefully shaven and burnt dark by sun. They gave out a smell of flocks and herds. The Prince talked to them cordially in his very stylised dialect, inquired about their families, the state of their livestock, the outlook for the crops. Then he asked, 'Have you brought anything?' And when the two answered yes, that it was in the room next door, the Prince felt a twinge of shame as he realised that the interview was a repetition of his own audiences with King Ferdinand. 'Wait five minutes and Ferrara will give you the receipts.' He put into their hands a couple of ducats each, worth more, probably, than what they had brought. 'Drink my health, will you?' and then went and looked at their produce: on the ground were four *caciocavallo* cheeses, each weighing roughly ten kilos; he gave them a careless glance; he loathed that particular cheese; there were six baby lambs, the last of the year's litter, with their heads lolling pathetically above the big gash through which their life-blood had flowed a few hours before. Their bellies had been slashed open too, and iridescent intestines hung out. 'May God receive his soul,' he thought, remembering the gutted soldier of a month before. Four pairs of chickens tied by the claws were twisting in terror under Bendicò's restless snout. 'Another example of pointless alarm,' he thought, 'the dog is no danger to them at all; he wouldn't even touch one of their bones as it would give him a belly-ache.'

All this blood and panic revolted him, however. 'Pastorello, take the chickens into the coop, will you, as there's no need of them in the larder; and another time take the baby lambs straight into the kitchen, will you; they make a mess here. And you, Lo Nigro, go and tell Salvatore to come and clean up and take away the cheeses. And open the window to let out the smell.'

Then Ferrara came and made out the receipts.

When the Prince went upstairs again, he found Paolo, his heir, the Duke of Querceta, waiting for him in his study on the red sofa where he proposed to take his siesta. The youth had screwed up all his courage to talk to him. Short, slim, olive-skinned, he seemed older than the Prince himself. 'I wanted to ask you, papa, how we're to behave with Tancredi when we next meet him.'

The Prince understood at once and felt a twinge of annoyance. 'What d'you mean? Has anything changed?'

'But papa, you can't possibly approve; he's gone to join those swine who're making trouble all over Sicily; things like that just aren't done.'

Personal jealousy, a bigot's resentment of his agnostic cousin, a dullard's at the other's zest, had taken political guise. The Prince was so indignant that he did not even ask his son to sit down. 'Better to make a fool of oneself than spend all day staring at horses' dung! I'm even fonder of Tancredi than I was before. And anyway what he's doing isn't as silly as all that. If in the future you're able to go on putting Duke of Querceta on your cards, and if you inherit any money when I'm gone, you will owe it to Tancredi and to others like him. Out with you now, and don't mention the subject to me again! I'm the only one who gives orders here.' Then he became kindlier and substituted irony for anger. 'Be off now, son, as I want to have a snooze. Go and talk politics with Guiscard, you'll understand each other.'

And as a shaken Paolo closed the door behind him, the Prince took off his frockcoat and boots, made the sofa creak under his weight and slid calmly off to sleep.

When he awoke, his valet came in with a newspaper and a letter on a tray. They had been sent up from Palermo by his brother-in-law Màlvica, brought by a mounted groom a short while before. Still a little dazed from his afternoon nap, the Prince opened the letter. 'My dear Fabrizio, I am writing to you in a state of utter collapse. Such dreadful news in the paper. The Piedmontese have landed. We are all lost. To-night I and my whole family will take refuge on a British man-o'-war. You will want to do the same, I am sure; if you wish I can reserve a berth or two for you. May God save our beloved King! As always, Ciccio.'

He folded up the letter, put it in his pocket and began laughing out loud. That ass Màlvica! He'd always been a rabbit. Not understanding a thing, and now panic-struck. Abandoning his palace to the mercy of servants; this time he'd really find it empty on his return. 'That reminds me, Paolo must go and stay down at Palermo; a house empty at a moment like this means a house lost. I'll tell him at dinner.'

He opened the newspaper. 'On the 11th of May an act of flagrant piracy culminated in the landing of armed men at Marsala. The latest reports say that the band numbers about eight hundred, and is commanded by Garibaldi. When these brigands set foot on land they were very careful to avoid any encounter with the royal troops, and moved off, as far as can be ascertained, in the direction of Castelvetrano, threatening peaceful citizens and spreading rapine and devastation, etc., etc. . . .'

The name of Garibaldi disturbed him a little. That adventurer all hair and beard was a pure Mazzinian. He had caused a lot of trouble already. 'But if that *Galantuomo* King of his has let him come down here it means they're sure of him. They'll curb him!'

Reassured, he combed his hair and had his shoes and frock-coat put on again. He thrust the newspaper into a drawer. It was almost time for Rosary, but the drawing-room was still empty. He sat down on a sofa, and as he waited noticed how the Vulcan on the ceiling was rather like the lithographs of Garibaldi he had seen in Turin. He smiled. 'Cuckold!'

The family was gathering. Silken skirts rustled. The youngest were still joking together. Behind the door could be heard the usual echo of controversy between servants and Bendicò determined to take part.

A ray of sunshine full of dust specks lit up the malicious monkeys.

He knelt down. '*Salve Regina, Mater misericordiae.*'

II
Donnafugata

'The trees! The trees!'

This shout from the leading carriage eddied back along the following four, almost invisible in clouds of white dust; and at every window perspiring faces expressed tired gratification.

The trees were only three, in truth, and eucalyptus at that, scruffiest of Mother Nature's children. But they were also the first seen by the Salina family since leaving Bisacquino at six that morning. It was now eleven, and for the last five hours all they had set eyes on were bare hillsides flaming yellow under the sun. Trots over level ground had alternated briefly with long slow trudges uphill and then careful shuffles down; both trudge and trot merging, anyway, into the constant jingle of harness bells, imperceptible now to the dazed senses except as sound equivalent of the blazing landscape. They had passed through crazed-looking villages washed in palest blue; crossed dry beds of torrents over fantastic bridges; skirted sheer precipices which no sage and broom could temper. Never a tree, never a drop of water; just sun and dust. Inside the carriages, tight shut against that sun and dust, the temperature must have been well over 120 degrees. Those desiccated trees yearning away under bleached sky bore many a message; that they were now within a couple of hours from their journey's end; that they were entering the family estates; that they could lunch, and perhaps even wash their faces in the verminous waters of the well.

Ten minutes later they reached the farm buildings of Rampinzeri; a huge pile, only used one month in the year by labourers, mules and cattle gathered there for the harvest. Over the great solid yet staved-in door a stone Leopard pranced in spite of legs broken off by flung stones; next to the main farm building a deep well, watched over by those eucalyptuses, mutely offered various services: as swimming pool, drinking trough, prison or cemetery. It slaked thirst, spread typhus, guarded the kidnapped

37

and hid the corpses both of animals and men till they were reduced to the smoothest of anonymous skeletons.

The whole Salina family alighted from their various carriages. The Prince, cheered by the thought of soon reaching his beloved Donnafugata, the Princess irritated and yet inert, part restored, however, by her husband's serenity; tired girls; boys excited by novelty and untamed by the heat; Mademoiselle Dombreuil, the French governess, utterly exhausted, remembering years spent in Algeria with the family of Marshal Bugeaud, moaning '*Mon Dieu, mon Dieu, c'est pire qu'en Afrique!*' and mopping at her turned-up nose; Father Pirrone, whose breviary-reading had lulled him into a sleep which had shortened the whole trip and made him the spryest of the party; a maid and two lackeys, city folk worried by the unusual aspect of the countryside; and Bendicò, who had rushed out of the last carriage and was baying at the funereal suggestions of rooks swirling low in the light.

All were white with dust to the eyebrows, lips or pigtails; whitish puffs arose around those who had reached the stopping-place and were dusting each other down.

Amid this dirt Tancredi's elegant spruceness stood out all the more. He had travelled on horseback and, reaching the farm half an hour before the carriages, had time to shake off dust, brush up and change his white cravat. While drawing some water from that well of many uses he had glanced for a second into the mirror of the bucket and found himself in good order, with the black patch over his right eye now more reminiscent than protective of a wound received three months before in the fighting at Palermo; with that other dark blue eye which seemed to have assumed the task of expressing enough sly gaiety for its mate in temporary eclipse; and with, above his cravat, a scarlet thread alluding discreetly to the red shirt he had once worn. He helped the Princess to alight, dusted the Prince's top hat with his sleeve, distributed sweets to his girl cousins and quips to the boys, almost genuflected before the Jesuit, returned the passionate hugs of Bendicò, consoled Mademoiselle Dombreuil, laughed at all, enchanted all.

The coachmen were walking the horses slowly round to freshen them up before watering, the lackeys laying tablecloths out on straw left over from the threshing, in the oblong of shade from the building. Luncheon began near the accommodating well. All round quivered the funereal countryside, yellow with stubble, black with burnt patches; the lament of cicadas filled the sky. It was like a death-rattle from parched Sicily at the end of August vainly awaiting rain.

An hour later they were all on the road again, refreshed. Although the horses were tired and going slower than ever, the last part of the journey seemed short; the landscape, no longer unknown, had lost its more sinister aspects. They began recognising places they knew well, arid goals of past excursions and picnics in other years – the Dragonara ravine, the Misilbesi crossroads; soon they would reach the shrine of Our Lady of Graces, turning-point of their longest walks from Donnafugata. The Princess had dozed off, the Prince, alone with her in the wide carriage, was beaming.

Never had he been so glad to be going to spend three months at Donnafugata as he was now, in that late August of 1860. Not only because at Donnafugata he loved the house, the people, the sense of feudal ownership still surviving there, but also because, unlike other times, he felt no regret for his peaceful evenings in the observatory, his occasional visits to Mariannina. The truth was he had found the spectacle offered by Palermo in the last three months rather nauseating. He would have liked to have had the fun of being the only one to understand the situation and accept that red-shirted 'bogey-man' Garibaldi; but he had to admit that second-sight was not a Salina monopoly. Everyone in Palermo seemed pleased; everyone except a mere handful of grumblers: his brother-in-law Màlvica, who had got himself arrested by Garibaldi's police and spent ten days in prison; his son Paolo, just as discontented but slightly more prudent, and now left behind at Palermo deep in some silly plot or other. Everyone else was making a great show of joy; wearing tricolour cockades on lapels, marching about in processions from morning till night, and above all talking, haranguing, declaiming; and if in the very first days of the occupation all this was given some sense of purpose by the acclamations greeting the few wounded passing through the main streets and by the shrieks of Bourbon police 'rats' being tortured in the side alleys, now that the wounded had recovered and the surviving 'rats' enrolled in the new police this hubbub, inevitable though he realised it to be, began to seem pointless and petty.

But he had to admit that all this was a mere surface manifestation of ill-breeding; the fundamentals of the situation, economic and social, were satisfactory, just as he had foreseen. Don Pietro Russo had kept his promises and not a shot had been heard near Villa Salina; and though a whole service of Chinese porcelain had been stolen from the palace in Palermo, that was merely due to the idiocy of Paolo, who had had it packed into a couple of cases which he had then left out in the palace courtyard during the shelling; a positive invitation for the packers themselves to cart it off.

The 'Piedmontese' (as the Prince continued to call them for reassurance, just as others called them 'Garibaldini' in exaltation or 'Garibaldeschi' in vilification) had paid a call at the house, if not precisely cap in hand as he had been told, at least with a hand at the visors of those red caps of theirs, as floppy and faded as those of any Bourbon officer.

About the 20th of June, announced twenty-four hours beforehand by Tancredi, appeared a general in a red tunic with black froggings. He was followed by an aide-de-camp and asked most politely for admission in order to admire the frescoes on the ceilings. In he was ushered without ado, as there had been sufficient warning to clear from one of the drawing-rooms a portrait of King Ferdinand II in full regalia and substitute for it a neutral *Pool of Bethsaida*; an operation combining advantages political and aesthetic.

The general was a quick-witted Tuscan of about thirty, talkative and inclined to show off; he had been well behaved and agreeable, had treated the Prince with all proper respect and even called him 'Excellency', in utter contradiction to one of the Dictator's first decrees; the aide-de-camp, a new recruit of nineteen, was a Milanese count, who fascinated the girls with his glittering boots and his slurred 'r's. With them came Tancredi, promoted, or rather created, captain on the field of battle; a little drawn from the pain of his wound, he stood there red-shirted and irresistible, showing an easy intimacy with the victors, an intimacy demonstrated by a mutual use of the familiar *tu*, lavished with childish fervour by the two officers from the mainland and returned in kind by Tancredi, though with a faint nasal twang that to the Prince seemed full of muted irony. While greeting them from heights of imperturbable courtesy, the Prince had in fact been much amused and quite reassured. So much so that three days later the two 'Piedmontese' had been invited to dinner; Carolina then had made a fine sight at the piano accompanying the singing of the general, who had risked, in homage to Sicily, Bellini's '*Vi ravviso, o luoghi ameni*' with Tancredi demurely turning over the pages of the score as if false notes didn't exist. The young Milanese count, meanwhile, was leaning over a sofa, chatting away about orange blossom to Concetta and revealing to her the existence of a writer she had never heard of, Aleardo Aleardi; she was pretending to listen though worrying really about the look of her cousin, whom the candlelight on the piano made even more languid than he was in reality.

It had been an idyllic evening and was followed by others equally cordial; during one of these the general was asked to try and obtain an exemption from the order expelling Jesuits for Father Pirrone, described as very aged and very ill; the general, who had taken a liking to the good priest, pretended to believe in his wretched state and agreed; he talked to political friends, pulled a string or two, and Father Pirrone stayed. Which went to confirm the Prince more than ever in the accuracy of his predictions.

The general was also most helpful about the complicated permits necessary in those troubled times for anyone wanting to move from place to place; and it was largely due to him that the Salina family was able to enjoy its annual sojourn in the country in that year of revolution. The young captain asked for a month's leave and set off with his uncle and aunt. Even apart from permits, the preparations for the Salina family's journey had been lengthy and complicated. Cryptic negotiations had to be conducted in the agent's office with 'persons of influence' from

Girgenti, negotiations ending in smiles, handclasps and the tinkle of coin. Thus a second and more useful permit had been obtained; though this was no novelty. Piles of luggage and food had to be collected too, and cooks and servants sent on three days ahead; then there was one of the smaller telescopes to be packed and Paolo persuaded to stay behind in Palermo. After this they were able to move off; the general and the little lieutenant came to wish them all Godspeed and bring them flowers; and as the carriages moved off from Villa Salina two scarlet-covered arms continued to wave for a long time; at a carriage window appeared the Prince's black top hat, but the little hand in black lace mittens which the young count had hoped to see remained in Concetta's lap.

The journey had lasted more than three days and been quite appalling. The roads, the famous Sicilian roads which had cost the Prince of Satriano the Lieutenant-Generalcy, were no more than tracks, all ruts and dust. The first night at Marineo, at the home of a notary and friend, had been more or less bearable, but the second at a little inn at Prizzi had been torture, with three of them to a bed, besieged by repellent local fauna. The third was at Bisacquino; no bugs there but to make up for that the Prince had found thirteen flies in his glass of *granita*, while a strong smell of excrement drifted in from the street and the privy next door, and all this had caused him most unpleasant dreams; waking at very early dawn amid all that sweat and stink he had found himself comparing this ghastly journey with his own life, which had first moved over smiling level ground, then clambered up rocky mountains, slid over threatening passes, to emerge eventually into a landscape of interminable undulations, all the same colour, all bare as despair. These early morning fantasies were the very worst that could happen to a man of middle age; and although the Prince knew that they would vanish with the day's activities he suffered acutely all the same, as he was used enough to them by now to realise that deep inside him they left a sediment of sorrow which, accumulating day by day, would in the end be the real cause of his death.

With the rising of the sun those monsters had gone back to their lairs in his unconscious; nearby now was Donnafugata and his palace, with its many-jetted fountains, its memories of saintly forebears, the sense it gave him of everlasting childhood. Even the people there were pleasant, simple and devoted. At this point a thought occurred: would they be just as devoted as before, after recent events? 'We'll soon see.'

Now at last they were nearly there. Tancredi's mischievous face appeared at the carriage window-sill. 'Uncle, Aunt, get ready, in five minutes we'll be there.' Tancredi was too tactful to precede the Prince into the town. He slowed his horse to a walk and proceeded in silence beside the leading carriage.

Beyond the short bridge leading into the town were waiting the authorities, surrounded by a few dozen peasants. As the carriages moved on to the bridge the municipal band struck up with frenzied enthusiasm *Noi siamo zingarelle* from 'Traviata', the first odd and endearing greeting by Donnafugata to its Prince in recent years; after this, at a warning by some urchin on the look-out, the bells of the Mother Church and of the Convent of the Holy Ghost filled the air with festive sound.

'Thanks be to God, everything seems as usual,' thought the Prince as he climbed out of his carriage. There was Don Calo-gero Sedàra, the mayor, with a tricolour sash bright and new as his job tight around his waist; Monsignor Trottolino, the arch-priest, with his big red face; Don Ciccio Ginestra, the notary, all braid and feathers, dressed up as captain of the National Guard; there was Don Totò Giambono, the doctor, and there was little Nunzia Giarritta, who offered the Princess a rather messy bunch of flowers, picked half an hour before in the palace gardens. There was Ciccio Tumeo, the Cathedral organist, who was not strictly speaking of sufficient standing to be there with the authorities but had come along all the same as friend and hunting companion of the Prince, and had had the excellent notion of bringing along with him, for the Prince's pleasure, his red pointer bitch Teresina, with two little brown spots above its eyes; a daring rewarded with a special smile from Don Fabrizio.

The latter was in high good humour and sincerely amiable; he and his wife had alighted to express their thanks, and against the tempestuous music of Verdi and the crashing of bells embraced the mayor and shook hands with all the others. The crowd of peasants stood there silent, but their motionless eyes emitted a curiosity that was in no way hostile, for the poor of Donnafugata really did have a certain affection for their tolerant lord who so often forgot to ask for their little rents of kind or money; also, used as they were to seeing the bewhiskered Leopard on the palace façade, on the church front, above the baroque fountains, on the majolica tiles in their houses, they were glad to set eyes now on the real animal in nankeen trousers, distributing friendly shakes of the paw to all, his features amiably wreathed in feline smiles. 'Yes, indeed; everything is the same as before, better, in fact, than before.' Tancredi, too, was the object of great curiosity; though everyone had known him for a long time, now he seemed to them transfigured; no longer did they see him as a mere unconventional youth, but as an aristocratic liberal, companion of Rosolino Pilo, wounded hero of the battle of Palermo. He was swimming in this noisy admiration like a fish in water; these rustic admirers were really rather fun; he talked to them in dialect, joked, laughed at himself and his wounds; but when he said 'General Garibaldi' his voice dropped an octave and he put on the rapt look of a choir-boy before the Monstrance; then to Don Calogero Sedàra, of whom he had vaguely heard as being active during the period of the liberation, he said in booming tones, 'Ah, Don Calogero, Crispi said lots of nice things to me about you.' After which he gave his arm to his cousin Concetta and moved off, leaving everyone abuzz.

The carriages, with servants, children and Bendicò, went on to the palace; but according to ancient usage, before the others set foot in their home they had to hear a *Te Deum* in the Duomo. This was anyway only a few paces off, and they moved there in procession, the new arrivals dusty but imposing, the authorities gleaming but humble. Ahead walked Don Ciccio Ginestra, the prestige of his uniform cleaving a path; he was followed by the Prince giving an arm to the Princess, and looking like a sated and pacified lion; behind them came Tancredi with on his right Concetta, who found this walk towards a church beside her cousin most upsetting and conducive to weepiness: a state of mind in no way alleviated by the dutiful young man's strong pressure on her arm, though its only purpose, alas, was to save her from potholes and ruts. The others followed in disorder. The organist rushed off so as to have time to deposit Teresina at home and be back at his resonant post at the moment of entry into the church. The bells were clanging away ceaselessly, and on the walls of the houses the slogans of 'Viva Garibaldi', 'Viva King Vittorio', 'Death to the Bourbon King', scrawled by an inexpert brush two months before were fading away as if wanting to merge back into the walls. Squibs were exploding all round as they moved up the steps, and as the little procession entered the church Don Ciccio Tumeo, who had arrived panting but in time, broke impetuously into the strains of Verdi's *Amami, Alfredo*.

The nave was packed with curious idlers between its squat columns of red marble; the Salina family sat in the choir, and during the short ceremony Don Fabrizio got up and made an impressive bow to the crowd; meanwhile the Princess was on the verge of swooning from heat and exhaustion; Tancredi, pretending to brush away flies, grazed more than once Concetta's blonde head. All was in order and after a short address by Monsignor Trottolino, they all genuflected to the altar, turned towards the doors and issued into the sun-dazed square.

At the bottom of the steps the authorities took their leave, and the Princess, acting under instructions whispered to her during the ceremony, invited the mayor, the arch-priest and the notary to dine that same evening. The arch-priest was a bachelor by profession and the notary one by vocation, so that for them the question of consorts did not arise; the invitation to the mayor was rather languidly extended to his wife; she was some peasant woman, of great beauty, but considered by her own husband as quite unpresentable in public for a number of reasons; thus no one was surprised at his saying that she was indisposed; but great was the amazement when he added' 'If Your Excellencies will allow I'll bring along my daughter Angelica, who's been talking for the past month of nothing but her longing to be presented to you now that she's grown up.' Consent was, of course, given; and the Prince, who had seen Tumeo peering at him from

behind the others' shoulders, called out to him, 'You come
too, of course, Don Ciccio, and bring Teresina.' And he added,
turning to the others, 'And after dinner, at nine o'clock, we shall
be happy to see all our friends.' For a long time Donnafugata
commented on these last words. And the Prince, who had found
Donnafugata unchanged, was found very much changed himself; for never before would he have issued so cordial an invitation: and from that moment, invisibly, began the decline of his
prestige.

The Salina palace was next door to the Mother Church. Its short
façade with seven windows on the square gave no hint of its vast
size, which extended three hundred yards back; the buildings
were of different styles, but all harmoniously grouped round
three great courtyards ending in a large garden. At the main
entrance in the square the travellers were subjected to new
demonstrations of welcome. Don Onofrio Rotolo, the family's
local steward, took no part in the official greetings at the entry
of the town. Educated under the rigid rule of the Princess
Carolina, he considered the '*vulgus*' as non-existent and the
Prince as resident abroad until the moment when he crossed the
threshold of his own palace. So there he stood, exactly two steps
outside the gates; very small, very old, very bearded, with a
much younger and plumper wife standing beside him, flanked
by lackeys and eight rangers with golden Leopards on their caps
and in their hands eight shot-guns of uncertain damaging power.
'I am happy to welcome Your Excellencies to your home. And
I beg to hand back the palace in the exact state in which it was
left to me.'

Don Onofrio Rotolo was one of the rare persons held in
esteem by the Prince, and perhaps the only one who had never
cheated him. His honesty bordered on mania, and spectacular
tales were told of it, such as the glass of *rosolio* wine once left
half-full by the Princess at the moment of departure, and found
a year later in exactly the same place with its contents evaporated
and reduced to a state of sugary lees, but untouched. 'For it is
an infinitesimal part of the Prince's patrimony and must not be
dispersed.'

After a proper exchange of greetings with Don Onofrio and Donna Maria the Princess, who was on her feet still only by sheer strength of will, went straight to bed, the girls and Tancredi hurried off to the tepid shade of the gardens, while the Prince and his steward went on a tour of the vast apartments. Everything was in perfect order; the pictures were clear of dust in their heavy frames, the old gilt bindings emitted discreet gleams, the high sun made the grey marbles glitter round the doorposts. Everything was in the state it had been for the last fifty years. Away from the noisy turbine of civil dissent Don Fabrizio felt refreshed, full of serene confidence, and glanced almost tenderly at Don Onofrio trotting along beside him. 'Don Onofrio, you're like one of those djinns standing guard over treasure, really you are; we owe you a great debt of gratitude.' In an earlier year the sentiment might have been the same but the words themselves would never have come to his lips; Don Onofrio looked at him in gratitude and surprise; 'My duty, Your Excellency, it's just my duty,' and to hide his emotion he scratched the back of his ear with the long nail on the little finger of his left hand.

After this the steward was put to the torture of tea. Don Fabrizio had two cups brought, and with death in his heart Don Onofrio had to swallow one. After this he began to recount the chronicles of Donnafugata: he had renewed the lease for the Aquila land two weeks before, on rather worse terms; he had had to meet heavy expenses for the repairs of the roof in the guest wing; but in the safe, at His Excellency's disposal, was the sum of three thousand two hundred and seventy-five ounces of gold, after paying all expenses, taxes and his own salary.

Then came the private news, all of which turned round the great novelty of the year: the rapid rise to fortune of Don Calogero Sedàra; six months ago a mortgage arranged by the latter with Baron Tumino had fallen in, and he had gained possession of the estate; thus by the loan of a thousand ounces of gold he now owned a property which yielded five hundred ounces a year; in April Don Calogero had also been able to buy, for practically nothing, a certain piece of land which contained a vein of much sought-after stone that he intended to exploit; he had also made some very profitable sales of grain at the period of confusion and famine after the landings. The voice of Don Onofrio filled with rancour. 'I've totted it up roughly on my fingers: Don Calogero's income will very shortly be equal to that of Your Excellency's here at Donnafugata.' With riches had also grown political influence. He had become head of the liberals in the town and also in the districts round; when the elections were held he was sure to be returned as deputy to Turin. 'And what airs they give themselves; not he, who is far too shrewd to do that, but his daughter who's just got back from college in Florence and goes around town in a crinoline with velvet ribbons hanging from her hat.'

The Prince was silent; the daughter, yes, that must be the Angelica who would be coming to dinner to-night; he was curious to see this dressed-up shepherdess; it was not true that nothing had changed: Don Calogero was as rich as he was! But deep down he had foreseen such things; they were the price to be paid.

Don Onofrio was disturbed by his master's silence, and imagined he had put the Prince out by telling him petty local gossip.

'Excellency, I ordered a bath to be prepared for you, it should be ready by now.' Don Fabrizio suddenly realised that he was tired; it was almost three o'clock, and he had been up and about for nine hours under that torrid sun and after that ghastly night. He felt his body covered in dust to the remotest creases. 'Thank you, Don Onofrio, for thinking of it; and for everything else. We shall meet to-night at dinner.'

He went up the internal staircase, passed through the tapestry hall, through the blue, the yellow drawing-rooms; lowered blinds filtered the light; in his study the Boulle clock ticked away discreetly. 'What peace, my God, what peace!' He entered the bathroom: small, white-washed, with a rough tiled floor and a hole in the middle to let the water out. The bath itself was a kind of oval trough, vast, of enamelled iron, yellow outside and grey in, propped on four heavy wooden feet. Hanging on a nail was a dressing-gown; fresh linen was laid out on a rush chair; and on another a suit which still showed creases from packing. Beside the bath lay a big piece of pink soap, a brush, a knotted handkerchief containing bran which would emit a sweet scent when soaked, and a huge sponge, one of those sent by the Salina agent. Through the unshaded window beat the savage sun.

He clapped his hands; two lackeys entered, each holding a pair of quivering pails, one of cold, the other of boiling water; they went to and fro a number of times; the trough filled up; he tried the temperature with a hand; it was all right. He ordered the servants out, undressed, got in. Under his huge bulk the water brimmed over a little. He soaped himself, rubbed himself; the warmth did him good, relaxed him. He was almost dozing off when he heard a knock at the door; Mimì, his valet, entered timidly. 'Father Pirrone is asking to see Your Excellency at once. He is waiting outside for Your Excellency to leave the bath-room.' The Prince was surprised; if there had been some accident he had better know at once. 'No, no, let him come in now.'

Don Fabrizio was alarmed by this haste of Father Pirrone; and partly from this and partly from respect for the priestly habit, he hurried to leave the bath expecting to get into his bath-robe before the Jesuit entered; but he did not succeed, and Father Pirrone came in at the very moment when, no longer veiled by soapy water, not yet shrouded by his bath-sheet, he was emerging quite naked, like the Farnese Hercules, and steaming as well, while water flowed in streams from neck, arms, stomach, and legs like the Rhône, the Rhine, the Danube and the Adige crossing and watering Alpine ranges. The sight of the Prince in a state of nature was quite new to Father Pirrone; the Sacrament of Penance had accustomed him to naked souls, but he was far less used to naked bodies; and he, who would not have blinked an eyelid at hearing the confession, say, of an incestuous intrigue, found himself flustered by this innocent but vast expanse of naked flesh. He stuttered an excuse and made to back out; but Don Fabrizio, annoyed at not having had time to cover himself, naturally turned his irritation against the priest. 'Now, Father, don't be silly; hand me that bath-robe, will you, and help me to dry, if you don't mind.' Then suddenly he remembered a discussion they had once had and went on: 'And take my advice, Father, have a bath yourself.' Satisfied at being able to give advice on hygiene to one who so often gave it to him on morals, he felt soothed. With the upper part of the bath-robe in his hands at last he began drying his hair, whiskers and neck, while with the lower end the humiliated Father Pirrone rubbed his feet.

When the peak and slopes of the mountain were dry, the Prince said, 'Now take a seat, Father, and tell me why you're in such a hurry to talk to me.' And as the Jesuit sat down he began some more intimate moppings on his own.

'Well, Excellency, I've been given a most delicate commission. One who is very dear to you indeed has opened her heart to me and charged me to tell you of her feelings, trusting, perhaps wrongly, that the consideration with which I am honoured . . .' Father Pirrone hesitated and hovered from phrase to phrase.

Don Fabrizio lost patience. 'Well, come on, Father, who is it? The Princess?' And his raised arm seemed to be threatening: in fact he was drying an armpit.

'The Princess is tired; she's asleep and I have not seen her. No, it is the Signorina Concetta.' Pause. 'She is in love.' A man of forty-five can consider himself still young till the moment comes when he realises that he has children old enough to fall in love. The Prince felt old age come over him in one blow; he forgot the huge distances still tramped out shooting, the *Gesummaria* he could still evoke from his wife, his freshness now at the end of a long and arduous journey. Suddenly he saw himself as a white-haired old man walking beside herds of grandchildren on billy-goats in the public gardens of Villa Giulia.

'Why ever did the silly girl go and tell you such a thing? Why not come to me?' He did not even ask who the man was; there was no need to.

'Your Excellency hides his fatherly heart almost too well under the mask of authority. It's quite understandable that the poor girl should be frightened of you and so fall back on the family chaplain.'

Don Fabrizio slipped on his long drawers and snorted; he foresaw long interviews, tears, endless bother. The silly girl was spoiling his first day at Donnafugata with her fancies.

'I know, Father, I know. Here no one really understands me. It's my misfortune.' He was sitting now on a stool with the fuzz

of fair hair on his chest dotted with pearly drops of water. Rivu-
lets were snaking over the tiles, and the room was full of the
milky smell of bran and the almond smell of soap. 'Well, what
should I say, in your opinion?'

The Jesuit was sweating in the heat of the little room, and
now that his message had been delivered would have liked to go
but he was held back by a feeling of responsibility. 'The wish to
found a Christian family is most agreeable to the eyes of the
Church. The presence of Our Lord at the marriage of Cana . . .'

'Let's keep to the point, shall we? I wish to talk about this
marriage, not about marriage in general. Has Don Tancredi
made any definite proposal, by any chance, and if so, when?'

For five years Father Pirrone had tried to teach the boy Latin;
for seven years he had put up with his quips and pranks; like
everyone else he had felt his charm. But Tancredi's recent political attitudes had offended him; his old affection was struggling
now with a new rancour. He did not know what to say. 'Well,
not a real proposal, exactly, no. But the Signorina Concetta is
quite certain: his attentions, his glances, his remarks, have all
become more and more open and frequent and quite convinced
the dear creature; she is sure that she is loved; but, being an
obedient and respectful daughter, she wishes me to find out
from you what her answer is to be if a proposal does come. She
thinks it imminent.'

The Prince felt a little reassured; how ever did a chit of a girl
like that think she had acquired enough experience to be able
to judge so surely the behaviour of a young man, particularly of
a young man like Tancredi? Perhaps it was just imagination,
one of those 'golden dreams' which convulse the pillows of
schoolgirls? The danger might not be so near.

Danger. The word resounded so clearly in his mind that he
gave a start of surprise. Danger. But danger for whom? He had
a great affection for Concetta; he liked her perpetual submission,
the placidity with which she yielded to the most unwelcome of
paternal suggestions: a submission and placidity, incidentally,
rather overvalued by him. His natural tendency to avoid any
threat to his own calm had made him miss the steely glint which
crossed her eyes when the whims she was obeying were really

too vexing. Yes, the Prince was very fond of this daughter of his. But he was even fonder of his nephew. Conquered for ever by the youth's affectionate chaff he had begun during the last few months to admire his intelligence too; that quick adaptability, that worldly penetration, that innate artistic subtlety with which he could use the demagogic terms then in fashion while hinting to initiates that for him, the Prince of Falconeri, it was only a momentary pastime; all this amused Don Fabrizio, and in people of his character and standing the fact of being amused makes up four-fifths of affection. Tancredi, he considered, had a great future; he could be the standard-bearer of a counter-attack which the nobility, under changed trappings, could launch against the new social state. To do this he lacked but one thing; money; this Tancredi did not have, none at all. And to get on in politics, now that a name counted less, would need a lot of money; money to buy votes, money to do the electors favours, money for a dazzling style of living. Style of living ... And would Concetta, with all those passive virtues of hers, be capable of helping an ambitious and brilliant husband to climb the slippery slopes of the new society? Timid, reserved, bashful as she was? Wouldn't she always remain just the pretty schoolgirl she was now, a leaden weight on her husband's feet?

'Can you see Concetta, Father, as ambassadress in Vienna or Petersburg?'

The question took Father Pirrone quite unawares. 'What has that to do with it? I don't understand.'

Don Fabrizio did not bother to explain; he plunged back into his silent thoughts. Money? Concetta would have a dowry, of course. But the Salina fortune would have to be divided into seven parts, unequal at that, in which the girls' would be the smallest. Well, then? Tancredi needed much more; Maria Santa Pau, for instance, with four estates already hers and all those uncles, priests and misers; or one of the Sutèra girls, so ugly but so rich. Love. Of course, love. Flames for a year, ashes for thirty. He knew what love was ... Anyway, Tancredi would always find women falling for him like ripe pears.

Suddenly he felt cold. The water on him had evaporated and the skin of his arms was icy. The ends of his fingers were crinkling. Oh, dear, what a lot of bothersome talk it would all mean. That must be avoided ... 'Now I have to go and dress, Father. Tell Concetta, will you, that I am not in the least annoyed, but that we'll talk about all this later when we're quite sure it's not all just the fancy of a romantic girl. *Au revoir*, Father.'

He got up and passed into the dressing-room. From the Mother Church next door rang a lugubrious funeral knell. Someone had died at Donnafugata, some tired body unable to withstand the deep gloom of Sicilian summer had lacked stamina to await the rains. 'Lucky person,' thought the Prince, as he rubbed lotion on his whiskers. 'Lucky person, with no worries now about daughters, dowries and political careers.' This ephemeral identification with an unknown corpse was enough to calm him. 'While there's death there's hope,' he thought; then he saw the absurd side of letting himself get into such a state of depression because one of his daughters wanted to marry. '*Ce sont leurs affaires, après tout*,' he thought in French, as he did when his cogitations persisted in playing pranks. He settled in an armchair and dropped off into a doze.

An hour later he awoke refreshed and went down into the garden. The sun was already low and its rays, no longer overwhelming, were lighting amiably on the araucarias, the pines, the lusty ilexes which were the glory of the place. From the end of the main alley, sloping gently down between high laurel hedges framing anonymous busts of broken-nosed goddesses, could be heard the gentle drizzle of spray falling into the fountain of Amphitrite. He moved swiftly towards it, eager to see it again. The waters came spurting in minute jets, blown from shells of Tritons and Naiads, from noses of marine monsters, spattering and pattering on the greenish surface, bouncing and bubbling, wavering and quivering, dissolving into laughing little gurgles; from the whole fountain, the tepid water, the stones covered with velvety moss, emanated a promise of pleasure that would never turn to pain. Perched on an islet in the middle of the round basin, modelled by a crude but sensual hand, a vigorous smiling Neptune was embracing a willing Amphitrite; her navel, wet with spray and gleaming in the sun, would be the nest, shortly, for hidden kisses in subaqueous shade. Don Fabrizio paused, gazed, remembered, regretted. He stood there a long while.

'Uncle, come and look at the foreign peaches. They've turned out fine. And leave these indecencies which are not for men of your age.'

Tancredi's affectionate mocking voice called him from his voluptuous torpor. He had not heard the boy come; he was like a cat. For the first time he felt a touch of rancour prick him at the sight of Tancredi; this fop with the pinched-in waist under his dark blue suit had been the cause of those sour thoughts of his about death two hours ago. Then he realised that it was not rancour, just disguised alarm: he was afraid the other would talk to him about Concetta. But his nephew's approach and tone was not that of one preparing to make amorous confidences to a man like himself. Don Fabrizio grew calm again; his nephew was looking at him with the affectionate irony which youth accords to age. 'They can allow themselves to be a bit nice to us, as they're so sure to be free of us the day after our funerals.' He went with Tancredi to look at the 'foreign peaches'. The grafting with German cuttings, made two years ago, had succeeded perfectly; there was not much fruit, a dozen or so, on the two grafted trees, but it was big, velvety, luscious-looking; yellowish, with a faint flush of rosy pink on the cheeks, like those of modest little Chinese girls. The Prince felt them with the delicacy for which his fleshy fingers were famous. 'They seem quite ripe. A pity there are too few for to-night. But we'll get them picked to-morrow and see what they're like.'

'There! that's how I like you, Uncle; like this, in the part of *agricola pius* – appreciating in anticipation of fruits of your own labours; and not as I found you a short while ago, gazing at all that shameless naked flesh.'

'And yet, Tancredi, these peaches are also products of love, of coupling.'

'Of course, but legal love, blessed by you as their master, and by Nino the gardener as notary. Considered, fruitful love. As for those,' he went on, pointing at the fountain whose shimmer could just be discerned through a veil of ilexes, 'd'you really think they've been before a priest?'

The conversation was taking a dangerous turn and Don Fabrizio hastily changed its direction. As they moved back up towards the house Tancredi began telling what he had heard of the love-life of Donnafugata: Menica, the daughter of Saverio the keeper, had let herself be put with child by her young man; the marriage would be rushed on now. Calicchio had just avoided being shot by an angry husband.

'But how d'you know such things?'

'I know, Uncle, I know. They tell me everything; they know I'll sympathise.'

When they reached the top of the steps, which rose from the garden to the palace with gentle turns and long landings, they could see the dusky horizon beyond the trees; over towards the sea huge, inky clouds were climbing up the sky. Perhaps the anger of God was satiated and the annual curse over Sicily nearly over? At that moment those clouds loaded with relief were being stared at by thousands of other eyes, sensed in the womb of the earth by billions of seeds.

'Let's hope the summer is over and that the rains are finally here,' said Don Fabrizio; and with these words the haughty noble to whom rain would only be a personal nuisance showed himself a brother to his roughest peasants.

The Prince had always taken care that the first dinner at Donna-fugata should bear the stamp of solemnity: children under fifteen were excluded from table, French wines were served, there was punch *alla Romana* before the roast; and the flunkeys were in powder and knee-breeches. On just one detail did he compromise; he never wore evening dress, lest he embarrass guests who would, obviously, possess none. That evening, in the 'Leopold' drawing-room, as it was called, the Salina family were awaiting the last arrivals. From under lace-covered shades the oil-lamps spread circumscribed yellow light: the vast equestrian portraits of past Salinas were as imposing and shadowy as their memories. Don Onofrio had already arrived with his wife, and so had the arch-priest who, with his light mantle folded back on his shoulders in sign of gala, was telling the Princess about tiffs at the College of Mary. Don Ciccio, the organist, had also arrived

(Teresina had already been tied to the leg of a scullery table) and was recalling with the Prince their fantastic bags in the Dragonara ravines. All was placid and normal when Francesco Paolo, the sixteen-year-old son, burst into the room and announced: 'Papa, Don Calogero is just coming up the stairs. In *tails*!'

Tancredi, intent on fascinating the wife of Don Onofrio, realised the import of the news a second before the others. But when he heard that fatal word he could not contain himself and burst into convulsive laughter. No laugh, though, came from the Prince on whom, one might almost say, this news had more effect than the bulletin about Garibaldi's landing at Marsala. That had been an event not only foreseen but also distant and invisible. Now, with his sensibility to presages and symbols, he saw revolution in that white tie and two black tails moving at this moment up the stairs of his own home. Not only was he, the Prince, no longer the major landowner in Donnafugata, but he now found himself forced to receive, when in afternoon dress himself, a guest appearing in evening clothes.

His distress was great; it still lasted as he moved mechanically towards the door to receive his guest. When he saw him, however, his agonies were somewhat eased. Though perfectly adequate as a political demonstration it was obvious that, as tailoring, Don Calogero's tail-coat was a disastrous failure. The stuff was excellent, the style modern, but the cut appalling. The Word from London had been most inadequately made flesh in a tailor from Girgenti to whom Don Calogero had gone with his tenacious avarice. The wings of his cravat pointed straight to heaven in mute supplication, his huge collar was shapeless, and, what is more, it is our painful but necessary duty to add that the mayor's feet were shod in buttoned boots.

Don Calogero advanced towards the Princess with a hand outstretched and still gloved. 'My daughter begs you to excuse her; she was not quite ready. Your Excellency knows how females are on these occasions,' he added, expressing in his near dialect a thought of Parisian levity, 'but she'll be here in a second; it's only a step from our place, as you know.'

The second lasted five minutes; then the door opened and in

came Angelica. The first impression was of dazed surprise. The Salina family all stood there with breath taken away; Tancredi could even feel the veins pulsing in his temples. Under the first shock from her beauty the men were incapable of noticing or analysing its defects, which were numerous; there were to be many for ever incapable of this critical appraisal. She was tall and well-made, on an ample scale; her skin looked as if it had the flavour of fresh cream which it resembled, her childlike mouth that of strawberries. Under a mass of raven hair, curling in gentle waves, her green eyes gleamed motionless as those of statues, and like them a little cruel. She was moving slowly, making her wide white skirt rotate around her, and emanating from her whole person the invincible calm of a woman sure of her own beauty. Only many months later was it known that at the moment of that victorious entry of hers she had been on the point of fainting from nerves.

She took no notice of the Prince hurrying towards her, she passed by Tancredi grinning at her in a daydream; before the Princess's armchair she bent her superb back in a slight bow, and this form of homage, unusual in Sicily, gave her for an instant the fascination of exoticism as well as that of local beauty.

'Angelica, my dear, it's so long since I've seen you. You've changed a lot; not for the worse!' The Princess could not believe her own eyes; she remembered the rather ugly and uncared-for thirteen-year-old girl of four years ago and could not make her tally with this voluptuous maiden before her. The Prince had no memories to reorganise; he only had forecasts to overturn; the blow to his pride dealt by the father's tail-coat was now repeated by the daughter's looks; but this time it was not a matter of black stuff but of milk-smooth white skin; and well-cut, yes, very well indeed! Old war horse that he was, the bugle-call of feminine beauty found him ready and he turned to the girl with the tone of gracious respect which he would have used to the Duchess of Bovino or the Princess of Lampedusa; 'How lucky we are, Signorina Angelica, to have gathered such a lovely flower in our home; and I hope that we shall have the pleasure of seeing you here often.'

'Thank you, Prince; I see that you are as kind to me as you

have always been to my dear father.' The voice was pretty,
low-pitched, a little too careful perhaps; Florentine schooling
had cancelled the sagging Girgenti accent; the only Sicilian
characteristic still in her speech was the harsh consonants,
which anyway toned in well with her clear but emphatic type
of beauty. In Florence she had also been taught to drop the
'Excellency'.

About Tancredi there seems little to be said; after being intro-
duced by Don Calogero, after manoeuvring the searchlight of
his blue eyes, after just managing to resist implanting a kiss on
Angelica's hand, he had resumed his chat with the Signora
Rotolo without taking in a word that the good lady said. Father
Pirrone, in a dark corner, was deep in meditation over Holy
Scripture, which that night appeared only in the guise of
Delilahs, Judiths and Esthers.

The central doors of the drawing-room were flung open and
the butler declaimed mysterious sounds announcing that dinner
was ready: '*Prann' pronn'*.' The heterogeneous group moved
towards the dining-room.

The Prince was too experienced to offer Sicilian guests, in
a town of the interior, a dinner beginning with soup, and he
infringed the rules of *haute cuisine* all the more readily as he
disliked it himself. But rumours of the barbaric foreign usage
of serving an insipid liquid as first course had reached the
notables of Donnafugata too insistently for them not to quiver
with a slight residue of alarm at the start of a solemn dinner
like this. So when three lackeys in green, gold and powder
entered, each holding a great silver dish containing a towering
macaroni pie, only four of the twenty at table avoided showing
pleased surprise; the Prince and Princess from foreknowledge,
Angelica from affectation and Concetta from lack of appetite.
All the others (including Tancredi, I regret to say) showed their
relief in varying ways, from the fluty and ecstatic grunts of the
notary to the sharp squeak of Francesco Paolo. But a
threatening circular stare from the host soon stifled these
improper demonstrations.

Good manners apart, though, the aspect of those monumental
dishes of macaroni was worthy of the quivers of admiration they

evoked. The burnished gold of the crusts, the fragrance of sugar and cinnamon they exuded, were but preludes to the delights released from the interior when the knife broke the crust; first came a spice-laden haze, then chicken livers, hard boiled eggs, sliced ham, chicken and truffles in masses of piping hot, glistening macaroni, to which the meat juice gave an exquisite hue of suède.

The beginning of the meal, as happens in the provinces, was quiet. The arch-priest made the sign of the Cross and plunged in head first without a word. The organist absorbed the succulent dish with closed eyes; he was grateful to the Creator that his ability to shoot hare and woodcock could bring him ecstatic pleasures like this, and the thought came to him that he and Teresina could exist for a month on the cost of one of these dishes; Angelica, the lovely Angelica, forgot little Tuscan black-puddings and part of her good manners and devoured her food with the appetite of her seventeen years and the vigour given by grasping her fork half-way up the handle. Tancredi, in an attempt to link gallantry with greed, tried to imagine himself tasting, in the aromatic forkfuls, the kisses of his neighbour Angelica, but he realised at once that the experiment was disgusting and suspended it, with a mental reserve about reviving this fantasy with the pudding; the Prince, although rapt in the contemplation of Angelica sitting opposite him, was the only one at table able to notice that the *demi-glace* was overfilled, and made a mental note to tell the cook so next day; the others ate without thinking of anything, and without realising that the food seemed so delicious because sensuality was circulating in the house.

All were calm and contented. All except Concetta. She had of course embraced and kissed Angelica, told her not to use the formal third person and insisted on the familiar *tu* of their infancy, but under her pale blue bodice her heart was being torn to shreds; the violent Salina blood came surging up in her, and beneath a smooth forehead she found herself brooding over day-dreams of poisoning. Tancredi was sitting between her and Angelica distributing, with the punctiliousness of one who feels in the wrong, his glances, compliments and jokes equally between both neighbours; but Concetta had an intuition, an animal intuition of the current of desire flowing from her cousin towards the intruder, and the little frown between her nose and forehead deepened; she wanted to kill as much as she wanted to die. But being a woman she snatched at details; Angelica's little finger in the air when her hand held her glass; a reddish mole on the skin of her neck; an attempt, half repressed, to remove with a finger a shred of food stuck in her very white teeth; she noticed even more sharply a certain coarseness of spirit; and to these details, which were really quite insignificant as they were cauterised by sensual fascination, she clung as trustingly and desperately as a falling builder's boy snatches at a leaden gutter; she hoped that Tancredi would notice too and be revolted by these obvious traces of difference in breeding. But Tancredi had already noticed them, and, alas! with no result. He was letting himself be drawn along by the physical stimulus of a beautiful woman to his fiery youth, and also by the (as-it-were) numerical excitement aroused by a rich girl in the mind of a man ambitious and poor.

At the end of dinner the conversation became general: Don Calogero told in bad Italian but with knowing insight some inside stories about the conquest of the province by Garibaldi; the notary told the Princess of a little house he was having built 'out of town'; Angelica, excited by light, food, Chablis and the obvious admiration she was arousing in every man around the table, asked Tancredi to describe some episodes of the 'glorious battle' for Palermo. She had put an elbow on the table and was leaning her cheek on her hand. Her face was flushed and she was perilously attractive to behold; the arabesque made by her forearm, elbow, finger and hanging white glove seemed exquisite to Tancredi and repulsive to Concetta. The young man, while continuing to admire, was describing the campaign as if it had all been quite light and unimportant; the night march on Gibilrossa, the scene between Bixio and La Masa, the assault on Porta di Termini. 'It was the greatest fun, signorina. Our biggest laugh was on the night of the 28th of May. The general needed a lookout post at the top of the convent at Origlione; we knocked, banged, cursed, knocked again: no one opened; it was an enclosed convent. Then Tassoni, Aldrighetti, I and one or two others tried to break down the door with our rifle buts. Nothing doing. We ran to fetch a beam from a shelled house nearby and finally, with a hellish din, the door gave way. We went in; not a soul in sight, but from a corner of the passage we heard desperate screams; a group of nuns had taken refuge in the chapel and were all crouching round the altar; I wonder *what* they feared at the hands of those dozen excited young men! They looked absurd, old and ugly in their black habits, with starting eyes, ready and prepared for . . . martyrdom. They were whining like bitches. Tassoni, who's a card, shouted: "Nothing doing, sisters, we've other things to think of; but we'll be back when you've some novices." And we all laughed fit to burst. Then we left them there, their tongues hanging out, to go and shoot at Royalists from the terraces above. Ten minutes later I was wounded.'

Angelica laughed, still leaning on her elbow, and showed all her pointed teeth. The joke seemed most piquant to her; that hint of rape perturbed her; her lovely throat quivered. 'What fine lads you must have been! How I wish I'd been with you!' Tancredi seemed transformed; the excitement of the story, the thrill of memory, mingling with the agitation produced by the girl's air of sensuality, changed him for an instant from the gentle youth he was in reality into a brutal and licentious soldier.

'Had you been there, signorina, we'd have had no need to wait for novices.'

Angelica had heard a lot of coarse talk at home; but this was the first time (and not the last) when she found herself the object of a sexual innuendo; the novelty of it pleased her, her laughter went up a tone, became strident.

At that moment everyone rose from the table; Tancredi bent to gather up the feather fan dropped by Angelica; as he rose to his feet he saw Concetta with face aflame and two little tears in the corners of her lids. 'Tancredi, one tells nasty tales like that to a confessor, not to young ladies at table; anyway when I'm there.' And she turned her back on him.

Before going to bed Don Fabrizio paused a moment on the little balcony of his dressing-room. Beneath lay the shadowed garden, sunk in sleep; in the inert air the trees seemed like fused lead; from the overhanging bell-tower came an elfin hoot of owls. The sky was clear of clouds; those which had greeted the dusk had moved away, maybe towards less sinful places, condemned by divine wrath to lesser penalties. The stars looked turbid and their rays scarcely penetrated the pall of sultry air.

The soul of the Prince reached out towards them, towards the intangible, the unattainable, which gives joy without laying claim to anything in return; as on many other occasions, he tried to imagine himself in those icy tracts, a pure intellect armed with a note-book for calculations: difficult calculations, but ones which would always work out. 'They're the only truly disinterested, the only really trustworthy creatures,' thought he in his worldly idiom; 'who worries about dowries for the Pleiads, a political career for Sirius, marital joys for Vega?' It had been a bad day; he realised it now, not only from a pressure in the pit of his stomach, but from the stars too; instead of seeing them disposed in their usual groupings he noticed a single pattern up there every time he raised his eyes: two stars above, the eyes; one beneath, the tip of a chin: mocking symbol of a triangular face which his mind projected into the constellations when it was disturbed. Don Calogero's tail-coat, Concetta's love, Tancredi's blatant infatuation, his own cowardice; even the threatening beauty of that girl Angelica; bad things; rubble preceding an avalanche. And Tancredi! The lad was right, agreed, and he would help him too; but Don Fabrizio had to admit that it was all slightly ignoble. And he himself was like Tancredi. 'Enough of that now, let's sleep on it.'

Bendicò in the shadow rubbed a big head against his knee; 'You see; you, Bendicò, are a bit like them, like the stars; happily incomprehensible, incapable of producing anxiety.' He raised the dog's head, which was almost invisible in the darkness. 'And then with those eyes of yours at the same level as your nose, with your lack of chin, such a head can't possibly evoke malignant spectres in the sky.'

Centuries-old tradition required that the day following their arrival the Salina family should visit the Convent of the Holy

Ghost to pray at the tomb of Blessed Corbèra, forebear of the
Prince and foundress of the convent, who had endowed it, there
lived a holy life and there died a holy death.

The Convent of the Holy Ghost had a rigid rule of enclosure
and entry was severely forbidden to men. That was why the
Prince particularly enjoyed visiting it, for he, as direct descendant of the foundress, was not excluded: and of this privilege,
shared only with the King of Naples, he was both jealous and
childishly proud.

This faculty of canonical intrusion was the chief, but not
the only reason, for his liking the Convent of the Holy Ghost.
Everything about the place pleased him, beginning with the
humble simplicity of the parlour, with its barrel vaulted ceiling
centred on the Leopard, its double gratings for interviews, a
little wooden wheel for passing messages in and out, and a heavy
door whose threshold he and the King were the only men in the
whole world allowed to cross. He liked the look of the nuns
with their wide wimples of purest white linen in tiny pleats
gleaming against the rough black robes; he was edified at hearing
for the hundredth time the Mother Abbess describe the Blessed
One's ingenuous miracles; at her showing the corner of the dank
garden where the saintly nun had suspended in the air a huge
stone which the Devil, irritated by her austerity, had flung at
her; he was astounded at the sight of the two famous and indecipherable letters framed on the wall of a cell, one to the Devil
from Blessed Corbèra, to convert him to virtue, and the other
the Devil's reply, expressing, it seems, his regret at not being
able to comply with her request: the Prince liked the almond
cakes which the nuns made up from an ancient recipe, he liked
listening to the Office chanted in choir, and he was even quite
happy to pay over to the community a not inconsiderable
portion of his own income, in accordance with the act of
foundation.

So that morning there were only happy people in the two
carriages moving towards the convent just outside the town. In
the first were the Prince, the Princess and their daughters
Carolina and Concetta; in the second his daughter Caterina,
Tancredi and Father Pirrone, both the latter of whom, of course,

would stay *extra muros* and wait in the parlour during the visit, consoled by almond cakes from the wooden wheel. Concetta looked serene, though a little absent-minded, and the Prince did his best to hope that yesterday's fancies had all blown over.

Entry into an enclosed convent is never a quick matter, even for one possessing the most sacred of rights. Nuns like to show a certain reluctance, formal maybe but prolonged, which gives more flavour to however certain an admission; and, although the visit had been announced beforehand, there was a considerable wait in the parlour. Towards the end of this Tancredi unexpectedly asked the Prince, 'Uncle, can't you get me in too? After all I'm half a Salina, and I've never been here before.'

Though pleased at heart by the request, the Prince shook his head decisively. 'But, my boy, you know only I and no other man can enter here.' It was not easy, however, to put Tancredi off: 'Excuse me, Nuncle; the rule says: *the Prince of Salina may enter together with two gentlemen of his suite if the Abbess so permits.* I read it again yesterday. I'll be the gentleman in your suite, I'll be your squire, I'll be whatever you like. Do ask the Abbess, please.' He was speaking with unusual warmth; perhaps he wanted a certain person there to forget his ill-considered chatter of the night before. The Prince was flattered. 'If you're so keen on it, dear boy, I'll see ...' But Concetta turned to her cousin with her sweetest smile: 'Tancredi, we passed a beam of wood lying in front of Ginestra's house. Go and fetch it, it'll get you in all the quicker.' Tancredi's blue eyes clouded and his face went red as a poppy, either from shame or anger. He tried to say something to the surprised Prince, but Concetta interrupted again, acidly now, and without a smile: 'Let him be, Father, he's only joking; he's been in one convent already, that ought to be enough for him; it's not right for him to enter this one of ours.' With a grinding of drawn bolts the door opened. Into the stuffy parlour entered the freshness of the cloister together with the murmur of assembled nuns. It was too late to ask questions, and Tancredi was left behind to walk up and down in front of the convent under the blazing sky.

The visit to the Holy Ghost was a great success. Don Fabrizio, from love of quiet, had refrained from asking Concetta the meaning of her words; doubtless just one of the usual tiffs between cousins; anyway the coolness between the two young people kept off bother, confabulations and decisions, so it had been welcome. On these premises the tomb of Blessed Corbèra was venerated with due respect by all, the nuns' watery coffee drunk with tolerance and the pink and greenish almond cakes crunched with satisfaction; the Princess inspected the vestment-press, Concetta talked to the nuns with her usual withdrawn kindliness and he, the Prince, left on the refectory table the ten ounces of gold that he offered every time he came. It was true that at the door Father Pirrone was found alone; but as he said that Tancredi had suddenly remembered an urgent letter and gone off on foot, no one took much notice.

On returning to the palace the Prince went up to the library, which was in the middle of the façade under the clock and lightning conductor. From the great balcony, closed against the heat, could be seen the square of Donnafugata, vast, shaded by dusty plane trees. Opposite were some house fronts of exuberant local design, rustic monstrosities in soap-stone, weathered by the years, upholding amid twists and curves balconies that were too small; other houses, among them that of Don Calogero Sedàra, hid behind prim Empire fronts.

Don Fabrizio walked up and down the immense room; every now and again glancing out at the square; on one of the benches donated by himself to the commune three old men were roasting in the sun; four mules stood tethered to a tree; a dozen or so urchins chased each other, shouting and brandishing wooden swords. Under the blazing mid-summer sun the view could not have been more typical. On one of his crossings past the window, however, his eye was drawn to a figure obviously urban – slim, erect, well-dressed. He screwed up his eyes. It was Tancredi; he recognised him, although already some way off, by the sloping shoulders and slim-fitting waist of his frockcoat. He had changed his clothes; he was no longer in brown as at the convent, but in Prussian blue, 'my seduction colour' as he himself called it. In one hand he held a cane with an enamel handle (doubtless the one bearing the Unicorn of the Falconeri and their motto

Semper purus) and he was walking with cat-like tread, as if taking care not to get his shoes dusty. Ten paces behind him followed a lackey carrying a tasselled box containing a dozen yellow peaches with pink cheeks. He sidestepped a sword-waving urchin, carefully avoided a urinating mule, and reached the Sedàras' door.

III

The Troubles of Don Fabrizio

THE RAINS HAD come, the rains had gone, and the sun was back on its throne like an absolute monarch kept off for a week by his subjects' barricades, and now reigning once again, choleric but under constitutional restraint. The heat braced without burning, the light domineered but let colours live; from the soil sprouted cautious clover and mint, and on faces diffident hopes.

Don Fabrizio, with his dogs Teresina and Arguto and his retainer Don Ciccio Tumeo, would spend long hours out shooting, from dawn till afternoon. The effort was out of all proportion to the results, for the most expert shot finds difficulty in hitting a target which is scarcely ever there, and it was rarely that the Prince was able to take even a brace of partridges home to the larder, or Don Ciccio to slap on his kitchen table a wild rabbit – promoted, *ipso facto* as usual in Sicily, to the rank of hare.

A big bag would anyway have been a secondary pleasure for the Prince; the joy of those days out shooting lay elsewhere, subdivided in many tiny episodes. It began with shaving in a room still dark, by candlelight that projected every gesture emphatically over the painted architecture on the ceiling; it was whetted by crossing sleeping drawing-rooms, by glimpses in the flickering light of tables with playing cards lying in disorder amid chips and empty glasses, and catching sight among them of a Jack of Spades waving a manly greeting: by passing through the motionless garden under a grey light in which the earliest birds were twisting and turning to shake the dew off their feathers; by gliding through the ivy-hung wicket gate: by escaping, in fact. And then in the street, blamelessly innocent still in the early light, he would find Don Ciccio smiling into his yellowed moustaches and swearing affectionately at the dogs; these, as they waited, were flexing their muscles under velvety fur. Venus still glimmered, like the bloom on a grape, damp and transparent, but one could already hear the rumble of the solar chariot climbing the last slope below the horizon; soon they would meet the first flocks moving towards them torpidly as tides, guided by stones thrown by leather-breeched shepherds; the wool looked soft and rosy in the early sun: then there would be obscure quarrels of precedence to be settled between sheep dogs and punctilious pointers, after which deafening interval they turned up a slope and found themselves in the immemorial silence of pastoral Sicily. All at once they were far from everything in space and still more in time. Donnafugata with its palace and its new rich was only a mile or two away, but seemed a dim memory like those landscapes sometimes glimpsed at the distant end of a railway tunnel; its troubles and splendours appeared even more insignificant than if they belonged to the past, for compared to this remote unchangeable landscape they seemed part of the future, made not of stone and flesh but of the substance of some dream of things to come, extracts from a Utopia thought up by a rustic Plato and apt to change any second into quite different forms or even not to exist at all; deprived thus of that charge of energy which everything in the past continues to possess, they could no longer be a worry.

Yes, Don Fabrizio had certainly had his worries those last two months; they had come from all directions, like ants making for a dead lizard. Some had crawled from crevices of the political situation; some been flung on him by other people's passions; and some (these had the sharpest bite) had sprung up within himself, from his irrational reactions, that is, to politics and the whims of others ('whims' was his name when irritated for what in calm he called 'passions'). He would review these worries every day, manoeuvre them, set them in column or extend them in open order on the parade ground of his own conscience, hoping to find in their evolutions a sense of finality that could reassure him; and not succeeding. In former years there had been far fewer bothers, and anyway his stay at Donnafugata had always been a period of rest; his worries used to drop their rifles, disperse into the windings of the valleys and settle down there quietly, so intent on munching bread and cheese that their warlike uniforms were forgotten and they could be mistaken for inoffensive peasants. This year, though, they had all stayed on parade in a body, like mutinous troops shouting and brandishing weapons, arousing in his home the dismay of a colonel who has given the order 'Fall out' only to find his battalion standing there in closer and more threatening order than ever.

The arrival had been all right, with bands, fireworks, bells, gipsy song and *Te Deum*; but afterwards! The bourgeois revolution climbing his stairs in Don Calogero's tail-coat, Angelica's beauty putting the shy grace of his Concetta in the shade, Tancredi rushing at the inevitable changes and even able to deck out his realistic motives with sensual infatuation; the scruples and deceptions of the Plebiscite; the endless little subterfuges he had to submit to, he, the Leopard, who for years had swept away difficulties with a wave of his paw.

Tancredi had been gone for more than a month and was now at Caserta bivouacking in the apartments of his King; from there every now and again he sent Don Fabrizio letters which the latter read with alternate frowns and smiles, then put away in the remotest drawer of his desk. He had never written to Concetta, though he did not forget to send her a greeting with his usual affectionate slyness; once he even wrote: 'I kiss the hands of all the little Leopardesses and particularly Concetta's', phrases censored by paternal prudence when the letter was read out to the assembled family. Angelica was now visiting them almost daily, more seductive than ever, accompanied by her father or some old witch of a maid: officially these visits were made to her friends the girls, but in fact their climax obviously came at the moment when she asked with apparent indifference, 'And what news of the Prince?' 'Prince' in Angelica's mouth did not, alas, mean him, Don Fabrizio, but the little Garibaldino captain; and this provoked a strange sensation in Salina, woven from the crude cotton of sensual jealousy to silken pleasure at his dear Tancredi's success; a sensation, when all was said and done, that was somewhat disagreeable. It was always he who answered this question; he would give a carefully considered account of what he knew, taking care, however, to present a well-arranged little bouquet of news from which his cautious tweezers had extracted both thorns (descriptions of many a jaunt to Naples, allusions to the lovely legs of Aurora Schwarzwald, dancer at the San Carlo) and premature buds ('send news of the Signorina Angelica' – 'In Ferdinand II's study I found a Madonna by Andrea del Sarto which reminded me of the Signorina Sedàra'). So he would put together an insipid picture of Tancredi which bore very little resemblance to the original, but did at least prevent anyone saying that he himself was acting either as spoilsport or pimp. These verbal precautions corresponded closely to his own feelings about Tancredi's considered passion, but they irritated him inasmuch as they wearied him; anyway they were only one sample of all the guile in language and behaviour he had been forced to adopt for some time; he thought with regret of the year before when he could say whatever went through his head, in the certainty that any silly remark would be treated as words from the Gospel and any unconsidered comment as princely carelessness. And now that he had begun regretting the past, he would find himself, in moments of worst humour, slithering quite a way down that perilous slope; once, as he was putting sugar in a cup of tea which Angelica was holding out to him, he realised that he was envying the chances open to a Fabrizio Salina and Tancredi Falconeri of three centuries before, who would have rid themselves of urges to bed down with the Angelicas of their day without ever going before a priest or giving a thought to such local girls' dowries (which were anyway then non-existent), or ever needing to keep respectable uncles on tenter-hooks about saying or suppressing appropriate remarks. The impulse of atavistic lust (which was not really all lust, but partly sensuality stemming from laziness) stung the civilised gentleman nearing fifty so sharply that it made him blush; somewhere, at infinite removes, he had been touched by scruples which he chose to call Rousseauesque, and felt deeply ashamed; from which might be deduced an even sharper revulsion against the social circumstances in which he was so inextricably involved.

The sensation of finding himself a prisoner in a situation evolving more rapidly than foreseen was particularly acute that morning. The night before, in fact, the stage coach bearing the irregular and scanty mail to Donnafugata in its canary-yellow box had brought a letter from Tancredi.

This proclaimed its importance even before reading, written as it was on sumptuous sheets of gleaming paper and in a harmonious script scrupulously tracing full strokes down and thin strokes up. It was obviously the 'clean copy' of any number of disordered drafts. In it the Prince was not addressed by the name of 'Nuncle' which had become dear to him; the wily youth had thought of a formula, 'dearest Uncle Fabrizio', which had a number of merits; of removing any suspicion of jesting on the verge of sacred ground, proclaiming from the very first line the importance of what was to follow, of allowing the letter to be shown to anyone and also of providing a link with ancient pre-Christian beliefs which attributed a binding power to the exact invocation of a name.

'Dearest Uncle Fabrizio', therefore, was informed that his 'most affectionate and devoted nephew' had for the last three months been a prey to the most violent love, and that neither 'the risks of war' (read: walks in the park of Caserta) nor 'the many attractions of a great city' (read: the charms of the dancer Schwarzwald) had been able even for an instant to drive from his mind and heart the image of the Signorina Angelica Sedàra (here a long procession of adjectives to exalt the beauty, grace, virtue and intellect of his beloved); then, in neat hieroglyphics of ink and sentiment, the letter went on to say that Tancredi had felt so conscious of his own unworthiness that he had tried to suffocate his ardour ('long but vain have been the hours during which, amid the clamour of Naples or the austere company of my comrades-in-arms, I have tried to repress my feelings'). But now love had overcome his reserve, and he was begging his dearly beloved uncle to deign to request Signorina Angelica's 'most esteemed father' for her hand, in his name and on his behalf. 'You know, Uncle, that all I can offer to the object of my affections is my love, my name, and my sword.' After this phrase, in connection with which it should not be forgotten that romanticism was then at high noon, Tancredi went on to long considerations of the expediency, nay the necessity of unions between families such as the Falconeri and the Sedàra (once he even dared write 'The House of Sedàra') being encouraged in order to bring new blood into old families, and also to level out classes, one of the aims of the current political movement in Italy. This was the only part of the letter that Don Fabrizio read with any pleasure; and not just because it confirmed his own previsions and crowned him with the laurels of a prophet, but also (it would be harsh to say 'above all') because the style, with its hints of subdued irony, magically evoked his nephew's face; the jesting nasal tone, the sparkling sly blue eyes, the mockingly polite smile. And when he realised that this little Jacobin sally was written out on exactly one single sheet of paper so that if he wanted he could let others read the letter while subtracting this revolutionary chapter, his admiration for Tancredi's tact knew no bounds. After a brief résumé of recent operations and an expression of the conviction that within a year they would be in Rome, 'predestined capital of the new Italy', he thanked his uncle for the care and affection given him in the past, and ended by excusing himself for daring to confide him with this charge 'on which my future happiness depends'. Then came greetings (for Don Fabrizio only).

A first reading of this extraordinary composition made Don Fabrizio's head spin: once again he noted how astoundingly fast all this had gone; put in modern terms he could be said to be in the state of mind of someone to-day who thinks he has boarded one of the easy-going old planes pottering between Palermo and Naples, and suddenly finds himself shut inside a Super Jet and realises he would be at his destination almost before there was time to make the sign of the Cross. Then the second affectionate layer of his nature came to the top, and he rejoiced at this decision of Tancredi which would assure him an ephemeral carnal satisfaction and a perennial financial peace. He paused then, for a moment, to note the youth's extraordinary self-confidence in presuming his own wish already accepted by Angelica; but all these thoughts were swept away eventually by a sense of humiliation at being forced to deal with Don Calogero about a subject so intimate, and also of vexation at having to conduct delicate negotiations next day, with the use, what was more, of precaution and cunning alien to his own, presumably leonine, nature.

Don Fabrizio only revealed the contents of this letter to his wife when they were lying in bed under the pale-blue glow from the glass-hooded oil-lamp. Maria Stella did not say a word at first, just made a series of signs of the Cross; then she remarked that she should have crossed herself with her left hand and not her right; after this supreme expression of amazement she loosed the thunderbolts of her eloquence. Sitting up in bed, her fingers rumpled the sheet while her words furrowed the lunar atmosphere of the enclosed room like angry scarlet torches: 'I'd so hoped he would marry Concetta! He's a traitor, like all liberals of his kind; first he betrayed his King, now he betrays us! He, with that double-face of his, those honeyed words and poisoned actions! That's what happens when one lets people into one's home who aren't of our own blood!' Here she let loose her cavalry charge in family scenes – 'I always said so, but no one would listen to me. I never could endure that fop! You just lost your head about him!' In reality the Princess too had been subject to Tancredi's charm, and she still loved him; but the pleasure of shouting 'I told you so' being the strongest any human being can enjoy, all truths and all feelings were swept along in its wake. 'And now he has even had the impertinence to ask you, his uncle and Prince of Salina, father of the very girl he has deceived, to carry his squalid message to that slut's rascally father! You mustn't do it, Fabrizio, you mustn't do it, you shan't do it, you mustn't do it!' Her voice went up in tone, her body began to stiffen.

Don Fabrizio, still lying on his back, gave a sideways glance to assure himself that the valerian was on the night table. The bottle was there with a silver spoon across the stopper; in the glaucous half-darkness of the room they shone like a reassuring beacon built to withstand storms of hysteria. For a moment he thought of getting out of bed and fetching them; but he compromised by just sitting up too; thus he reacquired a position of prestige. 'Now, Stella, my dear, don't be silly. You don't know what you are saying. Angelica is not a slut. She may become one, but for the moment she's a girl just like any other, prettier than others, and she simply wants to make a good marriage; she may even be a little in love with Tancredi, like everyone else. She'll have money, most of which was ours; but it's now well,

almost too well, taken care of by Don Calogero; and Tancredi
has great need of that; he's a gentleman, he's ambitious, he's a
perfect sieve with money. As for Concetta, he never actually said
a word to her; in fact, it's she who's treated him badly ever since
we got to Donnafugata. And he's not a traitor; he follows the
times, that's all, in his politics and in his private life; and anyway
he's a very lovable lad, you know that as much as I do, Stella my
dear.' Five huge fingers stroked the top of her tiny head. She
was sobbing now; having been sensible enough to drink a sip of
water, the fire of her rage had muted to self-pity. Don Fabrizio
began to hope that he would not have to get out of the warm
bed, face a barefoot crossing of the chilly room. Then to ensure
his future peace he pretended to be angry: 'And I'll have no
shouting in my own house, in my own room, in my own bed!
None of this "You do this" and "You won't do that": I decide;
I'd already decided long before it ever crossed your mind! That's
enough now!'

The hater of shouting was himself bawling with all the breath
in his great chest. Thinking he had a table in front of him, he
banged a great fist on his own knee, hurt himself and calmed
down too.

The Princess, alarmed, was now whining in a low voice like
a frightened puppy.

'Now, let's sleep. To-morrow I'm going out shooting and have
to get up early. Enough! What's decided is decided. Good night,
Stella, my dear.' He kissed his wife first on her forehead and then
on her lips. He lay down again and turned towards the wall. The
shadow of his recumbent form was projected on the silken walls
like the silhouette of a mountain range on a blue horizon.

Stella lay back too, and as her right leg grazed the left leg of
the Prince, she felt consoled and proud at having for a husband
a man so vital and so proud. What did Tancredi matter . . . or
even Concetta . . . ?

For the moment such tight-rope balancing was suspended, along
with all other thought, in the archaic and aromatic countryside
– if it could be called that – where he went shooting every
morning. The term 'countryside' implies soil transformed by

labour; but the scrub clinging to the slopes was still in the very same state of scented tangle in which it had been found by Phoenicians, Dorians and Ionians when they disembarked in Sicily, that America of antiquity. Don Fabrizio and Tumeo climbed up and down, slipped and were scratched by thorns, just as an Archedamos or Philostrates must have got tired and scratched twenty-five centuries before. They saw the same objects, their clothes were soaked with just as sticky a sweat, the same indifferent breeze blew steadily from the sea, moving myrtles and broom, spreading a smell of thyme. The dogs' sudden pauses for thought, their tension waiting for prey, were the very same as when Artemis was invoked for the chase. Reduced to these basic elements, its face washed clean of worries, life took on a tolerable aspect. That morning, shortly before reaching the top of the hill, Arguto and Teresina began the hieratic dance of dogs who have scented prey; stretching, stiffening, prudently raising paws, repressing barks; a few minutes later a tiny beige-coloured backside slid through the grass and two almost simultaneous shots ended the silent wait; at the Prince's feet Arguto placed an animal in its death throes.

It was a wild rabbit; its humble dun-coloured coat had been unable to save it. Horrible wounds lacerated snout and chest. Don Fabrizio found himself stared at by big black eyes soon overlaid by a glaucous veil; they were looking at him with no reproval, but full of tortured amazement at the whole ordering of things; the velvety ears were already cold, the vigorous paws contracting in rhythm, still-living symbol of useless flight; the animal had died tortured by anxious hopes of salvation, imagining it could still escape when it was already caught, just like so many human beings. While sympathetic fingers were still stroking that poor snout, the animal gave a last quiver and died; Don Fabrizio and Don Ciccio had had their bit of fun, the former not only the pleasure of killing but also the comfort of compassion.

When the sportsmen reached the top of the hill, there among the tamarisks and scattered cork-trees appeared the real Sicily again, the one compared to which baroque towns and orange groves are mere trifles: aridly undulating to the horizon in hillock after hillock, comfortless and irrational, with no lines that the mind could grasp, conceived apparently in a delirious moment of creation; a sea suddenly petrified at the instant when a change of wind had flung the waves into a frenzy. Donnafugata lay huddled and hidden in an anonymous fold of the ground, and not a living soul was to be seen; the only signs of the passage of man were scraggy rows of vines. Beyond the hills on one side was the indigo smudge of the sea, more mineral and barren, even, than the land. The slight breeze moved over all, universalising the smell of dung, carrion and sage, cancelling, suppressing, reordering each thing in its careless passage; it dried up the little drops of blood which were the only residue of the rabbit, far away it ruffled the locks of Garibaldi, and further still flung dust in the eyes of Neapolitan soldiers hurriedly reinforcing the battlements of Gaeta, deluded by a hope as vain as the rabbit's frenzied flight. The Prince and the organist rested under the circumscribed shadow of cork-trees; they drank tepid wine from wooden bottles with a roast chicken from Don Fabrizio's haversack, ate little cakes called *muffoletti* dusted with raw flour which Don Ciccio had brought with him, and local grapes so ugly to look at and so good to eat; with hunks of bread they satisfied the hungry dogs standing there in front of them, impassive as bailiffs bent on getting debts paid. Under the monarchic sun Don Fabrizio and Don Ciccio were dozing off.

But though a shot had killed the rabbit, though the bored rifles of General Cialdini were now dismaying the Bourbon troops at Gaeta, though the midday heat was making men doze off, nothing could stop the ants. Attracted by a few chewed grape skins spat out by Don Ciccio, along they rushed in close order, morale high at the chance of annexing this bit of garbage soaked with an organist's saliva. Up they came full of confidence, disordered but resolute; groups of three or four would stop now and again for a chat, exalting, perhaps, the ancient glories and future prosperity of ant hill Number Two under cork-tree Number Four on the top of Mount Morco; then once again they would take up their march with the others towards a buoyant future; the gleaming backs of those imperialists seemed to quiver with enthusiasm, while from their ranks no doubt rose the notes of an anthem.

By some association of ideas which it would be inopportune to pursue, the activity of these insects prevented the Prince from sleeping and reminded him of the days of the Plebiscite about Unification through which he had lived shortly before at Donnafugata itself. Apart from a sense of amazement, those days had left him many an enigma to solve; now, in sight of nature which, except for ants, obviously had no such bothers, he might perhaps find a solution for one of them. The dogs were sleeping stretched and crouched like figures in relief, the little rabbit hanging head down from a branch was swinging out diagonally under the constant surge of wind, but Tumeo, with the help of his pipe, still managed to keep his eyes open.

'And you, Don Ciccio, how did you vote on the twenty-first?'

The poor man started; taken by surprise at a moment when he was outside the stockade of precautions in which like each of his fellow townsmen he usually moved, he hesitated, not know-ing what to reply.

The Prince mistook for alarm what was really only surprise, and felt irritated. 'Well, what are you afraid of? There's no one here but us, the wind and the dogs.'

The list of reassuring witnesses was not really happily chosen; wind is a gossip by definition, the Prince was half Sicilian. Only the dogs were absolutely trustworthy and that only because they lacked articulate speech. But Don Ciccio had now recovered; his peasant astuteness had suggested the right reply – nothing at all. 'Excuse me, Excellency, but there's no point in your ques-tion. You know that everyone in Donnafugata voted "yes".'

Don Fabrizio did know this; and that was why this reply merely changed a small enigma into an enigma of history. Before the voting many had come to him for advice; all of them had been exhorted, sincerely, to vote 'yes'. Don Fabrizio, in fact, could not see what else there was to do: whether treating it as a *fait accompli* or as an act merely theatrical and banal, whether taking it as historical necessity or considering the trouble these humble folk might get into if their negative attitude were known. He had noticed, though, that not all had been con-vinced by his words; into play had come the abstract Machiavel-lianism of Sicilians, which so often induced these people, with all their generosity, to erect complex barricades on the most fragile of foundations. Like clinics adept at treatment based on fundamentally false analyses of blood and urine which they are too lazy to rectify, the Sicilians (of that time) ended by killing off the patient, that is themselves, by a niggling and hair-splitting rarely connected with any real understanding of the problems involved, or even of their interlocutors. Some of these who had made a visit *ad limina leopardorum* considered it impossible for a Prince of Salina to vote in favour of the Revolution (as the recent changes were still called in those remote parts), and they interpreted his advice as ironical, intended to effect a result in practice opposite to his words. These pilgrims (and they were the best) had come out of his study winking at each other – as far as their respect for him would allow – proud at having penetrated the meaning of the princely words, and rubbing their hands in self-congratulation at their own perspicacity just when this was most completely in eclipse.

Others, on the other hand, after having listened to him, went off looking sad and convinced that he was a turncoat or half-wit, more than ever determined to take no notice of what he said but to follow instead the age-old proverb about preferring a known evil to an untried good. These were reluctant to ratify the new national reality for personal reasons too; either from religious faith, or from having received favours from the former régime and not being sharp enough to insert themselves into the new one, or finally because during the upsets of the liberation period they had lost a few capons and sacks of beans, and been cuckolded either freely like Garibaldini volunteers or forcibly like Bourbon levies. He had, in fact, the disagreeable but distinct impression that about fifteen of them would vote 'no', a tiny minority certainly, but noticeable in the small electorate of Donnafugata. Taking into consideration that the people who came to him represented the flower of the inhabitants, and that there must also be some unconvinced among the hundreds of electors who had not dreamt of setting foot inside the palace, the Prince had calculated that Donnafugata's compact affirmative would be varied by about forty negative votes.

The day of the Plebiscite was windy and grey, and tired groups of youths had been seen going through the streets of the town with bits of paper covered with 'yes' stuck in the ribbons of their hats. Amid waste paper and refuse swirled by the wind they sang a few verses of *La Bella Gigugin* transformed into a kind of Arab wail, a fate to which any gay tune sung in Sicily is bound to succumb. There had also been seen two or three 'foreigners' (that is from Girgenti) installed in *Zzu* Menico's tavern, where they were declaiming Leopardi's lines on the 'magnificent and progressive destiny' of a renovated Sicily united to resurgent Italy. A few peasants were standing listening, mutely, stunned by overwork or starved by unemployment. These cleared their throats and spat continuously, but kept silent; so silent that it must have been then (as Don Fabrizio said afterwards) that the 'foreigners' decided to give Arithmetic precedence over Rhetoric in the Quadrivium arts.

The Prince went to vote about four in the afternoon, flanked on the right by Father Pirrone, on the left by Don Onofrio Rotolo; frowning and fair-skinned, he proceeded slowly towards the Town Hall, frequently putting up a hand to protect his eyes lest the breeze loaded with all the filth collected on its way should bring on the conjunctivitis to which he was subject; and he remarked to Father Pirrone that though the air would have been like a putrid pool without the wind, yet health-giving gusts did seem to drag up a lot of dirt with them. He was wearing the same black frockcoat in which two years before he had gone to pay his respects at Caserta to poor King Ferdinand, who had been lucky enough to die in time to avoid this day of dirty wind when the seal would be set on his own incapacity. But had it really been incapacity? One might as well say that a person succumbing to typhus dies of incapacity. He remembered the King busy putting up dykes against the floods of useless documents: and suddenly he realised how much unconscious appeal to pity there was in those unattractive features. Such thoughts were disagreeable, as are all those that make us understand things too late, and the Prince's face went solemn and dark as if he were following an invisible funeral car. Only the violent impact of his feet on loose stones in the street showed his internal conflict. It is superfluous to mention that the ribbon on his top hat was innocent of any piece of paper; but in the eyes of those who knew him a 'yes' and a 'no' alternated on the glistening felt.

On reaching a little room in the Town Hall used as the voting booth he was surprised to see all the members of the committee get up as his great height filled the doorway; a few peasants who had arrived before were put aside, and so without having to wait Don Fabrizio handed his 'yes' into the patriotic hands of Don Calogero Sedàra. Father Pirrone, though, did not vote at all, as he had been careful not to get himself listed as resident in the town. Don 'Nofrio, obeying the express desires of the Prince, gave his own monosyllabic opinion about the complicated Italian question; a masterpiece of concision carried through with the good grace of a child drinking castor oil. After which all were invited for 'a little glass' upstairs in the Mayor's study; but Father Pirrone and Don 'Nofrio put forward good reasons, one of abstinence, the other of stomach-ache, and remained below. Don Fabrizio had to face the party alone.

Behind the Mayor's writing desk gleamed a brand new portrait of Garibaldi and (already) one of King Victor Emmanuel hung, luckily, to the right; the first handsome, the second ugly; both, however, made brethren by prodigious growths of hair which nearly hid their faces altogether. On a small low table was a plate with some ancient biscuits blackened by fly droppings and a dozen little squat glasses brimming with *rosolio* wine: four red, four green, four white, the last in the centre: an ingenious symbol of the new national flag which tempered the Prince's remorse with a smile. He chose the white liquor for himself, presumably because the least indigestible and not, as some thought, in tardy homage to the Bourbon standard. Anyway, all three varieties of *rosolio* were equally sugary, sticky and revolting. His host had the good taste not to give toasts. But, as Don Calogero said, great joys are silent. Don Fabrizio was shown a letter from the authorities of Girgenti announcing to the industrious citizens of Donnafugata the concession of 2,000 lire towards sewage, a work which would be completed before the end of 1961 so the Mayor assured them, stumbling into one of those *lapsus* whose mechanism Freud was to explain many decades later; and the meeting broke up.

Before dusk the three or four easy girls of Donnafugata (there were some there too, not grouped but each hard at work on her own) appeared in the square with tricolour ribbons in their manes as protest against the exclusion of women from the vote; the poor creatures were jeered at even by the most advanced liberals and forced back to their lairs. This did not prevent the *Giornale di Trinacria* telling the people of Palermo four days later that at Donnafugata 'some gentle representatives of the fair sex wished to show their faith in the new and brilliant destinies of their beloved Country, and demonstrated in the main square amid great acclamation from the patriotic population'.

After this the electoral booths were closed and the scrutators got to work; late that night the shutters on the balcony of the Town Hall were flung open and Don Calogero appeared with a tricolour sash over his middle, flanked by two ushers with lighted candelabra which the wind snuffed at once. To the invisible crowd in the shadows below he announced that the Plebiscite at Donnafugata had had the following results:

Voters, 515; Voting, 512; Yes, 512; No, zero.

From the dark end of the square rose applause and hurrahs; on her little balcony Angelica, with her funereal maid, clapped lovely rapacious hands; speeches were made; adjectives loaded with superlatives and double consonants reverberated and echoed in the dark from one wall to another; amid thundering of fireworks messages were sent off to the King (the new one) and to the General; a tricolour rocket or two climbed up from the village into the blackness towards the starless sky. By eight o'clock all was over, and nothing remained except darkness as on any other night, always.

On the top of Monte Morco all was clear now, in bright light; but the gloom of that night still lay stagnant, deep in Don Fabrizio's heart. His discomfort had become more irksome, if vaguer; it had no connection at all with the great matters of which the Plebiscite marked the start of a solution: the major interests of the Kingdom (of the Two Sicilies) and of his own class, his personal privileges had come through all these events battered but still lively. In the circumstances he could not well expect more. No, his discomfort was not of a political nature and must have deeper roots somewhere in one of those reasons which we call irrational because they are buried under layers of self-ignorance. Italy was born on that sullen night at Donnafugata, born right there, in that forgotten little town, just as much as in the sloth of Palermo or the clamour of Naples; but an evil fairy, of unknown name, must have been present; anyway Italy was born and one could only hope that she would live on in this form; any other would be worse. Agreed. And yet this persistent disquiet of his must mean something; during that too brief announcement of figures, just as during those too emphatic speeches, he had a feeling that something, someone, had died, God only knew in what back-alley, in what corner of the popular conscience.

The cool air had dispersed Don Ciccio's somnolence, the massive grandeur of the Prince dispelled his fears; all that remained afloat now on the surface of his conscience was resentment, useless of course but not ignoble. He stood up, spoke in dialect and gesticulated, a pathetic puppet who in some absurd way was right.

'I, Excellency, voted "no". "No", a hundred times "no". I know what you told me: necessity, unity, expediency. You may be right; I know nothing of politics. Such things I leave to others. But Ciccio Tumeo is honest, poor though he may be, with his trousers in holes' (and he slapped the carefully mended patches on the buttocks of his shooting breeches) 'and I don't forget favours done me! Those swine in the Town Hall just swallowed up my opinion, chewed it and then spat it out transformed as they wanted. I said black and they made me say white! The one time when I could say what I thought that bloodsucker Sedàra went and annulled it, behaved as if I'd never existed, as if I never meant a thing, me, Francesco Tumeo La Manna son of the late Leonardo, organist of the Mother Church at Donnafugata, a better man than he is! To think I'd even dedicated to him a mazurka composed by me at the birth of that ...' (he bit a finger to rein himself in) 'that mincing daughter of his!'

At this point calm descended on Don Fabrizio, who had

finally solved the enigma; now he knew who had been killed at
Donnafugata, at a hundred other places, in the course of that
night of dirty wind: a new-born babe: good faith; just the very
child who should have been cared for most, whose strengthening
would have justified all the silly vandalisms. Don Ciccio's negative vote, fifty similar votes at Donnafugata, a hundred thousand
'no's' in the whole Kingdom, would have had no effect on the
result, have made it, in fact, if anything more significant; and
this maiming of souls would have been avoided. Six months
before they used to hear a rough despotic voice saying: 'Do what
I say or you're for it!' Now there was already an impression of
such a threat being replaced by a money-lender's soapy tones:
'But you signed it yourself, didn't you? Can't you see? It's quite
clear. You must do as we say, for here are the IOU's; your will
is identical with mine.'

Don Ciccio was still thundering on: 'For you nobles it's
different. *You* might be ungrateful about an extra estate, but *we*
must be grateful for a bit of bread. It's different again for profiteers like Sedàra with whom cheating is a law of nature. Small
folk like us have to take things as they come. You know, Excellency, that my father, God rest his soul, was gamekeeper at the
royal shoot of Sant' Onofrio back in Ferdinand IV's time, when
the English were here? It was a hard life, but the green royal
livery and the silver plaque conferred authority. Queen Isabella,
the Spaniard, was Duchess of Calabria then, and it was she who
had me study, made me what I am now, organist of the Mother
Church, honoured by Your Excellency's kindness; when my
mother sent off a petition to Court in our years of greatest need,
back came five gold ounces, sure as death, for they were fond of
us there in Naples, they knew we were decent folk and faithful
subjects; when the King came he used to clap my father on the
shoulder. "Don Lionà," he said, "I wish we'd more like you,
devoted to the throne and to my Person." Then the officer in
attendance used to hand out gold coin. Alms, they call it now,
that truly royal generosity; and they call it that so as not to give
any themselves; but it was just a reward for loyalty. And if those
holy Kings and lovely Queens are looking down at us from
heaven to-day, what'ld they say? "The son of Don Leonardo

Tumeo betrayed us!" Luckily the truth is known in Paradise!
Yes, Excellency, I know, people like you have told me, such
things from royalty mean nothing, they're just part of the job.
That may be true, in fact is true. But we got those five gold
ounces, that's a fact, and they helped us through the winter. And
now I could repay the debt my "no" becomes a "yes"! I used
to be a "faithful subject", I've become a "filthy Bourbonite".
Everyone's Savoyard nowadays! But I take "Savoyards" with
coffee!' And he dipped an invisible biscuit between finger and
thumb into an imaginary cup.

Don Fabrizio had always liked Don Ciccio, partly because of
the compassion inspired in him by all who from youth had
thought of themselves as dedicated to the Arts, and in old age,
realising they had no talent, still carried on the same activity at
lower levels, pocketing withered dreams; and he was also
touched by the dignity of his poverty. But now he also felt a
kind of admiration for him, and deep down at the very bottom
of his proud conscience a voice was asking if Don Ciccio had
not perhaps behaved more nobly than the Prince of Salina. And
the Sedàra, all the various Sedàra, from the petty one who viol-
ated arithmetic at Donnafugata to the major ones at Palermo
and Turin, had they not committed a crime by choking such
consciences? Don Fabrizio could not know it then, but a great
deal of the slackness and acquiescence for which the people of
the South were to be criticised during the next decade, was due
to the stupid annulment of the first expression of liberty ever
offered them.

Don Ciccio had said his say. And now his genuine but rarely
shown side of 'austere man of principle' was taken over by one
much more frequent and no less genuine, that of snob. For
Tumeo belonged to the zoological species of 'passive snob', a
species unjustly reviled nowadays. Of course the word 'snob'
was unknown in the Sicily of 1860; but just as tuberculosis
existed before Koch, so in that remote era there were people
for whom to obey, imitate and above all avoid distressing those
whom they considered of higher social rank than themselves was
the supreme law of life; snobbery, in fact, is the opposite of envy.
At that time a man of this type went under various names; he

was called 'devoted', 'attached', 'faithful'; and life was happy for him since a nobleman's most fugitive smile was enough to flood an entire day with sun; and accompanied by such affectionate appellatives, the restorative graces were more frequent than they are to-day. Now Don Ciccio's frankly snobbish nature made him fear causing Don Fabrizio distress, and he searched diligently round for ways to disperse any frowns he might be causing on the Prince's Olympian brow; the best means to hand was suggesting they should start shooting again; and so they did. Surprised in their afternoon naps, some wretched woodcock and another rabbit fell under the marksmen's fire, particularly accurate and pitiless that day as both Salina and Tumeo were identifying those innocent creatures with Don Calogero Sedàra. But the shots, the flying feathers, the shreds of skin glittering for an instant in the sun, were not enough to soothe the Prince that day; as the hours passed and return to Donnafugata drew near he felt more and more oppressed, bothered, humiliated at the thought of the imminent conversation with the plebeian Mayor, and his having called in his heart those woodcock and the rabbit 'Don Calogero' had been no use after all; though he had already decided to swallow the horrid toad he still felt a need for more information about his adversary, or rather, for a sounding out of public opinion about the step he was about to take. So for the second time that day Don Ciccio was surprised by a sudden point-blank question.

'Listen, Don Ciccio; you see so many people, what do they really think of Don Calogero at Donnafugata?'

Tumeo, in truth, felt he had already shown his opinion of the Mayor quite clearly; and he was just about to say so when into his mind came rumours he had heard about Tancredi making up to Angelica: and he was suddenly overwhelmed with regret at having let himself be drawn into expressing downright judgments which must certainly be anathema to the Prince if what he assumed was true; in another part of his mind, meanwhile, he was congratulating himself at not having said anything positive against Angelica; and the faint ache which he still felt in his right forefinger had the effect of a soothing balsam.

'After all, Excellency, Don Calogero Sedàra is no worse than lots of others who have come up in the last few months.' The homage was moderate but enough to allow Don Fabrizio to insist, 'You see, Don Ciccio, I'm most interested to know the truth about Don Calogero and his family.'

'The truth, Excellency, is that Don Calogero is very rich, and very influential too; that he's a miser (when his daughter was at college he and his wife used to eat a fried egg between them), but knows how to spend when he has to; and as every coin spent in the world must end in someone's pocket he now finds many people dependent on him; when he's a friend he really is a friend, one must say that for him: he lets his land on very harsh terms and the peasants kill themselves to pay, but a month ago he lent fifty gold ounces to Pasquale Tripi who had helped him at the time of the landings: without interest, too, which is the greatest miracle ever known since Santa Rosalia stopped the plague at Palermo. He's clever as the devil, too; Your Excellency should have seen him last April or May; up and down the whole district he went like a bat; by trap, horse, mule, foot, in rain or sun; and wherever he passed secret groups were formed, to prepare the way for those that were to come. He's a scourge of God, Excellency, a scourge of God. And we're only seeing the start of Don Calogero's career. In a few months he'll be Deputy in the Turin Parliament; in a few years, when church property is put up for sale, he'll pay next to nothing for the estates of Marca and Fondachello and become the biggest landowner in the province; that's Don Calogero, Excellency, the new man to be: a pity he has to be like that, though.'

Don Fabrizio remembered a conversation with Father Pirrone some months before in the sunlit observatory. What the Jesuit had predicted had come to pass. But wasn't it perhaps good tactics to insert himself into the new movement, make at least part use of it for a few members of his own class? The worry of his imminent interview with Don Calogero lessened.

'But the rest of his family, Don Ciccio, what are they really like?'

'Excellency, no one has laid eyes on Don Calogero's wife for years, except me. She only leaves the house to go to early Mass, the five o'clock one, when it's empty. There's no organ-playing

at that hour; but once I got up early just to see her. Donna
Bastiana came in with her maid, and as I was hiding behind a
confessional I could not see very much; but at the end of Mass
the heat was too great for the poor woman and she took off her
black veil. Word of honour, Excellency, she was lovely as the
sun, one can't blame Don Calogero, who's a beetle of a man,
for wanting to keep her away from others. But even in the best
kept houses secrets come out; servants talk; and it seems Donna
Bastiana is a kind of animal: she can't read or write or tell the
time by a clock, can scarcely talk; just a beautiful mare, voluptuous and uncouth; she's incapable even of affection for her own
daughter! Good for bed and that's all.'

Don Ciccio, who, as protégé of queens and follower of
princes, considered his own simple manners to be perfect, smiled
with pleasure. He had found a way of getting some of his own
back on the suppressor of his personality. 'Anyway,' he went on,
'one couldn't expect much else. You know whose daughter
Donna Bastiana is, Excellency?' He turned, rose on tiptoe,
pointed to a distant group of huts which looked as if they were
slithering off the edge of the hill, nailed there just by a wretched-
looking bell-tower: a crucified hamlet. 'She's the daughter of
one of your peasants from Runci, Peppe Giunta he was called,
so filthy and so crude that everyone called him Peppe "Mmerda"
... excuse the word, Excellency.' Satisfied, he twisted one of
Teresina's ears round a finger. 'Two years after Don Calogero
had eloped with Bastiana they found him dead on the path to
Rampinzeri, with twelve bullets in his back. Always lucky, is
Don Calogero, for the old man was getting above himself and
demanding, they say.'

Much of this was known to Don Fabrizio and had already
been balanced up in his mind; but the nickname of Angelica's
grandfather was new to him; it opened a profound historical
perspective, and made him glimpse other abysses compared to
which Don Calogero himself seemed a garden flowerbed. The
Prince began to feel the ground giving way under his feet; how
ever could Tancredi swallow this? And what about himself? He
found himself trying to work out the relationship between the
Prince of Salina, uncle of the bridegroom, and the grandfather

of the bride; he found none, there wasn't any. Angelica was just Angelica, a flower of a girl, a rose merely fertilised by her grandfather's nickname. *Non olet*, he repeated, *non olet*; in fact *optime foeminam ac contuberninum olet.*

'You've mentioned everything, Don Ciccio, crude mothers and faecal grandfathers, but not what interests me: the Signorina Angelica.'

The secret of Tancredi's matrimonial intentions, although embryonic until a few hours before, would certainly have been told then had it not luckily been camouflaged. No doubt the young man's frequent visits to Don Calogero's home had been noticed, as also his ecstatic smiles and little attentions, normal and insignificant in a city but symptoms of violent passion in the eyes of virtuous folk at Donnafugata. The main scandal had been the first; the old men cooking in the sun and the children duelling in the dust had seen all, understood all, and repeated all; and on the aphrodisiac and seductive properties of those dozen peaches had been consulted the most expert witches and abstruse treatises on potions, chiefly that by Rutilio Benincasa, the Aristotle of the rustic proletariat. Luckily there had come about a phenomenon relatively frequent amongst Sicilians; malice had masked truth; everyone had built up a puppet of a libertine Tancredi fixing his lascivious desires on Angelica; he was manoeuvring to seduce her, that was all. The thought of any possible marriage between a Prince of Falconeri and a granddaughter of Peppe 'Mmerda' did not even cross the minds of these country folk, who thus rendered to feudal families a homage equivalent to that rendered by a blasphemer to God. Tancredi's departure had cut short these fantasies and they were not mentioned again. In this respect Tumeo had been like the others, so he greeted the Prince's question with the amused air assumed by older men when discoursing on the follies of the young.

'As to the Signorina, Excellency, there's nothing to say about her; she speaks for herself; her eyes, her skin, her figure are all there to be seen and appreciated by anyone. Don Tancredi has understood the language they speak, I think; or shouldn't I suggest such a thing? She has all the beauty of the mother with none of the grandfather's stink of manure; and she's intelligent, too.

You've seen how those few years in Florence have transformed her completely? A real lady she's become,' went on Don Ciccio, insensitive to subtleties in such matters. 'A complete lady. When she returned from school and invited me home she played my old mazurka; badly, but it was a delight to watch her, those black locks, those eyes, those legs, that breast . . . Uuh! No stink of manure there! Her sheets must smell like paradise!'

The Prince was vexed; so touchy is the pride of class, even in a moment of decline, that these orgiastic praises of his future niece's allurements offended him; how dared Don Ciccio express himself with such lascivious lyricism about a future Princess of Falconeri? It is true, of course, that the poor man knew nothing as yet; he would have to be told all: but anyway the news would be public in three hours. He decided at once and turned to Tumeo a smile feline but friendly. 'Calm yourself, my dear Don Ciccio, calm yourself; at home I have a letter from my nephew charging me to ask for Signorina Angelica's hand in matrimony on his behalf; so from now on you will talk of her with your usual respect. You are the first to know the news, but for that privilege you must pay; when we get back to the palace you'll be locked up with Teresina in the gun-room; you'll have time to clean and oil all the guns, and you will be set at liberty only after Don Calogero's visit; I want nothing to leak out before.'

Taken by surprise like this, all Don Ciccio's snobberies and precautions collapsed together like a group of skittles hit in the middle. All that survived was age-old feeling.

'How foul, Excellency! A nephew of yours ought not to marry the daughter of those who're your enemies, who have stabbed you in the back! To try to seduce her, as I thought, was an act of conquest; this is unconditional surrender. It's the end of the Falconeri and of the Salina too.'

Having said this he bent his head and longed in anguish for the earth to open under his feet. The Prince had gone purple, even his ears, even the whites of his eyes seemed flushed with blood. He clenched his fists and took a step towards Don Ciccio. But he was a man of science, used, after all, to seeing at times the pros and cons; and anyway under that leonine aspect he was a sceptic. He had put up with so much that day already; the result of the Plebiscite, the nickname of Angelica's grandfather, those bullets in the back. And Tumeo was right; in him spoke clear tradition. But the man was a fool: this marriage was not the end of everything, but the beginning of everything. It was in the very best of traditions.

His fists unclenched; the marks of his nails were impressed on his palms. 'Let's go home, Don Ciccio, there are some things you can't understand. Now, you'll remember what we agreed, won't you?'

And as they climbed down towards the road, it would have been difficult to tell which of the two was Don Quixote and which Sancho Panza.

When Don Calogero's arrival was announced at exactly half-past four the Prince had not yet finished his toilet; he sent a message asking the Mayor to wait a minute in his study and went on placidly embellishing himself. He plastered his hair with *Lemo-liscio*, Atkinson's 'Lime Juice and Glycerine', a dense whitish lotion which arrived in cases from London and whose name suffered the same ethnic changes as songs: he rejected the black frockcoat and chose instead a very pale lilac one which seemed more in keeping with the presumably festive occasion; he dallied a little longer to tweak out with pincers an impudent fair hair which had succeeded in escaping that morning in his hurried shave: he had Father Pirrone called; before leaving the room he took off a table an extract from the *Blätter für Himmelsforschung* and with the rolled-up pamphlet made the sign of the Cross, a gesture of devotion which in Sicily has a non-religious meaning more often than is realised.

As he crossed the two rooms preceding the study he tried to imagine himself as an imposing leopard with smooth scented skin preparing to tear a timid jackal to pieces; but by one of those involuntary associations of ideas which are the scourge of natures like his, he found flicking into his memory one of those French historical pictures in which Austrian marshals and generals, covered with plumes and decorations, are filing in surrender past an ironical Napoleon; they are more elegant, undoubtedly, but it is the squat little man in the grey topcoat who is the victor; and so, put out by these inopportune memories of Mantua and Ulm, it was an irritated Leopard that entered the study.

Don Calogero was standing there, very small, very badly shaved; he would have looked like a jackal had it not been for eyes glinting intelligence; but as this intelligence of his had a material aim opposed to the abstract one to which the Prince's was supposed to tend, this was taken as a sign of slyness. Devoid of the instinct for choosing the right clothes for the occasion which was innate in the Prince, the Mayor had thought it proper to dress up almost in mourning; he was nearly as black as Father Pirrone, but while the latter was sitting in a corner with the marmoreally abstract air of priests who wish to avoid influencing the decisions of others, the Mayor's face expressed a sense of avid expectancy almost painful to behold. They plunged at once into the skirmish of insignificant words which precede great verbal battles. But it was Don Calogero who launched the main attack.

'Excellency,' he asked, 'have you had good news from Don Tancredi?' In little towns in those days the Mayor was always able to examine the post unofficially and maybe he had been warned by the unusually elegant writing paper. The Prince, when this occurred to him, began to feel annoyed.

'No, Don Calogero, no. My nephew's gone mad . . .'

But there exists a deity who is protector of princes. He is called Courtesy. And he often intervenes to prevent Leopards from unfortunate slips. But he has to be paid heavy tribute. As Pallas intervened to curb the intemperances of Odysseus, so Courtesy appeared to Don Fabrizio and stopped him on the brink of the abyss; but the Prince had to pay for his salvation by becoming explicit for just once in his life. With perfect naturalness, without a second's hesitation, he ended the phrase; '. . . mad with love for your daughter, Don Calogero. So he wrote to me yesterday.'

The Mayor preserved a surprising equanimity. He gave a slight smile and began examining the ribbon on his hat; Father Pirrone's eyes were turned to the ceiling as if he were a master mason charged with judging its solidity. The Prince was put out: that silence on both their parts even deprived him of the petty satisfaction of arousing surprise. So it was with relief that he realised Don Calogero was about to speak.

'I knew it, Excellency, I knew it. They were seen to kiss on Tuesday, 25th of September, the day before Don Tancredi's departure. In your garden, near the fountain. Laurel hedges aren't always as thick as people think. For a month I've been waiting for your nephew to make some move, and I'd just been thinking now of coming to ask Your Excellency about his intentions.'

Don Fabrizio felt assailed by numbers of stinging hornets. First, as is proper to every man not yet decrepit, that of carnal jealousy. So Tancredi had tasted that flavour of strawberries and cream which would always be unknown to him! Then came a sense of social humiliation at finding himself an accused instead of a bearer of good news. Third, personal vexation, that of one who thought he had everything in his control and then finds much has been happening without his knowledge. 'Don Calogero, let's not change the cards we have on the table. Remember, it was *I* who called *you*. I wished to tell you of a letter from my nephew which arrived yesterday. In it he declares his passion for your daughter, a passion of whose intensity I ...' (Here the Prince hesitated a moment, because lies are sometimes difficult to tell before gimlet eyes like the Mayor's) '... I was completely ignorant till now; and at the end of it he charges me to ask you for Signorina Angelica's hand.'

Don Calogero went on smiling impassively; Father Pirrone had transformed himself from architectural expert into Moslem sage, and with four fingers of his right hand crossed in four fingers of his left was rotating his thumbs around each other, turning and changing their direction with a great display of choreographic fantasy. The silence lasted a long time; the Prince lost patience. 'Now, Don Calogero, it is I who am waiting for you to declare your intentions.'

The Mayor's eyes had been fixed on the orange fringe of the Prince's armchair; for an instant he covered them with his right hand, then raised them; now they looked candid, brimming with amazed surprise, as if that action had really changed them.

'Excuse me, Prince' (by the sudden omission of 'Excellency' Don Fabrizio knew that all was happily consummated) 'but joy and surprise had taken my words away. I'm a modern parent, though, and can give no definite answer until I have questioned the angel who is the consolation of our home. But I also know how to exercise a father's sacred rights. All that happens in Angelica's heart and mind is known to me, and I think I can say that Don Tancredi's affection, which honours us all, is sincerely returned.'

Don Fabrizio was overcome with sincere emotion; the toad had been swallowed; the chewed head and gizzards were going down his throat; he still had to crunch up the claws, but that was nothing compared to the rest; the worst was over. With this sense of liberation he began to feel his affection for Tancredi coming to the fore again, and thought of those narrow blue eyes of his glittering as they read the happy reply; he imagined, or recalled rather, the first months of a love match with the frenzies and acrobatics of the senses braced and sustained by all the hierarchies of angels, benevolent though surely surprised. And he foresaw Tancredi's security of life later on, his chances for developing talents whose wings would have been clipped by lack of money.

The nobleman rose to his feet, took a step towards the surprised Don Calogero, raised him from his armchair, clasped him to his breast; the Mayor's short legs were suspended in the air. For a moment that room in a remote Sicilian province looked like a Japanese print of a huge violet iris with a hairy fly hanging from a petal. When Don Calogero touched the floor again, Don Fabrizio thought, 'This won't do, I really must give him a pair of English razors.'

Father Pirrone switched off the turbine of his thumbs; he got up and squeezed the Prince's hand. 'Excellency, I evoke the protection of God on this marriage; your joy has become mine.' To Don Calogero he extended the tips of his fingers without a word. Then with a knuckle he tapped the barometer hanging on the wall: it was falling; bad weather ahead. He sat down and opened his breviary.

'Don Calogero,' said the Prince, 'the love of these two young people is the basis, the sole foundation of their future happiness. That we all know. But we men of a certain age, men of experience, have to think of other things, too. There is no point in my telling you how illustrious is the family of Falconeri; it came to Sicily with Charles of Anjou, flourished under the Aragonese, the Spanish, the Bourbon kings (if I may name them in your presence) and I am sure that it will also prosper under the new dynasty from the mainland (which God preserve).' (It was impossible to tell how much the Prince was being ironic or how much just mistaken.) 'They were Peers of the Realm, Grandees of Spain, Knights of Santiago, and when they have a fancy to be Knights of Malta they need only raise a finger and Via Condotti turns them out a diploma all fresh from the oven, without a word of complaint. So far at least.' (This perfidious insinuation was entirely lost on Don Calogero, who was quite ignorant of the statutes of the Sovereign Hierosalamitan Order of St John.) 'I am sure that your daughter will ornament still more by her rare beauty the ancient trunk of the Falconeri and emulate by her virtue that of the saintly princesses of the line, the last of whom, my sister, God rest her soul, will certainly bless the bride and groom from Heaven.' Again Don Fabrizio felt moved, remembering his dear Giulia whose wasted life had been a perpetual sacrifice to the frenzied extravagances of Tancredi's father. 'As for the boy, you know him; and if you did not, I am here to guarantee him in every possible way. There is endless good in him, and it is not only I who say so. Isn't that true, Father Pirrone?'

The excellent Jesuit, dragged from his reading, found himself suddenly facing an unpleasant dilemma. He had been Tancredi's confessor and he knew quite a number of his little failings: none very serious, of course, but such as to detract quite a good deal from the endless goodness of which the Prince had spoken; and all such (he almost felt like saying) as to guarantee an unwavering marital infidelity. This, of course, could not actually be said both for sacramental reasons and from worldly expediency. On the other hand he liked Tancredi, and though he disapproved of the wedding with all his heart he would never say a word which could either impede it or in any way cloud its course. He took refuge in Prudence, most tractable of the cardinal virtues. 'The fund of goodness in our dear Tancredi is great indeed, Don Calogero, and, sustained by Divine Grace and by the earthly virtues of Signorina Angelica, he may one day become a good Christian husband.' The prophecy, risky but prudently conditional, passed muster.

'But, Don Calogero,' went on the Prince, chewing on the last gristly bits of toad, 'if it is pointless to tell you of the antiquity of the Falconeri, it is unfortunately also pointless, since you already know it, to tell you that my nephew's economic circumstances are not equal to the greatness of his name. Don Tancredi's father, my brother-in-law Ferdinando, was not what is called a provident parent; his magnificent scale of life, and the irresponsibility of his administrators, have gravely shaken the patrimony of my dear nephew and former ward; the great estates around Mazzara, the pistachio woods of Ravanusa, the mulberry plantations of Oliveri, the palace in Palermo, all, all have gone; that you know, Don Calogero.'

Don Calogero did indeed know that; it had been the greatest migration of swallows in living memory: a thought which still brought terror, though not prudence, to the entire Sicilian nobility, while it was a font of delight for all the Sedàras. 'During the period of my guardianship all I succeeded in saving was the villa, the one near my own, by juridical quibbles and also thanks to a sacrifice or two on my own part which I made joyfully, both in memory of my sainted sister Giulia and because of my own affection for the dear lad. It's a fine villa; the staircase was designed by Marvuglia, the drawing-rooms frescoed by Serenario; but at the moment the room in best repair can scarcely be used as a stall for goats.'

The last shreds of toad had been nastier than he had expected: but they had gone down too, in the end. Now he had only to wash out his mouth with some phrase which was pleasant as well as sincere. 'But, Don Calogero, the result of all these disasters, of all this heart-burning, has been Tancredi. There are certain things known to people like us; and maybe it is impossible to obtain the distinction, the delicacy, the fascination of a boy like him without his ancestors having romped through half a dozen fortunes. At least so it is in Sicily; it's a kind of law of nature, like those regulating earthquakes and drought.'

He paused a moment as a lackey came in bearing two lighted lamps on a tray. As they were being set in place the Prince caused a silence charged with resigned concern to reign in the study. 'Tancredi is no ordinary boy, Don Calogero,' he went on. 'He is far more than merely gentlemanly and elegant; though he has not studied much, he knows about the important things; men, women, the feel and sense of the times. He is ambitious and rightly so; he will go far; and your Angelica, Don Calogero, will be lucky to mount the ladder with him. Also, in Tancredi's company one may have moments of irritation, but never of boredom; and that means a great deal.'

It would be an exaggeration to say that the Mayor appreciated the worldly subtleties of this part of the Prince's speech; on the whole it merely confirmed him in his summary conviction of Tancredi's shrewdness and opportunism; and what he needed at home was a man astute and able, no more. He thought himself, he felt himself to be the equal of anyone; and he was even rather sorry to notice in his daughter a genuine affection for the handsome youth.

'Prince, all these things I knew, and others too. And they don't matter to me at all.' He wrapped himself round once more in a cloak of sentimentality. 'Love, Excellency, love is all, as I know myself.' And he may have been sincere, poor man, if his probable definition of love were admitted. 'But I'm a man of the world and I want to put my cards on the table too. There's no point in talking about my daughter's qualities; she's the blood in my heart, the liver in my guts: I've no one else to leave what I have, and what's mine is hers. But it's only right that the young people should know what they can count on at once. In the marriage contract I will assign to my daughter the estate of Settesoli, of 644 *salmi*, that is 1010 *hectares* as they want us to call them nowadays, all corn, first-class land, airy and cool; and 180 *salmi* of olive groves and vineyards at Gibildolce; and on the wedding day I will hand over to the bridegroom twenty linen sacks each containing 10,000 ounces of gold. I'll only have a stick or two left myself,' he added, knowing well he would not and not wanting to be believed, 'but a daughter's a daughter. And with that they can do up all the staircases by Marruggia and all the ceilings by Sorcionario that exist. Angelica must be properly housed.'

Ignorant vulgarity exuded from his every pore; even so the two listeners were astounded; Don Fabrizio needed all his self-control not to show surprise; Tancredi's coup was far bigger than he had ever imagined. A sensation of revulsion came over him again, but Angelica's beauty, the bridegroom's grace, still managed to veil in poetry the crudeness of the contract. Father Pirrone did let his tongue cluck on his palate; then, annoyed at having shown his own amazement, he tried to rhyme the improvident sound by making his chair and shoes squeak and by crackling the leaves of his breviary but failed completely; the impression remained.

Luckily an impromptu remark from Don Calogero, the only one in the conversation, got both of them out of the embarrassment. 'Prince,' he said, 'I know that what I am about to say will have no effect on you who descend from the loves of the Emperor Titus and Queen Berenice; but the Sedàra are noble too; till I came along we've been an unlucky lot, buried in the provinces and undistinguished, but I have the documents in order, and one day it will be known that your nephew has married the Baronessina Sedàra del Biscotto; a title granted by His Majesty Ferdinand IV on his rights from Mazzara port. I've put the papers through; there's only one link missing.'

A hundred years ago this business of a missing link, of getting such papers 'through' was an important element in the lives of many Sicilians, causing alternating exaltation and depression to thousands of respectable or not so respectable folk; but the subject is too important to be treated fleetingly, and we will content ourselves with saying here that Don Calogero's heraldic impromptu gave the Prince the incomparable artistic satisfaction of seeing a type realised in all its details; and that he gave a depressed laugh ending in a sweetish taste of nausea.

After this the conversation drifted off into a number of aimless ruts; Don Fabrizio remembered Tumeo shut up in the darkness of the gun-room; for the nth time in his life he deplored the length of country calls and ended by wrapping himself in hostile silence. Don Calogero understood, promised to return next morning with Angelica's undoubted consent, and said goodbye. He was accompanied through two of the drawing-rooms, embraced again, and began descending the stairs while the Prince, towering above, watched getting smaller this little conglomeration of ill-cut clothes, money and cunning brashness who was now to become almost part of his family.

Holding a candle in his hand he then went to free Tumeo, who was sitting resignedly in the dark smoking his pipe. 'I'm sorry, Don Ciccio, but you'll understand, I had to do it.'

'I do understand, Excellency, I do indeed. Did everything go off all right?'

'Perfectly, couldn't be better.' Tumeo mouthed some congratulations, put the leash back on the collar of Teresina, sleeping exhausted by the hunt, and picked up the game-bag.

'Take those woodcock of mine too, won't you? They're not enough for us all, anyway. Good-bye, Don Ciccio, come and see us soon. And excuse everything.' A powerful clap on the shoulder served as sign of reconciliation and a reminder of power; the last faithful retainer of the House of Salina went off to his own poor rooms.

When the Prince returned to his study he found that Father Pirrone had slipped away to avoid discussions. And he went towards his wife's room to tell her all that had happened. The sound of his vigorous rapid steps announced his arrival ten yards ahead. He crossed the girls' sitting-room; Carolina and Caterina were winding a skein of wool, and as he passed got to their feet and smiled; Mademoiselle Dombreuil hurriedly took off her spectacles and replied demurely to his greeting; Concetta had her back to him; she was embroidering and, not hearing her father's steps, did not even turn.

IV
Love at Donnafugata

As MEETINGS DUE to the marriage contract became more frequent, Don Fabrizio found an odd admiration growing in him for Sedàra's qualities. He became used to the ill-shaven cheeks, the plebeian accent, the odd clothes and the persistent odour of stale sweat, and he began to realise the man's rare intelligence. Many problems that had seemed insoluble to the Prince were resolved in a trice by Don Calogero; free as he was from the shackles imposed on many other men by honesty, decency and plain good manners, he moved through the forest of life with the confidence of an elephant which advances in a straight line, rooting up trees and trampling down lairs, without even noticing scratches of thorns and moans from the crushed. Reared and tended in pleasant vales traversed by courteous wafts of 'please', 'I'd be so grateful', 'how kind', the Prince, when chatting to Don Calogero, found himself on an open heath swept by searing winds, and although continuing in his heart to prefer defiles in the hills, he could not help admiring this vital surge which drew from the ilexes and cedars of Donnafugata chords never heard before.

Bit by bit, almost without realising it, Don Fabrizio told Don Calogero about his own affairs, which were numerous, complex and little understood by himself; this was not due to any defect of intelligence but to a kind of contemptuous indifference about matters he considered low, though deep down this attitude was really due to laziness and the ease with which he had always got out of difficulties by selling off a few more hundred of his thousands of acres.

Don Calogero's advice, after listening to the Prince's report and mentally setting it in order, was both opportune and immediately effective; but the eventual result of such advice, cruelly efficient in conception, and feeble in application by the kindly Don Fabrizio, was that as years went by the Salina were to acquire a reputation as extortioners of their own dependants, a

reputation quite unjustified in reality but which helped to
destroy their prestige at Donnafugata and Querceta, without in
any way halting the collapse of the family fortunes.

It is only fair to mention that more frequent contact with the
Prince had a certain effect on Sedàra too. Until that moment he
had met aristocrats only on business of buying and selling or
through their very rare and long-brooded invitations to parties,
circumstances in which this most singular of social classes does
not show at its best. During such meetings he had formed the
opinion that the aristocracy consisted entirely of sheep-like
creatures, who existed merely in order to give up their wool to
his shears and their names and incomprehensible prestige to his
daughter. But since getting to know Tancredi during the period
after Garibaldi's landing he had found himself dealing, unexpectedly, with a young noble as cynical as himself, capable of
striking a sharp bargain between his own smiles and titles and
the attractions and fortunes of others, while knowing how to
dress up such 'Sedàra-ish' actions with a grace and fascination
which he, Don Calogero, felt he did not himself possess, but
which influenced him without realising it and without his being
able in any way to discern its origins. When he got to know
Don Fabrizio better he found there again the pliability and incapacity for self-defence that were characteristic of his imaginary
sheep-noble, but also a strength of attraction different in tone,
but similar in intensity, to young Falconeri's; he also found a
certain energy with a tendency towards abstraction, a disposition
to seek a shape for life from within himself and not in what
he could wrest from others. This abstract energy made a deep
impression on Don Calogero, although with a direct impact not
filtered through words as has been attempted here; much of this
fascination, he noticed, simply came from good manners, and
he realised how agreeable can be a well-bred man, for at heart
he is only someone who eliminates the unpleasant aspects of so
much of the human condition and exercises a kind of profitable
altruism (a formula in which the usefulness of the adjective made
him tolerate the uselessness of the noun). Gradually Don Calogero came to understand that a meal in common need not
necessarily be all munching and grease stains; that a conversation

may well bear no resemblance to a dog fight; that to give precedence to a woman is a sign of strength and not, as he had believed, of weakness; that sometimes more can be obtained by saying 'I haven't explained myself well' than 'I can't understand a word'; and that the adoption of such tactics can result in a greatly increased yield from meals, arguments, women and questioners.

It would be rash to affirm that Don Calogero drew an immediate profit from what he had learnt; he did manage from then on to shave a little better and feel a little less aghast at the amount of soap used for laundering, no more; but from that moment there began, for him and his family, that process of continual refining which in the course of three generations transforms innocent boors into defenceless gentry.

Angelica's first visit to the Salina family as a bride-to-be was impeccably stage-managed. Her bearing was so perfect that it might have been suggested word for word by Tancredi, but this was ruled out by the slow communications of the period; one possible explanation was that he had given her some suggestions even before their official engagement: a risky hypothesis for one able to measure the young Prince's foresight but not entirely absurd. Angelica arrived at six in the evening, dressed in pink and white; her soft black tresses were shadowed by a big straw hat of late summer on which bunches of artificial grapes and gilt heads of corn discreetly evoked the vineyards of Gibildolce and the granaries of Settesoli. She sloughed off her father in the entrance hall; then with a swirl of wide skirts floated lightly up the numerous steps of the inner staircase and flung herself into the arms of Don Fabrizio; on his whiskers she implanted two big kisses which were returned with genuine affection; the Prince paused perhaps just a second longer than necessary to breathe in the scent of gardenia on adolescent cheeks. After this Angelica blushed, took half a step back: 'I'm so, so happy . . .' then came close again, stood on tiptoe, and murmured into his ear 'Nuncle!'; a highly successful line, comparable in its perfect timing to Eisenstein's business with the pram, and which, explicit and secret as it was, set the Prince's simple heart aflutter and yoked him to the lovely girl for ever. Meanwhile Don Calogero

was coming up the stairs, and said how very sorry his wife was
she could not be present but the night before she had slipped at
home and twisted her left foot, which was most painful. 'Her
ankle's like a melon, Prince.' Don Fabrizio, exhilarated by the
verbal caress, and forewarned by Tumeo's revelations that his
offer would never be put to the proof, said that he would give
himself the pleasure of calling upon the Signora Sedàra at once,
a suggestion which dismayed Don Calogero and made him, in
order to reject it, think up a second indisposition of his spouse's,
this time a violent headache which forced the poor woman to
stay in the dark.

Meanwhile the Prince gave his arm to Angelica. They crossed
a number of dark salons, just lit enough by the dim glimmer of
oil-lamps for them to see their way; but at the end of the splendid
perspective of rooms glittered the 'Leopold' drawing-room
where the rest of the family was gathered, and their procession
through empty darkness towards a light centre of intimacy had
the rhythm of a Masonic initiation.

The family was crowding round the door; the Princess had
withdrawn her own reservations before the wrath of her husband, who had not so much rejected them as blasted them to
nullity; she kissed her lovely future niece again and again and
squeezed her to her bosom with such energy that the girl found
stamped on her skin the setting of the famous Salina ruby neck-
lace which Maria Stella had insisted on wearing, though it was
daylight, in sign of a major celebration. The sixteen-year-old
Francesco Paolo was pleased at having this exceptional chance
of kissing Angelica too, under the impotently jealous eyes of his
father. Concetta was particularly affectionate; her joy was so
intense that the tears even came to her eyes. The other sisters
drew close around her with noisy gaiety just because they were
not moved. Even Father Pirrone, who in his saintly way was not
insensible to female fascination in which he saw an undeniable
proof of Divine Goodness, felt all his own opposition melt away
before the warmth of her grace (with a small 'g'); and he
murmured to her: '*Veni, sponsa de Libano*' (he had to check
himself to avoid other warmer verses rising to his memory).
Mademoiselle Dombreuil, as befits a governess, wept with

emotion, kneading the girl's plump shoulders in her disappointed fingers and crying: '*Angelicà, Angelicà, pensons à la joie de Tancrède*'. Only Bendicò, in contrast to his usual sociability, crouched behind a console table and growled away in the back of his throat until energetically called to task by an indignant Francesco Paolo with still quivering lips.

Lighted candles had been set on twenty-four of the forty-eight branches of the chandelier, and each of these candles, white and at the same time ardent, seemed like a virgin in the throes of love; the twin-coloured Murano flowers on their stem of curved glass looked down, admired the girl who entered, and gave her a fragile and iridescent smile. The great fireplace was lit more in sign of joy than to warm the tepid room, and the light of the flames quivered on the floor, loosing intermittent gleams from the dull gold of the furniture; it really did represent the domestic hearth, symbol of home, and its brands were sparks of desire, its embers ardours contained.

The Princess, who possessed to an eminent degree the faculty of reducing emotions to a minimum common denominator, began narrating sublime episodes from Tancredi's childhood; so insistent was she about these that it really began to seem as if Angelica should consider herself lucky to be marrying a man who had been so reasonable at the age of six as to submit to necessary enemas without a fuss, and bold at twelve as to have stolen a handful of cherries. As this episode of banditry was being recalled, Concetta burst out laughing. 'That's a habit Tancredi hasn't yet been able to rid himself of,' she said, 'd'you remember, Papa, how a couple of months ago he took those peaches you'd been so looking forward to?' Then she suddenly looked dour, as if she were chairwoman of an association for the owners of damaged orchards.

Don Fabrizio's voice quickly put such trifling in its place: he talked of Tancredi as he now was, of the quick attentive youth, always ready with a remark which enraptured those who loved him and exasperated everyone else; he told of Tancredi's introduction to the Duchess of Sansomething-or-other during a visit to Naples, and how she had been so taken with him that she wanted him to visit her morning, noon and night, whether she happened to be in her drawing-room or her bed; all because, said she, no one knew how to tell *les petits riens* like Tancredi; and although Don Fabrizio hurriedly added that Tancredi could have been no more than sixteen at the time and the duchess over fifty, Angelica's eyes flashed, for she had definite information about the habits of Palermitan youths and strong intuitions about those of Neapolitan duchesses.

Anyone deducing from this attitude of Angelica that she loved Tancredi would have been mistaken; she had too much pride and too much ambition to be capable of that annihilation, however temporary, of one's own personality without which there is no love; apart from that she was too young and inexperienced to be able as yet to appreciate his genuine qualities, all subtle nuances: but although she did not love him, she was in love with him, a very different thing; his blue eyes, his affectionate teasing, certain suddenly serious tones of his voice gave her, even in memory, quite a definite turn, and just then her one longing was to be enfolded by his hands; once enfolded she would forget and substitute them, as in fact happened, but for the moment she yearned for his clutch. So the revelation of this possible love-affair (which was, in fact, non-existent) gave her a twinge of that most absurd of tortures, retrospective jealousy; a twinge soon dissipated, however, by a cool appraisal of the advantages, erotic and otherwise, of her marriage to Tancredi.

Don Fabrizio went on praising Tancredi. In his affection he got to the point of talking about him as a kind of Mirabeau. 'He's begun early and well,' said he, 'and will go far.' Angelica's smooth forehead bowed in assent. Actually she did not care at all about Tancredi's political future; she was one of the many girls who consider public events as part of a separate universe and could not even imagine that a speech by Cavour might in time, through thousands of minute links, influence her own life and change it. She was thinking, 'We've got the money and that's enough for us; as to going far . . .' Such youthful simplicities she was to discard completely when years later she became one of the most venomous string-pullers for Parliament and Senate.

'And then, Angelica, you have no idea yet how amusing Tancredi is! He knows everything, sees an unexpected side

everywhere. When one's with him and he's on form, the world
seems even funnier than it usually does, sometimes more serious,
too.' That Tancredi was amusing Angelica already knew; that he
was capable of revealing new worlds she not only hoped but had
some reason to suspect ever since that 25th of September last,
day of that famous kiss, the only one officially noted, in the
shelter of that treacherous laurel hedge, for it had been something much subtler and tastier, entirely different from the only
other sample in her experience, one given her over a year before
by a gardener's boy at Poggio Cajano. But Angelica cared very
little about the wit or even the intelligence of her fiancé, far less
in any case than did sweet old Don Fabrizio – really *so* sweet,
though so 'intellectual' too. In Tancredi she saw her chance of
gaining a fine position in the noble world of Sicily, a world
which to her was full of marvels very different to those which it
contained in reality; and she also wanted him as a lively partner
in bed. If he was superior in spirit too, all the better; but she
on her part didn't bother much about that. There was always
amusement to be had. In any case those were ideas for the future;
for the moment, whether witty or stupid, she would have liked
to have had him there, stroking at least her neck under the tresses
as he had once done.

'Oh God, oh God, how I wish he were with us now!'

The exclamation moved them all, both by its evident sincerity
and the ignorance that caused her to make it, and brought that
very successful first visit to an end. For shortly afterwards Angelica and her father made their farewells: preceded by a stable lad
with a lighted lantern the uncertain gold of whose gleams set
alight the red of fallen plane leaves, father and daughter returned
to their home, entry into which had been prevented for Peppe
'Mmerda' by bullets tearing into his kidneys.

Now that Don Fabrizio felt serene again, he had gone back to
his habit of evening reading. In autumn, after the Rosary, as it
was now too dark to go out, the family would gather round the
fire waiting for dinner, and the Prince, standing up, would read
out to his family a modern novel in instalments, exuding dignified benevolence from every pore.

These were just the years when novels were helping to form those literary myths which still dominate European minds today; but in Sicily, partly because of its traditional impermeability to anything new, partly because of the general ignorance of any language whatsoever, partly also, it must be said, because of a vexatious Bourbon censorship working through the Customs, no one had heard of Dickens, Eliot, Sand, Flaubert or even Dumas. A couple of Balzac's volumes had, through various subterfuges, it is true, reached the hands of Don Fabrizio, who had appointed himself family censor; he had read them and then lent them in disgust to a friend he didn't like, saying that they were by a writer with a talent undoubtedly vigorous but also wild and 'obsessed' (to-day he would have said monomaniac); a hurried judgment, obviously, but not without a certain acuteness. The level of these readings was therefore somewhat low, conditioned as it was by respect for the girls' virginal shyness, the Princess's religious scruples and the Prince's own sense of dignity, which would have energetically rejected letting his united family hear any 'filth'.

It was about the 10th of November and getting towards the end of their stay at Donnafugata. The rain was pouring down and a gale slapping gusts of rain angrily on the window panes; in the distance could be heard a roll of thunder; every now and again a few drops found their way down the primitive Sicilian chimney, sizzled a moment on the fire and dotted with black the glowing brands of olive wood. He was reading *Angiola Maria* and that evening had just reached the last few pages; the description of the heroine's journey through the icy Lombard winter froze the Sicilian hearts of the young ladies even in their warm armchairs. All of a sudden there was a great scuttle in the room next door, and in came Mimi the footman panting hard. 'Excellency,' he cried, forgetting all his style. 'Excellency, Signorino Tancredi's arrived! He's in the courtyard seeing his luggage unloaded. Think of it! Madonna, in this weather!' And off he rushed.

Surprise swept Concetta into a time which no longer corresponded with reality, and 'Darling!' she exclaimed. But the very sound of her own voice led her back to the comfortless present

and, of course, such a brusque change from a secret warm climate
to an open frozen one was most painful; luckily the exclamation
was submerged in the general excitement and not heard.

Preceded by Don Fabrizio's long steps they all rushed towards
the stairs; the dark drawing-rooms were hurriedly crossed; down
they went; the great gate was flung wide on to the outer stairs
and the courtyard below; the wind rushed in, making the can-
vases of the portraits quiver and sweeping with it dampness and
a smell of earth; against a sky lit by flashes of lightning the trees
in the garden swayed and rustled like torn silk. Don Fabrizio
was just about to pass through the front door, when on the top
step outside appeared a heavy shapeless mass; it was Tancredi
wrapped in the huge blue cloak of the Piedmontese Cavalry, so
soaked that he must have weighed a ton and looked quite black.
'Careful, Nuncle; don't touch me, I'm a sponge!' The light of
the lantern on the stairs showed a glimpse of his face. He came
in, undid the chain which held the cloak at the collar, and let
fall the garment which flopped on the floor with a squelch. He
smelt like a wet dog; for the last three days he had not taken off
his boots; but to Don Fabrizio, embracing him, he was the lad
more beloved than his own sons, for Maria Stella a dear nephew
basely calumniated, for Father Pirrone the sheep always lost and
always found, for Concetta a dear ghost resembling her lost love.
Even Mademoiselle Dombreuil kissed him with her mouth, so
unused to caresses, and cried, poor girl, '*Tancrède, Tancrède, pensons à la joie d'Angelicà*', so few strings had her own bow, forced
as she always was to echo the joy of others. Bendicò also found
again its dear comrade in play, one who knew better than anyone
else how to blow into a snout through a closed fist; but it showed
its ecstasy in its own doggy way by leaping frenziedly round the
room and taking no notice of its beloved.

It was a moving moment, this grouping of the family around
the returned youth, all the dearer as he was not really a member
of it, all the happier as he was coming to gather both love and a
sense of perennial security; a moving moment — but a long one
too. When the first transports were spent, Don Fabrizio noticed
that on the threshold were standing two other figures, also drip-
ping and also smiling. Tancredi noticed them too and began to

laugh. 'Excuse me, all of you, but the excitement quite made
me forget. Aunt,' he said, turning to the Princess, 'I've allowed
myself to bring a dear friend, Count Carlo Cavriaghi; anyway,
you know him, he used often to come up to the villa when he
was with the general; and this other is Lancer Moroni, my servant.' The soldier smiled all over his dull, honest face, and stood
there at attention while the water dripped from the thick cloth
of his overcoat down on to the floor. But the young Count did
not stand at attention; taking off his soaking shapeless cap he
kissed the Princess's hand, smiled and dazzled the girls with his
little blond moustaches and his unsuppressible slurred 'r'. 'And
to think they told me that it never rained down here! Heavens,
the last two days we might have been in the sea itself.' Then he
became serious, 'But, Falconeri, where is the Signorina Angelica? You've dragged me all the way here from Naples to show
me her. I see many a beauty, but not her.' He turned to Don
Fabrizio. 'You know, Prince, according to him she's the Queen
of Sheba! Let's go at once to worship this creature *formosissima
et nigerrima*. Come on, you stubborn oaf!'

By such talk he brought the language of the officers' mess into
the proud hall with its double row of armoured and beribboned
ancestors; and everyone was amused. But Don Fabrizio and
Tancredi knew how things stood: they knew Don Calogero,
they knew his Beautiful Beast of a wife, the incredible state of
that rich man's home; things unknown to candid Lombardy.

Don Fabrizio intervened. 'Listen, Count; you thought it
never rained in Sicily and now you can see it's pouring. We
wouldn't like you to think there isn't pneumonia in Sicily too,
and then find yourself in bed with a high temperature. Mimì,'
he said to the footman, 'light the fire in the Signorino Tancredi's
room and in the green room of the guest wing. Prepare the little
room next door for the soldier. And you, Count, go and get
thoroughly dry and change your clothes. I'll send you up some
punch and biscuits. And dinner is at eight, in two hours.' Cavriaghi was too used to military service not to bow at once to the
voice of authority; he saluted and followed meekly behind the
footman. Behind him Moroni dragged along the military boxes
and curved sabres in their green flannel wrappings.

Meanwhile Tancredi was writing, 'Dearest Angelica, I've come, and for you. I'm head over heels in love, but also wet as a frog, filthy as a lost dog, and hungry as a wolf. The very minute I've cleaned myself up and consider myself worthy of appearing before the loveliest creature in the world, I will hurry over to you; in two hours. My respects to your dear parents. To you . . . nothing for the moment.' The text was submitted to the approval of the Prince; the latter had always been an admirer of Tancredi's epistolary style; he laughed, and approved in full. Donna Bastiana would have plenty of time to catch some other imaginary disease; and the note was at once sent opposite.

Such was the general zest and jollity that a quarter of an hour was enough for the two young men to dry, clean up, change uniforms and meet once again in the 'Leopold Room' around the fire; there they drank tea and brandy and let themselves be admired. At that period nothing could have been less military than the families of the Sicilian aristocracy; no Bourbon officers had ever been seen in the drawing-rooms of Palermo, and the few Garibaldini who had penetrated them gave more the impression of picturesque scarecrows than real military men. So those two young officers were in fact the first the Salina girls had ever seen close to; in their double-breasted uniforms, Tancredi's with the silver buttons of the Lancers, Carlo's with the gilt ones of the Bersaglieri, the first with a high black velvet collar bordered with orange, the other with crimson, they sat stretching towards the embers legs encased in blue cloth and black cloth. On their sleeves were the silver and gold stars amid twirls and dashes and endless loops; a delight for girls used only to severe frockcoats and funereal tail-coats. The edifying novel lay upside down behind an armchair.

Don Fabrizio did not quite understand; he remembered both the young men in lobster red and very carelessly turned out. 'But don't you Garibaldini wear red shirts any longer?'

The two turned on him as if a snake had bitten them. 'Garibaldini, Garibaldini indeed, Uncle! We were once and now that's over! Cavriaghi and I, thanks be to God, are officers in the regular army of His Majesty, King of Sardinia for another few months, and shortly to be of Italy. When Garibaldi's army broke up we had the choice: to go home or stay in the King's army. He and I and a lot of others went into the *real* army. We couldn't stand that rabble long, could we, Cavriaghi?'

'Heavens, what dreadful people! Good for ambushes and looting, that's all! Now we're with decent fellows, and we're proper officers!' And he plucked at his little moustache with a grimace of adolescent disgust.

'We had to drop rank, you know, Nuncle. They didn't seem to think much of our military experience. From captain I've become lieutenant again, as you see!' And he showed the two stars on his shoulder straps. 'He from being lieutenant is now second lieutenant. But we're as happy as if we'd got promotion. With these uniforms we're now respected in quite another way.'

'I should think so,' interrupted Cavriaghi; 'people aren't afraid we'll steal their chickens.'

'You should have seen what it was like from Palermo here, when we stopped at post stations to change horses! All we had to say was "Urgent orders on His Majesty's service" and horses appeared like magic; and we'd show them our orders, which were actually the bills of the Naples hotel wrapped up and sealed!'

Having had their say on military changes, they passed on to more general subjects. Concetta and Cavriaghi had sat down together a little apart and the young Count showed her the present which he had brought her from Naples: Aleardo Aleardi *Canti* magnificently bound for the purpose. A princely crown was deeply incised in the dark blue leather with her initials, C.C.S. beneath. Below that again, in large, vaguely Gothic, lettering, were the words *Sempre sorda* – For ever deaf.

Concetta was amused and laughed. 'Why deaf, Count? C.C.S. hears perfectly well!'

The face of the young Count flamed with boyish passion. 'Deaf, yes, deaf, Signorina, deaf to my sighs and deaf to my groans! And blind, too, blind to the begging in my eyes! If you only knew what I suffered when you left Palermo to come here; not a wave, not a sign as the carriage vanished down the drive. And you expect me not to call you deaf! "Cruel" is what I really should have written.'

His somewhat literary excitement was chilled by the girl's reserve. 'Count, you must be very tired after your long journey; your nerves are not quite in order: calm yourself. Why not read me a nice poem?'

While the Bersagliere was reading out the gentle verses in a voice charged with emotion and amid pauses full of distress, Tancredi in front of the fireplace was taking from his pocket a small blue satin box. 'Here's the ring, Nuncle, the ring I'm giving to Angelica; or rather the one you're giving her *via* me.' He pressed the clasp and there was a dark sapphire cut in a clear octagon and clustering close round it a multitude of tiny pure diamonds. A slightly gloomy jewel, but in close harmony with the funereal taste of the times, and one obviously worth the two hundred gold ounces sent by Don Fabrizio. In reality it had cost a good deal less; in those months of fleeing and sacking, superb jewels were to be picked up cheap in Naples; from the difference in price had come a brooch, a memento for Schwarzwald. Concetta and Cavriaghi were also called to admire it, but did not move, as the young Count had already seen it and Concetta was putting off that pleasure till later. The ring went from hand to hand, was admired, praised, and Tancredi congratulated on his foreseeable good taste. Don Fabrizio asked, 'But what about the measurements; we'll have to send the ring to Girgenti to have it cut to the right size.' Tancredi's eyes glittered with fun. 'There's no need for that, Nuncle; the measurement is exact; I'd taken it before.' And Don Fabrizio was silent; here, he recognised, was a master.

The little box had done the whole round of the fireplace and come back to the hands of Tancredi when from behind the door was heard a subdued 'May I?' It was Angelica. In the rush and excitement she had snatched up, to protect her from the pouring rain, one of those huge peasants' capes of rough cloth called *scappolare*. Wrapped in its stiff dark blue folds her body looked very slim; under the wet hood her green eyes looked anxious, bewildered, and voluptuous.

The sight of her, and the contrast between the beauty of her face and the rusticity of her clothes, was like a whip-lash to Tancredi; he got up, ran to her without a word and kissed her on the mouth. The box which he held in his right hand tickled her bent neck. Then he pressed the spring, took the ring, put it on her engagement finger; the box dropped to the ground. 'There, darling, that's for you, from your Tancredi.' Then irony broke in, 'And thank Nuncle for it, too.' Then he embraced her again; sensual anticipation made them both tremble; the room, the bystanders, seemed very far away; and he felt as if by those kisses he were taking possession of Sicily once more, of the lovely faithless land which now, after a vain revolt, had surrendered to him again, as always to his family, its carnal delights and golden crops.

As the result of this welcome arrival the family's return to Palermo was put off and there followed two weeks of enchantment. The gale which had accompanied the journey of the two officers had been the last of a series. After it came the resplendent St Martin's summer which is the real season of pleasure in Sicily; weather luminous and blue, oasis of mildness in the harsh progression of the seasons, inveigling and leading on the senses with its sweetness, luring to secret nudities by its warmth. Not that there was any erotic nudity at the palace of Donnafugata, just an air of excited sensuality all the sharper for being carefully restrained. Eighty years before the Salina palace had been a meeting place for those obscure pleasures which appealed to the dying eighteenth century; but the severe regency of the Princess Carolina, the neo-religious fervour of the Restoration, the straightforward sensuality of Don Fabrizio had eventually caused its bizarre extravagances to be forgotten; the little powdered demons had been put to flight; they still existed, of course, but only as sleeping embryos, hibernating under piles of dust in some attic of the vast building. The lovely Angelica's entry into the palace had made them stir a little, as may be remembered; but it was the arrival of two young men in love which really awoke the instincts lying dormant in the house; and these now showed themselves everywhere, like ants woken by the sun, no longer poisonous, but livelier than ever. Even the architecture, the rococo décor itself, evoked thoughts of fleshly curves and taut erect breasts; and every opening door seemed like a curtain rustling in a bed-alcove.

Cavriaghi was in love with Concetta; but boy that he was, not only in appearance like Tancredi but deep within, his love found expression in the easy rhythms of poets such as Prati and Aleardi, and in dreaming of moonlight elopements whose logical sequence he did not dare contemplate and which anyway Concetta's 'deafness' obviated from the start. Who can tell whether in the seclusion of that green room of his he did not abandon himself to more definite hopes? Certain it is that to the love-scenery of that autumn in Donnafugata his only contribution was the sketching in of clouds and evanescent horizons and not the creation of architectural masses. The two girls, Carolina and Caterina, however, played their parts excellently in the symphony of desires traversing the whole palace that November and mingling with the murmur of the fountains, the pawing of the horses on heat in the stables, and the tenacious burrowing of nuptial nests by wood-worms in the old furniture. The two girls were young and attractive and, though with no particular loves of their own, found themselves immersed in the currents emanating from the others; often the kiss which Concetta denied to Cavriaghi, the embrace from Angelica which left Tancredi unsatisfied would reverberate around the girls and graze their untouched bodies; and they too would find themselves dreaming about locks of hair damp with sweat, about whimpers of pleasure. Even poor Mademoiselle Dombreuil, by dint of functioning as lightning conductor, was drawn into the turbid and laughing vortex, as psychiatrists become infected and succumb to the frenzies of their patients. When after a day of hide and seek and moralising ambushes she lay down on her lonely bed, she would stroke her own withered breasts and mutter indiscriminate invocations to Tancredi, to Carlo, to Fabrizio . . .

Centre and motor of this sensual agitation were, of course, one couple, Tancredi and Angelica. Their certain marriage, though not very close, extended its reassuring shadow in anticipation on the parched soil of their mutual desires. Difference of class made Don Calogero consider their long periods alone together as quite normal with the nobility, and made Princess Maria Stella think habitual to those in the Sedàras' rank of life the frequency of Angelica's visits and a freedom of bearing which she would certainly not have found proper in her own daughters. And so Angelica's visits to the palace became more and more frequent until they were almost constant, and she ended by being only accompanied there formally by her father, who would at once proceed to the business quarters for the finding or weaving of hidden plots, or by a maid who vanished into the servants' hall to drink coffee and bore the unlucky palace domestics.

Tancredi wanted to show Angelica the whole palace with its inextricable complex of guest rooms, state rooms, kitchens, chapels, theatres, picture galleries, odorous saddling rooms, stables, stuffy conservatories, passages, stairs, terraces and porticos, and particularly of a series of abandoned and uninhabited apartments which had not been used for many years and formed a mysterious and intricate labyrinth of their own. Tancredi did not realise, or he realised perfectly well, that he was drawing the girl into the hidden centre of the sensual cyclone; and Angelica at that time wanted whatever Tancredi did. Their wanderings through the seemingly limitless building were interminable; they would set off as if for some unknown land, and unknown indeed it was because in many of those apartments and corners not even Don Fabrizio had ever set foot – a cause of great satisfaction to him, for he used to say that a house of which one knew every room wasn't worth living in.

The two lovers embarked for Cythera on a ship made of dark and sunny rooms, of apartments sumptuous or squalid, empty or crammed with remains of heterogeneous furniture. They would set off accompanied by Cavriaghi or by Mademoiselle Dombreuil, sometimes by both (Father Pirrone with the wisdom of his Order had always refused to go); outer decency was saved. But in the palace of Donnafugata it was not difficult to mislead anyone wanting to follow; this just meant slipping into one of the very long, narrow and tortuous passages, with grilled windows which could not be passed without a sense of anguish, turning through a gallery, up some handy stair, and the two young people were far away, invisible, alone as if on a desert island. All that remained to survey them was some faded pastoral portrait created blind by the painter's inexperience, or a shepherdess glancing down consentingly from an obliterated fresco.

Cavriaghi, in any case, soon tired, and when he found his route leading through a room he knew or some staircase down into the garden would slip off, both to please his friend and to go and sigh over Concetta's ice-cold hands. The governess would hang on longer, but not indefinitely; for some time her unanswered calls could be heard fading farther and farther away, '*Tancrède, Angelicà, où êtes-vous?*' Then silence would fall again, except for the scuffle of rats in the ceilings above, or the rustle of some centuries-old forgotten letter sent wandering by the wind over the floor; excuses for pleasant frights, for the reassuring contact of flesh to flesh. And with them always, cunning and tenacious, was Eros, drawing the young couple further and further into a game full of charm and risk. Both of them were still very near childhood, and they enjoyed the game in itself, enjoyed being followed, being lost, being found again; but when they reached each other their sharpened senses would overwhelm them, and his five fingers entwining in hers with that gesture dear to indecisive sensualists, the gentle rub of fingertips on the pale veins of the back of the hand, would shake up their whole being, prelude more insinuating caresses.

Once she had hidden behind an enormous picture propped on the floor; and for a short time *Arturo Corbera at the Siege of Antioch* formed a protection for the girl's hopeful anxiety; but when she was found, with her smile veincd in cobwebs and her hands veiled in dust, she was clasped tight, and though she kept on saying again and again, 'No, Tancredi, no,' her denial was in fact an invitation, for all he was doing was to stare with his blue eyes into her green ones. One luminous cold morning she was trembling in a dress that was still summery; he squeezed her to him, to warm her, on a sofa covered in tattered silk: her scented breath moved the hair on his forehead; they were moments ecstatic and painful, during which desire became a torment, restraint upon it a delight.

The rooms in the abandoned apartments had neither a definite layout nor a name; and like the explorers of the New World they would baptise the rooms they crossed with the names of their joint discoveries. A vast bedroom in whose alcove stood the ghost of a bed adorned with a baldacchino hung with skeleton ostrich feathers was remembered afterwards as 'the feather room'; a staircase with steps of smooth crumbling slate was called by Tancredi 'the staircase of the lucky slip'. A number of times they really did not know where they were; all this twisting and turning, backing and following, pauses full of murmuring contact, made them lose their way so that they had to lean out of some paneless window to gather from an angle of the courtyard or a view of the garden which wing of the palace they were in. But sometimes they could not find their way even so, as the window did not give on to one of the great courts but on to some inner yard, anonymous itself and never entered, marked only by the corpse of some cat or the usual little heap of spaghetti and tomato sauce vomited or flung there; and from another window they would find themselves looking into the eyes of some pensioned-off old maidservant. One afternoon inside a cupboard they found four *carillons*, those music-boxes which delighted the affected simplicity of the eighteenth century. Three of these, buried in dust and cobwebs, remained mute; but the last, which was more recent and shut tighter into its dark wooden box, started up its cylinder of bristling copper, and the little tongues of raised steel suddenly produced a delicate tune, all in clear silvery tones – the famous *Carnival of Venice*; they kissed in rhythm with those notes of disillusioned gaiety, and when their embrace loosened were surprised to notice that the notes had ceased for some time and their action had left no other trace than a memory of that ghostly music.

Once the surprise was of a different kind. In one of the rooms in the old guest wing they noticed a door hidden by a wardrobe; the centuries-old lock soon gave way to fingers pleasantly entwined in forcing it: behind it a long narrow staircase wound up in gentle curves of pink marble steps. At the top was another door, open, and covered with thick but tattered padding; then came a charming but odd little apartment, of six small rooms gathered round a medium-sized drawing-room, all, including the drawing-room, with floors of whitest marble sloping away slightly towards a small lateral gutter. On the low ceilings were some very unusual reliefs in coloured stucco, luckily made almost indecipherable by damp; on the walls hung big surprised-

looking mirrors, hung too low, one shattered by a blow almost
in the middle, and each fitted with contorted rococo candle-
brackets. The windows gave on to a segregated courtyard, a kind
of blind and deaf well, which let in a grey light and had no other
outlet. In every room and even in the drawing-room were wide,
too wide sofas, showing nails from which traces of silk had
been torn away; spotty arm-rests; on the fireplaces were delicate
intricate little marble intaglios, naked figures in paroxysm, but
martyred by some furious hammer. The damp had marked the
walls high up and also perhaps low down at a man's height,
where it had assumed strange shapes, odd thickness, dark tints.
Tancredi, disturbed, would not let Angelica touch a cupboard
in the drawing-room wall, and opened it himself. It was deep
but empty except for a roll of dirty stuff standing upright in a
corner; inside was a bundle of small whips, switches of bull's
muscle, some with silver handles, others wrapped half-way up
in a charming old silk, white with little blue stripes, on which
could be seen three rows of blackish marks; and metal instruments for inexplicable purposes. Tancredi was afraid, also of
himself. 'Let's go, my dear, there's nothing interesting here.'
They shut the door carefully, went down the stairs again in
silence, and put the wardrobe back where it was before; and all
the rest of that day Tancredi's kisses were very light as if given
in a dream and in expiation.

After the Leopard, in fact, the whip seemed the most frequent
object at Donnafugata. The day after their discovery of the enigmatic little apartment the two lovers found another little whip.
This was not actually in the secret apartment but in the venerated
one called the Rooms of the Saint-Duke, where in the middle
of the seventeenth century a Salina had withdrawn as if into a
private monastery, there to do penance and prepare his own
journey towards Heaven. They were small low rooms, with
floors of humble brick, and white-washed walls, like those of
the poorest peasants. The last of these opened on to a balcony
which overlooked the yellow expanse of estate after estate, all
immersed in sad light. On one wall was a huge crucifix, over life
size; the head of the martyred God touched the ceiling, the
bleeding feet grazed the floor; the wound in the ribs seemed

like a mouth prevented by brutality from pronouncing the words
of ultimate salvation. Next to the Divine Body there hung from
a nail a lash with a short handle, from which dangled six strips
of now hardened leather ending in six lumps of lead as big as
walnuts. This was the 'discipline' of the Saint-Duke. In that
room Giuseppe Corbera Duke of Salina had scourged himself
alone, in sight of his God and his estates, and it must have seemed
to him that the drops of his own blood were about to rain down
on the land and redeem it; in his holy exaltation it must have
seemed that only through this expiatory baptism could that earth
really become his, blood of his blood, flesh of his flesh, as the
saying is. But now many pieces of it had gone for ever and a
large number of those to be seen from up there belonged to
others, to Calogero even; to Don Calogero, thus to Angelica,
thus to his future son-in-law. This proof of ransom through
beauty, parallel to that other ransom through blood, made
Tancredi's head swim. Angelica was kneeling and kissing the
pierced feet of Christ. 'There,' said Tancredi, 'you're like that
whip there, used for the same ends.' He showed her the whip;
and since Angelica did not understand and raised her smiling
head, lovely but vacuous, he bent down and as she knelt gave
her a rough kiss which made her moan, for it bruised her lip and
rasped her palate.

So the pair of them spent those days in dreamy wanderings,
in the discovery of hells redeemed by love, of forgotten paradises
profaned by love itself. The dangers of stopping the game and
drawing the prize became more and more pressing for both; in
the end they searched no longer, but went off absorbed into the
remotest rooms, those from which no cry could reach anyone
from the outside world. But there never would be a cry; only
invocations and low whimpers. There they would both lie, close
but innocent, pitying each other. The most dangerous places for
them were the rooms of the old guest wing; private, in good
order, each with its neat rolled-up mattress which would spread
out again at a mere touch of the hand. One day, not Tancredi's
mind which had no say in the matter, but all his blood had
decided to put an end to it; that morning Angelica, like the
beautiful bitch that she was, had said, 'I'm your novice,' recalling

to him with the clarity of an invitation their first mutual onrush of desire; and already the woman had surrendered and offered, already the male was about to overwhelm the man, when the church bell clanged almost straight down on their prone bodies, adding its own throb to the others; their interlaced mouths disentangled for a smile. They came to themselves; and next day Tancredi had to leave.

Those were the best days in the lives of Tancredi and Angelica, lives later to be so variegated, so erring, against the inevitable background of sorrow. But of that they were still unaware, in their pursuit of a future which they deemed more concrete than it turned out to be, made of nothing but smoke and wind. When they were old and uselessly wise their thoughts would go back to those days with insistent regret; they had been days when desire was always present because always overcome, when many beds had been offered and refused, when the sensual urge, because restrained, had for one second been sublimated in renunciation, that is into real love. Those days were the preparation for a marriage which, even erotically, was no success; a preparation, however, in a way sufficient to itself, exquisite and brief; like those overtures which outlive the forgotten operas they belong to and hint in delicate veiled gaiety at all the arias which later in the opera are to be developed undeftly, and fail.

When Angelica and Tancredi returned to the world of the living from their exile in the universe of extinct vices, forgotten virtues and, above all, perennial desire, they were greeted with amiable irony. 'How silly of you, children, to get so dusty. What a state you're in, Tancredi!' would smile Don Fabrizio; and his nephew would go off to get himself dusted down. Cavriaghi sat astride a chair, conscientiously smoking a cheroot, looked at his friend washing his face and neck, and snorted at seeing the water turn black as coal. 'I don't deny it, Falconeri; the Signorina Angelica is the loveliest girl I've ever seen; but that's not a justification: heavens, do restrain yourself a bit; to-day you've been alone together three whole hours; if you're so much in love then get married at once and don't let people laugh at you. You should have seen the face the father made today when he came out of his office and found you were still sailing about in that ocean of rooms! Brakes, my dear fellow, brakes, that's what you need! You Sicilians have so few of 'em!'

He pontificated away, enjoying inflicting his wisdom on his older comrade, on 'deaf' Concetta's cousin. But Tancredi, as he dried his hair, was furious; to be accused of having no brakes, he who had enough to stop a train! On the other hand the good Bersagliere was not entirely in the wrong; appearances had to be thought of too; though now he had gone moralist like this from envy it was obvious that his courtship of Concetta was getting nowhere. And then Angelica! The delicious taste of blood today when he'd bitten the inside of her lip! That soft bending of hers under his embrace! But it was true, there was no sense in it all really. 'Tomorrow we'll go and visit the church with a full escort of Father Pirrone and Mademoiselle Dombreuil!'

Angelica meanwhile was changing her dress in the girls' room. '*Mais Angélica, est-il Dieu possible de se mettre dans un tel état?*' Mademoiselle Dombreuil was wailing indignantly, as the lovely creature, in undervest and petticoats, was washing her arms and neck. The cold water subdued her excitement and she had to admit to herself that the governess was right; was it worth getting so tired and so dusty and making people smile? For what? Just to be gazed in the eyes, to be stroked by those slender fingers, little more . . . and her lip was still smarting. 'That's enough now. To-morrow we'll stay in the drawing-room with the others.' But next day those same eyes, those same fingers would cast their spell again, and the two would go back once more to their wild games of hide and seek.

The paradoxical result of all these separate but convergent resolutions was that at dinner in the evening the pair most in love were the calmest, reposing on their illusory good intentions for next day; and they would muse ironically on the love relationships of the others, however minor. Concetta had disappointed Tancredi; when at Naples he had felt a certain remorse about her and that was why he had brought Cavriaghi along with him, in the hope the Milanese might replace him with his cousin. Pity also played a part in his foresight; in a subtle but easy-going way, astute as he was, he had seemed when he arrived almost to be commiserating with her at his own abandonment; and he pushed forward his friend. Nothing doing; Concetta unravelled her little spool of schoolgirl gossip and looked at the sentimental little Count with icy eyes behind which there seemed almost a certain contempt. A silly girl that; no good making any more efforts. What more did she want, anyway? Cavriaghi was a handsome lad, well set up, with a good name and flourishing dairy-farms in Brianza; in fact he was one about whom could be used that rather chilling term 'a good match'. Ah: so Concetta wanted him, Tancredi, did she? He had wanted her too once; she was less beautiful, much less rich than Angelica, but she had something in her which the girl from Donnafugata would never possess. But life is a serious matter, devil take it! Concetta must have realised that. Why had she begun treating him so badly, then? Turning on him at the Holy Ghost Convent; and so many times afterwards. The Leopard, yes, the Leopard, of course; but there must be limits even for that proud beast. 'Brakes is what you want, my dear cousin, brakes! You Sicilian girls have so few of 'em!'

Angelica, though, in her heart agreed with Concetta; Cavriaghi lacked pep; after loving Tancredi, to marry Cavriaghi would be like a drink of water after a taste of this Marsala in front of her. Concetta, of course, understood that from her own experience. But those other two sillies, Carolina and Caterina, were making fishes' eyes at Cavriaghi, wriggling and languishing every time he went near them. Well, then! With her own lack of family scruples she just could not understand why one of the two didn't try and nab the little Count from Concetta for herself. 'Boys at that age are like dogs; one only has to whistle and they come straight away. Silly girls! With all those scruples and taboos and pride, in the end they won't get anyone.'

In the smoking-room, conversations between Tancredi and Cavriaghi, the only two smokers in the house and so the only exiles, also assumed a certain tone. The little Count ended by confessing to his friend the failure of his own amorous hopes. 'She's too beautiful, too pure for me; she doesn't love me; it was rash of me to hope; but I'll leave here with a regret like a dagger in my heart. I've not even dared to make a definite proposal. I feel that to her I'm just a worm, and she's right. I must find myself a she-worm to put up with me.' And his nineteen years made him laugh at his own discomfiture.

From the height of his own assured happiness Tancredi tried to console him: 'You see, I've known Concetta all her life: she's the sweetest creature in the world; a mirror of all the virtues; but she's a little too reserved, too withdrawn, I'm afraid she has too high an opinion of herself; and then she's Sicilian to the very marrow: she's never left here; she might never feel at home in a place where one has to arrange a week ahead for a plate of macaroni!'

Tancredi's little joke, one of the earliest expressions of national unity, brought a smile from Cavriaghi again; pains and sorrows did not stay with him long. 'But I'd have laid in *cases* of your macaroni for her, of course! Anyway what's done is done; I only hope your uncle and aunt, who've been so sweet to me, won't take against me for having thrust myself among you pointlessly.' He was reassured quite sincerely, for Cavriaghi had made himself liked by everyone except Concetta (and perhaps liked by Concetta too, in a way) for the boisterous good humour which he combined with the most plaintive sentimentality; then they talked of something else, that is they talked of Angelica.

'You know, Falconeri, you *are* a lucky dog! To go and find a jewel like Signorina Angelica in this pigsty (excuse my calling it that, my dear fellow). What a beauty, good God, what a beauty! Lucky rascal, leading her round for hours in the remotest corners of this house as huge as our own cathedral! And not only lovely, but clever and cultured too; and good as well; one can see that in her eyes, in that sweet innocence of hers.'

Cavriaghi went on ecstatically about Angelica's goodness, under Tancredi's amused glance. 'The really good person in all this is you yourself, Cavriaghi.' The phrase slipped unnoticed over that Milanese optimism. Then, 'Listen,' said the young Count, 'you'll be leaving in a few days; don't you think it's time I was introduced to the mother of the young baroness?'

This was the first time – and from a Lombard voice – that Tancredi heard his future wife called by a title. For a second he did not realise who the other was referring to. Then the prince in him rebelled. 'Baroness? what d'you mean, Cavriaghi?

She's a dear, sweet creature whom I love and that's quite enough.'

That it really was 'quite enough' was not actually true; but Tancredi was perfectly sincere; with his atavistic habit of great possessions it seemed to him that the estates of Gibildolce and Settesoli, all those bags of gold, had been his since the time of Charles of Anjou, always.

'I'm sorry but I don't think you'll be able to meet Angelica's mother; she's leaving to-morrow for the vapour baths at Sciacca; she's very ill, poor thing.'

He stubbed the end of his cheroot in an ashtray. 'Let's go into the drawing-room, shall we? We've been bears here for long enough.'

One day about that time Don Fabrizio received a letter from the Prefect of Girgenti, written in a style of extreme courtesy, announcing the arrival at Donnafugata of the Cavaliere Aimone Chevalley di Monterzuolo, Secretary to the Prefecture, who wanted to talk to him, the Prince, about a subject very close to the Government's heart. Surprised, Don Fabrizio sent off his son, Francesco Paolo, to the post-station next day to receive the *missus dominicus* and invite him to stay at the palace, an act both of hospitality and of true compassion, consisting in not abandoning the body of the Piedmontese to the thousands of little creatures who would have tortured him in the cave-hostelry of *Zzu* Menico.

The post coach arrived at dusk with an armed guard on the box and a few glum faces inside. From it also alighted Chevalley di Monterzuolo, recognisable at once by his scared look and wary simper. He had been in Sicily for a month, in the most persistently native part of the island what was more, bounced there straight from his little property near Montferrat. Timid and congenitally bureaucratic, he found himself much out of his element. His head had been stuffed with the tales of brigands by which Sicilians love to test the nervous resistance of new arrivals, and for a month he had seen every usher in his office as a murderer, and every wooden paper cutter on his desk as a dagger; for a month, too, the oily cooking had upset his inside.

There he stood now, in the twilight, with his valise of beige cloth, peering at the very unpromising aspect of the street in the midst of which he had been dumped. The inscription 'Corso Vittorio Emmanuele', whose blue letters on a white ground adorned the half-ruined house opposite him, was not enough to convince him that he was in a place which was, after all, part of his own nation; and he did not dare to ask the way from any of the peasants propped against walls like caryatids, in his certainty of not being understood and his fear of a gratuitous knife in the guts, still dear to him however upset.

When Francesco Paolo came up and introduced himself he screwed up his eyes at first as he thought himself done for: but the fair-haired youth's calm honest air reassured him a little, and when he realised that he was being invited to stay with the Salina he was both surprised and relieved. The dark journey to the palace was enlivened by a running contest between Piedmontese and Sicilian courtesies (the two most punctilious in Italy) over the valise, which in the end was borne by both knightly contenders, though very light.

On reaching the palace the bearded faces of the armed rangers standing about in the first courtyard once more disturbed the soul of Chevalley di Monterzuolo; while the distant cordiality of the Prince's greeting, together with the evident luxury of the rooms he glimpsed, flung him into contrary worries. Member of one of those families of Piedmontese squireens which live in their own land with dignity and narrow means, it was the first time he found himself a guest at a great house, and this redoubled his shyness; meanwhile the bloodthirsty anecdotes he had been told at Girgenti, the staggeringly insolent aspect of the townsfolk here, the 'bravos' (as he called them to himself) encamped in the courtyard, filled him with terror; so that he went down to dinner in the grip of contrasting fears, at finding himself in an ambience above his normal habits and at feeling an innocent traveller in a bandit's trap.

At dinner he ate well for the first time since setting foot on Sicilian shores, and the charm of the girls, the austerity of Father Pirrone and the grand manner of Don Fabrizio convinced him that the palace of Donnafugata was not the lair of Capraro the bandit, and that he would probably leave there alive. His greatest consolation was the presence of Cavriaghi, who, he was told, had been staying there for ten days and looked in excellent health and also on excellent terms with that young Falconeri, a friendship between a Sicilian and a Lombard which seemed almost miraculous to him. At the end of dinner he went up to Don Fabrizio and requested a private interview as he wished to leave again next morning; but the Prince clapped him on the shoulder and with a most Leopard-like smile exclaimed, 'Not at all, my dear Cavaliere, you're in my home now and I'll hold you as hostage for as long as I like; you won't leave to-morrow morning, and to be quite sure of it I shall deprive myself of the pleasure of a private talk with you until the afternoon.' This phrase, which would have terrified the excellent Secretary three hours before, now rather cheered him. That evening Angelica was not there, and so they played a hand of whist; at a table with Don Fabrizio, Tancredi and Father Pirrone, he won two rubbers and gained three lire and thirty-five centimes; after which he withdrew to his own room, enjoyed the cleanliness of the linen and fell into the trustful sleep of the just.

Next morning Tancredi and Cavriaghi led him around the garden, showed him the picture gallery and tapestry collection. They also trotted him a little round the town; under the honey-coloured sun of that November day it seemed less sinister than it had the night before; he even saw a smile here and there, and Chevalley di Monterzuolo began to reassure himself about rustic Sicily. Tancredi noticed this and was at once assailed by the singular island itch to tell foreigners' tales which, however horrifying, were unfortunately quite true. They were passing in front of a jolly building with a façade decorated in crude stucco work.

'That, my dear Chevalley, is the home of Baron Mútolo; now it's closed and empty as the family live in Girgenti since the baron's son was captured by brigands ten years ago.'

The Piedmontese began to tremble. 'Poor things, I wonder how much they paid to free him.'

'No, no, they didn't pay a thing; they were in financial straits already and had no ready money, like everybody else here. But they got the boy back all the same; by instalments, though.'

'What do you mean, Prince?'

'By instalments, I said, by instalments; bit by bit. First arrived the index finger of his right hand. A week later his left foot; and finally in a great big basket, under a layer of figs (it was August), the head; its eyes were staring and there was congealed blood on the corner of the lips. I didn't see it, I was a child then; but I'm told it wasn't a very pretty sight. The basket was left on that very step there, the second one up to the door, by an old woman with a black shawl on her head; no one recognised her.'

Chevalley's eyes went rigid with horror; he had already heard the story before this, but seeing now in the sunshine the very step on which the bizarre gift had been put was a different matter. His bureaucratic mind came to his help. 'What an inept police those Bourbons had. Very soon, when our carabinieri come along, they'll put an end to all this.'

'No doubt, Chevalley, no doubt.'

Then they passed in front of the Civic Club, which had its daily show of iron chairs and men in mourning under the shade of the plane trees in the Square. Bows, smiles. 'Take a good look, Chevalley, impress the scene on your memory; twice a year or so one of these gentlemen here is left stone dead on his own little armchair; a rifle shot in the uncertain light of dusk, and no one ever knows who it was that shot him.' Chevalley felt the need to lean on Cavriaghi's arm so as to sense a little northern blood near him.

Shortly afterwards, at the top of a steep alley, through multi-coloured festoons of drawers out to dry, they saw the simple baroque front of a little church. 'That's Santa Ninfa. The parish priest was killed in there five years ago as he was saying Mass.'

'Horrors! Shooting in church!'

'Oh, no shooting, Chevalley. We are too good Catholics for misbehaviour of that kind. They just put poison in the communion wine; more discreet, more liturgical, I might say. No one ever knew who did it; the priest was a most excellent person; he had no enemies.'

Like a man who wakes up in the night to see a skeleton sitting at the foot of the bed in his own trousers, and saves himself from panic by forcing himself to believe it's just a joke by drunken friends, so Chevalley took refuge in the idea that he was having his leg pulled. 'Very amusing, Prince, really entertaining; you should write novels, you know; you tell these stories very well.' But his voice was trembling; Tancredi took pity on him, and although on their way home they passed three or four places all of which were most evocative, he abstained from telling their tales, and talked about Bellini and Verdi, perennial curative unctions for national wounds.

At four in the afternoon the Prince sent to tell Chevalley that he was waiting for him in his study. This was a small room with walls lined by glass cases containing grey partridges with pink claws, rarities, stuffed trophies of past shoots. One wall was ennobled by a high, narrow bookcase, crammed full of back numbers of mathematical reviews. Above the great armchair meant for visitors hung a constellation of family miniatures; Don Fabrizio's father, Prince Paolo, dark complexioned and sensual lipped as a Moor, with the cordon of St Januarius diagonally across his black court uniform; Princess Carolina as a widow, with her fair hair heaped into a towering dressing and severe blue eyes; the Prince's sister, Giulia, Princess of Falconeri, sitting on a bench in a garden, with the crimson splodge of a small parasol laid on the ground to her right and to her left the yellow splodge of Tancredi at three years old offering her wild flowers (Don Fabrizio had thrust this miniature into his pocket secretly while the bailiffs were making their inventory for the sale at Villa Falconeri). Beneath that was his eldest son, Paolo, in tight white leather breeches, just about to mount an arrogant horse with a curving neck and flashing eyes; then various unidentifiable uncles and aunts, covered with jewels or pointing sorrowfully at the bust of some extinct dear one. But in the centre of the constellation, acting as a kind of Polar star, shone a bigger miniature; this was of Don Fabrizio himself at the age of about twenty, with his very young wife leaning her head on his shoulder in an act of complete loving abandon. She was dark-haired, he rosy in the blue and silver uniform of the Royal Guards, smiling with pleasure, his face framed in his first and very fair long whiskers.

Chevalley, as soon as he sat down, began explaining the mission with which he had been charged. 'After the happy annexation, I mean after the glorious union of Sicily and the Kingdom of Sardinia, the Turin Government intends to nominate a number of illustrious Sicilians as Senators of the Kingdom. The provincial authorities have been charged with drawing up a list of personalities to be proposed for the Central Government's examination, and eventually for the royal nomination, and, of course, at Girgenti your name was mentioned at once, Prince; a name illustrious for its antiquity, for the personal prestige of its bearer, for scientific merit; and also for the dignified and liberal attitude assumed during recent events.' The little speech had been prepared for some time; it had been even the object of a number of pencil notes in a little book which was now in the hip pocket of Chevalley's trousers. But Don Fabrizio gave no sign of life; his eyes could only just be glimpsed through his heavy lids. Motionless, the great paw with its blondish hairs completely covered a dome of St Peter's in alabaster on the table.

Accustomed by now to the slyness of the loquacious Sicilians whenever anything is suggested to them, Chevalley did not let himself be discouraged. 'Before sending the list to Turin my superiors thought it proper to inform you in person and see if this proposal met with your approval. To ask for your assent, for which the Government much hopes, has been the object of my mission here; a mission which has also given me the honour and the pleasure of getting to know you and your family, this magnificent palace, and picturesque Donnafugata.'

Flattery always slipped off the Prince like water off leaves in fountains: it is one of the advantages enjoyed by men who are at once both proud and used to being so. 'This fellow here seems to be under the impression he's come to do me a great honour,' he was thinking. 'To me, who am what I am, among other things a peer of the Kingdom of Sicily, which must be more or less the same as a Senator. It's true that one must value gifts in relation to those who offer them; when a peasant gives me his bit of cheese he's making me a bigger present than the Prince of Làscari when he invites me to dinner. That's obvious. The difficulty is that the cheese is nauseating. So all that remains is the heart's gratitude which can't be seen and the nose wrinkled in disgust which can be seen only too well.'

Don Fabrizio's ideas about the Senate were very vague; in spite of every effort his thoughts kept leading him back to the Roman Senate; to Senator Papirius breaking a staff on the head of an ill-mannered Gaul, to a horse, Incitatus, made a senator by Caligula, an honour which even his son Paolo might have thought excessive. He was irritated at finding recurring to him insistently a phrase which was sometimes used by Father Pirrone: 'Senatores boni viri, senatus autem mala bestia.' Nowadays there was also an Imperial Senate in Paris, though that was only an assembly of profiteers with big salaries. There was or had been a senate in Palermo, too, though it had only been a committee of civil administrators – what administrators! Low work for a Salina. He decided to be frank. 'But Cavaliere, do explain what being a senator means; the newspapers under our last monarchy never allowed information about the constitutional systems of other Italian states to be printed, and a week's visit of mine to Turin some years ago was not enough to enlighten me. What is it? A simple title of honour? A kind of decoration, or are there legislative, deliberative functions?'

The Piedmontese, representative of the only liberal State in Italy, rose to the bait. 'But, Prince, the Senate is the High Chamber of the Kingdom! In it the flower of Italy's politicians, picked by the wisdom of the Sovereign, will examine, discuss, approve or disapprove the laws proposed by the Government for the progress of the country; it functions at the same time as spur and as brake; it incites good actions and prevents bad ones. When you have accepted a seat in it, you will represent Sicily on an equality with the other elected deputies, you will make us hear the voice of this lovely country which is only now sighting the modern world, with so many wounds to heal, so many just desires to be granted.'

Chevalley would perhaps have continued for some time in this tone if Bendicò from behind the door had not asked 'the wisdom of his Sovereign' to admit him. Don Fabrizio made as

if to get to his feet and open the door, but slowly enough to allow
the Piedmontese time to open it himself; Bendicò meticulously
sniffed around Chevalley's trousers, after which, having decided
this was a good man, the dog lay down under the window
and slept.

'Just listen to me, Chevalley, will you? If it were merely a
question of some honorific, of a simple title to put on a visiting
card, no more, I should be pleased to accept; I feel that at this
decisive moment for the future of the Italian State it is the duty
of us all to support it, and to avoid any impression of disunity in
the eyes of those foreign States which are watching us with alarm
or hope, both of them unjustified, but that do at the moment
exist.'

'Well, then, Prince, why not accept?'

'Be patient now, Chevalley, I'll explain in a moment; we
Sicilians have become accustomed, by a long, a very long
hegemony of rulers who were not of our religion and did not
speak our language, to split hairs. If we had not done so we'd
never have coped with Byzantine tax gatherers, with Berber
Emirs, with Spanish Viceroys. Now the bent is endemic, we're
made like that. I said "support", I did not say "participate". In
these last six months, since your Garibaldi set foot at Marsala,
too many things have been started without our being consulted
for you now to ask a member of the old governing class to help
develop them and carry them through. I do not wish to discuss
now if what was done was good or bad; for my part I believe
much of it to have been bad; but I'd like to tell you at once what
you'll only understand after spending a year among us.

'In Sicily it doesn't matter about doing things well or badly;
the sin which we Sicilians never forgive is simply that of "doing"
at all. We are old, Chevalley, very old. For over twenty-five
centuries we've been bearing the weight of superb and heterogeneous civilisations, all from outside, none made by ourselves,
none that we could call our own. We're as white as you are,
Chevalley, and as the Queen of England; and yet for two thousand five hundred years we've been a colony. I don't say that
in complaint; it's our fault. But even so we're worn out and
exhausted.'

Chevalley was disturbed now. 'But that is all over, isn't it? Now Sicily is no longer a conquered land, but a free part of a free State.'

'The intention is good, Chevalley, but it comes too late; and I've already said that it is mainly our fault. You talked to me a short while ago about a young Sicily sighting the marvels of the modern world; for my part I see instead a centenarian being dragged in a bath-chair round the Great Exhibition in London, understanding nothing and caring about nothing, whether it's the steel factories of Sheffield or the cotton spinneries of Manchester, and thinking of nothing but drowsing off again on beslobbered pillows with a pot under the bed.'

He was still talking quietly, but the hand around St Peter's had tightened; later the tiny cross surmounting the dome was found snapped. 'Sleep, my dear Chevalley, sleep, that is what Sicilians want, and they will always hate anyone who tries to wake them, even in order to bring them the most wonderful of gifts: I must say, between ourselves, that I have strong doubts whether the new kingdom will have many gifts for us in its luggage. All Sicilian self-expression, even the most violent, is really wish-fulfilment; our sensuality is a hankering for oblivion, our shooting and knifing a hankering for death; our languor, our exotic ices, a hankering for voluptuous immobility, that is for death again; our meditative air is that of a void wanting to scrutinise the enigmas of Nirvana. From that comes the power among us of certain people, of those who are half awake: that is the cause of the well-known time lag of a century in our artistic and intellectual life; novelties attract us only when they are dead, incapable of arousing vital currents; from that comes the extra-ordinary phenomenon of the constant formation of myths which would be venerable if they were really ancient, but which are really nothing but sinister attempts to plunge us back into a past that attracts us only because it is dead.'

Not all of this was understood by the good Chevalley; and the last phrase he found particularly obscure; he had seen the variously painted carts being drawn along by horses covered with feathers, he had heard tell of the heroic puppet theatres, but he too had thought they were genuine old traditions. He said, 'Aren't you exaggerating a little, Prince? I myself have met emigrant Sicilians in Turin, Crispi, for example, who seemed anything but asleep.'

The Prince said irritably, 'When there are so many of us there are bound to be exceptions: in any event, I've already mentioned some of us as half awake. As for this young man Crispi, not I, certainly, but you perhaps may be able to see if as an old man he doesn't fall back into our voluptuous torpor; they all do. Anyway, I've explained myself badly; I said Sicilians, I should have added Sicily, the atmosphere, the climate, the landscape of Sicily. Those are the forces which have formed our minds together with and perhaps more than alien pressure and varied invasions: this landscape which knows no mean between sensuous sag and hellish drought; which is never petty, never ordinary, never relaxed, as should be a country made for rational beings to live in; this country of ours in which the inferno round Randazzo is a few miles from the beauty of Taormina Bay; this climate which inflicts us with six feverish months at a temperature of 104. Count them, Chevalley, count them; May, June, July, August, September, October; six times thirty days of sun sheer down on our heads; this summer of ours which is as long and glum as a Russian winter and against which we struggle with less success. You don't know it yet, but fire could be said to snow down on us as on the accursed cities of the Bible. If a Sicilian worked hard in any of those months he would expend energy enough for three. Then water is either lacking altogether or has to be carried from so far that every drop is paid for by a drop of sweat; and when the rains come, they are always tempestuous and set dry torrents to frenzy, drown beasts and men on the very spot where two weeks before both had been dying of thirst.

'This violence of landscape, this cruelty of climate, this continual tension in everything, and even these monuments of the past, magnificent yet incomprehensible because not built by us and yet standing round us like lovely mute ghosts; all those rulers who landed by main force from all directions, who were at once obeyed, soon detested and always misunderstood; their sole means of expression works of art we found enigmatic and taxes we found only too intelligible, and which they spent elsewhere. All these things have formed our character, which is thus conditioned by events outside our control as well as by a terrifying insularity of mind.'

The ideological inferno evoked in this little study disturbed Chevalley even more than the bloodthirsty tales of that morning. He tried to say something, but Don Fabrizio was now too worked up to listen.

'I don't deny that a few Sicilians may succeed in breaking the spell once off the island; but they would have to leave it very young; by twenty it's too late; the crust is formed; they will remain convinced that their country is basely calumniated like all other countries, that the civilised norm is here, the oddities elsewhere. But do please excuse me, Chevalley, I've let myself be led on and I've probably bored you. You haven't come all this way to hear Ezekiel deplore the misfortunes of Israel. Let us return to the subject of our conversation: I am most grateful to the Government for having thought of me for the Senate and I ask you to express my most sincere gratitude to them. But I cannot accept. I am a member of the old ruling class, inevitably compromised with the Bourbon régime, and bound to it by chains of decency if not of affection. I belong to an unlucky generation, swung between the old world and the new, and I find myself ill at ease in both. And what is more, as you must have realised by now, I am without illusions; what would the Senate do with me, an inexperienced legislator who lacks the faculty of self-deception, essential requisite for anyone wanting to guide others? We of our generation must draw aside and watch the capers and somersaults of the young around this ornate catafalque. Now you need young men, bright young men, with minds asking "how" rather than "why", and who are good at masking, at blending I should say, their obvious personal interests with vague public ideals.' He was silent, left St Peter's alone. Then he went on: 'May I give you some advice to hand on to your superiors?'

'That goes without saying, Prince; it will certainly be heard with every consideration; but I still venture to hope that instead of advice you may give your consent.'

'There is a name I should like to suggest for the Senate: that of Calogero Sedàra. He has more the qualities to sit there than I have; his family, I am told, is an old one or soon will be: he has more than what you call prestige, he has power; he has outstanding practical merits instead of scientific ones; his attitude during the May crisis was not so much irreproachable as actively useful; as to illusions, I don't think he has any more than I have, but he's clever enough to know how to create them when needed. He's the man for you. But you must be quick, as I've heard that he intends to put up as candidate for the Chamber of Deputies.'

There had been much talk about Sedàra at the Prefecture. His activities both as mayor and private citizen were well known. Chevalley gave a start; he was an honest man and his esteem for the legislative chambers was paralleled by the purity of his intentions; so he thought it best not to say a word in reply; and he did well not to compromise himself as, ten years later, Don Calogero did in fact gain the Senate. But though honest, Chevalley was no fool; he certainly lacked those quick wits which in Sicily usurp the name of intelligence, but he could assess slowly and firmly and also he had not the southern insensibility to the distress of others. He understood Don Fabrizio's bitterness and discomfort, he reviewed for an instant the misery, the abjection, the black indifference of which he had been witness for the last month. During the past few hours he had envied the Salina opulence and grandeur, but now his mind went back tenderly to his own little vineyard, his Monterzuolo near Casale, ugly, mediocre, but serene and alive. And he found himself pitying this prince without hopes as much as the children without shoes, the malaria-ridden women, the guilty victims whose names reached his office every morning; all were equal fundamentally, all were comrades in misfortune segregated in the same well.

He decided to make a last effort. As he got up his voice was charged with emotion. 'Prince, do you seriously refuse to do all in your power to alleviate, to attempt to remedy the state of physical squalor, of blind moral misery in which this people of yours lies? Climate can be overcome, the memory of evil régimes cancelled, for the Sicilians must want to improve; if honest men withdraw the way will be open for those with no scruples and no vision, for Sedàra and his like; and then everything will be as before for yet more centuries. Listen to your conscience, Prince, and not to the proud truths that you have spoken. Collaborate.'

Don Fabrizio smiled at him, took him by the hand, made him sit beside him on the sofa. 'You're a gentleman, Chevalley, and I consider it a privilege to have met you; you are right in all you say; your only mistake was saying "the Sicilians must want to improve." I'll tell you a personal anecdote. Two or three days before Garibaldi entered Palermo I was introduced to some British naval officers from one of the warships then in harbour to keep an eye on things. They had heard, I don't know how, that I own a house down on the shore facing the sea, with a terrace on its roof from which can be seen the whole circle of hills around the city; they asked to visit this house of mine and look at the landscape where Garibaldini were said to be operating, as they could get no clear idea from their ships. In fact Garibaldi was already at Gibilrossa. They came to my house, I accompanied them up on to the roof; they were simple youths in spite of their reddish whiskers. They were ecstatic about the view, the vehemence of the light; they confessed, though, that they had been horrified at the squalor, decay, filth of the streets around. I didn't explain to them that one thing was derived from the other, as I have tried to with you. Then one of them asked me what those Italian volunteers were really coming to do in Sicily. *"They are coming to teach us good manners!"* I replied in English. *"But they won't succeed, because we are gods."*

'I don't think they understood, but they laughed and went off. That is my answer to you too, my dear Chevalley; the Sicilians never want to improve for the simple reason that they think themselves perfect; their vanity is stronger than their misery; every invasion by outsiders, whether so by origin or, if Sicilian, by independence of spirit, upsets their illusion of achieved perfection, risks disturbing their satisfied waiting for nothing; having been trampled on by a dozen different peoples, they think they have an imperial past which gives them a right to a grand funeral.

'Do you really think, Chevalley, that you are the first who has hoped to canalise Sicily into the flow of universal history? I wonder how many Moslem imâms, how many of King Roger's knights, how many Swabian scribes, how many Angevin barons, how many jurists of the Most Catholic King have conceived the same fine folly; and how many Spanish viceroys too, how many of Charles III's reforming functionaries! And who knows now what happened to them all! Sicily wanted to sleep in spite of their invocations; for why should she listen to them if she herself is rich, if she's wise, if she's civilised, if she's honest, if she's admired and envied by all, if, in a word, she is perfect?

'Now even people here are repeating what was written by Proudhon and some German Jew whose name I can't remember, that the bad state of things here and elsewhere, is all due to feudalism; that it's my fault, as it were. Maybe. But there's been feudalism everywhere, and foreign invasions too. I don't believe that your ancestors, Chevalley, or the English squires or the French seigneurs governed Sicily any better than did the Salina. The results were different. The reason for the difference must lie in this sense of superiority that dazzles every Sicilian eye, and which we ourselves call pride while in reality it's blindness. For the moment, for a long time to come, there's nothing to be done. I'm sorry; but I cannot lift a finger in politics. It would only get bitten. These are things one can't say to a Sicilian; and if you'd said them yourself, I too would have objected.

'It's late, Chevalley; we must go and dress for dinner. For a few hours I have to act the part of a civilised man.'

Chevalley left early next morning and Don Fabrizio, who had arranged to go out shooting, was able to accompany him to the post-station. With them was Don Ciccio Tumeo, carrying on his shoulders the double weight of two shot-guns, his and Don Fabrizio's, and within himself the bile of his own trampled virtue.

In the livid light of five-thirty in the morning Donnafugata was deserted and seemed despairing. In front of every house the refuse of squalid meals accumulated along leprous walls; trembling dogs were routing about with a greed that was always disappointed. An occasional door was already open and the cumulative stench of sleep spread out into the street; by glimmering wicks mothers scrutinised the lids of their children for trachoma; almost all were in mourning and many had been the wives of those carcasses one stumbles over on the turns of mountain tracks. The men were coming out gripping their hoes to look for someone who might give them work, God willing; subdued silence alternated with exasperated screams of hysterical voices; away over towards the Convent of the Holy Ghost a tinny dawn was beginning to tinge leaden clouds.

Chevalley thought: 'This state of things won't last; our lively new modern administration will change it all.' The Prince was depressed. 'All this shouldn't last; but it will, always; the human "always" of course, a century, two centuries ... and after that it will be different, but worse. We were the Leopards and Lions; those who'll take our place will be little jackals, hyenas; and the whole lot of us, Leopards, jackals and sheep, we'll all go on thinking ourselves the salt of the earth.' They thanked each other and said good-bye. Chevalley hoisted himself up on the post-carriage, propped on four wheels the colour of vomit. The horse, all hunger and sores, began its long journey.

Day had just dawned: the little light that managed to pass through quilted clouds was held up once more by the immemorial filth on the windows. Chevalley was alone; amid bumps and shakes he moistened the tip of his index finger with saliva and cleaned a pane for the width of an eye. He looked out; in front of him, under the ashen light, the landscape lurched to and fro, irredeemable.

V

Father Pirrone Pays a Visit

FATHER PIRRONE's origins were rustic; he had been born at San Cono, a tiny hamlet which is now, thanks to the autobus, almost a satellite-star in the solar system of Palermo, but a century ago belonged as it were to a planetary system of its own, being four or five cart-hours from the Palermo sun.

The father of our Jesuit had been overseer of two properties which the Abbey of Sant' Eleuterio thought it owned in the territory of San Cono. An overseer's job was then most perilous for the health both of soul and body, as it necessitated odd acquaintanceships and the knowledge of many a tale which might bring on ills that could suddenly stretch the patient dead beneath some rustic wall, with all those stories inside him lost irrevocably to idle curiosity. But Don Gaetano, Father Pirrone's father, had managed to avoid this occupational disease by rigorous hygiene based on discretion and a careful use of preventive remedies; and he had died peacefully of pneumonia one bright Sunday in February when a soughing wind was stripping the almond blossom. He left his widow and three children (two girls and the priest) relatively well off; like the wise man he was, he had managed to save up some of the incredibly meagre salary paid by the Abbey, and at the moment of his demise owned a few almond trees at the end of the valley, a row or two of vines on the slopes, and some stony pasturage farther up: all poor stuff, of course, but enough to confer a certain weight amid the depressed economy of San Cono. He was also owner of a small, rigidly square house, blue outside and white in, four rooms down and four up, at the very entrance of the village on the Palermo road.

Father Pirrone had left this house at the age of sixteen, when his successes at the parish school and the benevolence of the mitred Abbot of Sant' Eleuterio had set him on the road towards the archiepiscopal seminary; but every few years he had returned there, to bless the marriage of one of his sisters or to give a (in the worldly sense) superfluous absolution to the dying Don Gaetano, and he had come back now, at the end of February 1861, for the fifteenth anniversary of his father's death; on a day gusty and clear, just like that other one.

Getting there had meant a five hours' shaking in a cart with his feet dangling behind a horse's tail; but once he had overcome his nausea at the patriotic pictures newly painted on the cart panels, culminating in a rhetorical presentation of a flame-coloured Garibaldi arm in arm with an aquamarine Santa Rosalia, they had been a pleasant five hours. The valley rising from Palermo to San Cono mingles the lushness of the coast with the harshness of the interior, and is swept by sudden gusts of cleansing wind famous for being able to deviate the best-aimed bullets, so that marksmen faced with these ballistic problems preferred to go elsewhere. Then the carter, who had known the dead man well, launched out into lengthy reminiscences of his merits, reminiscences which, although not always adapted to a son's and a priest's ear, had flattered his practised listener.

His arrival was greeted with happy tears. He embraced and blessed his mother, whose deep widow's weeds set off nicely her white hair and rosy hue; and greeted his sisters and nephews, looking askance among the latter at Carmelo, who had had the bad taste to put a tricolour cockade on his cap in token of rejoicing. As soon as he got into the house he was assailed as always by sweet youthful memories. Nothing was changed, from the red brick floor to the sparse furniture; the same light entered the small narrow windows; Romeo, the dog, barking briefly in a corner, was exactly like another hound, its great-great-grandfather, his companion in violent play; and from the kitchen arose the centuries-old aroma of simmering stew of essence of tomatoes, onions and mutton, for macaroni on festive occasions. Everything expressed the serenity achieved by the dead man's labours.

Soon they moved off to church for the commemorative Mass. That day San Cono looked its best, basking almost proudly in its exhibition of different manures. Sly goats with dangling black udders and numbers of little Sicilian piglets, dark and slim as

minute colts, were running among the people and up the steep
tracks; and as Father Pirrone had become a kind of local glory,
many women, children and even youths crowded round him to
ask for his blessing or remind him of old days.

After a re-orientating gossip in the sacristy by the parish priest
and attendance at Mass he moved to the tombstone in a side
chapel; the women kissed the marble amid sobs, the son prayed
aloud in his archaic Latin; and when they got home the macaroni
was ready and much enjoyed by Father Pirrone, whose palate
had not been spoilt by the culinary delicacies of Villa Salina.

Then towards evening his friends came to greet him and met
in his room. A three-branched bronze lantern hung from the
ceiling and spread a dim light from its oil burners; in a corner
was the bed with its vari-coloured mattress and stifling pink and
yellow quilt; another corner of the room, the 'barn', was divided
off by high stiff matting hiding honey-coloured corn taken
weekly to the mill for the family needs; on the walls hung pock-
marked engravings, St Antony exhibiting the Divine Infant, St
Lucia her gouged-out eyes, and St Francis Xavier haranguing
crowds of plumed and naked Indians; outside, in the starry dusk,
the wind blew and in its way was the only one to commemorate
the dead. In the centre of the room under the lamp was a big
squat brazier surrounded by a strip of polished wood on which
people put their feet; all around, on hemp chairs, sat the guests.
There were the parish priest, the two Schirò brothers, local
landowners, and Don Pietrino the old herbalist; they came looking glum and remained looking glum, because, while the
women were busy below, they sat talking of politics, hoping to
hear consoling news from Father Pirrone who came from
Palermo and must know a lot as he lived with the 'nobles'.
The desire for news had been appeased and that for consolation
disappointed, for their Jesuit friend, partly from sincerity and
partly also from tactics, painted for them a very black future.
The Bourbon tricolour still hung over Gaeta but the blockade
was tight and the powder magazines in the fortress were being
blown up one by one, and nothing could be saved there now,
except honour: not much, that is; Russia was friendly but distant, Napoleon III shifty and close, and of the risings in Basilicata

and Terra di Lavoro the Jesuit spoke little because deep down
he was rather ashamed of them. They must, he told them, face
up to the reality of this atheistic and rapacious Italian state now
in formation, to these laws of expropriation, to conscription
which would spread from Piedmont all the way down here, like
cholera. 'You'll see,' was his not very original conclusion, 'you'll
see they won't even leave us eyes to weep with.'

These words were followed by the traditional chorus of rustic
complaints. The Schirò brothers and the herbalist already felt
the new fiscal grip; the former had had extra contributions and
additions here and there, the latter an overwhelming shock; he
had been called to the Town Hall and told that if he didn't pay
twenty lire every year he wouldn't be allowed to sell his potions.
'But I go and gather the grasses, these holy herbs God made,
with my own hands in the mountains, rain or shine, on certain
days and nights of the year. I dry them in the sun which belongs
to everybody and I grind them up myself, with my own grandfather's mortar. What have you people at the Town Hall to do
with it? Why should I pay you twenty lire? Just for nothing
like that?'

The words came muffled from a toothless mouth, but his eyes
were dark with genuine rage. 'Am I right or not, Father? You
tell me!'

The Jesuit was fond of him; he remembered him as a man
already grown, in fact already bent from continual wandering
and stooping, when he himself had been a boy throwing stones
at the birds; and he was also grateful because he knew that when
the old man sold one of his potions to women he always said
they would be useless without many an Ave and Gloria. But he
prudently preferred to ignore what was in the potions, or the
hopes with which the clients asked for them.

'You're right, Don Pietrino, a hundred times right. Why, of
course! But if those people didn't take money off you and other
poor souls like you, how could they afford to make war on the
Pope and steal what's his?'

The conversation meandered on in the mild lamplight,
quivering as the wind penetrated the heavy shutters. Father Pirrone expatiated on the future and the inevitable confiscation of

ecclesiastical property; good-bye then to the mild rule of the
Abbey in these parts: good-bye to the plates of soup distributed
in bad winters; and when the younger Schirò had the imprudence to say that a few poor peasants might perhaps get some
land of their own, his voice froze into sharp contempt. 'You'll
see, Don Antonino, you'll see. The Mayor will buy everything
up, pay the first instalments, and then do just what he likes. It's
already happened in Piedmont!'

They ended by going off scowling even more than when
they'd come, and with enough complaints to last two months.
The only one to stay was the herbalist, who would not be going
to bed that night as there was a new moon and he had to gather
rosemary on the Pietrazzi rocks; he had brought a lantern with
him and would be setting off straight from there.

'But tell me, Father, you who live with the nobles, what do
they say about all these great doings? What does the Prince of
Salina say, so tall and touchy and proud?'

Father Pirrone had more than once asked himself this question, and it was not an easy one to answer, particularly as he
had taken little notice or interpreted as exaggeration what Don
Fabrizio had told him one morning in the Observatory nearly a
year ago. He knew now, but could find no way of translating it
into comprehensible terms for Don Pietrino who, though far
from a fool, had more understanding of the anti-catarrhal, laxat-
ive, and even aphrodisiac properties of his herbs than of such
abstractions.

'You see, Don Pietrino, the "nobles", as you call them, aren't
so easy to understand. They live in a world of their own, created
not directly by God but by themselves during centuries of highly
specialised experiences, of their own worries and joys; they have
a very strong collective memory, and so they're put out or
pleased by things which wouldn't matter at all to you and me,
but which to them seem vitally connected with their heritage
of memories, hopes, caste fears. Divine Providence has willed
that I should become a humble member of the most glorious
Order in an Eternal Church whose eventual victory has been
assured; you are at the other end of the scale, by which I don't
mean the lowest but the most different. When you find a thick

bush of marjoram or a well-filled nest of Spanish flies (you look for those too, Don Pietrino, I know) you are in direct communication with the natural world which the Lord created with undifferentiated possibilities of good and evil until man could exercise his own free will on it; and when you're consulted by evil old women and eager young girls, you are plunging back into the dark abyss of centuries that preceded the light from Golgotha.'

The old man looked at him in amazement; he had wanted to know if the Prince of Salina was satisfied or not with the latest changes, and the other was talking to him about aphrodisiacs and light from Golgotha. 'All that reading's driven him off his head, poor man.'

'But the "nobles" aren't like that; all they live by has been handled by others. They find us ecclesiastics useful to reassure them about eternal life, just as you herbalists are here to procure them soothing or stimulating drinks. And by that I don't mean they're bad people; quite the contrary. They're just different; perhaps they appear so strange to us because they have reached a stage towards which all those who are not saints are moving, that of indifference to earthly goods through surfeit. Perhaps it's because of that they take so little notice of things that are of great importance to us; those on mountains don't worry about mosquitoes in plains, nor do the people in Egypt about umbrellas. Yet the former fear landslides, the latter crocodiles, which are no worry to us. For them new fears have appeared of which we're ignorant; I've seen Don Fabrizio get quite testy, wise and serious though he is, because of a badly ironed collar to his shirt; and I know for certain that the Prince of Làscari didn't sleep for a whole night from rage because he was wrongly placed at one of the Viceroy's dinners. Now don't you think that a human being who is put out only by bad washing or protocol must be happy, and thus superior?'

Don Pietrino could understand nothing at all now: all this was getting more and more nonsensical, what with shirt collars and crocodiles. He was still upheld, though, by a basis of good rustic commonsense. 'But if that's what they're like, Father, they'll all go to Hell.'

'Why? Some will be lost, others saved, according to how they've lived in that conditioned world of theirs. Salina himself, for instance, might just scrape through; he plays his own game decently, follows the rules, doesn't cheat. God punishes those who voluntarily contravene the Divine Laws which they know and turn voluntarily down a bad road; one who goes his own way, so long as he doesn't misbehave along it, is always all right. If you, Don Pietrino, sold hemlock instead of mint, knowingly, you'd be for it; but if you thought you'd picked the right one, old Zana would die the noble death of Socrates and you'd go straight to Heaven with a cassock and wings of purest white.'

The death of Socrates was too much for the herbalist; he had given up and was fast asleep. Father Pirrone noticed this and was pleased, for now he would be able to talk freely without fear of being misunderstood; and he felt a need of talking, so as to fix into a pattern of phrases some ideas obscurely milling in his head.

'And they do a lot of good, too. If you knew, for instance, the families otherwise homeless that find shelter in those palaces! And the owners ask for no return, not even immunity from petty theft. They do it not from ostentation but from a sort of obscure atavistic instinct which prevents them doing anything else. Although it may not seem so, they are in fact less selfish than many others; the splendour of their homes, the pomp of their receptions, have something impersonal about them, something not unlike the grandeur of churches and of liturgy, something which is in fact *ad maiorem gentis gloriam*, and that redeems a great deal: for every glass of champagne drunk by themselves they offer fifty to others; when they treat someone badly, as they do sometimes, it is not so much their personality sinning as their class affirming itself. *Fata crescunt*. For instance, Don Fabrizio has protected and educated his nephew Tancredi and so saved a poor orphan who would have otherwise been lost. You say that he did it because the young man is a noble too, and that he wouldn't have lifted a finger for anyone else. That's true, but why should he lift a finger if sincerely, in the deep roots of his heart, he considers all "others" to be botched attempts, china figurines come misshapen from the potter's hands and not worth putting to the test of fire.

'You, Don Pietrino, if you weren't asleep at this moment, would be jumping up to tell me that the nobles are wrong to have this contempt of others, and that all of us, equally subject to the double slavery of love and death, are equal before the Creator; and I would have to agree with you. But I'd add that not only nobles are to be blamed for despising others, since that is quite a general vice. A university professor despises a parish schoolmaster even if he doesn't show it, and since you're asleep I can tell you without reticence that we clergy consider ourselves superior to the laity, we Jesuits superior to the other clergy, just as you herbalists despise tooth-pullers who in their turn deride you. Doctors on the other hand jeer at both tooth-pullers and herbalists, and are themselves treated as fools by their patients who expect to be kept alive with hearts or livers in a hopeless state; to magistrates lawyers are just bores who try to delay the course of law, and on the other hand literature is full of satires against the pomposity, indolence and often worse of those very judges. The only people who also despise themselves are labourers; when they've learnt to jeer at others the circle will be closed and we'll start all over again.

'Have you ever thought, Don Pietrino, how many names of jobs have become insults? From trooper and fishwife to *reitre* or *pompier* in French? People don't think of the merits of troopers or fishwives; they just look at their marginal defects and call them all rough and profane; and as you can't hear me, I may tell you that I'm perfectly aware of the exact current meaning of the word "Jesuit".

'Then these nobles put a good face on their own disasters: I've seen one who'd decided to kill himself next day, poor man, looking beaming and happy as a boy on the eve of his first Communion; while if you, Don Pietrino, had to drink one of your own herb drinks, you'd make the village ring with your laments. To rage and mock is gentlemanly; to grumble and whine is not. In fact I could give you a recipe: if you meet a "gentleman" who's querulous, look up his family tree; you'll soon find a dead branch.

'It's a class difficult to suppress because it's in continual renewal and because if needs be it can die well, that is it can throw out a seed at the moment of death. Look at France; they let themselves be massacred with elegance there and now they're back as before. I say as before, because it is differences of attitude, not estates and feudal rights, which make a noble.

'They tell me that in Paris nowadays there are Polish counts who've been forced into exile and poverty by revolts and despotism; they drive cabs, but frown so at their middle-class customers that the poor things get into the cab, without knowing why, as humbly as dogs in church.

'And I can tell you too, Don Pietrino, that if, as has often happened before, this class were to vanish, an equivalent one would be formed straight away with the same qualities and the same defects; it might not be based on blood any more, but possibly on ... on, say, length of time in a place, or pretended knowledge of some text presumed sacred.'

At this point his mother's steps were heard on the wooden stairs; she laughed as she came in. 'Who d'you think you're talking to, son? Can't you see your friend's fast asleep?'

Father Pirrone looked a little abashed; he did not reply but just said, 'I'll go outside with him now. Poor man, he's got to spend all night out in the cold.' He took the wick from the lantern and lit it from one of the ceiling lamps, getting up on tiptoe and splashing his cassock with oil; then he put it back and shut its little gate. Don Pietrino was sailing in dreams; saliva was dribbling from a lip and spreading over his collar. It took some time to wake him up. 'Excuse me, Father, but you were saying such confusing things.' They smiled, went downstairs, and out. Night submerged the little house, the village, the valley; the nearby mountains could just be seen, surly as always; the wind had calmed but it was very cold; the stars were glittering away, producing thousands of degrees of heat which were not enough to warm one poor old man. 'Poor Don Pietrino! Would you like me to go and get you another cloak?'

'Thank you, I'm used to it. We'll meet to-morrow, then you'll tell me what the Prince of Salina feels about the Revolution.'

'I can tell you that at once and in a few words; he says there's been no revolution and that all will go on as it did before.'

'More fool he! Doesn't it seem a revolution to you when the

Mayor wants me to pay for the grass God created and which I gather myself? Or have you gone off your head too?'

The light of the lantern went jerking off and eventually vanished into shadows thick as felt.

Father Pirrone thought what a mess the world must seem to one who knew neither mathematics nor theology. 'Oh, Lord, only Thy Omniscience could have devised so many complications.'

Another sample of these complications faced him next morning. When he went down, ready to say Mass in the parish church, he found his sister Sarina chopping onions in the kitchen. The tears in her eyes seemed bigger than her activity warranted.

'What is it, Sarina? Any trouble? Don't let it depress you; the Lord afflicts and consoles.'

His affectionate tone dissipated the remains of the poor woman's reserve; she began sobbing loudly, with her face on the greasy table-top. Among the sobs could always be heard the same words, 'Angelina, Angelina . . . If Vincenzino knew he'd kill them both . . . Angelina . . . He'd kill them both!'

His hands thrust into his wide black sash, with only his thumbs showing, Father Pirrone stood looking at her. It wasn't difficult to understand; Angelina was Sarina's adolescent daughter; Vincenzino, whose fury was so feared, was her father and his brother-in-law; the only unknown part of the equation was the name of the other person involved, Angelina's presumed lover.

The Jesuit had seen her for the first time the day before as a full-grown girl, after having left her a snivelling child seven years before. She seemed about eighteen and was very plain indeed, with the jutting mouth of so many peasant girls around these parts, and frightened dog's eyes. He had noticed her on his arrival and in his heart in fact made rather uncharitable comparisons between her, plebeian as the diminutive of her own name, and Angelica, sumptuous as that name from Ariosto, who had recently disturbed the peace of the Salina household.

The trouble must be serious and here he was right in the middle of it; he remembered what Don Fabrizio had once said: every time one sees a relative one finds a thorn; then he was

sorry for having remembered that. He extracted his right hand
from his sash, took off his hat and clapped his sister's quivering
shoulder. 'Come on now Sarina, don't do that! Luckily, I'm
here. Crying's no use. Where is Vincenzino?' Vincenzino had
gone off to Rimato to see the Schiròs' ranger. All the better;
they could talk things over without fear of surprise. Between
sobs, sucked tears and nose snuffling, out the whole squalid
story came; Angelina (or rather 'Ncilina) had let herself be
seduced; the disaster had happened during St Martin's Summer;
she used to go to meet her lover in Donna Nunziata's hayloft;
now she'd been with child three months; in a panic she had
confessed all to her mother; soon her belly would begin
showing and Vincenzino would raise hell. 'He'll kill me too,
he will, because I didn't tell him; he's what they call "a man
of honour"!'

In fact with his low forehead, ornamental quiffs of hair on the
temples, lurching walk and perpetual swelling of the right
trouser pocket where he kept a knife, it was obvious at once that
Vincenzino was 'a man of honour', one of those violent cretins
capable of any havoc.

Now Sarina was overcome by a new fit of sobbing, stronger
than the first because she'd been seized by renewed remorse
for having been unworthy of her husband, that mirror of
chivalry.

'Sarina, Sarina, stop it now! Don't do that! The young man
must marry her, he will marry her. I'll go to his home, talk to
him and his family, everything will be all right. Then Vincenzino will know only about the engagement and his precious
honour will remain intact. But I must know who the man is. If
you know, tell me.'

His sister raised her head; her eyes now showed another fear,
no longer the animal one of the knife thrusts, but a more
restricted, keener one which the brother could not for the
moment place.

'It was Santino Pirrone! Turi's son! And he did it out of
spite, spite against me, against our mother, against our father's
memory! I've never spoken to him, they all said he was a good
boy – but he's a swine, a true son of that double-dishonoured

father of his. I remembered afterwards; I always used to see him passing here in November with two friends and a red geranium behind his ear. Red of hell, that was, red of hell!'

The Jesuit took a chair and sat down next to the poor woman. Obviously he would have to be late for Mass. This was serious. Turi, the father of the seducer Santino, was an uncle of his; the brother, in fact the elder brother, of his dead father. Twenty years ago he had worked together with the dead man in his job as overseer, just at the moment of the latter's greatest and most meritorious activity. Later the brothers had quarrelled, one of those family quarrels we all know with deeply entangled roots, impossible to cure because neither side speaks out clearly, each having much to hide. The fact was that when the dead man acquired the little almond grove, his brother Turi had said that half of it really belonged to him because half the money for it, or half the work, he had put in himself; but the deeds bore only the name of the dead Gaetano. Turi stormed up and down the roads of San Cono foaming at the mouth. The dead man's prestige was in danger, friends came between and the worst was avoided; the almond grove remained Gaetano's property, but the gulf between the two branches of the Pirrone family became unbridgeable; Turi did not even go to his brother's funeral and was referred to simply as the 'swine' in his sister's house. The Jesuit had been told of all this by letters dictated to the parish priest and had formed some ideas of his own about it which he did not express from filial reverence. The little almond grove now belonged to Sarina.

It was all quite obvious; no love or passion played any part; just a dirty trick to revenge another dirty trick. But it could be set right; the Jesuit thanked Providence for having brought him to San Cono at that very time. 'Listen, Sarina, I'll settle all this in a couple of hours, but you've got to help me; half of Chibbaro' (that was the almond grove) 'must go as 'Ncilina's dowry. There's no other way out of it; the silly girl has been the ruin of you.' And he thought how the Lord to bring about His justice can even use bitches in heat.

Sarina lost her temper. 'Half of Chibbaro! To that swine, never! Better dead!'

'All right. Then after Mass I'll go and talk to Vincenzino. Don't be afraid, I'll try and calm him down.' He put his hat back on his head and his hands into his belt; and waited patiently, sure of himself.

Any version of Vincenzino's furies, even though revised and expurgated by a Jesuit priest, was always beyond poor Sarina, who began weeping for the third time; gradually her sobs lessened and then stopped. She got up: 'May God's will be done; you fix it, it's beyond me. But our lovely Chibbaro! All that sweat of our father's!'

Her tears were just about to start again, but the priest had already gone.

After celebrating the Divine Sacrifice and accepting coffee from the parish priest, the Jesuit went straight to his Uncle Turi's home. He had never been there but knew it was a shack at the very top of the village near Mastro Ciccu the blacksmith's. He soon found it, and as there were no windows and the door was open to let in a little sun, he stopped on the threshold. In the darkness inside he could see heaps of mules' harness, saddle-bags, sacks; Don Turi earned his living as a mule driver, now helped by his son.

'*Dorâzio!*' called Father Pirrone. This was an abbreviation of the form of *Deo Gratias* (*agamus*) used by clerics asking permission to enter. An old man's voice shouted, 'Who is it?' and someone got up at the back of the room and came towards the door. 'It's your nephew, Father Saverio Pirrone. I wanted to talk to you if I may.'

It was not much of a surprise for Turi; a visit by Father Pirrone or some representative must have been expected for at least two months. Uncle Turi was a vigorous, straight-backed old man baked through and through by sun and hail, with the sinister furrows on his face which troubles trace on people who are not good.

'Come in,' he said without a smile. He stood aside and even went grudgingly through the action of kissing the priest's hand. Father Pirrone sat down on one of the big wooden saddles. The place looked very wretched indeed: two chickens were grubbing away in a corner and everything smelt of manure, wet washing and evil poverty.

'Uncle, we've not met for years, but that's not all my fault; I'm seldom at home, as you know, but you never come near my mother, your sister-in-law; I'm sorry to hear that.'

'I'll never set foot in that house again. Just passing it turns my stomach! Turi Pirrone never forgets an injury, even after twenty years!'

'Oh, yes, of course, yes indeed. But here I am today like the dove from Noah's Ark, to assure you that the flood is over. I'm very glad to be here and I was very happy yesterday when they told me at home that your son Santino is engaged to my niece Angelina; they are two fine young people, I'm told, and their union will put an end to the quarrel between our families which, if I may say so, has always grieved me.'

Turi's face expressed a surprise too obvious not to be false. 'If it weren't for your habit, Father, I'd say you were lying. You must have been listening to tales from those females of yours. Santino has never spoken to Angelina in his life: he's far too good a son to go against his father's wish.'

The Jesuit admired the old man's astuteness and the smoothness of his lying.

'Apparently, Uncle, I've been misinformed; why, they told me that you'd agreed on the dowry and would both be coming to our place today to make it official. But the nonsense these idle females talk! Even if it's not true, though, it does show what's in those good hearts of theirs. Well, Uncle, there's no point in my staying here; I'm going straight home to reprove my sister. Very pleased to find you so well.'

The old man's face was beginning to show a certain greedy interest. 'Wait, Father. Give us another laugh with this gossip of yours; what dowry were the females talking of?'

'Oh, I don't know! I think I heard something about half of Chibbaro! 'Ncilina, they said, was very dear to them and no sacrifice was too much to ensure peace in the family!'

Don Turi stopped laughing. He got up, 'Santino!' he began bawling as loudly as if calling a recalcitrant mule. And as no one came he shouted louder still, 'Santino, blood of the Madonna, where are you?' Then, when he saw Father Pirrone quiver, he put a hand over his mouth with a gesture unexpectedly servile.

Santino was seeing to the animals in the adjacent yard. He entered shyly, with a curry-comb in his hand. He was a fine-looking lad of twenty-two, tall and slim like his father, with eyes not yet embittered. He had seen the Jesuit pass through the village the day before as had everyone else and he recognised him at once. 'This is Santino. And this is your cousin Father Saverio Pirrone. You can thank God the Reverend Father is here, or I'd have cut your ears off. What's all this love-making without your own father knowing? Children are born for their parents and not to run after skirts.'

The young man looked ashamed, perhaps not from disobedience but because of his father's past consent, and did not know what to say; he got out of the difficulty by putting the curry-comb on the floor and going to kiss the priest's hand. The latter showed his teeth in a smile and sketched a benediction. 'God bless you, my son, though I don't think you deserve it.'

The old man continued, 'As your cousin here has gone on begging me I've given my consent in the end. Why didn't you tell me before, though? Now clean yourself up and we'll go down to Angelina's now.'

'A moment, Uncle, just a moment.' It occurred to Father Pirrone that he ought to say a word to the 'man of honour' who knew nothing as yet. 'Back home they'll be sure to want to get things ready; anyway they told me they'd be expecting you at seven this evening. Come then, and it'll be a pleasure to see you.' And off he went, embraced by father and son.

When Father Pirrone got back to the little square house he found his brother-in-law Vincenzino already home, so all he could do to reassure his sister was wink at her from behind her proud husband's back; but as they were both Sicilians that was quite enough. Then he told his brother-in-law that he wanted to talk to him, and the two went off to the scraggy little pergola at the back. The swaying edge of the Jesuit's cassock traced a kind of uncrossable mobile frontier around him; the fat buttocks of the 'man of honour' waggled, perennial symbol of threatening pride. Their conversation was actually quite different from what

the priest had foreseen. Once assured of the imminence of 'Ncilina's marriage, the 'man of honour' showed complete indifference about what her behaviour had been. But at the first
mention of the proposed dowry his eyes rolled, the veins in his
temples swelled and the lurch in his walk became more marked;
from his mouth came a gurgle of low obscene oaths and
announcements of murderous intentions; his hand, which had
not made a single gesture in defence of his daughter's honour,
began clutching the right pocket of his trousers to show that in
defence of his almond trees he was ready to spill the very last
drop of other people's blood.

Father Pirrone let the stream of abuse run out, merely making
quick signs of the Cross at the frequent curses; of the gesture
announcing a massacre he took no notice at all. During a pause
he put in: 'Of course I want to contribute to a general settlement
too. You know the private agreement ensuring me the ownership of whatever was due to me from our father's estate? I'll send
that back to you from Palermo, torn up.'

This balsam had an immediate effect. Vincenzino, intent on
computing the value of the anticipated inheritance, was silent;
and through the cold sunny air came the cracked notes of a song
which had suddenly burst from 'Ncilina as she swept out her
uncle's room.

In the afternoon Uncle Turi and Santino came to pay their
visit, quite spruced up and wearing very white shirts. The
engaged couple sat on chairs side by side and broke out now and
again into loud wordless giggles in each other's faces. They were
really pleased, she at 'settling' herself and having this big handsome male at her disposal, he at following his father's advice and
now owning not only half an almond grove but a slave too. And
no one now found the red geranium he had put in his buttonhole
to have any connection with hell.

Two days later Father Pirrone left for Palermo. As he jogged
along he went over impressions that were not entirely pleasant;
that brutish love-affair come to fruition in St Martin's Summer, that wretched half almond grove reacquired by means of
calculated courtship, seemed to him the rustic poverty-struck

equivalent of other events recently witnessed. Nobles were
reserved and incomprehensible, peasants explicit and clear; but
the Devil twisted them both round his little finger all the same.

At the Villa Salina he found the Prince in excellent spirits.
Don Fabrizio asked if he had enjoyed his four days away and if
he had remembered to give his mother his, the Prince's, greetings. He knew her, in fact; she had stayed at the villa six years
before and pleased both the Prince and Princess by her serene
widowhood. The Jesuit had entirely forgotten about the greetings and was silent; then he said that his mother and sister had
charged him with bearing His Excellency their respects, which
was a fib rather than a lie. 'Excellency,' he added then, 'I wanted
to ask you if you could give orders for me to have a carriage
tomorrow; I must go to the Archbishopric to ask for a dispensa-
tion; a niece of mine has got engaged to her cousin.'

'Of course, Father Pirrone, of course, if you wish; but I have
to go down to Palermo myself the day after tomorrow, you
could come with me – or are you really in such a rush?'

VI
A Ball

THE PRINCESS MARIA STELLA climbed into the carriage, sat down on the blue satin cushions and gathered around her as many rustling folds of her dress as she could. Meanwhile Concetta and Carolina were also getting in; they sat down in front of her, their identical pink dresses exhaling a faint scent of violets. Then a heavy foot on the running board made the barouche heel over on its high springs; Don Fabrizio was getting in too. The carriage was crammed, waves of silk, hoops of three crinolines, billowed, clashed, mingled almost to the height of their heads; beneath was a tight press of footgear, the girls' silken slippers, the Princess's russet ones, the Prince's patent leather pumps: each suffered from the other's feet and could find nowhere to put his own.

The mounting steps were folded, the footman given his orders. 'To Palazzo Ponteleone.' He got back on to the box, the groom holding the horses' bridles moved aside, the coachman gave an imperceptible click of his tongue, and the barouche slid into motion.

They were going to a ball.

Palermo at the moment was passing through one of its intermittent periods of social gaiety; there were balls everywhere. After the coming of the Piedmontese, after the Aspromonte affair, now that spectres of violence and spoliation had fled, the few hundred people who made up 'the world' never tired of meeting each other, always the same ones, to exchange congratulations on still existing.

So frequent were the various and yet identical parties that the Prince and Princess of Salina had moved to their town palace for three weeks so as not to have to make the long drive from San Lorenzo almost every night. The ladies' dresses would arrive from Naples in long black cases like coffins, and there would be an hysterical coming and going of milliners, hairdressers and shoemakers; of exasperated servants carrying excited notes to fitters. The Ponteleone ball was to be one of the most important of that short season; important for all concerned because of the standing of the family, the splendour of the palace and the number of guests; particularly important for the Salina who would be presenting to 'society' Angelica, their nephew's lovely bride-to-be. It was still only half-past ten, rather early to appear at a ball if one is Prince of Salina, whose arrival should be timed for when a fête is at its height. But this time they had to be early if they wanted to be there for the entry of the Sedàras, who were the sort of people ('they don't *know* yet, poor things') to take literally the times on the gleaming invitation card. It had taken a good deal of trouble to get one of those cards sent to them; no one knew them, and the Princess Maria Stella had been obliged to make a visit to Margherita Ponteleone ten days before; all had gone smoothly, of course, but even so it had been one of those little thorns that Tancredi's engagement had inserted into the Leopard's delicate paws.

The short drive to Palazzo Ponteleone took them through a tangle of dark alleys, and they went at walking pace; Via Salina, Via Valverde, down the Bambinai slope, so gay in daytime with its little shops of waxen figures, so dreary by night. The horse-shoes sounded muffled amid the dark houses asleep or pretending to sleep.

The girls, incomprehensible beings for whom a ball is fun and not a tedious worldly duty, were chatting away gaily in low voices; the Princess Maria Stella felt her bag to assure herself she'd brought her little bottle of sal volatile; Don Fabrizio was enjoying in anticipation the effect of Angelica's beauty on all those who did not know her and of Tancredi's luck on all those who knew him too well. But a shadow lay across his contentment; what about Don Calogero's tail-coat? Certainly not like the one worn at Donnafugata; he had been put into the hands of Tancredi, who had dragged him off to the best tailor and even been present at fittings. Officially the result had seemed to satisfy him the other day; but in confidence he had said, 'The coat is the best we can do; Angelica's father lacks *chic*.' That was undeniable; but Tancredi had guaranteed a perfect shave and decently polished shoes. That was something.

Where the Bambinai slope comes out by the apse of San
Domenico the carriage stopped; there was a faint tinkle and
round the corner appeared a priest bearing a ciborium with the
Blessed Sacrament; behind, a young acolyte held over him a
white canopy embroidered in gold; in front another bore a big
lighted candle in his left hand and in his right a little silver bell
which he was shaking with obvious enjoyment. These were the
Last Sacraments; in one of those barred houses someone was in
a death agony. Don Fabrizio got out and knelt on the pavement,
the ladies made the sign of the Cross, the tinkling faded into the
alleys tumbling down towards San Giacomo, and the barouche,
with its occupants given a salutary warning, set off again towards
its destination, now close by.

They arrived, they alighted in the portico; the coach vanished
into the immensity of the courtyard, whence came the sound of
pawing horses and the gleams of equipages arrived before.

The great stairs were of rough material but superb proportions;
from every step country plants spread rustic scents; on the landing between flights the amaranthine liveries of two footmen,
motionless under their powder, set a note of bright colour in
the pearly grey surroundings. From two high little grated windows came a gurgle of laughter and childish murmurs; the small
Ponteleone grandchildren, excluded from the party, were looking on, making fun of the guests. The ladies smoothed down
silken folds; Don Fabrizio, *gibus* under an arm, was head and
shoulders above them, although a step behind. At the door of
the first drawing-room they met their host and hostess; he, Don
Diego, white-haired and paunchy, saved from looking plebeian
only by his caustic eyes, she, Donna Margherita, with, between
coruscating tiara and triple row of emeralds, the hooked features
of an old priest.

'You've come early! All the better! But don't worry, *your*
guests haven't appeared yet.' A new thorn pierced the sensitive
fingertips of the Leopard. 'Tancredi's here already too.' There
in the opposite corner of the drawing-room was standing their
nephew, black and slim as an adder, surrounded by three or four
young men whom he was making roar with laughter at little

tales that were quite certainly indecent; but his eyes, restless as ever, were fixed on the entrance door. Dancing had already begun and through three, four, five antechambers came notes of an orchestra from the ballroom.

'We're also expecting Colonel Pallavicino, who did so well at Aspromonte.'

This phrase from the Prince of Ponteleone was not as simple as it sounded. On the surface it was a remark without political meaning, mere praise for the tact, the delicacy, the respect, the tenderness almost with which the Colonel had got a bullet fired into General Garibaldi's foot; and for the accompaniment too, the bowing, kneeling and hand-kissing of the wounded Hero lying under a chestnut tree on a Calabrian hillside, smiling from emotion and not from irony as he might well have done (for Garibaldi, alas, lacked a sense of humour).

At an intermediate stage of the princely psyche the phrase had a technical meaning and was intended to praise the Colonel for the aptness of his dispositions, the timely deployment of his battalions, and his ability to carry out successfully against the same adversary what Landi had so unaccountably failed to do at Calatafimi. At heart, though, Ponteleone thought that the Colonel 'did so well' by managing to stop, defeat, wound and capture Garibaldi, in so doing saving the compromise so laboriously achieved between the old state of things and the new.

Evoked, created almost by the approving words and still more approving thoughts, the Colonel now appeared at the top of the stairs. He was moving amid a tinkle of epaulettes, chains and spurs in his well-padded, double-breasted uniform, a plumed hat under his arm and his left wrist propped on a curved sabre. He was a man of the world with graceful manners, well-versed, as all Europe knew by now, in hand-kissings dense with meaning; every lady whose fingers were brushed by his perfumed moustaches that night was able to re-evoke from first-hand knowledge the historical incident so highly praised in the popular press.

After sustaining the shower of praise poured over him by the Ponteleone, after shaking the two fingers held out to him by Don Fabrizio, Pallavicino merged into the scented froth of a group of ladies. His consciously virile features emerged above snowy white shoulders, and an occasional phrase came over. 'I sobbed, Countess, sobbed like a child'; or 'He looked fine and serene as an archangel.' The male sentimentality enchanted ladies reassured already by the musketry of his Bersaglieri.

Angelica and Don Calogero were late, and the Salina family were thinking of plunging into the other rooms when Tancredi was seen to detach himself from his little group and move like a dart towards the entrance: the expected pair had arrived. Above the ordered swirl of her pink crinoline Angelica's white shoulders merged into strong soft arms; her head looked small and proud on its smooth youthful neck adorned with intentionally modest pearls. And when from the opening of her long kid glove she drew a hand which though not small was perfectly shaped, on it was seen glittering the Neapolitan sapphire.

In her wake came Don Calogero, a rat escorting a rose: though his clothes had no elegance, this time they were at least decent. His only mistake was wearing in his buttonhole the Cross of the Order of the Crown of Italy recently conferred on him; but this soon vanished into one of the secret pockets in Tancredi's tail-coat.

Her fiancé had already taught Angelica to be impassive, that fundamental of distinction ('You can be expansive and noisy only with me, my dear; with all others you must be the future Princess of Falconeri, superior to many, equal to all'), and so she greeted her hostess with a totally unspontaneous but highly successful mixture of virginal modesty, neo-aristocratic hauteur and youthful grace.

The Palermitans are Italians after all, and so particularly responsive to the appeal of beauty and the prestige of money; apart from which Tancredi, however attractive, being also notoriously penniless, was considered an undesirable match (mistakenly, as was seen afterwards when too late); and so he was appreciated more by married women than by marriageable girls. This merging of merits and demerits now had the effect of Angelica being received with unexpected warmth. One or two young men might well have regretted not having dug up for themselves so lovely an amphora brimming with coin: but

Donnafugata was a fief of Don Fabrizio's, and if he had found that treasure there and then passed it to his beloved Tancredi, one could no more be jealous of that than of his finding a sulphur mine on his land; it was his property, there was nothing to be said.

But even this transient resentment melted before the rays of those eyes. At one moment there was quite a press of young men wanting to be introduced and to ask for a dance; to each one of them Angelica dispensed a smile from her strawberry lips, to each she showed her card in which every polka, mazurka and waltz was followed by the possessive signature: Falconeri. There was also a general attempt by young ladies to get on familiar terms; and after an hour Angelica found herself quite at her ease among people who had not the slightest idea of her mother's crudity or her father's rapacity.

Her bearing did not contradict itself for an instant; never was she seen wandering about alone with head in the clouds, never did her arms move from her body, never was her voice raised above the murmur (quite high anyway) of the other ladies. For Tancredi had told her the day before, 'Now darling, we (and so you too now) are more attached to our houses and furniture than we are to anything else; and nothing offends us more than carelessness about those; so look at everything and praise everything; anyway Palazzo Ponteleone is worth it; but as you're not just a girl from the provinces whom everything surprises, always put a little reserve into your praise; admire, but always compare with some archetype seen before and known to be outstanding.' The long visits to the palace at Donnafugata had taught Angelica a great deal, so that evening she admired every tapestry, but said that the ones in Palazzo Pitti had a finer border; she praised a Madonna by Dolci but remembered that the Grand Duke's had a more expressive melancholy; even of the slice of tart brought her by an attentive young gentleman she said that it was excellent, almost as good as that of 'Monsù Gaston', the Salina chef. And as Monsù Gaston was positively the Raphael of cooks, and the tapestries of Palazzo Pitti the Monsù Gaston of hangings, no one could complain, in fact everyone was flattered by the comparison; and so from that evening she began to acquire the reputation of a polite but inflexible art expert which was to accompany her quite unwarrantably throughout her long life.

While Angelica reaped laurels, Maria Stella gossiped on a sofa with two old friends, and Concetta and Carolina froze with their shyness the politest partners. Don Fabrizio was wandering round the rooms; he kissed the hands of ladies he met, numbed the shoulders of men he wanted to greet, but could feel ill-humour creeping slowly over him. First of all he didn't like the house; the Ponteleone hadn't done it up for seventy years, it was still the same as in the time of Queen Maria Carolina, and he, who considered himself to have modern tastes, was indignant. 'Good God, with Diego's income it wouldn't take long to sweep away all these consoles, all these tarnished mirrors! Then order some decent rosewood and plush furniture, and so live in comfort himself and stop making his guests go round catacombs like these. I'll tell him so in the end.' But he never told Diego, for these opinions only stemmed from his mood and his tendency to contradiction; they were soon forgotten and he himself never changed a thing either at San Lorenzo or Donnafugata. Meanwhile, however, they served to increase his disquiet.

The women at the ball did not please him either. Two or three among the older ones had been his mistresses, and seeing them now, weighed down by years and daughters-in-law, it was an effort to imagine them as they were twenty years before, and he was annoyed at the thought of having thrown away his best years in chasing (and catching) such slatterns. The younger women weren't up to much either, except for one or two: the youthful Duchess of Palma, whose grey eyes and gentle reserve he admired, Tutú Làscari also, with whom, had he been younger, he might well have found himself in unique and exquisite harmony. But the others ... it was a good thing that Angelica had emerged from the shades of Donnafugata to show these Palermitans what a really lovely woman was like.

There was something to be said for his strictures; what with the frequent marriages between cousins in recent years due to sexual lethargy and territorial calculations, with the dearth of proteins and overabundance of starch in the food, with the total lack of fresh air and movement, the drawing-rooms were now filled with a mob of girls incredibly short, improbably dark, unbearably giggly. They were sitting around in huddles, letting out an occasional hoot at an alarmed young man, and destined, apparently, to act only as background to three or four lovely creatures such as the fair-haired Maria Palma, and the exquisite Eleonora Giardinelli, who glided by like swans over a frog-filled pool.

The more of them he saw the more put out he felt; his mind, conditioned by long periods of solitude and abstract thought, at one moment, as he was passing through a long gallery where a numerous colony of these creatures had gathered on the central *pouf*, got into a kind of hallucination; he felt like a keeper in a zoo looking after some hundred female monkeys; any moment he expected to see them clamber up the chandeliers and hang there by their tails, swinging to and fro, showing off their behinds and loosing a stream of nuts, shrieks and grins at pacific visitors below.

A religious evocation, oddly enough, drew him away from this zoologic vision. For from the group of crinolined monkeys rose a monotonous, continuous sacred cry. 'Maria! Maria!' the poor creatures were perpetually exclaiming. 'Maria, what a lovely house!' 'Maria, what a handsome man Colonel Pallavicino is!' 'Maria, how my feet are aching!' 'Maria, I'm so hungry! When does the supper room open?' The name of the Virgin, invoked by that virginal choir, echoed throughout the gallery and changed the monkeys back into women, for the *ouistiti* of the Brazilian forests had not yet, as far as he knew, been converted to Catholicism.

Slightly nauseated, the Prince passed into the room next door, where were encamped the rival and hostile tribe of men; the younger were off dancing and those now there were only the older ones, all of them his friends. He sat down a little among them; there, instead of the name of the Queen of Heaven being taken in vain, the air was turgid with commonplaces. Among these men Don Fabrizio was considered an 'eccentric'; his interest in mathematics was taken almost as sinful perversion, and had he not been actually Prince of Salina and known as an excellent horseman, a tireless shot and a fair womaniser, his parallaxes and telescopes might have exposed him to the risk of outlawry. Even so they did not say much to him, for his cold blue eyes, glimpsed under the heavy lids, put would-be talkers off, and he often found himself isolated, not, as he thought, from respect, but from fear.

He got up; his melancholy had now changed to black gloom. He had been wrong to come to this ball; Stella, Angelica, his daughters, could easily have coped with it alone, and he at this moment would have been happily ensconced in his study next to the terrace in Villa Salina, listening to the tinkling of the fountain and trying to catch comets by their tails. 'Anyway, I'm here now; it would be rude to leave. Let's go and have a look at the dancing.'

The ballroom was all golden; smoothed on cornices, stippled on door-frames, damascened pale, almost silvery, over darker gold on door panels and on the shutters which covered and annulled the windows, conferring on the room the look of some superb jewel-case shut off from an unworthy world. It was not the flashy gilding which decorators slap on nowadays, but a faded gold, pale as the hair of certain nordic children, determinedly hiding its value under a muted use of precious material intended to let beauty be seen and cost forgotten. Here and there on the panels were knots of rococo flowers in a colour so faint as to seem just an ephemeral pink reflected from the chandeliers.

That solar hue, that variegation of gleam and shade, made Don Fabrizio's heart ache as he stood black and stiff in a door-way: this eminently patrician room reminded him of country things; the chromatic scale was the same as that of the vast wheat fields around Donnafugata, rapt, begging for pity from the tyrannous sun; in this room, too, as on his estates in mid-August, the harvest had been gathered long ago and stacked elsewhere, leaving, as here now, a sole reminder in the colour of burnt up useless stubble. The notes of the waltz in the warm air seemed to him but a stylisation of the incessant winds harping their own sorrows on those parched surfaces, to-day, yesterday, to-morrow, for ever and for ever. The crowd of dancers among whom he could count so many near to him in blood if not in heart, began to seem unreal, made of the raw material of lapsed memories, more labile even than that of disturbing dreams. From the ceiling the gods, reclining on gilded couches, gazed down smiling and inexorable as a summer sky. They thought themselves eternal; but a bomb manufactured in Pittsburgh, Penn., was to prove the contrary in 1943.

'Fine, Prince, fine! They don't do things like this nowadays, with gold leaf at its present price!' Sedàra was standing beside him; his quick eyes were moving over the room, insensible to its charm, intent on its monetary value.

Quite suddenly Don Fabrizio felt a loathing for him; to the rise of this man and a hundred others like him, to their obscure intrigues and their tenacious greed and avarice, was due the sense of death looming darkly over these palaces; it was due to him and his colleagues, to their rancour and sense of inferiority, their incapacity for putting out blooms, that the black clothes of the men dancing reminded Don Fabrizio of crows veering to and fro above lost valleys in search of putrid prey. He felt like giving a sharp reply and telling him to get out of his way. But he couldn't; the man was a guest, he was the father of that dear girl Angelica; and maybe, too, he was just as unhappy as others.

'Fine, Don Calogero, fine. But our young couple's the finest of all.' Tancredi and Angelica were passing in front of them at that moment, his gloved right hand on her waist, their outspread arms interlaced, their eyes gazing into each other's. The black of his tail-coat, the pink of her interweaving dress, looked like some unusual jewel. They were the most moving sight there, two young people in love dancing together, blind to each other's defects, deaf to the warnings of fate, deluding themselves that the whole course of their lives would be as smooth as the ball-room floor, unknowing actors set to play the parts of Juliet and Romeo by a director who had concealed the fact that tomb and poison were already in the script. Neither was good, each self-interested, turgid with secret aims; yet there was something sweet and touching about them both; those murky but ingenuous ambitions of theirs were obliterated by the words of jesting tenderness he was murmuring in her ear, by the scent of hair, by the mutual clasp of those bodies destined to die.

The two young people drew away, other couples passed, less handsome, just as moving, each submerged in their passing blindness. Don Fabrizio felt his heart thaw; his disgust gave way to compassion for all these ephemeral beings out to enjoy the tiny ray of light granted them between two shades, before the cradle, after the last spasms. How could one inveigh against those sure to die? It would be as vile as those fish vendors insulting the condemned in the Piazza del Mercato sixty years before. Even the female monkeys on the *poufs*, even those old boobies of friends were poor wretches, condemned and touching as the cattle lowing through city streets at night on their way to the slaughter-house; to the ears of each of them would one day come that tinkle he had heard three hours before behind San Domenico. Nothing could be decently hated except eternity.

And then these people filling the rooms, all these faded women, all these stupid men, these two vainglorious sexes were part of his blood, part of himself; only they could really understand him, only with them could he be at ease. 'I may be more intelligent, I'm certainly more cultivated than they are, but I come from the same stock, with them I must make common cause.'

He noticed Don Calogero talking to Giovanni Finale about a possible rise in the price of cheese and how in the hope of this beatific event his eyes had gone liquid and gentle. Don Fabrizio could slip away without remorse.

Till that moment accumulated irritation had given him energy; now, with relaxed nerves, weariness overcame him; it was already two o'clock. He looked round for a place where he could sit down quietly, far from men, beloved and brothers, all right in their way, but always tiresome. He soon found it; the library, small, silent, lit and empty. He sat down, then got up to drink some water which he found on a side table. 'Only water is really good,' he thought like a true Sicilian; and did not dry the drops left on his lips. He sat down again; he liked the library and soon felt at his ease there; it did not oppose his taking possession, for it was impersonal as are rooms little used; Ponteleone was not a type to waste his time in there. He began looking at a picture opposite him, a good copy of Greuze's *Death of the Just Man*; the old man was expiring on his bed amid welters of clean linen, surrounded by afflicted grandsons, and by grand-daughters raising arms towards the ceiling. The girls were pretty, and provoking: and the disorder of their clothes suggested sex more than sorrow; they, it was obvious at once, were the real subject of the picture. Even so, Don Fabrizio was surprised for a second at Diego always having this melancholy scene before his eyes; then he reassured himself by thinking that the other probably entered that room only once or twice a year.

Immediately afterwards he asked himself if his own death would be like that; probably it would, apart from the sheets being less impeccable (he knew that the sheets of those in their death agony are always dirty with spittle, ejections, medicine marks . . .) and it was to be hoped that Concetta, Carolina and his other women folk would be more decently clad. But the same, more or less. As always the thought of his own death calmed him as much as that of others disturbed him: was it perhaps because, when all was said and done, his own death would in the first place mean that of the whole world?

From this he went on to think that he must see to repairing the tomb of his ancestors at the Capuchins. A pity corpses could no longer be hung up by the neck in the crypt and watched slowly mummifying; he'd look magnificent on that wall, tall and big as he was, terrifying girls by the set smile on his parchment face, by his long, long white nankeen trousers. But no, they'd dress him up in party clothes, perhaps in this very evening coat he was wearing now . . .

The door opened. 'Nuncle, you're looking wonderful this evening. Black suits you perfectly. But what are you looking at? Are you paying court to death?'

Tancredi was arm in arm with Angelica; both of them were still under the sensual influence of the dance, and were tired. Angelica sat down and asked Tancredi for a handkerchief to mop her brow; Don Fabrizio gave her his. The two young people looked at the picture with complete lack of interest. For both of them death was purely an intellectual concept, a facet of knowledge as it were and no more, not an experience which pierced the marrow of their bones. Death, oh, yes, it existed of course, but was something that happened to others. The thought occurred to Don Fabrizio that it was inner ignorance of this supreme consolation which makes the young feel sorrows much more sharply than the old; the latter are nearer the safety exit.

'Prince,' said Angelica, 'we'd heard you were here; we came to have a little rest, but also to ask you something. I hope you won't refuse it.' Her eyes were full of sly laughter, her hand was resting on Don Fabrizio's sleeve. 'I wanted to ask you to dance the next mazurka with me. Do say yes, now, don't be naughty; we all know you used to be a great dancer.' The Prince was very pleased and felt suddenly quite spry. The Capuchins' crypt indeed! His hairy cheeks quivered with pleasure. The idea of the mazurka rather alarmed him, though; that military dance, all heel-banging and turns, was not for his joints. To kneel before Angelica would be a pleasure, but what if he found it difficult to get up afterwards?

'Thank you, my dear girl: you're making me feel young again. I'll be happy to obey you; but not the mazurka; grant me the first waltz.'

'You see, Tancredi, how good Nuncle is? No nonsense about him, like you. You know, Prince, he didn't want me to ask you; he's jealous.'

Tancredi laughed. 'When one has such a smart good-looking uncle one's quite right to be jealous. Anyway this time I won't oppose it.' They all three smiled, and Don Fabrizio could not make out if they had thought up this suggestion to please him or to mock him. It didn't matter; they were dear creatures all the same.

As she was going out Angelica slid a finger over the cover of an armchair. 'Pretty, these; a good colour, but those at your home, Prince . . .' The ship was taking its usual course.

Tancredi intervened. 'That's enough, Angelica. We both love you quite apart from your knowledge of furniture. Leave the chairs alone and come and dance.'

As he was going into the ballroom, Don Fabrizio saw that Sedàra was still talking to Giovanni Finale. He heard market terms; they were comparing the prices of wheat. The Prince foresaw an invitation soon to Margarossa, the estate which Finale was ruining by his agricultural experiments.

Angelica and Don Fabrizio made a magnificent couple. The Prince's huge feet moved with surprising delicacy and never were his partner's satin slippers in danger of being grazed. His great paw held her waist with vigorous firmness, his chin leant on the black waves of her hair; from Angelica's bust rose a delicate scent of *bouquet à la Maréchale*, and above all an aroma of young smooth skin. A phrase of Tumeo came back to him: 'Her sheets must smell like paradise.' A crude, vulgar phrase, but accurate. Lucky Tancredi . . .

She talked. Her natural vanity was as appeased as her tenacious ambition. 'I'm so happy, Nuncle. Everyone's been so kind, so sweet. Tancredi's an angel; and you're an angel, too. I owe all this to you, Nuncle; even Tancredi. For if you hadn't agreed, I don't know what would have happened.'

'I've nothing to do with it, my dear; all this is due to yourself alone.'

It was true; no Tancredi could ever have resisted that beauty united to that income. He would have married her whatever happened. A twinge crossed his heart: the thought of Concetta's haughty yet defeated eyes. But that was a brief little pain; at every twirl a year fell from his shoulders; soon he felt back at the age of twenty, when in that very same ballroom he had danced with Stella before he knew disappointment, boredom and the rest. For a second, that night, death seemed to him once more 'something that happens to others'.

So absorbed was he in memories which dovetailed so well with his present feelings that he did not notice how all of a sudden he and Angelica were dancing alone. Instigated, perhaps, by Tancredi, the other couples had stopped and were watching; the two Ponteleone were there too, looking touched; they were old and perhaps understood. Stella was old too, but she was gazing on dully from beneath a doorway. When the band stopped there was nearly a round of applause; but Fabrizio had too leonine an air for anyone to risk such an impropriety.

When the waltz was over Angelica suggested that Don Fabrizio should come and take supper at her and Tancredi's table. He would have much liked to, but at that moment the memories of his own youth were too vivid for him not to realise how tiresome supper with an old uncle would have been then, with Stella only a yard or so away. Lovers want to be alone, or at least with strangers; never with older people, worst of all with relations.

'Thank you, Angelica, but I'm not hungry. I'll take something standing up. Go with Tancredi, don't worry about me.'

He waited a moment for the two young people to draw away, then he too went into the supper room. A long, narrow table was set at the end, lit by the famous twelve silver-gilt candelabra given to Diego's grandfather by the Court of Madrid at the end of his embassy in Spain; on tall pedestals of gleaming metal six alternating figures of athletes and women held above their heads silver-gilt shafts crowned by the flames of twelve candles. The sculptor had hinted skilfully at the serene ease of the men and the graceful effort of the girls in upholding the disproportionate weight. Twelve pieces of first-class quality ... 'I wonder how much land they're worth,' that wretch Sedàra would have said. Don Fabrizio remembered Diego showing him one day the cases for each of those candles, vast green morocco affairs with the tripartite shield of Ponteleone and the entwined initials of the donors stamped on the sides in gold.

Beneath the candelabra, beneath the five tiers bearing towards the distant ceiling pyramids of home-made cakes that were never touched, spread the monotonous opulence of buffets at big balls: coraline lobsters boiled alive, waxy *chaud-froids* of veal, steely-lined fish immersed in sauce, turkeys gilded by the ovens' heat, rosy *foie-gras* under gelatine armour, boned woodcocks reclining on amber toast decorated with their own chopped guts, dawn-tinted galantine, and a dozen other cruel, coloured delights. At the end of the table two monumental silver tureens held limpid soup, the tint of burnt amber. To prepare this supper the cooks must have sweated away in the vast kitchens from the night before.

'Dear me, what an amount! Donna Margherita knows how to do things well. But it's not for me!'

Scorning the table of drinks, glittering with crystal and silver on the right, he moved left towards that of the sweetmeats. Huge sorrel *babas*, *Mont Blancs* snowy with whipped cream, cakes speckled with white almonds and green pistachio nuts, hillocks of chocolate-covered pastry, brown and rich as the top soil of the Catanian plain from which, in fact, through many a twist and turn they had come, pink ices, champagne ices, coffee ices, all *parfaits* and falling apart with a squelch at a knife cleft; a melody in major of crystallised cherries, acid notes of yellow pineapple, and green pistachio paste of those cakes called 'Triumphs of Gluttony', shameless 'Virgins' cakes' shaped like breasts. Don Fabrizio asked for some of these, and as he held them on his plate looked like a profane caricature of Saint Agatha claiming her own sliced-off breasts. 'Why ever didn't the Holy Office forbid these puddings when it had the chance? "Triumphs of Gluttony" indeed! (Gluttony, mortal sin!) Saint Agatha's sliced-off teats sold by convents, devoured at dances! Well! Well!'

Round the room smelling of vanilla, wine, *chypre*, wandered Don Fabrizio looking for a place. Tancredi saw him from his table and clapped a hand on a chair to show there was room there; next to him was Angelica, peering at the back of a silver dish to see if her hair was in place. Don Fabrizio shook his head in smiling refusal. He went on looking; from a table he heard the satisfied voice of Pallavicino, 'The most moving moment of my life . . .' By him was an empty place. What a bore the man was! Wouldn't it be better, after all, to listen to Angelica's refreshing if forced cordiality, to Tancredi's dry wit? No: better bore oneself than bore others.

With a word of apology he sat down next to the Colonel, who got up as he arrived – a small sop to Salina pride. As he savoured the subtle mixture of blancmange, pistachio and cinnamon in the puddings he had chosen, Don Fabrizio began conversing with Pallavicino and realised that, beyond those sugary phrases meant perhaps only for ladies, the man was anything but a fool. He too was a 'gentleman', and the fundamental scepticism of his class, smothered usually by the impetuous Bersaglieri flames on his lapel, came peering out again now that he found himself in surroundings like those into which he was born, away from the inevitable rhetoric of barracks and admirers.

'Now the Left wants to string me up because last August I ordered my men to open fire on the General. But can you tell me, Prince, what else I could have done in view of the written orders I was carrying? I must confess though, when at Aspromonte I found myself facing that mob of a few hundred ragamuffins, some looking like out-and-out fanatics, others scowling like professional agitators, I was pleased my instructions coincided so with my own feelings. If I hadn't given orders to fire those people would have hacked us to pieces, my soldiers and me; that wouldn't have mattered much, of course. But in the end it would have meant French and Austrian intervention, and that would have had endless repercussions, including the collapse of this Italian Kingdom of ours which has got itself put together in some miraculous way, quite how I can't for the life of me understand. And I can tell you another thing in confidence: those musket shots of ours were a particular help to ... Garibaldi himself! They freed him from the rabble hanging round him, all those creatures like Zambianchi who were making use of him for ends that may have been generous but were certainly inept, with the Tuileries or Palazzo Farnese behind them. Very different types those were to the ones who landed with him at Marsala, who did believe, the best of them, that Italy could be created by repeating 1848. And he knows that, the General does, for when I was making him the genuflection that has caused so much comment, he shook my hand with a warmth that must surely be unusual towards a man who's just fired a bullet into one's foot a few minutes before. And d'you know what he said to me in a low voice, he who was the one really decent person on the whole wretched mountainside? "Thank you, Colonel." Thank you for what, I ask you? For laming him for life? Obviously not; but for having brought home to him so clearly the bluster, the cowardice, worse maybe, of those followers of his.'

'Forgive me saying so, Colonel, but don't you think all the

hand-kissing, cap-doffing and compliments went a little far?'

'No, frankly. For they were all genuine acts of respect. You should have seen him, that poor great man, stretched out under a chestnut tree, suffering in body and still more in mind. A sad sight! He showed himself plainly as what he's always been, a child, in spite of beard and wrinkles, a simple adventurous little boy; it was difficult for me not to feel moved at having had to shoot at him. Why shouldn't I, anyway? Usually I kiss only ladies' hands; on that occasion, Prince, I was kissing a hand for the salvation of the Kingdom, also a lady to whom we soldiers owe homage.'

A footman passed; Don Fabrizio told him to bring a slice of *Mont Blanc* and a glass of champagne. 'And you, Colonel, aren't you taking anything?'

'Nothing to eat, thank you. Perhaps I'll drink a glass of champagne too.'

Then he went on, obviously unable to take his mind off a memory which, consisting as it did of a little shooting and a lot of skill, was exactly the sort that attracts men of his type. 'The General's men, as my Bersaglieri disarmed them, were cursing away, and d'you know who at? At him, the only one of them who'd actually paid in his own person. Foul, but natural really; they saw that childlike yet large personality, the only one capable of covering up their obscure intrigues, slipping out of their grasp. And if my own courtesies were superfluous, I'd be pleased even so at having done them; we in Italy can never go too far with sentiment and hand-kissing; they're the most effective political arguments we have.'

He drank the wine brought him, but that seemed to increase his bitterness even more. 'Have you been on the mainland since the Kingdom was founded? You're lucky. It's not a pretty sight. Never have we been so disunited as since we've been reunited. Turin doesn't want to cease being a capital. Milan finds our administration inferior to the Austrians', Florence is afraid the works of art there will be carried off, Naples is moaning about the industries she's lost and here, here in Sicily, some huge irrational disaster is growing up ... For the moment, due partly to your humble servant, no one mentions red shirts any more; but they'll be back again. When they've vanished, others of different colours will come; and then red ones once again. And how will it end? There's Italy's Lucky Star they say. But you know better than me, Prince, that even fixed stars are so only in appearance.' Perhaps he was a little tipsy, making such prophecies. But at such disquieting prospects Don Fabrizio felt his heart contract.

The ball went on for a long time still, until six in the morning; all were exhausted and wishing they had been in bed for at least three hours; but to leave early was like proclaiming the party a failure and offending the host and hostess who had taken *such* a lot of trouble, poor dears.

The ladies' faces were livid, their dresses crushed, their breaths heavy. 'Maria! How tired I am! Maria! How sleepy!' Above their disordered cravats the faces of the men were yellow and lined, their mouths stained with bitter saliva. Their visits to a disordered little room near the band alcove became more frequent; in it were disposed a row of twenty vast vats; by that time nearly all were brimful, some spilling over. Sensing that the dance was nearing its end, the sleepy servants were no longer changing the candles in chandeliers, and the short stubs diffused a different, smoky, ill-omened light. In the empty supper room were only dirty plates, glasses with dregs of wine which the servants, glancing around, would hurriedly drain; through the cracks in the shutters filtered a plebeian light of dawn.

The party was crumbling away and around Donna Margherita there was already a group saying good-bye. 'Heavenly! A dream! Like the old days!' Tancredi was hard put to wake Don Calogero who, with head flung back, had gone off to sleep on an armchair apart; his trousers were rucked up to his knees and above his silken socks showed the ends of his drawers, a most rustic sight. Even Colonel Pallavicino had circles under his eyes, declaring, though, to whoever wished to listen, that he was not going home and would move straight from Palazzo Ponteleone to his headquarters; such in fact was the iron tradition followed by officers invited to a ball.

When the family had settled into its carriage (the dew had made the cushions damp) Don Fabrizio said that he would walk home; a little fresh air would do him good, he had a slight headache. The truth is that he wanted to draw a little comfort from gazing at the stars. There were still one or two up there, at the zenith. As always, seeing them revived him; they were distant, they were omnipotent and at the same time they were docile to his calculations; just the contrary to humans, always too near, so weak and yet so quarrelsome.

There was already a little movement in the streets, a cart or two with rubbish heaped four times the height of the tiny grey donkey dragging it along. A long open wagon came by stacked with bulls killed shortly before at the slaughter-house, already quartered and exhibiting their intimate mechanism with the shamelessness of death. At intervals a big thick red drop fell on to the paving-stones.

At the crossroads he glimpsed the sky to the east, above the sea. There was Venus, wrapped in her turban of autumn mist. She was always faithful, always awaiting a Don Fabrizio on his early morning outings, at Donnafugata before a shoot, now after a ball.

Don Fabrizio sighed. When would she decide to give him an appointment less ephemeral, far from stumps and blood, in her own region of perennial certitude?

VII
Death of a Prince

DON FABRIZIO had always known that sensation. For a dozen years or so he had been feeling as if the vital fluid, the faculty of existing, life itself in fact and perhaps even the will to go on living, were ebbing out of him slowly but steadily, as grains of sand cluster and then line up one by one, unhurried, unceasing, before the narrow neck of an hour-glass. In some moments of intense activity or concentration this sense of continual loss would vanish, to reappear impassively in brief instants of silence or introspection; just as a constant buzzing in the ears or ticking of a pendulum superimpose themselves when all else is silent, assuring us of always being there, watchful, even when we do not hear them.

With the slightest effort of attention he used to notice at all other times too, the rustling of the grains of sand as they slid lightly away, the instants of time escaping from his mind and leaving him for ever. But this sensation was not, at first, linked to any physical discomfort. On the contrary this imperceptible loss of vitality was itself the proof, the condition so to say, of a sense of living; and for him, accustomed to scrutinising limitless outer space and to probing vast inner abysses, the sensation was in no way disagreeable; this continuous whittling away of his personality seemed linked to a vague presage of the rebuilding elsewhere of a personality (thanks be to God) less conscious and yet broader. Those tiny grains of sand were not lost; they were vanishing, but accumulating elsewhere to cement some more lasting pile. Though 'pile', he had reflected, was not the exact word, for it suggested weight; nor was 'grain of sand' either for that matter. They were more like the tiny particles of watery vapour exhaled from a narrow pond, mounting then into the sky to great clouds, light and free.

Sometimes he was surprised that the vital reservoir could still contain anything at all after all those years of loss. 'Not even were it big as a Pyramid . . .' On other occasions, more frequent, he had felt a kind of pride at being the only one to notice this continual escape, while no one around him seemed to sense it in the same way; and this had made him feel a certain contempt for others, as an old soldier despises a conscript who deludes himself that sizzling bullets are just harmless flies. Such things are never confessed, no one knows why, but left for others to sense; and no one around him had ever sensed them at all, none of his daughters with their dreams of a world beyond the tomb identical with this life, all complete with judges, cooks and convents; not even Stella who, though devoured by the canker of diabetes, had still clung pitiably to this vale of tears.

Perhaps only Tancredi had understood for an instant, when he had said with that subdued irony of his, 'You, Nuncle, are courting death.' Now the courtship was ended; the lovely lady had said a definite 'yes' to an elopement, to a reserved compartment on the train.

For this was different now, quite different. Sitting in an armchair, his long legs wrapped in a blanket, on the balcony of the Hotel Trinacria, he felt life flowing from him in great pressing waves with a spiritual roar like that of the Rhine Falls. It was noon on a Monday at the end of July, and away in front of him spread the sea of Palermo, compact, oily, inert, improbably motionless, crouching like a dog trying to make itself invisible at its master's threats; but up there the static perpendicular sun was straddling it and lashing at it pitilessly. The silence was absolute. Under the high, high light Don Fabrizio heard no other sound but that inner one of the life gushing from him.

He had arrived that morning, a few hours before, from Naples, where he had gone to consult a specialist, Professor Sémmola. Accompanied by his forty-year-old daughter, Concetta, and his grandson Fabrizietto, he had had a dreary journey, slow as a funeral procession. The bustle of the port of departure and that of arrival at Naples, the acrid smell of the cabin, the incessant clamour of that paranoiac city, had exasperated him with the querulous exasperation which tires and prostrates the very weak while arousing an equivalent exasperation in good folk with years of life ahead. He had insisted on returning by land; a sudden decision which the doctor had tried to oppose:

but he had been adamant, and so overwhelming was the shadow of his prestige still that he had had his way.

The result was that he had been forced to spend thirty-six hours cooped up in a scorching hot box, suffocated by the smoke of tunnels repetitive as feverish dreams, blinded by the sun in open patches stark as sad realities, humiliated by the innumerable squalid services he had to ask of his alarmed grandson. They crossed evil-looking landscapes, accursed mountain ranges, torpid malarial plains, those landscapes of Calabria and Basilicata which seemed barbarous to him while they were actually just like those of Sicily. The railway line had not yet been completed; in its last tract near Reggio it made a wide detour through Metaponto across lunar deserts called sarcastically by the athletic and voluptuous names of Croton and Cybaris. Then, at Messina, after the deceitful smile of the Straits had been given a lie by the parched slopes of Cape Pelorus, there was another detour, long and cruel as legal arrears. They had gone down to Catania, clambered up again towards Castro Giovanni; the locomotive, as it panted up those fabulous slopes, seemed about to die like an over-forced horse; then after a noisy descent they reached Palermo. On the arrival platform were the usual masks of family faces with painted smiles of pleasure at the journey's happy outcome. It was in fact from the would-be consoling smiles of those awaiting him at the station, from their pretence – a bad pretence – at an air of gaiety, that there suddenly came home to him what had been the real diagnosis of Sémmola, who to him had spoken only reassuring phrases; and it was then, after getting down from the train, as he was embracing his daughter-in-law buried in widow's weeds, his children showing their teeth in smiles, Tancredi with anxious eyes, Angelica with silken bodice tight over mature breasts, it was then that he heard the crash of the cascade.

Probably he fainted, for he did not remember how he had reached the carriage; he found himself lying in it with his legs contracted, only Tancredi with him. The carriage had not yet moved, and from outside came voices of his family in confabulation. 'It's nothing.' 'The journey was too long.' 'Any of us might faint in this heat.' 'It would be too tiring for him to go up to the

villa.' He was perfectly lucid again now: he noticed a serious
conversation going on between Concetta and Francesco Paolo,
Tancredi's elegance, his brown and beige check suit, his brown
bowler; and he noticed too how for once his nephew's smile
was not mocking but touched with sad affection; from this he
got the bitter-sweet sensation that his nephew loved him and
also knew him to be done for, since that perpetual irony had
been driven off by tenderness. The carriage moved off and
turned to the right. 'But where are we going, Tancredi?' His
own voice surprised him. It seemed to echo that inner booming.

'Nuncle, we're going to the Hotel Trinacria; you're tired and
the villa's a long way; you can have a night's rest and get home
to-morrow. Don't you think so?'

'Then let's go to our place by the sea, that's even nearer.'

But it wasn't possible; the house was not in order, as he knew
well; it was only used for occasional luncheons by the sea; there
wasn't even a bed in it.

'You'll be better at the hotel, Uncle; you'll have every comfort there.' They were treating him like a new-born baby; and
he had just about a new-born baby's strength.

The first comfort he found at the hotel was a doctor, called
in a hurry, perhaps during his black-out. But it was not the one
who always treated him, Doctor Cataliotti, with big white cravat
under smiling face and rich gold spectacles; this was a poor
devil, doctor to the slum quarter around, impotent witness of a
thousand wretched death-agonies. Above a torn frockcoat
stretched his long, haggard face stubbled with white hair, the
disillusioned face of a famished intellectual; when he took a
chainless watch from his pocket, the false gilt showed marks of
verdigris. He too was a poor goat-skin flask worn through by
the jostle of the mule path and scattering without realising its
last drops of oil. He felt the pulse-beats, prescribed camphor
drops, showed his decayed teeth in a smile meant to be reassuring
and which was pitiable instead, and shuffled off.

The drops soon arrived from a chemist nearby; they did him
good; he felt a little less weak, but the impetus of escaping time
did not lessen.

Don Fabrizio looked at himself in the wardrobe mirror: he

recognised his own suit more than himself; very tall and emaciated, with sunken cheeks and three days' growth of beard; he looked like one of those maniac Englishmen who amble round the vignettes in books by Jules Verne which he used to give Fabrizietto as Christmas presents. A Leopard in very bad trim. Why, he wondered, did God not want anyone to die with their own face on? For the same happens to us all: we all die with a mask on our features; even the young; even that blood-daubed soldier, even Paolo, when he'd been raised from the cobbles with taut crumpled features as passers-by rushed in the dust after his runaway horse. And if in him, an old man, the crash of escaping life was so powerful, what a tumult there must have been as the brimming reservoirs emptied in a second out of those poor young bodies.

An absurd rule of enforced camouflage – he would have liked to contravene it as much as he could; but he felt that he was unable, that to hold up a razor would have been like holding up his own desk, before. 'Call a barber, will you?' he said to Francesco Paolo. But at once he thought, 'No. It's a rule of the game; hateful but formal. They'll shave me afterwards.' And he said out loud, 'It doesn't matter; we'll think about that later.' The idea of the utter abandon of his corpse, with a barber crouched over it, did not disturb him.

A waiter came in with a basin of warm water and a sponge, took off his coat and shirt and washed his face and hands, as one washes a child, as one washes the dead. Smuts from the day and a half's train journey turned the water a funereal black. The low room was suffocating; the heat fomented smells, brought out the mustiness of ill-dusted plush; the ghosts of dozens of crushed cockroaches were manifested in a faint medicinal odour; by the night table tenacious memories of stale and varied urine overcast the room. He had the shutters opened: the hotel was in shadow, but a blinding light was reflected from the metallic sea; better, though, than that prison stink. He asked for an armchair to be taken on the balcony; leaning on someone's arm he dragged himself out, and sat down after those few steps with the sensation of relief he used to feel once on sitting down after four hours of shooting in the mountains. 'Tell everyone to leave me in peace;

I feel better; I want to sleep.' He did feel sleepy; but he found that to give way to drowsiness now would be as absurd as eating a slice of cake immediately before a longed-for banquet. He smiled. 'I've always been a wise gourmet.' And he sat there, immersed in that great outer silence, in that terrifying inner rumble.

He could turn his head to the left; beside Monte Pellegrino could be seen a cleft in the circle of hills and, beyond, two hillocks at whose feet lay his home. Unreachable to him as this was, it seemed very far away; he thought of his own observatory, of the telescopes now destined to years of dust; of poor Father Pirrone, who was dust too; of the paintings of his estates, of the monkeys on the hangings, of the big brass bedstead in which his dear Stella had died; of all those things which now seemed to him humble however precious, just braided metal, woven threads and canvas with sap and earth, which he had kept alive and would shortly be plunged, through no fault of their own, into a limbo of abandon and oblivion. His heart tightened, he forgot his own agony thinking of the imminent end of those poor dear things. The inert row of houses behind him, the wall of hills, the sun-scourged distance, prevented him thinking clearly even of Donnafugata; it seemed like a house in a dream, no longer his; all he had of his own now was this exhausted body, those slate tiles under his feet, that surging of dark water towards the abyss. He was alone, a shipwrecked man adrift on a raft, prey of untameable currents.

There were his sons, of course. The only one who resembled him, Giovanni, was no longer here. Every couple of years he sent greetings from London; he had ceased dealing with coal and moved on to diamonds; just after Stella's death a short letter had come addressed to her and soon after a little parcel with a bracelet. Ah, yes. He too had 'courted death', in fact by leaving everything he had done his best to organise for himself as much of death as he could while actually going on living. But the others . . . There were his grandchildren, too, of course; Fabrizietto, youngest of the Salina, so handsome, so lively, so dear . . .

So odious. With his double dose of Màlvica blood, with his good-time instincts, with his tendency to middle-class smartness. It was useless to try and avoid the thought, but the last of the Salina was really he himself, this gaunt giant now dying on a hotel balcony. For the significance of a noble family lies entirely in its traditions, that is in its vital memories; and he was the last to have any unusual memories, anything different from those of other families. Fabrizietto would only have banal ones like his schoolfellows, of snacks, of spiteful little jokes against teachers, horses bought with an eye more to price than quality; and the meaning of his name would change more and more to empty pomp, embittered by the gadfly thought that others could outdo him in outward show. He would go hunting for a rich marriage when that would have become a commonplace routine and no longer a predatory adventure like Tancredi's. The tapestries of Donnafugata, the almond groves of Ragattisi, even, who knew, the fountain of Amphitrite, might suffer a grotesque metamorphosis from the age-old muted things they had been into pots of quickly-swallowed *foie gras*, or can-can girls transient as their own rouge. And he himself would be only a memory of a choleric old grandfather who had collapsed one July afternoon just in time to prevent the boy going off to Livorno for sea-bathing. He had said that the Salina would always remain the Salina. He had been wrong. The last Salina was himself. That fellow Garibaldi, that bearded Vulcan, had won after all.

From the room next door, open on to the same balcony, Concetta's voice reached him, 'We simply must; he's got to be called. I should never forgive myself if he weren't.' He understood at once; they were talking of a priest. For a moment he had an idea of refusing, of lying, of starting to shout that he was perfectly well, that he needed nothing. But soon he realised how ridiculous all that would be: he was the Prince of Salina and as a Prince of Salina he must die with a priest by his side. Concetta was right. Why should he avoid what was longed for by thousands of other dying people? And he fell silent, waiting to hear the little bell with the Last Sacraments. It soon came; the parish church of the Pietà was almost opposite. The gay silvery tinkle came climbing up the stairs, flowed along the passage, became sharp as the door opened; preceded by the hotel manager, a Swiss, flustered at having a dying man on his hands, in came

Father Balsamo, the parish priest, bearing the Blessed Sacrament in a leather-sheathed pyx. Tancredi and Fabrizietto raised the armchair, bore it back into the room; the others were kneeling. He signed more than said, 'Away, away.' He wanted to confess. Things should be done properly or not at all. Everyone went out, but when he was about to speak he realised he had nothing to say; he could remember some definite sins, but they seemed so petty as not to be worth bothering a worthy priest about on a hot day. Not that he felt himself innocent; but his whole life was blameworthy, not this or that single act: and now he no longer had time to say so. His eyes must have expressed an uneasiness which the priest took for contrition; as in fact in a sense it was. He was absolved; his chin seemed to be propped on his chest, for the priest had to kneel down to place the Host between his lips. Then there was a murmur of the immemorial syllables which smooth the way, and the priest withdrew.

The armchair was not pulled back on to the balcony. Fabrizietto and Tancredi sat down next to him and held each of his hands; the boy was staring at him with the natural curiosity of one present at his first death-agony and no more; this dying person was not a man, he was a grandfather, which is a very different thing. Tancredi squeezed his hand tightly and talked to him, talked a great deal, talked gaily; he explained projects with which he was associated, commented on political developments; he was a Deputy, had been promised the Legation in Lisbon, knew many a secret and savoury tale. His nasal voice, his subtle vocabulary sketched a futile arabesque over the ever noisier surging away of the waters of life. The Prince was grateful for the gossip; and he squeezed Tancredi's hand with a great effort though with almost no perceptible result. He was grateful, but did not listen. He was making up a general balance sheet of his whole life, trying to sort out of the immense ash-heap of liabilities the golden flecks of happy moments. These were: two weeks before his marriage, six weeks after; half an hour when Paolo was born, when he felt proud at having prolonged by a twig the Salina tree (the pride had been misplaced, he knew that now, but there had been some genuine self-respect in it); a few talks with Giovanni before the latter vanished (a few monologues, if the truth were told, during which he had thought to find in the boy a kindred mind); and many hours in the observatory, absorbed in abstract calculations and the pursuit of the unreachable. Could those latter hours be really put down to the credit side of life? Were they not some sort of anticipatory gift of the beatitudes after death? It didn't matter, they had existed.

Below in the street, between the hotel and the sea, a barrel-organ had halted and was playing away in the avid hope of touching the hearts of foreigners who, at that season, were not there. It was grinding out *You who Opened Your Wings to God* from 'Lucia di Lammermoor'. What remained of Don Fabrizio thought of all the rancour mingling with all the torture, at that moment, throughout Italy, from mechanical music of this kind. Tancredi, intuitive as ever, ran to the balcony, threw down a coin, waved for the barrel-organ to stop. The outer silence closed in again, the clamour within him grew huge.

Tancredi. Yes, much on the credit side came from Tancredi; that sympathy of his, all the more precious for being ironic; the aesthetic pleasure of watching him manoeuvre amid the shoals of life, the bantering affection whose touch was so right. Then dogs; Fufi, the fat pug of his childhood, the impetuous poodle Tom, confidant and friend, Speedy's gentle eyes, Bendicò's delicious nonsense, the caressing paws of Pop, the pointer at that moment searching for him under bushes and garden chairs and never to see him again; then a horse or two, these already more distant and detached. There were the first few hours of returns to Donnafugata, the sense of tradition and the perennial expressed in stone and water, of time congealed; a few care-free shoots, a cosy massacre or two of hares and partridges, some good laughs with Tumeo, a few minutes of compunction at the convent amid odours of must and confectionery. Anything else? Yes, there were other things: but these were only grains of gold mixed with earth: moments of satisfaction when he had made some biting reply to a fool, of content when he had realised that in Concetta's beauty and character was prolonged the true Salina strain; a few seconds of frenzied passion; the surprise of Arago's letter spontaneously congratulating him on the accuracy of his difficult calculations about Huxley's comet. And – why not? –

the public thrill of being given a medal at the Sorbonne, the exquisite sensation of one or two fine silk cravats, the smell of some macerated leathers, the gay voluptuous air of a few women passed in the street, of one glimpsed even yesterday at the station of Catania, in a brown travelling dress and suède gloves, mingling amid the crowds and seeming to search for his exhausted face through the dirty compartment window. What a noise that crowd was making! 'Sandwiches!' '*Il Corriere dell'Isola*'. And then the panting of the tired breathless train . . . and that appalling sun as they arrived, those lying faces, the crashing cataracts . . .

In the growing dark he tried to count how much time he had really lived. His brain could not cope with the simple calculation any more; three months, three weeks, a total of six months, six by eight, eight-four . . . forty-eight thousand . . . $\sqrt{840,000}$. He summed up. 'I'm seventy-three years old, and all in all I may have lived, really lived, a total of two . . . three at the most.' And the pains, the boredom, how long had they been? Useless to try and make himself count those; the whole of the rest; seventy years.

He felt his hand no longer being squeezed. Tancredi got up hurriedly and went out . . . Now it was not a river erupting over him but an ocean, tempestuous, all foam and raging white-flecked waves . . .

He must have had another stroke for suddenly he realised that he was lying stretched on the bed. Someone was feeling his pulse; from the window came the blinding implacable reflection of the sea; in the room could be heard a faint hiss; it was his own death-rattle, but he did not know it. Around him was a little crowd, a group of strangers staring at him with frightened expressions. Gradually he recognised them: Concetta, Francesco Paolo, Carolina, Tancredi, Fabrizietto. The person holding his pulse was Doctor Cataliotti; he tried to smile a greeting at the latter but no one seemed to notice; all were weeping except Concetta; even Tancredi, who was saying: 'Uncle, dearest Nuncle!'

Suddenly amid the group appeared a young woman; slim, in brown travelling dress and wide bustle, with a straw hat trimmed with a speckled veil which could not hide the sly charm of her face. She slid a little suède-gloved hand between one elbow and another of the weeping kneelers, apologised, drew closer. It was she, the creature for ever yearned for, coming to fetch him; strange that one so young should yield to him; the time for the train's departure must be very close. When she was face to face with him she raised her veil, and there, chaste but ready for possession, she looked lovelier than she ever had when glimpsed in stellar space.

The crashing of the sea subsided altogether.

VIII
Relics

ANYONE PAYING a visit to the old Salina ladies would be apt to find at least one priest's hat on the hall chairs. All three were spinsters and their household had been rent by secret struggles for power, so that each one, a strong character in her own way, wanted a separate confessor of her own. It was still the custom in that year, 1910, for confessions to take place at home, and these penitents' scruples required frequent repetition. Add to this little platoon of confessors the chaplain who came every morning to celebrate Mass in the private chapel, the Jesuit in charge of the general spiritual direction of the household, the monks and priests who came to draw alms for this or that parish or good work, and it will be readily understood why there was such an incessant coming and going of clerics, and why the antechamber of Villa Salina was often reminiscent of one of those Roman shops around Piazza della Minerva which display in their windows every imaginable ecclesiastical headgear, from flaming red for Cardinals to cindery black for country priests.

On that particular afternoon of May 1910 the parade of hats was quite unprecedented. The presence of the Vicar-General of the Archdiocese of Palermo was announced by his huge hat of fine beaver in a delicate shade of fuchsia, placed on a separate chair, with next to it a single glove, the right hand one, in woven silk of the same delicate hue; his secretary's of gleaming long-haired black plush, the crown circled by a narrow violet cord; those of two Jesuit Fathers, subdued tenebrous felts, symbols of modesty and reserve. The chaplain's headgear lay on an isolated chair, as was proper for a person undergoing inquiry.

The meeting that day was no unimportant matter. In accordance with Papal instructions the Cardinal Archbishop had begun an inspection of the private chapels of his archdiocese, to reassure himself about the merits of those allowed to hold services there, the conformity of liturgy and decoration with the canons of the Church, and the authenticity of relics venerated in them. The

Salina chapel was the best known in the city and one of the first which His Eminence proposed to visit. And it was in order to arrange for this event, fixed for next morning, that Monsignor the Vicar-General had called at Villa Salina. Unfortunate rumours about that chapel, seeped through many a filter, had reached the archiepiscopal Curia; not, of course, anything about the merits of the owners or of their right to carry out their religious duties in their own home; such subjects were beyond discussion. Nor was there any doubt thrown on the propriety or continuity of services held there, for these were as near perfection as may be, except perhaps for an overwhelming and perfectly comprehensible reluctance on the part of the Salina ladies to let anyone be present at the sacred rites who was outside their close family circle. The Cardinal's attention had been drawn to a picture venerated in the villa, and to the relics, the dozens of relics, exposed in the chapel. There were the most disturbing rumours about the authenticity of these, and it was desired that their genuineness be proved. The chaplain, an ecclesiastic of some culture and high hopes, had been reprimanded severely for not having kept the old ladies sufficiently on the alert; he had had, as it were, a 'dressing-down of the tonsure'.

The meeting was taking place in the main drawing-room of the villa, the one of the monkeys and cockatoos. On a sofa covered with blue material interwoven with pink, a purchase of thirty years earlier that clashed with the evanescent tints of the precious wall-hangings, sat the Signorina Concetta with Monsignor the Vicar-General on her right; on each side of the sofa in two similar armchairs were the Signorina Carolina and one of the Jesuits, Father Corti, while the Signorina Caterina, whose legs were paralysed, was in a wheel chair, and the other ecclesiastics had to be content with chairs covered in the same material as the walls, which seemed then far less valuable than the envied armchairs.

The three sisters were all around seventy, and Concetta was not the eldest; but the struggle for power which has been hinted at earlier had ended some time ago with the rout of her adversaries, so no one would now have dared contest her functions as mistress of the house.

She still showed the vestiges of past beauty; heavy and imposing in her stiff clothes of black watered silk, she wore her
snow-white hair raised on her head so as to show her almost
unfurrowed brow; this, together with contemptuous eyes and a
resentful line above her nose, gave her an air that was authoritarian, almost imperial; so much so that a nephew of hers, having
caught sight in some book or other of a picture of a famous
Czarina, used to call her in private 'Catherine the Great'; an
unsuitable name made quite innocent by the complete purity of
Concetta's life and her nephew's total ignorance of Russian
history.

The conversation lasted an hour, coffee had been taken and it
was getting late. Monsignor reassumed his arguments: 'It is His
Eminence's paternal wish that Mass celebrated in private should
conform to the purest rites of Holy Mother Church, and that is
why in his pastoral care he is visiting your chapel first, for he
knows your house to be a beacon for the laity of Palermo and
he desires that the authenticity of all objects venerated there
should bring even more edification to yourselves and to all
devout souls.' Concetta was silent, but Carolina, the elder sister,
exploded, 'Now we're to appear as accused before our friends,
are we? This idea of inspecting our chapel, excuse me for saying
so, Monsignor, should never have so much as passed through
His Eminence's head.'

Monsignor laughed, amused. 'Signorina, you cannot imagine
how gratifying your vehemence is to me; as the expression of a
simple and absolute faith, most acceptable to the Church and
certainly to Our Lord Himself; and only in order to make this
faith flower yet more abundantly and to purify it has the Holy
Father recommended these inspections, which have already
been taking place for some months throughout the Catholic
world.'

The reference to the Holy Father was not, actually, very
opportune; Carolina was one of those Catholics who consider
themselves to be in closer possession of religious truths than the
Pope himself; and a few moderate declarations of Pius X, the
abolition of some secondary feast days in particular, had already

exasperated her. 'This Pope would do better to mind his own business.' Then she began to wonder if she hadn't gone too far, crossed herself and muttered a *Gloria Patri*.

Concetta intervened. 'Don't let yourself be drawn into saying things you don't think, Carolina. Or what sort of impression will Monsignor take away with him?'

The latter was actually smiling more than ever; here before him, he was thinking, was a little girl grown old in narrow ideas and arid acts of piety. Benignly he indulged her.

'Monsignor will take away the impression of having been in the company of three devout ladies,' said he.

Father Corti, the Jesuit, tried to relax the tension. 'I, Monsignor, am among those who can best confirm your words; Father Pirrone, whose memory is venerated by all that knew him, often used to tell me when I was a novice of the devout atmosphere in which the ladies grew up: the name of Salina should anyway be a guarantee for that.'

Monsignor wanted to get down to facts. 'Well, Signorina Concetta, now everything's clear, I should like, with your permission, to visit the chapel in order to prepare His Eminence for the marvels of faith he will see tomorrow morning.'

In Prince Fabrizio's time there had been no chapel in the villa; the whole family used to go out to church on feast days, and even Father Pirrone had to walk quite a step every morning to say his own Mass. But after the death of Prince Fabrizio, when, as a result of various complications of inheritance which would be boring to narrate, the villa became the exclusive property of the three sisters, they at once thought of setting up their own oratory. They chose an out-of-the-way drawing-room, which with its half columns of imitation granite stuck into the walls was vaguely reminiscent of a Roman basilica; they obliterated an unsuitable mythological fresco from the centre of the ceiling; decked up an altar. And all was ready.

When Monsignor entered, the chapel was lit by the late afternoon sun, which fell full on the altar and the picture above so venerated by the Salina ladies. It was a painting in the style of Cremona, and represented a slim and very attractive young woman with eyes turned to heaven and an abundance of brown hair scattered in gracious disorder on half-bare shoulders; in her right hand she was gripping a crumpled letter, with an expression of anxious expectancy not unconnected to a certain sparkle in her glistening eyes; behind her was a green and gentle Lombard landscape. No Holy Child, no crowns, no snakes, no stars, none in fact of those symbols which usually accompany the image of Mary; the painter must have trusted that virginal expression as being enough to recognise her by. Monsignor drew nearer, went up one of the altar steps and stood there, without crossing himself, looking at the picture for a minute or two, his face all smiling admiration as if he were an art critic. Behind him the sisters made signs of the Cross and murmured an *Ave Maria*.

Then the prelate came down the steps again, turned round and said, 'A fine painting, that; very expressive.'

'A miraculous icon, Monsignor, most miraculous!' explained Caterina, poor ill creature, leaning from her ambulating instrument of torture.

'It has done so many miracles!' Carolina pressed on. 'It represents the Madonna of the Letter. The Virgin is on the point of consigning the holy missive invoking her Divine Son's protection on the people of Messina; a protection which has been gloriously conceded, as is shown by the many miracles during the earthquake of two years ago.'

'A fine picture, Signorina; whatever it represents it's a pretty thing and should be treated carefully.' Then he turned to the relics; seventy-four of them, they completely covered the two walls on each side of the altar. Each was enclosed in a frame which also contained a card with information about it and a number referring to the documents of authentication. These documents themselves, many voluminous and hung with seals, were locked into a damask-covered chest in a corner of the chapel. There were frames of worked and smooth silver, frames of bronze and coral, frames of tortoiseshell; in filigree, rare woods, box-wood, in red and blue velvet; large, tiny, square, octagonal, round, oval; frames worth a fortune and frames bought at the Bocconi stores; all collected by those devoted souls in their religious exaltation as custodians of supernatural treasures.

The real creator of this collection had been Carolina; she had found somewhere a certain Donna Rosa, a huge old woman, half-nun, with useful connections in all the churches, convents and charity foundations of Palermo and its surroundings. It had been this Donna Rosa who had brought up to Villa Salina every few months a relic of a saint wrapped in tissue paper. She had managed, she would say, to get some dilapidated parish or decayed family to part with it. The name of the seller was not given merely because of understandable, in fact praiseworthy, discretion; and anyway there were the proofs of authenticity which she brought and always handed over, clear as daylight, written out in Latin or mysterious characters she called Greek or Syriac. Concetta, administrator and bursar, would pay. Then came a search and adaptation of frames. And once again the impassive Concetta would pay. There was a period, a couple of years ago, when the collecting mania even disturbed Caterina's and Carolina's sleep; in the morning they would recount to each other dreams of miraculous discoveries, with the hope that they would be realised, as did indeed sometimes happen after the dreams had been confided to Donna Rosa. What Concetta dreamt no one knew. Then Donna Rosa died and the influx of relics stopped almost completely; anyway, by then, there was a certain superfluity.

Monsignor glanced rather hurriedly at one or two of the nearest frames. 'Treasures,' he said, 'treasures! What lovely frames!' Then congratulating them on the fine 'display' (such was his word), and promising to return next day with His Eminence ('yes, at nine exactly') he genuflected, crossed himself towards a modest Madonna of Pompeii hung on a side wall, and left the oratory. Soon the seats were bereft of hats, and the ecclesiastics climbed into the three carriages from the Archbishopric, with their black horses, which had awaited them in the courtyard. Monsignor made a point of asking the chaplain, Father Titta, to share his own carriage, much to the latter's solace. The carriages moved off, and Monsignor was silent; they drove by the sumptuous Villa Falconeri, with its flowering bougainvillaea drooping over the walls of the splendidly kept gardens; and when they reached the slope down to Palermo amid the orange groves, Monsignor spoke. 'And so you, Father Titta, have actually said Mass for years in front of the picture of that girl? That girl with a rendezvous and waiting for her lover? Now don't tell me you too believed it was a holy icon.'

'Monsignor, I am to blame, I know. But it's not easy to gainsay the Signorina Carolina. That you cannot know.'

Monsignor shivered at the memory. 'My son, you've put your finger on it; and that will be taken into consideration.'

Carolina had gone off to pour out her rage in a letter to Chiara, her married sister in Naples; Caterina, tired by the long and painful conversation, had been put to bed; Concetta went back to her own solitary room. This was one of those rooms (so numerous that one might be tempted to say it of all rooms) which have two faces, one with a mask that they show to ignorant visitors, the other which is only revealed to those in the know, the owner in particular to whom all its squalid essence is manifest. This particular room was airy and looked over the broad garden; in a corner was a high bed with four pillows (Concetta suffered from heart trouble and had to sleep almost sitting up): no carpets, but a fine white floor with intricate yellow tiles; a valuable money chest with dozens of little drawers covered with hardstone and worked stucco: the desk, central table and all the furniture in breezy local inlay work, with figures of huntsmen, dogs and game in amber-colour on a rose-wood background: furniture considered by Concetta herself as antiquated and even in bad taste and which, sold at auction after her death, is to-day the pride of a prosperous shipping agent when his wife serves cocktails to envious friends. On the walls were portraits, water-colours, sacred images. All was clean, all ordered. Two things only, perhaps, might have appeared unusual: in the corner opposite the bed towered four enormous wooden cases painted in green, each with a big padlock; and in front of these, on the floor, was a heap of mangy fur. To the lips of an ingenuous visitor the little room might have brought a smile, so suggestive was it of an old maid's affectionate care.

To one who knew the facts – Concetta herself – it was an inferno of mummified memories. The four green cases contained dozens of day and night shirts, dressing-gowns, pil-low-cases, sheets carefully divided into 'best' and 'second-best': the trousseau collected by Concetta herself fifty years before. Now those padlocks were never opened for fear incongruous demons might leap out, and under the ubiquitous Palermo damp the contents grew yellow and decayed, useless for ever and for anyone. The portraits were of dead people no longer loved, the photographs of friends who had hurt her in their lifetime, the only reason they were not forgotten in death; the water-colours showed houses and places most of which had been sold, or rather stupidly bartered away by spendthrift nephews. Anyone looking carefully into the heap of moth-eaten fur would have noticed two erect ears, a snout of black wood, and two astonished eyes of yellow glass; it was Bendicò, dead for forty-five years, embalmed for forty-five years, nest now of spiders' webs and moth, detested by the servants who had been imploring Con-cetta for dozens of years to have it thrown on the rubbish heap; but she always refused, reluctant to detach herself from the only memory of her past which aroused no distressing sensations.

But the distressing sensations of today (at a certain age every day punctually produces its own) all referred to the present. Much less devout than Carolina, much more sensitive than Caterina, Concetta had understood the meaning of the Vicar-General's visit and foreseen the consequences; orders to take away all or nearly all the relics, the changing of the picture above the altar, an eventual reconsecration of the chapel. She had never really believed in the authenticity of these relics, and had paid up with the indifference of a father settling a bill for toys which are of no interest to himself but help to keep the children quiet. To her the removal of these objects was a matter of indifference; what did touch her, the day's real thorn, was the appalling figure the Salina family would now cut with ecclesiastical authorities, and soon with the entire city. The Church kept its secrets much better than anyone else in Sicily, but that did not mean much yet; all would be spread round in a month or two; as everything spreads on this island which should have as its symbol not the Trinacria but the Ear of Dionysius at Syracuse which makes the lightest sigh resound for fifty yards. And the Church's esteem

meant a lot to her. The prestige of her name had slowly disap-
peared, the family fortune, divided and subdivided, was at best
equivalent to that of any number of other lesser families and
very much smaller than that of some rich industrialists. But in
the Church, in their relations with it, the Salina had maintained
their pre-eminence. What a reception His Eminence had given
the three sisters when they went to make their Christmas visit!
Would that happen now?

A maid entered: 'Excellency, the Princess is just arriving. Her
motor-car is in the courtyard.' Concetta got up, tidied her hair,
threw a black lace shawl over her shoulders, resumed her imperial air, and reached the entrance hall just as Angelica was
climbing the last steps of the outer staircase. She suffered from
varicose veins; her legs, which had always been a little short,
scarcely upheld her, and she was climbing up leaning on the
arm of her own footman whose black topcoat swept the stairs.
'Concetta, darling!' 'Angelica, dear! It's so long since we've
met!' In fact only five days had gone by since her last visit, but
the intimacy between the two cousins, an intimacy similar in
closeness and feeling to that which was to bind Italians and
Austrians in their opposing trenches a few years later, was such
that five days really could seem a long time.
    Angelica, now nearly seventy, still showed many traces of
beauty; the illness which was to transform her into a wretched
spectre three years later was already active, but still secreted deep
in her blood; her green eyes were what they had been before,
only slightly dulled by the years, and the wrinkles on her neck
were hidden by the soft black folds of the hood and veil which
she, a widow for the last three years, wore not without a certain
nostalgic coquetry. 'You see,' she said to Concetta as they moved
entwined towards a drawing-room, 'you see, with these imminent celebrations of the fiftieth anniversary of The Thousand
there's never a minute's peace. Just imagine, a few days ago they
told me I'd been put on the Committee of Honour; a homage
to dear Tancredi's memory, of course, but such a lot for me to
do! Finding lodgings for veterans coming from all over Italy,
arranging invitations for the grandstand without offending any-

one; taking care to invite the mayor of every commune in the island. Oh, by the way, dear: the Mayor of Salina is a clerical and has refused to march past; so I thought at once of your nephew, of Fabrizio; he came to visit me, and I pinned him down there and then. He couldn't refuse. So at the end of the month we'll see him filing past dressed to the nines down Via Libertà in front of a big placard with "Salina" on it in letters a foot high. Don't you think it's a good idea? A Salina rendering homage to Garibaldi! A fusion of old and new in Sicily! I've thought of you too, darling; here's your invitation for the grandstand, right next to the royal box.' And she pulled out of her Parisian bag a piece of cardboard in Garibaldi red, the very same colour as the strip of silk worn for a time by Tancredi above his collar. 'Carolina and Caterina won't be too pleased,' she went on in her arbitrary way, 'but I only had one place; anyway you have more right to it than they have; you were Tancredi's favourite cousin.'

She talked a lot and she talked well; forty years of living with Tancredi, however tempestuous and interrupted, had been more than long enough to rub off the last traces of Donnafugata accent and manners; she had camouflaged herself even to the point of copying that graceful twining of the fingers which had been one of Tancredi's characteristics. She read a lot; on her table the latest books by Anatole France and Bourget alternated with D'Annunzio and Serao; and she had the reputation in the drawing-rooms of Palermo of being an expert on the architecture of the Châteaux of the Loire, about which she would often discourse with somewhat hazy enthusiasm, contrasting, perhaps unconsciously, their Renaissance serenity with the restless baroque of the palace at Donnafugata, against which she nurtured an aversion inexplicable to anyone who knew nothing of her meek and slighted youth.

'But what a head I have, my dear! I was forgetting to tell you that Senator Tassoni will soon be coming here; he's staying with me at Villa Falconeri and wants to meet you; he was a great friend of poor Tancredi's, a comrade-in-arms too, and he's heard Tancredi talk of you, it seems. Our dear Tancredi!' The handkerchief with its narrow black border came out of her bag, and she dried a tear in eyes that were still fine.

Concetta had been inserting, as always, an occasional phrase of her own into Angelica's continual flow; but at the name of Tassoni she was silent. Once again she saw a scene, very distant but quite clear, as if through the other end of a telescope: the big white table surrounded by all those people now dead; near her Tancredi, dead too — as anyway, really, she was herself; his brutal anecdote. Angelica's hysterical laughter, her own no less hysterical tears. It had been the turning-point of her life, that; the road she had taken then had led her here, to this desert not even inhabited by extinct love or spent rancour.

'Oh, I've heard of the bother you're having with the Curia. What a nuisance they are! But why didn't you tell me before? I could have done something; the Cardinal is always very good to me. I'm afraid that it's too late now. But I'll pull some strings. Anyway, it'll all blow over.'

Senator Tassoni, who arrived soon after, was a brisk and spruce old man. His wealth, which was great and growing, had been acquired by competition and hard struggle, and instead of making him flabby it had kept him in a state of continual energy which now seemed to conquer the years and made him almost fiery. From the few months spent with Garibaldi's southern army he had acquired a military bearing destined never to be discarded. Blended with courtesy it formed a philtre which had gained him many successes in the past, and which now, joined to the number of his securities, was of great use for getting his own way with the boards of banks and cotton factories; half Italy and a great part of the Balkan countries sewed on their own buttons with thread made by Tassoni & Co.

'Signorina,' he was saying to Concetta as he sat beside her on a low stool suitable for a page, which was just why he had chosen it, 'Signorina, a dream of my distant youth is now being realised. How often in those icy nights camping out on the Volturno or around the ramparts of besieged Gaeta, how often our unforgettable Tancredi used to talk of you! I seemed to know you already, to have frequented this house amid whose walls his untamed youth was passed, and I am happy to be able, though with such delay, to lay my homage at the feet of her who was the consolation of one of the purest heroes of our Risorgimento.'

Concetta was unused to conversations with people she had
not known since infancy; she was also no lover of literature; so
she had no immunity against rhetoric and was in fact open to its
fascination. The Senator's words moved her; she forgot that old
anecdote of half a century ago, she no longer saw in Tassoni a
violator of convents, a jeerer at poor terrified nuns, but an old
man, Tancredi's sincere friend who talked of him with true
affection, one who brought to her a shadow, a message from the
dead man across the morass of time which the dead can so seldom cross. 'And what did my dear cousin tell you about me?'
she asked in a low voice, with a shyness that brought to life once
more the eighteen-year-old girl from that bundle of black silk
and white hair.

'Ah, so many things! He talked of you almost as much as of
Donna Angelica! She for him was love, you were the image
of his sweet youth, that youth which for us soldiers passes so
soon.'

Again an icy hand froze her old heart; but now Tassoni had
raised his voice, and turned to Angelica. 'D'you remember,
Princess, what he said at Vienna ten years ago?' He turned back
towards Concetta to explain. 'I was there with the Italian delega-
tion for the Trade Treaty; Tancredi put me up at the embassy
like the warm-hearted friend and comrade he was, with that
great gentleman's affability of his. Perhaps seeing a comrade-in-
arms again in that hostile city had moved him, for he told us so
much about his past. In the back of a box at the Opera, between
one act and another of *Don Giovanni*, he confessed, in his incom-
parably ironic way, a sin, an unpardonable sin, which he said
he'd committed against you, yes, against you, Signorina.' He
interrupted himself a second to gain time to set his surprise. 'He
told us how one evening, during dinner at Donnafugata, he had
allowed himself to invent a story and tell it to you; a tale of
war connected with the fighting round Palermo; and how you
believed it and were offended because the story was rather out-
spoken for the customs of fifty years ago. You had reproved him.
"She was so sweet," said he, "as she fixed me with those angry
eyes of hers and as her lips swelled with anger so prettily, like a
puppy's; she was so sweet that if I hadn't controlled myself I'd

have kissed her there and then in front of twenty people and that terrible old uncle of mine!" You, Signorina, will have forgotten it; but Tancredi remembered it well, he had such delicacy of feeling; he also remembered it because it happened on the very day he met Donna Angelica for the first time.' And he sketched towards the Princess one of those gestures of homage, with his right hand dropping away through the air, whose Goldoniesque tradition was preserved then only among Senators of the Kingdom.

The conversation continued for some time, but it could not be said that Concetta took any great part in it. The sudden revelation penetrated into her mind slowly and did not make her suffer much at first. But when the visitors had said good-bye and left and she was alone, she began seeing more clearly and so suffering more. The spectres of the past had been exorcised for years; though they were of course to be found hidden in everything, and it was they that made food taste bitter and company seem boring: but it was a long time since they had shown their faces; now they came leaping out, with the ghastly grins of irreparable wrongs. It would, of course, be absurd to say that Concetta still loved Tancredi; love's eternity lasts but a year or two, not fifty. But as one who has recovered from smallpox fifty years before still bears its marks on the face although he may have forgotten the pain of the disease, so she bore in her own oppressed life now the wounds of a bitter disappointment that had become almost part of history, so much part in fact that its fiftieth anniversary was being celebrated officially.

Until to-day, on the rare occasions when she thought over what had happened at Donnafugata that distant summer, she had felt upheld by a sense of martyrdom, of wrong endured, of resentment against a father who had neglected her, and of torturing emotion on account of that other dead man. Now, however, these second-hand feelings which had formed the skeleton of her whole mode of thought were also collapsing. There had been no enemies, just one single adversary, herself; her future had been killed by her own imprudence, by the reckless Salina pride; and now, just at the moment when her memories had come alive again after so many years, she found herself even without the solace of being able to blame her own unhappiness on others, a solace which is the last protective device of the desperate.

If Tassoni had told the truth, then the long hours spent in savouring her hatred before her father's picture, her hiding of every photograph of Tancredi so as not to be forced to hate him too, had been stupidity – worse, cruel injustice; and she suffered now at the memory of Tancredi's warm and imploring tone as he had begged his uncle to allow him into that convent; they had been words of love towards her, words not understood, routed by her pride which at her harshness had drawn back with their tails between their legs like whipped puppies. From the timeless depth of her being a black pain came welling to spatter her all over at that revelation of the truth.

But was it the truth? Nowhere has truth so short a life as in Sicily; a fact has scarcely happened five minutes before its genuine kernel has vanished, been camouflaged, embellished, disfigured, annihilated by imagination and self-interest; shame, fear, generosity, malice, opportunism, charity, all the passions, good as well as evil, fling themselves on the fact and tear it to pieces; very soon it has vanished altogether. And poor Concetta was hoping to find the truth of feelings that had never been expressed but only glimpsed half a century before! The truth no longer existed. Precarious fact, though, had been replaced by irrefutable pain.

Meanwhile Angelica and the Senator were driving the short distance back to Villa Falconeri. Tassoni was worried: 'Angelica,' he said (they had had a very short affair thirty years before, and kept the intimacy, for which there is no substitute, conferred by a few hours spent between the same pair of sheets), 'I'm afraid I disturbed your cousin in some way; did you notice how silent she was towards the end of the visit? I hope I didn't, she's such a dear.'

'I should think you have hurt her, Vittorio,' said Angelica, exasperated by a double though imaginary jealousy, 'she was madly in love with Tancredi; but he never took any notice of her.' And so a new spadeful of soil fell on the tumulus of truth.

*   *   *

The Cardinal of Palermo was a truly holy man; and even now, after he has been dead a long time, his charity and his faith are still remembered. While he was alive, though, things were different; he was not a Sicilian, he was not even a southerner or a Roman; and many years before he had tried to leaven with nordic activity the inert and heavy dough of the island's spiritual life in general and the clergy's in particular. Flanked by two or three secretaries from his own parts he had deluded himself, those first years, that he could remove abuses and clear the soil of its more flagrant stumbling-blocks. But soon he had to realise that he was, as it were, firing into cotton-wool; the little hole made at the moment was covered after a few seconds by thousands of tiny fibres and all remained as before, the only additions being cost of powder, ridicule at useless effort and deterioration of material. Like everyone who in those days wanted to change anything in the Sicilian character he soon acquired the reputation of being a fool (which in the circumstances was exact) and had to content himself with doing good works, which only diminished his popularity still further if they involved those benefited in making the slightest effort themselves, such as, for instance, visiting the archiepiscopal palace.

So the aged prelate who set out on the morning of the fourteenth of May to visit Villa Salina was a good man but a disillusioned one, who had in the end assumed towards those in his own diocese an attitude of contemptuous pity (which was sometimes, after all, unjust). This made him adopt brusque and cutting ways that dragged him even farther into the swamps of unpopularity.

The three Salina sisters were, as we know, deeply offended by the inspection of their chapel; but, childish and above all feminine in mind, they also drew a certain undeniable satisfaction from the thought of receiving in their home a Prince of the Church, at being able to show him the grandeur of the Salina which in good faith they thought still intact, and above all at seeing a kind of sumptuous red bird moving round their rooms for half an hour and admiring the varied and harmonising tones of its differing purples and heavy shot silk. But the poor creatures were destined to be disappointed even of this last modest hope.

When they, having descended the external staircase, saw His Eminence alight from his carriage, they realised that he was in informal dress. Only the tiny purple buttons on the severe black cassock indicated his high rank; in spite of his expression of injured goodness, the Cardinal was no more imposing than the Archpriest of Donnafugata. He was polite but cold, mingling almost too ably a show of respect for the Salina name and the individual virtues of the ladies themselves with a contempt for their inept and formalised devotions. To the Vicar-General's exclamations about the beauty of the decorations in the rooms they passed he did not answer a word; he refused to accept any of the refreshments prepared for him ('Thank you, Signorina, only a little water; to-day is the eve of my Holy Patron's feast day'), he did not even sit down. He went to the chapel, bowed a second before the Madonna of Pompeii, made a hurried inspection of the relics. Then he blessed with pastoral benignity the mistresses of the house and the servants kneeling in the entrance hall, and said to Concetta, who bore on her face the signs of a sleepless night, 'Signorina, for three or four days no Divine Service can be held in the chapel, but I will see that it is reconsecrated as soon as possible. It seems to me that the picture of the Madonna of Pompeii could well take the place of the one now above the altar, which can join the fine works of art I have admired while passing through your rooms. As for the relics, I am leaving behind Don Pacchiotti, my secretary and a most competent priest; he will examine the documents and tell you the results of his researches; and what he decides will be as if I had decided it myself.'

Benignly he let everyone kiss his ring, then climbed into the heavy carriage together with his small suite.

The carriage had not yet reached the Falconeri turning before Carolina, with cheeks taut and darting eyes, exclaimed 'This Pope must be a Turk', while Caterina had to be given smelling salts. Meanwhile Concetta was chatting calmly to Don Pacchiotti, who had in the end accepted a cup of coffee and a *baba*.

Then the priest asked for the keys of the case of documents, requested permission and withdrew into the chapel, after first taking from his bag a small hammer and saw, a screw-driver, a

magnifying glass and a couple of pencils. He had been a pupil of
the Vatican School of Palaeography; and he was also Piedmontese. His labours were long and meticulous; the servants who
passed by the chapel door heard the knocks of a hammer, the
squeak of screws, and sighs. Three hours later he re-emerged
with his cassock full of dust and his hands black, but with a
pleased look and a serene expression on his bespectacled face.
He apologised for carrying a big wicker basket. 'I took the
liberty of appropriating this to put in what I'd discarded; may I
set it down here?' And he placed his burden in a corner; it was
overflowing with torn papers and cards, little boxes containing
bits of bone and gristle. 'I am happy to say that I have found five
relics which are perfectly authentic and worthy of being objects
of devotion. The rest are there,' he said, pointing at the basket.
'Could you tell me, Signorina, where I can brush myself down
and wash my hands?'

Five minutes later he reappeared and dried his hands on a big
towel on whose border pranced a Leopard in red thread. 'I forgot
to say that the frames are all laid out on the chapel table; some
of them are really lovely.' He said good-bye. 'Ladies, my
respects.' But Caterina refused to kiss his hand.

'And what are we to do with the things in the basket?'

'Just whatever you like, ladies; keep them or throw them on
the rubbish heap; they have no value whatsoever.' And when
Concetta wanted to order a carriage to drive him back, he said,
'Don't worry about that, Signorina; I'll lunch with the Ora-
torians a few steps away; I don't need a thing.' And putting his
instruments back into his bag, off he went on light feet.

Concetta withdrew to her room; she felt no emotion whatsoever; she seemed to be living in a world familiar yet alien, which
had already ceded all the impulses it could give and consisted
now only of pure forms. The portrait of her father was just a
few square inches of canvas, the green cases just a few square
yards of wood. Later she was brought a letter. The envelope had
a black seal with a big coronet in relief.

'Darling Concetta, I've heard of His Eminence's visit and am
so glad a few relics could be saved. I hope to get the Vicar-

General to come and say the first Mass in the reconsecrated chapel. Senator Tassoni is leaving to-morrow and recommends himself to your *bon souvenir*. I'll be coming over to visit you soon. Meanwhile a warm embrace to you and to Carolina and Caterina too. Ever, Angelica.'

Still she could feel nothing; inner emptiness was total; but she did sense an unpleasant atmosphere exhaling from the heap of furs. That was to-day's distress: even poor Bendicò was hinting at bitter memories. She rang the bell. 'Annetta,' she said, 'this dog has really become too moth-eaten and dusty. Take it out, throw it away.'

As the carcass was dragged off, the glass eyes stared at her with the humble reproach of things discarded in the hope of final riddance. A few minutes later what remained of Bendicò was flung into a corner of the yard visited every day by the dustman. During the flight down from the window its form recomposed itself for an instant; in the air there seemed to be dancing a quadruped with long whiskers, its right foreleg raised in imprecation. Then all found peace in a little heap of livid dust.

Places of My Infancy

A MEMORY

SUMMER 1955

Contents

I

WITH EVERYONE, I think, memories of early childhood consist of a series of visual impressions, many very clear but lacking any sense of chronology. To write a 'chronicle' of one's own childhood is, it seems, impossible; however honest one might set out to be one would eventually give a false impression, often with glaring anachronisms. I shall therefore adopt the method of grouping my subjects together, so trying to give an overall impression in space rather than by sequence of time. I will touch on the background of my childhood and of the people forming part of it; also of my feelings, though I will not try to follow the development of these from their origins.

I can promise to say nothing that is untrue, but I shall not want to say *all*; and I reserve the right to lie by omission. Unless I change my mind.

One of the oldest memories I can set exactly in time, as it is connected with a fact verifiable historically, goes back to the 30th of July 1900, and so to the time when I was a few days over three and a half years old.

I was with my mother in her dressing-room, with her maid (probably Teresa from Turin). It was a rectangular room whose windows gave on to a pair of balconies projecting from the shorter sides, one of them looking over a narrow garden that separated our house from the Oratory of S. Zita, the other over a small inner courtyard. The dressing-table, kidney-shaped, with a pink material showing through its glass top and legs enwrapped in a kind of white lace petticoat, was set facing the balcony overlooking the little garden; on it, as well as brushes and toilet implements, stood a big mirror in a frame also made of mirror, decorated with stars and other glass ornaments which were a delight to me.

It was about eleven in the morning, I think, and I can see the great light of summer coming through the open French windows, whose shutters were closed.

My mother was combing her hair with the help of her maid,

and I do not know what I could have been doing, sitting on the floor in the middle of the room. I don't know if my nurse, Elvira the Sienese, was with us too, but I think not.

Suddenly we hear hurried steps coming up the little inner staircase communicating with my father's apartments on the lower or *mezzanine* floor directly beneath; he enters without knocking, and utters some phrase in an excited tone. I remember his manner very well, but not his words nor their sense.

I can 'see' still, though, the effect they produced; my mother dropped the long-handled silver brush she was holding, Teresa said; '*Bon Signour!*', and the whole room was in consternation.

My father had come to announce the assassination of King Umberto at Monza the evening before, the 29th of July 1900. I repeat that I 'see' every streak of light and shade from the balcony, 'hear' my father's excited voice, the sound of the brush falling on the glass table-top, good Teresa's exclamation in Piedmontese, that I 'feel' the sense of dismay which overwhelmed us; but all this remains personal, detached from the news of the King's death. The historic meaning, as it were, was told me later, and may serve to explain the persistence of the scene in my memory.

Another of the memories which I can clearly distinguish is that of the Messina earthquake (28th December 1908). The shock was certainly felt at Palermo, but I have no memory of that; I suppose it did not interrupt my sleep. But I can see distinctly the hands of my grandfather's big English pendulum-clock, which was then incongruously located in the big winter drawing-room, stopped at the fatal hour of twenty past five; and I can still hear one of my uncles (I think Ferdinando who was mad about watchmaking) explain to me that it had been stopped by an earthquake during the night. Then I remember that same evening, about half-past seven, being in my grandparents' dining-room (I used often to be present at their dinner as it took place before mine) when an uncle, probably the same Ferdinando, came in with an evening paper which announced 'serious damage and numerous victims at Messina from this morning's earthquake'.

I speak of 'my grandparents' dining-room', but I should say

my grandmother's, because my grandfather had been dead a year and a month.

This memory is much less lively visually than the first, though much more exact on the other hand from the point of view of a 'thing that happened'.

Some days later there arrived from Messina my cousin Filippo who had lost his father and mother in the earthquake. He went to stay with my cousins the Piccolos, together with his cousin Adamo, and I remember going there to pay him a visit on a bleak rainy winter's day. I remember that he had a camera (already!) which he had taken care to keep with him as he escaped from the ruins of his house in Via della Rovere, and how on a table by a window he drew the outlines of warships and discussed with Casimiro the calibre of the guns and the emplacement of the turrets; his insouciant attitude amid the dreadful misadventures he had undergone was criticised at the time by his family, though it was charitably ascribed to shock resulting from the disaster – this was said to be prevalent among all the survivors of Messina. It was later more accurately put down to a cold nature which only caught fire in addressing technical questions such as, precisely, photography and the turrets on the early dreadnoughts.

I can still see my mother's grief when, quite a few days later, came news of her sister Lina's and her brother-in-law's bodies having been found. I can see my mother, dressed in a short cape of moiré Astrakhan, sobbing in a big armchair in the green drawing-room, an armchair in which no one ever sat, though it's the very one in which I 'see' my great-grandmother sitting. Big army wagons were going round the streets collecting clothes and blankets for refugees; one passed along Via di Lampedusa and I handed woollen blankets from one of our balconies over to a soldier standing up on a cart and almost level with the balcony. This soldier was an artilleryman, with orange braid on his blue forage cap; I can still see his rubicund face and hear his 'Thank you, m'boy,' in a mainland accent. I have a memory, too, of a rumour going round that the refugees, who were lodged everywhere, even in boxes at theatres, were behaving 'most indecently' among themselves, and of my father saying with a smile, 'They feel an urge to replace the dead,' an allusion which I understood perfectly.

I retain no clear recollection of my Aunt Lina, who died in the earthquake; (her demise opened the sequence of tragic deaths among my mother's sisters, which provides a sampling of the three kinds of death by violence – accident, murder and suicide). She seldom came to Palermo: I do remember her husband, though, with his lively pair of eyes behind his glasses, and an unkempt, grizzled little beard.

There is another day also clearly stamped on my memory; I cannot get the date exactly, but it was certainly a long time before the Messina earthquake and shortly after King Umberto's death, I think. We were guests of the Florios at their villa of Favignana, at the height of summer. I remember Erica, my nurse, coming to wake me up earlier than usual, about seven, hurriedly passing a sponge full of cold water over my face and then dressing me with great care. I was dragged downstairs, went out through a little side-door to the garden, then made to climb up on to the villa's main entrance veranda overlooking the sea, and reached by a flight of some six or seven steps. I remember the blinding sun of that early morning of July or August. On the veranda, which was protected from the sun by great curtains of orange cloth swelling and flapping like sails in the sea breeze (I can still hear the sound), my mother, Signora Florio (the 'divinely lovely' Franca) and others were sitting on cane-chairs. In the centre of the group sat a very old, very bent lady with an aquiline nose, enwrapped in widow's weeds which were waving wildly about in the wind. I was brought before her; she said a few words which I did not understand and, bending down even farther, gave me a kiss on the forehead. (I must have been very small indeed if a lady sitting down had to bend down even farther to kiss me.) After this I was taken back to my room, stripped of my finery, re-dressed in more modest garments and led on to the beach to join the Florio children and others: with them I bathed and we stayed for a long time under a broiling sun playing our favourite game, which was searching in the sand for pieces of deep red coral occasionally to be found there.

That afternoon it was revealed that the old lady had been Eugénie, ex-Empress of the French, whose yacht was anchored off Favignana; she had dined with the Florios the night before (without of course my knowing anything about it) and had paid a farewell visit at seven next morning, (thus with imperial nonchalance inflicting real torture on my mother and on Signora Florio), in the course of which her hosts had wished to present to her the younger members of the household. It appears that the words she uttered before kissing me were: '*Quel joli petit!*'

During these last few days (mid-June, 1955) I have been rereading Stendhal's *Henri Brulard*. I had not read it since long ago in 1922, when I must have still been obsessed by 'explicit beauty' and 'subjective interest', for I remember not liking the book.

Now I cannot but agree with anyone who judges it to be Stendhal's masterpiece; it has an immediacy of feeling, an obvious sincerity, a remarkable attempt to sweep away accumulated memories and reach the essence. And what lucidity of style! What a mass of reflections, the more precious for being common to all men!

I should like to try and do the same. Indeed it seems obligatory. When one reaches the decline of life it is imperative to try and gather together as many as possible of the sensations which have passed through our particular organism. Few can succeed in thus creating a masterpiece (Rousseau, Stendhal, Proust) but all should find it possible to preserve in some such way things which without this slight effort would be lost for ever. To keep a diary, or write down one's own memories at a certain age, should be a duty 'State-imposed'; material thus accumulated would have inestimable value after three or four generations; many of the psychological and historical problems that assail humanity would be resolved. There are no memoirs, even those written by insignificant people, which do not include social and graphic details of first-rate importance.

The extraordinary interest that Defoe's novels aroused is due to the fact that they are near-diaries, brilliant though apocryphal. What, one wonders, would genuine ones have been like? Imagine, say, the diary of a Parisian procuress of the *Régence*, or the memories of Byron's valet during the Venetian period!

I shall try to follow the *Henri Brulard* method as closely as possible, even in describing the 'seedlings' of the principal scenes.

But I find I cannot follow Stendhal in 'quality' of memory. He interprets his childhood as a time when he was bullied and tyrannised. For me childhood is a lost paradise. Everyone was good to me – I was king of the home – even people later hostile to me were then '*aux petits soins*'.

So the reader (who won't exist) must expect to be led meandering through a lost Earthly Paradise. If it bores him, I don't mind.

II
Casa Lampedusa

FIRST OF ALL, our home. I loved it with utter abandon, and still love it now when for the last twelve years it has been no more than a memory. Until a few months before its destruction I used to sleep in the room where I was born, five yards away from the spot where my mother's bed had stood when she gave me birth. And in that house, in that very room maybe, I was glad to feel a certainty of dying. All my other homes (very few, actually, apart from hotels) have merely been roofs which have served to shelter me from rain and sun, not homes in the traditional and venerable sense of that word. And especially the one I have now, which I don't like at all, which I bought to please my wife and which I'm delighted to have bequeathed to her, because the fact is it's not my house.

So it will be very painful for me to evoke my dead Beloved as she was until 1929 in her integrity and beauty, and as she continued after all to be until 5th April 1943, the day on which bombs brought from beyond the Atlantic searched her out and destroyed her.

The first impression that remains with me is that of her vastness, and this impression owes nothing to the magnifying process which affects all that surrounds one's childhood, but to actual reality. When I saw the area covered by the unsightly ruins I found they were about 1600 square yards in extent. With only ourselves living in one wing, my paternal grandparents in another, my bachelor uncles on the second floor, for twenty years it was all at my disposal, with its three courtyards, four terraces, garden, huge staircases, halls, corridors, stables, little rooms on the *mezzanine* for servants and offices – a real kingdom for a boy alone, a kingdom either empty or sparsely populated by figures unanimously well-disposed.

At no point on earth, I'm sure, has sky ever stretched more violently blue than it did above our enclosed terrace, never has sun thrown gentler rays than those penetrating the half-closed shutters of the 'green drawing-room', never have damp-marks

215

on a courtyard's outer walls presented shapes more stimulating to the imagination than those at my home.

I loved everything about it: the irregularity of its walls, the number of its drawing-rooms, the stucco of its ceilings, the nasty smell from my grandparents' kitchen, the scent of violets in my mother's dressing-room, the stuffiness of its stables, the good feel of polished leather in its tack-rooms, the mystery of some unfinished apartments on the top floor, the huge coach-house in which our carriages were kept; a whole world full of sweet mysteries, of surprises ever renewed and ever fresh.

I was its absolute master and would run continually through its vast expanses, climbing the great staircase from the courtyard to the loggia on the roof, from which could be seen the sea and Mount Pellegrino and the whole city as far as Porta Nuova and Monreale. And knowing how by devious routes and turns to avoid inhabited rooms, I would feel alone and dictatorial, followed often only by my friend Tom running excitedly at my heels, with his red tongue dangling from his dear black snout.

The house (and I prefer to call it a house rather than a palace, a word which has been debased in Italy, applied as it is nowadays even to blocks fifteen storeys high) was tucked away in one of the most secluded streets of old Palermo, in Via di Lampedusa, at number 17, the uneven number's evil omen then serving only to add a pleasantly sinister flavour to the joy that it dispensed. (When later the stables were transformed into storerooms we asked for the number to be changed, and it became 23 when the end was near; so number 17 had after all been lucky.)

The street was secluded but not so very narrow, and well paved; nor was it dirty as might be thought, for opposite our entrance and along the whole length of the building extended the old Pietrapersia palace which had no shops or dwellings on the ground floor, its austere, clean front in local white and yellow punctuated by numerous windows protected by enormous grilles, conferring on it the dignified and gloomy air of an old convent or state prison. The bomb explosions later flung many of those heavy grilles into our rooms opposite, with what happy effect on the old stucco work and Murano chandeliers can be imagined.

But if Via di Lampedusa was decent enough, for the whole length of our house at least, the streets into it were not; Via Bara all'Olivella, leading into Piazza Massimo, was crawling with poverty and squalid cellars, and depressing to pass along. It became slightly better when Via Roma was cut through, but there always remained a good stretch of filth and horrors to traverse.

The façade of the house had no particular architectural merit: it was white with wide borders round windows of sulphur yellow, in purest Sicilian style of the seventeenth and eighteenth centuries in fact. It extended along Via di Lampedusa for some seventy yards or so, and had nine big balconies on the front. There were two gateways almost at the corners of the building, of enormous width as they used to be made in olden days to allow carriages to turn in from narrow streets. And in fact there was easy room even for the four-horsed teams which my father drove with mastery to race-meetings at La Favorita.

Just inside the main gate which we always used, the first on the left as one faces the façade, almost at the corner of Via Bara, and separated from the corner of the building by no more than a couple of yards' frontage on to which opened the grilled window of the porter's lodge, one entered a short paved gateway, its two side walls of white stucco supported by a low step. On the left was the porter's nook (which led through to his living quarters), with the fine mahogany door in the middle of which there was a big opaque glass pane with our coat of arms. And immediately after, still on the left preceding the two steps and the entrance to the 'grand staircase', with its double-leaved doors also in mahogany and glass (clear this time and devoid of any coat of arms), right in front of the right-hand stairway there was a colonnade of fine grey Billiemi stone that supported the overhanging *tocchetto* or gallery. Beyond this gate in fact lay the main courtyard, cobbled and divided into sections by rows of flagstones. At the far end three great arches, also supported on columns of Billiemi stone, bore a terrace which linked the two wings of the house at that point.

Beneath the first colonnade, to the right of the entrance gates there were several plants, mostly palms, in wooden tubs varnished green, and at the end there was a plaster statue of some Greek god or other, standing. Also at the end, and parallel to the entrance, there was the door to the tack-room.

The main staircase was a very fine one, all in grey Billiemi, with two flights of fifteen steps or so each, set between yellowish walls. Where the second flight began there was a wide oblong landing with two mahogany doors, one facing each flight of stairs; the one giving on to the first flight led to the quarters of the mezzanine devoted to the Administration and called 'the Accounts Office', the other to a minute cubby-hole wherein the footmen used to change their livery.

These two doors were decorated with a cornice also in Billiemi of Empire style, and they were surmounted at the height of the first floor each one with bulging little gilt balconies, which both opened on to the little entrance hall to our grand-parents' apartments.

I forgot to say that just past the entrance to the stairs, but on the exterior, in the courtyard, hung the red cord of a bell which the porter was supposed to ring in order to warn servants of their mistress's return, or the approach of visitors. The number of rings, which the porters gave with great skill, obtaining, I don't know how, sharp separate strokes without any tiresome tinkling, was rigorously laid down by protocol; four strokes for my grandmother the princess and two for her visitors, three for my mother the duchess and one for her visitors. But misunder-standings would occur, so that when at times my mother, grand-mother and some friend picked up on the way entered in the same carriage a real concert would ring out of four plus three plus two strokes which were never ending. The masters, my grandfather and father, left and returned without any bell ring-ing for them at all.

The second flight of stairs came out on to the wide luminous *tocchetto*, which was a gallery with the spaces between its columns filled in, for reasons of comfort, by big windows with opaque lozenge-shaped panes. This contained a few sparse pieces of furniture, some big portraits of ancestors, and a large table to the left on which were put letters on arrival (it was there I read a postcard addressed to my uncle Ciccio from Paris, on which

some French tart had written: '*Dis à Moffo qu'il est un mufle*'),
two pretty chests and a plaster statue of Pandora on the point of
opening the fatal box, surrounded by plants. At the end, facing
the head of the stairs, there was a door, always closed, which
gave directly on to the 'green drawing-room' (a door which
much later was to become the entrance to our quarters), and to
the right of the stairs, the entrance to the 'great hall', guarded
by an ever-open door, in embroidered red brocade, the upper
part displaying our coat of arms and that of the Valdina in colour
in the glass.

The 'great hall' was immense, flagged in white and grey
marble, with three balconies over Via di Lampedusa and one
over the Lampedusa courtyard, a dead-end extension of Via
Bara. It was divided by an arch which split it in two unequal
parts, the first smaller and the second vastly bigger. To my parents' great regret, its decoration was entirely modern, as in 1848
a shell had destroyed the fine painted ceiling and irreparably
damaged the wall-frescoes. For a long time, it seems, a fig tree
flourished there. The hall was done up when my grandfather
married, that is in 1866 or '67, all in white stucco with a wainscot
of grey marble. In the centre of the ceiling of each of the two
parts a coat of arms was depicted; opposite the entrance there
was a big walnut table on which visitors left their hats and capes;
then there were a few chests and the odd chair. It was in this
great hall that the footmen waited, lounging in their chairs and
ready to hurry out into the *tocchetto* at the sound of that bell
below.

After coming in by the door in red brocade which I've mentioned, if one turned towards the left-hand wall, one found
another door similarly covered but in green, which gave access
to our apartment; if one turned left one had to go on through
until on the right one reached a little staircase and a door leading
to my grandparents' quarters, beginning actually with the 'little
room' with the two little balconies which overlooked the stairs.

A door with green hangings gave on to the ante-chamber,
with six portraits of ancestors hung above its balcony entrance
and its two doors, walls of grey silk, and the odd piece of dark
furniture. And from there the eye fell on a perspective of

drawing-rooms extending one after the other for the length of the façade. Here for me began the magic of light, which in a city with so intense a sun as Palermo is concentrated or variegated according to the weather, even in narrow streets. This light was sometimes diluted by the silk curtains hanging before balconies, or heightened by beating on some gilt frame or yellow damask chair which reflected it back; sometimes, particularly in summer, these rooms were dark, yet through the closed blinds filtered a sense of the luminous power that was outside; or sometimes at certain hours a single ray would penetrate straight and clear as that of Sinai, populated with myriads of dust particles and going to vilify the colours of carpets, uniformly ruby-red throughout all the drawing-rooms: a real sorcery of illumination and colour which entranced my mind for ever. Sometimes I rediscover this luminous quality in some old palace or church, and it would wrench at my heart were I not ready to brush it aside with some 'wicked joke'.[1]

After the ante-chamber came the '*lambris*' room, so called because its walls were covered half-way up by panelling of inlaid walnut; next the so-called 'supper' room, its walls covered with dark flowered orange-coloured silk, part of which still survives as wall-coverings in my wife's room now. And there was the great ballroom with its enamelled floor and its ceiling on which delicious gold and yellow twirls framed mythological scenes where with rude energy and amid swirling robes crowded all the deities of Olympus.

After that came my mother's boudoir, very lovely, its ceiling scattered with flowers and branches of old coloured stucco, in a design gentle and corporeal as a piece of music by Mozart.

And after that one entered my mother's bedroom, which was very big; the principal wall where[2] there was the room at the corner of the house with a balcony (the last one) on Via Lampedusa, and one on the garden of the oratory of Santa Zita. The decorations in wood, stucco and paint in this room were among the finest in the house.

1 In English in the Italian text. (Trs.)
2 The Italian text here appears to be corrupted. (Trs.)

From the drawing-room known as the '*lambris*' room, going left one entered the 'green drawing-room', which led into the 'yellow drawing-room', and hence into a room which started out as my day-nursery, later to be turned into a little red drawing-room, the room which we most frequented, and which later became a library. This place had on the left (entering from the yellow drawing-room) a window on to the great courtyard and in the same wall a glass-panelled door giving on to the terrace. At right angles with these openings there was first a door (later bricked up) which led into a little room which used to be my grandfather's bathroom (it even had a marble bathtub) and which served as repository for my toys, and another glass-panelled door giving on to the small terrace.

III
The Journey

BUT THE HOUSE in Palermo had dependencies in the country which multiplied its charms. These were four; Santa Margherita Belice, a villa at Bagherìa, a palace at Torretta and a country house at Raitano. Then there was also the old home of the family at Palma and the castle of Montechiaro, but to those we never went.

The favourite was Santa Margherita, in which we would spend long months even of winter. It was one of the loveliest country houses I have ever seen. Built in 1680, it had been completely restored about 1810 by Prince Cutò on the occasion of a long sojourn there made by Ferdinand IV and Maria Carolina, forced to reside in Sicily during the years Murat was reigning in Naples. Afterwards, though, it had not been abandoned as were all other houses in Sicily, but constantly looked after, restored and enriched until the days of my grandmother Cutò, who, having lived in France until the age of twenty, had not inherited the Sicilian aversion for country life; she was in residence there almost continuously and brought it 'up-to-date' (for the Second Empire, of course, which was not very different from the general standard of comfort throughout Europe until 1914).

The charm of adventure, of the not wholly comprehensible, which is so much part of my memories of Santa Margherita, began with the journey there. This was an enterprise full of discomforts and delights. At that time there were no automobiles; around 1905 the only one that circulated around Palermo was old Signora Giovanna Florio's '*électrique*'. A train left the Lolli railway station at ten past five in the morning. So we had to get up at half-past three. Awakening at that hour was always nasty and made all the more miserable for me by the fact that it was the time at which I was given castor oil when I had stomachache. Servants and cooks had already left the day before. We were bundled into two closed landaus: in the first my father and mother, the governess Anna I, let's say, and myself; in the second Teresa, or Concettina maybe, my mother's maid, Ferrara, our accountant, a native of Santa Margherita and coming to spend the holidays with his family, and Paolo, my father's valet. Another vehicle followed I think, with luggage and hampers for luncheon.

It was usually about the end of June and dawn would be just spreading over the deserted streets. Across Piazza Politeama and Via Dante (then called Via Esposizione) we reached the Lolli railway station, where we packed into the train for Trapani. Trains then had no corridors, and so no lavatories; and when I was very small there was brought along for my use a chamber-pot in ghastly brown china bought on purpose and flung out of the window before reaching our destination. The ticket-collector would do his rounds by grappling along the exterior of the carriages, and all at once we would see his braided cap and black-gloved hand rising outside.

For hours then we crossed the lovely, desperately sad land-scape of western Sicily; it must have been I think just exactly the same as Garibaldi's Thousand had found it on landing – Carini, Cinisi, Zucco, Partinico; then the line went along the sea, the rails seeming laid on the sand itself; the sun, already hot, was broiling us in our iron box. Thermos flasks did not exist, and there were no refreshments to be expected at any station. The train next cut inland, among stony hills and fields of mown corn, yellow as the manes of lions. Eventually at eleven we reached Castelvetrano, then far from being the spry, thrusting little town it is now; it was a dreary place, with open drains and pigs walking in the main street; and flies by the billion. At the station, which had already been roasting under the sun for six hours, were waiting our carriages, two landaus fitted with yellow curtains.

At half-past eleven we set off again; for an hour as far as Partanna the road was level and easy, across fine, cultivated country; we began to recognise places we knew, a pair of majol-ica negroes' heads on the entrance pillars of a villa, an iron cross commemorating a murder; as we drew closer beneath Partanna, however, the scene changed: three Carabinieri appeared, a sergeant and two troopers on horseback, the napes of their necks protected by patches of white stuff like horsemen in Fattori's pictures, who were to accompany us all the way to Santa

Margherita. The road became mountainous: around us unrolled the immeasurable scenery of feudal Sicily, desolate, breathless, oppressed by a leaden sun. We looked about for a tree under whose shade to lunch; but there were only scraggy olives which gave no shelter from the sun. Eventually an abandoned peasant's hut was found, half in ruins, but its windows carefully closed. In its shade we alighted and ate; succulent things mostly. Slightly apart, the Carabinieri, who had bread, meat, cakes and bottles sent over to them, made a gay luncheon of their own, untroubled by the burning sun. At the end of the meal the sergeant would come up holding a brimming glass: 'I thank Your Excellencies on behalf of myself and my men!' And he took a gulp of wine which must have had a temperature of 104 degrees.

But one of the soldiers had remained on foot watchfully prowling round the hut.

Back we got into the carriages. It was now two o'clock – the truly ghastly hour of the Sicilian countryside in summer. We were moving at walking pace, for the slope down towards the Belice river was now starting. All were silent, and the only sound to be heard through the stamp of hooves was the voice of a Carabiniere humming ''La Spagnola sa amar cosi''.[1] Dust rose. Then we were across the Belice, a real and proper river for Sicily – it even had water in its bed – and began the interminable ascent at walking pace; bend succeeded bend eternally in the chalky landscape.

It seemed never-ending, and yet it did end. At the top of the slope the horses stopped, steaming with sweat; the Carabinieri dismounted, we too alighted to stretch our legs. Then we set off again at a trot.

My mother was now beginning to warn me.

'Watch out now, soon on the left we'll see La Venaría.'

In fact we were now passing over a bridge, and there on the left at last glimpsed a little verdure, some bamboo, even a patch or so of orange-grove. This was Le Dàgali, the first Cutò property on our road. And behind Le Dàgali was a steep hill, traversed

1 'That's how a Spanish woman loves.' (Trs.)

to the top by a wide alley of cypresses leading to La Venaría, a hunting lodge of ours.

We were not far off now. My mother, on tenterhooks because of her love for Santa Margherita, could no longer sit still and kept on craning out of one window or another. 'We're nearly at Montevago.' 'We're home!' Across Montevago we drove, first nucleus of life seen after four hours on the road. What a nucleus though! Wide deserted streets, houses weighed down equally by poverty and by implacable sun, not a living soul, only a few pigs and some cats' carcasses.

But once past Montevago everything improved. The road was straight and level, the countryside smiling. 'There's the Giambalvo villa! There's the Madonna of Graces and its cypresses!' and she even hailed the cemetery with delight. Then the Madonna of Trapani. 'We've arrived – there's the bridge!'

It was five in the afternoon. We had been travelling for twelve hours. On the bridge were lined up the municipal band, which broke into a lively polka. Exhausted as we were, with eyebrows white from dust and throats parched, we forced ourselves to smile and thank. A short drive through the streets and we came out into the piazza, saw the graceful lines of our home, and entered its gateway; first courtyard, passageway, second courtyard. We had arrived. At the bottom of the external staircase stood a little group of retainers, headed by our excellent agent Don Nofrio, tiny beneath his white beard and flanked by his powerful wife. 'Welcome!' 'We're so pleased to have arrived!'

Up in one of the drawing-rooms Don Nofrio had prepared crushed ice and lemon drinks, badly made but a blessing all the same. I was dragged off by Anna to my room and plunged, reluctant, into a tepid bath which the agent, peerless man, had thought of having ready, while my wretched parents faced the hordes of acquaintances already beginning to arrive.

IV
The House

SET IN the middle of the town, right on the leafy square, it spread over a vast expanse and contained about a hundred rooms, large and small. It gave the impression of an enclosed and self-sufficient entity, of a kind of Vatican as it were, that included state-rooms, living-rooms, quarters for thirty guests, servants' rooms, three great courtyards, stables and coach-houses, a private theatre and church, a large and very lovely garden, and a big orchard.

And what rooms they were! Prince Niccolò had had the good taste, almost unique for his time, not to ruin the eighteenth-century salons. In the state apartments every door was framed on both sides by fantastic friezes in grey, black or red marble, whose harmonious asymmetry sounded a gay fanfare at everyone passing from one room to another. From the second courtyard a wide balustraded staircase of green marble, in a single flight, led up to a terrace on which opened the great entrance doors, surmounted by the belled cross of the Cutò arms.

These led into a broad entrance hall, its walls entirely covered with two ranks, one above the other, of pictures representing the Filangeri family from 1080 until my grandmother's father; all lifesize standing figures in a great variety of costume, from a Crusader's to a Gentleman's-in-Waiting to Ferdinand II, pictures which in spite of their mediocre workmanship filled the big room with lively familiar presences. Beneath each, in white letters on a black background, were written their names and titles, and the chief events of their lives. 'Riccardo, defended Antioch against the Infidels.' 'Raimondo, wounded in the defence of Acre'; another Riccardo, 'chief instigator of the Sicilian Revolt' (that is, of the Sicilian Vespers), Niccolò I 'led two Hussar regiments against the Gallic hordes in 1796'.

Above each door or window, however, there were the panoramic maps of the 'fiefs', then still almost all present and correct. In all four corners were bronze statues of warriors in armour, a concession to the taste of the period, each holding on high a simple oil lamp. On the ceiling Jupiter, wrapped in a lilac cloud, blessed the embarkation of Roger as he prepared to sail from his native Normandy for Sicily; and tritons and water-nymphs frolicked around galleys ready to set forth on mother-of-pearl seas.

Once this proud overture was passed though, the house was all grace and charm, or rather gentleness veiled its pride as courtesy does that of an aristocrat. There was a library, its books shut inside cupboards of that decorative eighteenth-century Sicilian style called 'Monastic', not unlike the more florid Venetian, but cruder and less sweetened. There was nearly every work of the Enlightenment in tawny leather and gilt binding: *L'Encyclopédie*, Fontenelle, Helvétius, Voltaire in Kehl's great edition (if Maria Carolina read that, what must she have thought?), then *Victoires et Conquêtes*, a collection of Napoleonic bulletins and campaign reports which were my delight in the long silence-filled summer afternoons as I read them sprawled on one of those over-large 'poufs' which occupied the centre of the ballroom. An odd library, in fact, if one considers that it had been formed by a man as reactionary as that Prince Niccolò. Also to be found there were bound collections of the satirical journals of the Risorgimento, *Il Fischietto* and *Lo Spirito Folletto*, some exquisite editions of Don Quixote, of La Fontaine, that rare history of Napoleon with Norvins' charming illustrations (a book I still have); and among moderns the complete works, or almost, of Zola, whose yellow covers showed up glaringly on that mellow background, and a few other lesser novels; but there was also *I Malavoglia*, with an autographed dedication.

* * *

I do not know whether I have managed so far to convey the idea that I was a boy who loved solitude, who liked the company of things more than of people. This being the case it will easily be understood how ideal for me was life at Santa Margherita. I would wander through the vast ornate house (twelve people in three hundred rooms) as in an enchanted wood. A wood with no hidden dragons, full of happy marvels, even in the jesting names of the rooms: the 'aviary' room, its walls covered in rough crinkled white silk, on which amid infinite festoons of flowering branches glittered tiny multi-coloured birds painted in by hand; the '*ouistiti*' room where on similar tropical trees swung sly and hairy monkeys; 'the rooms of Ferdinando' which evoked at first in me the idea of a fair smiling uncle of mine, but which had actually kept this name because they had been the private apartments of the cruel and jocular *Re Nasone*, as was also shown by the huge Empire '*lit-bateau*', whose mattress was covered in a kind of morocco leather casing, apparently used on royal beds instead of an under blanket; green morocco leather, closely stamped with the triple gilt lilies of Bourbon, and looking like an enormous book. The walls were covered in silk of paler green, with vertical stripes, one shiny and one mat with tiny lines, just like the one in the green drawing-room of our house in Palermo. Then in the 'tapestry hall', the only one with some sinister association later, hung eight big tapestries on subjects taken from *Gerusalemme Liberata*. In one of these, representing an equestrian joust between Tancredi and Argante, one of the two horses had a strangely human look which I was to link in my mind later with Poe's *House of the Metzengersteins*. This particular tapestry, actually, is still in my possession.

The evenings, oddly enough, we always spent in the ballroom, an apartment in the centre of the first floor with eight balconies looking out over the piazza and four over the first courtyard. It was reminiscent of the ballroom of our house in Palermo; here, too, gold was the dominating note of the room. The walls, on the other hand, were pale green, almost entirely covered with hand-embroidered flowers and golden leaves, and the bases of pillars and the shutters vast as front doors were covered completely in dull gold-leaf with decorations in brighter gold. And when on winter evenings (we actually spent two winters at Santa Margherita, which my mother was loth to leave) we sat in front of the central fireplace, by the glow of a few petrol lamps whose light picked out capriciously a few flowers on the walls and flames in the shutters, we seemed to be enclosed in some magician's cave. I can definitely place the date of one of these evenings because I remember that newspapers were brought in announcing the fall of Port Arthur.

These evenings were not always restricted to the family alone; in fact they seldom were. My mother wanted to keep up her parents' tradition of being on cordial terms with the local notables, and many of these would dine with us in turn, while twice a week everyone met to play *scopone* in the ballroom. My mother had known them since childhood and liked them all; to me they seemed what perhaps they were not, good people without exception. Among them there was a native of Palermo forced by his wretched financial condition to emigrate to Santa Margherita, where he had a tiny house and an even tinier patch of ground; he was a practised shot, had been a close friend of my grandfather's, and enjoyed particularly favourable treatment; I think he used to lunch with us every day and was the only one to call my mother '*tu*', which she returned with a respectful '*lei*'. He was a straight-backed, wiry old man, with blue eyes and long white sprouting moustaches, distinguished and even elegant in his well-cut if threadbare clothes. I suspect now that he may have been a bastard of the Cutò family, some uncle of my mother's in fact. He would play the piano and tell wonderful tales of shooting out in the wilds and woods with my grandfather, of the prodigious acumen of his gun-dogs (Diana and Furetta) and of alarming but ever innocuous encounters with the brigand bands of Leone and Capraro. Then there was Nenè Giaccone, a big local landowner, with his flamboyant little goatee and insatiable vivacity; he was highly esteemed in the town as a great *viveur* because he spent two months of every year in Palermo at the Hotel Milano, on Via Emerico Amari, opposite the side façade of the Politeama – this was considered fast.

There was the Cavaliere Mario Rossi, a little man with a small black beard; he was an old post-office clerk who talked of nothing but Frascati ('You must realise, duchess, that Frascati is almost Rome') where his duties had taken him for a few months. There was Ciccio Neve, with his big rubicund face and muttonchop whiskers à la Franz-Josef, who lived with a mad sister (when one knows a Sicilian village well one discovers innumerable lunatics); there was Catania the schoolmaster, bearded like Moses; and another landowner, Montalbano, the typical rustic lordling, obtuse and gross, the father, I believe, of the present

Communist member of Parliament; Giorgio di Giuseppe, the intellectual of the company, from beneath whose windows passers-by at night heard him playing Chopin's nocturnes on the piano; Giambalvo, hugely fat and full of fun; Doctor Monteleone with a little black beard, who had studied in Paris and often spoke of the Rue Monge where he had had the oddest adventures; Don Colicchio Terrasa, very old and almost wholly peasant, with his son Totò, a great trencherman; and many others who were seen more rarely.

It will be noticed these were one and all men. Wives, daughters, sisters stayed at home, both because women in the country (in 1905–14) did not pay social calls, and also because their husbands, fathers and brothers did not consider them presentable. My mother and father would go and visit them once a season, and with Mario Rossi, whose wife was a Bilella and famous for her gastronomic arts, they would even take luncheon now and again; sometimes after a complex system of signals and warnings, she would send over by a small boy, who came galloping across the piazza under the broiling sun, an immense tureen full of macaroni done with barley in the Sicilian mode with chopped meat, eggplant and basil, which was, I remember, truly a dish fit for rustic and primitive gods. The boy had precise orders to set this on the dining table when we were already sitting down and, before leaving, he would say: ''*A signura raccumanna: 'u cascavaddu*' ('The signora recommends: cacciocavallo cheese'); an injunction perhaps sage but never obeyed.

The one exception to this absence of women was Margherita, the daughter of Nenè Giaccone the *viveur*; a pretty girl with auburn hair like her father, she had been educated at the Sacred Heart and was to be seen every now and then.

In contrast to the cordial relations with the townsfolk, those with the authorities were strained; the Mayor, Don Pietro Giaccone, was not on the visiting list, and neither was the parish priest, for all that the Cutò family had the benefice in their gift. The Mayor's absence is explained by the continuous feuding with the Town Hall over 'civic customs'. The Mayor was also a ladies' man and for a while he kept a trollop who passed herself off for a Spaniard, Pepita; he had unearthed her in a café-concert at Agrigento (!) and she drove about the streets of the town in a trap drawn by a grey pony. One day, as my father was standing outside the front entrance, he saw the couple passing in their elegant equipage; and with the unerring eye he had for these things he noticed that the wheel-hub had come away from its mounting and the wheel was on the point of falling off; so although he was not acquainted with the Mayor and their relations were strained, he ran after the trap shouting: 'Cavaliere look out, your right wheel's coming off.'

The Mayor stopped, saluted with his whip and said: 'Thank you. I'll see to it.' And he resumed his way without dismounting. Another twenty yards and the wheel did indeed go off after its own purposes, and the Mayor was rudely thrown to the ground together with Pepita in her pink chiffon dress. They were but slightly hurt. The following day four partridges arrived and a visiting card: 'Cav. Pietro Giaccone, Mayor of Santa Margherita Belice, to thank for the good but unheeded advice.' But this symptom of a thaw had no sequel.

V
The Garden

IN THE Santa Margherita house, the last and biggest of the three courtyards was the 'courtyard of the palms'; it was planted all over with the tallest of palm trees which in that season were laden with clusters of unfertilised dates. Entering it from the passage leading from the second courtyard, one had on one's right the long and low line of the building that housed the stables with, beyond it, the riding-school. In the centre of the courtyard, to the left of the stables and riding-school, stood two high pillars in porous yellow stone, adorned with masks and scrolls, which opened on to flights of steps leading down into the garden. They were short flights (a dozen or so steps in all) but in that space the baroque architect had found ways of expressing a freakish and whimsical turn of mind, alternating high and low steps, subjecting the flights to the most unexpected distortions, creating superfluous little landings with niches and benches so as to produce in this small space a variety of possible joinings and separations, of brusque rejections and affectionate reconciliations, which imparted to the staircase the atmosphere of a lovers' tiff.

The garden, like so many others in Sicily, was designed on a level lower than the house, I think so that advantage could be taken of a spring welling up there. It was very large and, when seen from a window of the house, perfectly regular in its complicated system of alleys and paths. It was all planted out with ilex and araucaria, the alleys bordered with myrtle hedges; and in the furnace of summer, when the jet of the spring dwindled, it was a paradise of parched scents of origanum and calamint, as are so many gardens in Sicily that seem made to delight the nose rather than the eyes.

The long alleys surrounding it on all four sides were the only straight ones in the whole garden, for in the rest the designer (who must surely have been the whimsical architect of the stairs) had multiplied twists, turns, mazes and corridors, contributing to give it that tone of graceful mystery which enveloped the whole house. All these cross-alleys, however, came out eventually on to a big central clearing, the one where the spring had been found; this, now enclosed in an ornate prison, lightened with its spurts a great fountain in the centre of which, on an islet of artificial ruins, a dishevelled and ungirt goddess of Abundance poured torrents of water into a deep basin forever crossed by friendly ripples. It was bounded by a balustrade, surmounted here and there by tritons and nereids sculptured in the act of diving with movements that were disordered in each individual statue but fused into a scenic whole. All round the fountain were stone benches, darkened by centuries-old moss, protected from sun and wind by a tangle of foliage.

But for a child the garden was brim full of surprises. In a corner was a big conservatory filled with cacti and rare shrubs, the kingdom of Nino, head gardener and my great friend, he, too, redhaired like so many at Santa Margherita, perhaps owing to the Norman Filangeri. There was a bamboo thicket, growing thick and sturdy around a secondary fountain, in the shade of which was an open space for games, with a swing from which long before my time Pietro Scalea, later Minister of War, fell and broke his arm. In one of the side alleys, embedded in the wall, was a big cage destined at one time for monkeys, in which my cousin Clementina Trigona and I shut ourselves one day, a Sunday morning when the garden was open to the townsfolk who stopped in mute amazement to gaze, uncertainly, at these dressed-up simians. There was a 'dolls' house', built for the diversion of my mother and her four sisters, made of red brick, with window frames in *pietra serena*; now, with its roof and floors fallen in, it was the only disconsolate corner of the big garden, the remainder of which Nino kept in admirable order with every tree well pruned, every alley yellow-pebbled, every bush clipped.

Every two weeks or so a cart came up from the nearby Belice with a big barrel full of eels, which were unloaded into the secondary fountain (the one of the bamboos), that served as a fishpond, when the cook sent for them to be scooped out with little nets according to the needs of the kitchen.

Everywhere at corners of alleys rose figures of obscure gods, usually noseless; and as in every self-respecting Eden there was a serpent hidden in the shadows, in the shape of some castor-oil shrubs (lovely in other ways with their oblong green leaves bordered in red) which one day gave me a nasty surprise when, crushing the berries of a fine vermilion bunch, I recognised upon the air the smell of the oil that, at that happy age, was the only real shadow on my life. My beloved Tom was following me, and I held out my besmirched hand for him to sniff; I still can see the kindly and reproachful way in which he puckered half of his black lip, as well brought-up dogs do when they want to show their disgust without giving offence to their masters.

A garden, I have said, full of surprises. But the whole of Santa Margherita was that, full of cheerful little traps. One would open a door on a passage and glimpse a perspective of rooms dim in the shade of half-pulled shutters, their walls covered with French prints representing Bonaparte's campaigns in Italy; at the top of the stairs leading to the second floor was a door that was almost invisible, so narrow was it and flush with the wall, and behind this was a big room crammed with old pictures hung right up to the very top of the walls, as in prints of the Paris *Salon* in the eighteenth century. One of the ancestral portraits in the first room was hinged, and behind lay my grandfather's gun-rooms, for he was a great shot.

The trophies shut in glass cabinets were local only: crimson-footed partridges, disconsolate-looking woodcock, coots from the Belice; but a big bench with scales, little measures for preparing cartridges, glass-fronted cupboards full of multi-coloured cartridge-cases, coloured prints showing more dangerous adventures (I can still see a bearded explorer in white fleeing screaming before the charge of a greenish rhinoceros), all these were enchantments to an adolescent. On the walls also hung prints and photographs of gun-dogs, pointers and setters, showing the calm of all canine faces. The guns were ranged in big racks, ticketed with numbers corresponding to a register in which were recorded the shots fired from each. It was from one of these guns, I think a lady's, with two richly damascened barrels, that I fired, in the garden, the first and last shots of my sporting career; one of the bearded keepers forced me to shoot at some innocent redbreasts; two fell, unfortunately, with blood on their tepid grey plumage; and as they were still quivering the keeper wrung their necks with his fingers.

In spite of my readings of '*Victoires et Conquêtes*', and '*L'épée de l'intrépide général comte Delort rougie du sang des ennemis de l'Empire*' this scene horrified me: apparently I only like blood when metamorphosed into printer's ink. I went straight to my father, to whose orders this slaughter of the Innocents was due, and said that never again would I fire on any creature.

Ten years later I was to kill a Bosnian with a pistol and who knows how many other Christians by shellfire. But this never made on me a tenth of the impression left by those two wretched robins.

There was also the 'carriage-room', a great, dark chamber, in which stood two enormous eighteenth-century *carrosses*, one gala, all gilt and glass, with doors on whose panels, against a yellow background, were painted pastoral scenes in '*vernis Martin*'; its seats, for at least six persons, were of faded taffeta; the other, a travelling carriage, was olive-green with gilt edgings and coats of arms on the door panels, and was upholstered in green Morocco leather. Beneath the seats there were lined cupboards intended, I think, for provisions on a journey, but now containing only a solitary silver dish.

Then there was the 'children's kitchen' with a miniature range and a set of copper cooking implements to scale, which my grandmother had installed in a vain attempt to inveigle her daughters into learning to cook.

And then there was the church and the theatre, with the fairy-tale passages by which they were reached, but of those I will speak later.

Amid all these splendours I slept in a completely bare room overlooking the garden, called the 'pink room' because of the colour of its varnished plaster; on one side was a dressing-room with a strange oval brass bath raised on four high wooden legs. I remember the baths which I was made to take in water that had starch dissolved in it or bran in a little bag from which when wet came a scented, milky drip; *bains de son*, bran baths, traces of which can be found in memoirs of the Second Empire, a habit which had evidently been handed on to my mother by my grandmother.

In a room nearby, identical to mine, but blue, slept a succession of governesses, Anna I and Anna II, who were German, and Mademoiselle, who was French. At my bedhead hung a kind of Louis Seize showcase in white wood, enclosing three ivory statuettes of the Holy Family on a crimson background. This case has been miraculously salvaged and now hangs at the bedhead of the room in which I sleep at my cousin Piccolo's villa at Capo d'Orlando. In that villa, too, I retrieve not only the 'Holy Family' of my infancy, but a trace, faint certainly but unmistakable, of my childhood; and so I love going there.

VI

The Church and the Theatre

THERE WAS also the church, which was then the cathedral of Santa Margherita. From the carriage-room one turned left and, up a few steps, reached a wide passage ending in a kind of school-room with benches, blackboards, and relief maps, where my mother and aunts had done their lessons as children.

It was at Santa Margherita, at the not-so-tender age of eight, that I was taught to read. To begin with, others read aloud to me; on alternate days, that is Tuesdays, Thursdays and Saturdays, 'Sacred History' and a kind of potted version of the Bible and the Gospels; and on Mondays, Wednesdays and Fridays, classical mythology. So I acquired a 'solid' knowledge of both these disciplines; I am still capable of saying how many, and who, were the brothers of Joseph and of finding my way among the complicated family squabbles of the Atrides. Before I learnt to read for myself my grandmother was forced by her own goodness to read aloud for an hour from *The Queen of the Caribbean* by Salgari; and I can still see her trying hard not to fall asleep as she read out about the prowess of the Black Pirate and the swashbuckling of Carmaux.

Eventually it was decided that this religious, classic, and adventuresome culture, vicariously imparted, could not last much longer, and that I was to be handed over to Donna Carmela, an elementary schoolmistress at Santa Margherita. Nowadays elementary schoolmistresses are smart lively young ladies, who chatter about Pestalozzi's and James's pedagogic studies and want to be called '*Professoressa*'. In 1905, in Sicily, an elementary schoolmistress was an old woman more than half-peasant, with her spectacled head wrapped up in a black shawl; but actually this one was a most expert teacher, and within two months I knew how to read and write and had lost my doubts about double consonants and accented syllables. For whole weeks, in the 'blue room' separated from my pink room only by the passage, I had to carry out articulated dictations – ar-ti-cu-la-ted dic-ta-tions – and repeat dozens of times, 'di, do, da, fo, fa, fu, *qui* and *qua* don't take an accent.' Blessed labours! Thanks

to them it will never be my lot, as it has been the lot of a
distinguished senator, to be surprised at the frequency with
which newspapers and handbills incur the error of slipping an
extra b into 'Republic'.

When I had learnt to write Italian my mother taught me to
write French; I already spoke it and had often been to Paris and
in France, but it was now that I learnt to read French. I can still
see my mother sitting with me at a desk, writing slowly and very
clearly *le chien, le chat, le cheval* in the columns of an exercise book
with a shiny blue cover, and teaching me that what the French
pronounce as 'ch' the Italians pronounce as 'sh', 'like "scirocco
and Sciacca"', she would say. From then on, until my school-
days, I spent all my afternoons in my grandparents' apartments
at Via di Lampedusa, reading behind a screen. At five o'clock
my grandfather would call me into his study to give me my afternoon refreshment – a hunk of hard bread and a large glass of cold
water. This has remained my favourite drink ever since.

Before reaching the school-room there were two doors on the
left which led to three guest-rooms; these were most favoured
because they gave on to the terrace on which the entrance stairway abutted. On the right of the carriage-room, between two
white console tables, was a big yellow door. From this one
entered a small oblong room, its chairs and various tables loaded
with images of Saints; I can still see a big china dish in the middle
of which lay the head of St John the Baptist, lifesize, with blood
coagulated in the bottom. From this room one entered a gallery
at the level of a high first storey, looking straight on to the High
Altar, which was surrounded by a superb railing of flowery gilt.
In this gallery were prie-dieux, chairs, and innumerable rosaries,
and from it every Sunday at eleven we attended High Mass, sung
without excessive fervour. The church itself was a fine spacious
one, I remember, in Empire style, with large, ugly frescoes in
white stucco work on the ceiling, as in the Olivella church in
Palermo which it resembled, albeit on a smaller scale.

From this same carriage-room which, I now remember, was
a kind of revolving stage for the least frequented part of the
house, one penetrated to the right into a series of passages,

cubby-holes and staircases that gave one a sense of having no
outlet, like certain dreams – and eventually reached the corridor
of the theatre. This was a real and proper theatre, with two tiers
each of twelve boxes, as well as a main box and, of course, the
stalls. The auditorium, capable of holding at least three hundred
people, was all white and gold, with its seats and the walls of
boxes lined in very light blue velvet. The style was Louis Seize,
restrained and elegant. In the centre was the equivalent of the
royal box, that is, our box, surmounted by an enormous shield
of gilt wood, containing the belled cross set on a double-headed
eagle's breast. And the drop-curtain, rather later in date, represented the defence of Antioch by Riccardo Filangeri (a defence
which, according to Grousset, was far less heroic than the painter
gave one to believe).

The auditorium was lit by gilt petrol lamps set on brackets
projecting under the first tier of boxes.

The best of it was that this theatre (which of course also had a
public entrance from the piazza) was often used.

Every now and again a company of actors would arrive; these
were strolling players who, generally in summer, moved on carts
from one village to the other, staying two or three days in each
to give performances. In Santa Margherita where there was a
proper theatre they stayed longer, two or three weeks.

At ten in the morning the leading actor would call in frockcoat and top hat to ask for permission to perform in the theatre;
he would be received by my father or, in his absence, by my
mother, who of course gave permission, refused any rent (or
rather made a contract for a token rental of fifty *centesimi* for the
two weeks), and also paid a subscription for our own box. After
which the leading actor left, to return half-an-hour later and
request a loan of furniture. These companies travelled, in fact,
with a few bits of painted scenery but no stage furniture, which
would have been too costly and inconvenient to carry about.
The furniture was granted, and in the evening we would recognise our armchairs, tables and wardrobes on the stage (they
were not our best, I'm sorry to say). They were handed back
punctually at the moment of departure, sometimes so garishly

revarnished that we had to ask other companies to desist from this well-intentioned practice. Once, if I remember right, the leading lady also called on us, a fat good-natured Ferrarese of about thirty who was to play *La Dame aux Camélias* for the closing night. Finding her own wardrobe unsuitable for the solemnity of the occasion she came to ask my mother for an evening dress: and so the Lady of the Camellias appeared in a very low-cut robe of Nile green covered in silver spangles.

These companies wandering round country villages have now vanished, which is a pity. The scenery was primitive, the acting obviously bad; but they played with gusto and fire and their 'presence' was certainly more life-like than are the pallid shades of fifth-rate films now shown in the same villages.

Every night there was a play, and the repertoire was most extensive; the whole of nineteenth-century drama passed on that stage; Scribe, Rovetta, Sardou, Giacometti and Torelli. Once there was even a *Hamlet*, the first time in fact that I ever heard it. And the audience, partly of peasants, were attentive and warm in their applause. At Santa Margherita, at least, these companies did good business, with theatre and furniture free and their draught-horses put up and foddered in our stables.

I used to attend every night, except on one night of the season called 'black night', when some French *pochade*, reputed indecent, was shown. Next day our local friends came to report on this libertine performance, and were usually very disappointed as they had expected something much more salacious.

I enjoyed it all enormously, and so did my parents. The better companies at the end of their season were offered a kind of rustic garden party with a simple but abundant buffet out in the garden, which cheered up the stomachs, often empty I fear, of those excellent strolling players.

But already in the last year in which I spent a long period at Santa Margherita, 1921, companies of actors no longer came, and instead flickering films were shown. The war had killed off, among others, these poor and picturesque wandering companies which had their own artistic merits and were, I have an idea, the training school of many a great Italian actor and actress of the nineteenth century, Duse among others.

VII
Excursions

OF ALL the walks around Santa Margherita, that towards Montevago was our most frequent, for it ran level, was the right length (about two miles each way), and had a definite if not attractive goal; Montevago itself.

Then there was a walk in the opposite direction, on the main road towards Misilbesi; one passed under a huge umbrella pine and then over the Dragonara bridge, surrounded unexpectedly by thick, wild verdure which reminded me of scenes from Ariosto as I imagined them at that period from Doré's illustrations. The landscape around Misilbesi had a ruffianly air about it suggestive of violence and hardship of a sort I imagined was no longer to be found in Sicily; a few years ago I noticed a by-road near Santa Ninfa (called Rampinzeri) in which I recognised the same ruffianly yet amiable aspect I associated with Misilbesi. On reaching Misilbesi, a sunbaked cross-roads marked by an old house with three dusty and deserted tracks that seemed to be leading to Hades rather than to Sciacca or Sambuca, we generally returned by carriage as our usual four miles were by then greatly exceeded.

The carriage had followed us at walking pace, stopping every now and again so as not to overtake us and then rejoining us unhurriedly; phases of silence and of disappearance alternating according to the turns of the road, before we were caught up with a clatter.

In autumn our walks had as goal the vineyard of Toto Ferrara, where we would sit on stones and eat the sweetest mottled grapes (vine grapes, for in 1905 table grapes were scarcely ever cultivated in our region), after which we entered a room in semi-darkness; at the end of it a lusty young man was jerking like a madman inside a barrel, his feet squashing the grapes whose greenish juice could be seen flowing down a wooden channel, while the air was filled with a heavy smell of must.

'Dance, and provençal song, and sunburnt mirth.'[1]

1 Keats: Ode to a Nightingale.

241

No, no 'mirth' at all; in Sicily there was none, there never is even now during work: the Tuscan girls singing their *stornelli* at vintage, the threshing punctuated by feasting, song and love-making round Leghorn, these are things unknown; all work is *'na camurrìa*[1], a blasphemous contravention of the eternal repose granted by the gods to our 'lotus-eaters'.

On rainy afternoons of autumn our walk was confined to the public gardens. These were set at the northern limit of the town, on a hillside overlooking the great valley which is probably the main east-west axis of Sicily and is certainly one of its few outstanding geographical features.

These gardens had been given to the municipality by my grandfather and were of quite infinite melancholy; a longish alley bordered by young cypresses and old ilexes led to a bare open space facing a small shrine of the Madonna of Trapani, with a flower bed of parched yellow bamboos in the middle and on the left a kind of kiosk-temple with a round dome from which to gaze at the view.

And it was worth gazing at. Opposite stretched a vast range of low mountains, all yellow from reaping, with blackish patches of burnt stubble, so that one had a vivid impression of a monstrous crouching beast. On the flanks of this lioness or hyena (according to the eye of the beholder) could just be made out villages whose greyish-yellow stone was scarcely distinguishable from the background: Poggioreale, Contessa, Salaparuta, Gibellina, Santa Ninfa, all weltering in poverty and dog-days, and in an ignorance against which they never reacted with even the faintest of flickers.

The little shrine at the other side of the open space in the gardens was a target for anti-clerical manifestos by Santa Margherita's law students, there on vacation. Often could be seen written up in pencil strophes from Carducci's 'Hymn to Satan': '*Salute, o Satana, o ribellione, o forza vindice della ragione.*'[2] And when my mother (who knew the 'Hymn to Satan' by heart and whose lack of admiration for it was due to aesthetic reasons

1 In Sicilian, venereal disease and, by extension, vexation, affliction.
2 'Greetings, oh Satan, oh rebellion, oh avenging force of reason.'

alone) next morning sent Nino our gardener to put a coat of whitewash over the modestly sacrilegious verses, others appeared two days later: '*Ti scomunico, o prete, vate di lutti e d'ire*'[1] and other volleys which the good Giosuè[2] thought it his duty to discharge against citizen Mastai.[3]

On the slope below the kiosk could be gathered capers, which I did regularly at the risk of breaking my neck; and around there also, it seems, were to be found those Spanish flies whose pulverised heads make such a potent aphrodisiac. I was sure at the time that these flies were there; but whom I heard this from, or when or how, remains a mystery. Never in my life, at any rate, have I set eyes on Spanish flies, dead or alive, whole or in powder.

Such were our daily, not very exacting, walks. Then there were longer, more complicated ones, our excursions.

The chief excursion of all was that to La Venaría, a hunting lodge on a spur just before Montevago. This was an excursion always made with local guests twice or so in a season, and was never without an element of comedy. A decision would be reached: 'Next Sunday, lunch at Venaría'. And in the morning off we would set at ten o'clock, ladies in carriages, men on donkeys. Although all or almost all the men owned horses or at least mules, the use of donkeys was traditional; the only rebel was my father, who got round the difficulty by declaring himself to be the one person capable of driving, on those roads, the dog-cart conveying the ladies and bearing also in the dog-cages secreted under the box, bottles and cakes for the guests' luncheon.

Amid laughter and jest the company would take the road to Montevago. In the middle of the dusty group was the dog-cart in which my mother, with Anna or whichever Mademoiselle was with us, Margherita Giaccone and some other lady, tried to shelter from the dust with grey veils of almost Moslem thickness; around would prance the donkeys (or rather '*'i scecche*', for in

1 'I excommunicate you, oh priest, prophet mourning and wrath.'
2 Carducci.
3 Pope Pius IX.

Sicilian donkeys are almost always feminine, like ships in English), their ears flapping. There were real falls, genuine donkeys' mutinies, and pretended falls due to love of the picturesque. We crossed Montevago, arousing vocal protests from every dog in the place, reached the Dàgari bridge, dropped down into the adjacent depression and began climbing.

The avenue was really grandiose; about three hundred yards long, it went straight up towards the top of the hill, bordered on each side by a double row of cypresses; not adolescent cypresses like those of San Guido, but great trees[1] almost a hundred years old, whose thick branches spread their austere scent in every season. The rows of trees were interrupted every now and again by sets of benches, and once by a fountain with a great mask emitting water at intervals. Under the odorous shade we climbed towards La Venaría, bathed in full sunshine high above.

It was a hunting lodge built at the end of the eighteenth century, considered 'tiny', though actually it must have had at least twenty rooms. Built on top of the hill, on the opposite side to the one by which we approached, it looked sheer across the valley, the same valley to be seen from the public gardens, which from higher up seemed vast and even desolate.

Cooks had left that morning at seven and had already prepared everything; when a boy look-out announced the group's approach they thrust into the ovens their famous *timbales* of macaroni *alla Talleyrand*, (the only macaroni which keeps for a period), so that when we arrived we had scarcely time to wash our hands before going straight out on to the terrace, where two tables had been laid in the open air. In the *timbales* the macaroni were steeped in the lightest glaze and, beneath the savoury crust of flaky pastry, absorbed the flavour of the prosciutto and truffles sliced into match-like slivers.

Huge cold bass with mayonnaise followed, then stuffed turkey and avalanches of potatoes. One might expect strokes from over-eating. A fat guest, Giambalvo, nearly did pass out once: but a pailful of cold water in his face and a prudent nap in a shady room saved him. Next, all was put to rights by the arrival of one

1 Now felled by later owners.

of those iced cakes at which Marsala, the cook, was a past-master. Wines, as always in sober Sicily, were of no importance. The guests expected them, of course, and liked their glasses filled to the brim, ('no collars' they would call to the footman) but in the absence of a collar to their glasses they emptied but one, at the most two.

After dusk we descended homewards.

I have spoken of excursions in the plural; in fact our only real excursion, thinking it over, was that to La Venaría. In the first years there were others, of which however I have kept only rather vague memories; though the word 'vague' is not quite exact; a better phrase would be 'difficult to describe'. The visual impression has remained vivid in my mind but was not then linked to any word. We must have taken the carriage out to Sciacca, for instance, to lunch with the Bertolinos when I was five or six years old; but of the luncheon, the people we met, the journey, I have no memory at all. On the other hand of Sciacca itself, or rather of its promenade above the sea, such a photographic, complete and precise image has remained stamped on my mind that when I returned there a couple of years ago, for the first time after more than fifty years, I was easily able to compare the scene under my eyes with the old one that had remained in my mind, and note the many similarities and the few differences.

As always memories refer particularly to memories of 'light'; at Sciacca I see a very blue, almost black, sea glinting furiously beneath the midday sun, in one of those skies of high Sicilian summer which are misty with heat, a balustrade over a sheer drop to the sea, a kind of kiosk, to the left of which was a café – which is still there.

Looming skies with scudding rain-clouds, on the other hand, remind me of a small country house, Cannitello, near Catania, set on a steep hillside reached by a zig-zagging road which, I don't know why, horses had to ascend at a gallop. I see a landau with dusty blue cushions (the very fact they were blue showed that the carriage was not our own but hired), my mother sitting in a corner, panic-stricken herself but trying to reassure me, while beside us the stunted trees whirled past and vanished with the speed of wind, and the coachman's incitements mingled with whip cracks and frenzied tingling of collar-bells (no, that carriage was certainly not ours).

Of the house where we were going I retain a memory of what I can now say was its gentlemanly but poverty-stricken air; obviously I did not formulate this economic-social judgment at the time, but I can say it in all serenity now, examining the mental photograph recently retrieved from the archives of memory.

I have spoken of the people who belonged to the household at Santa Margherita; I have yet to mention the guests who came to stay for a period of days or weeks.

I have to say that these guests were few; there were no motor-cars then, or rather three or four at most in the whole of Sicily, and the ghastly state of the roads induced the owners of the *rarae aves* to use them only in towns. Santa Margherita was a long way from Palermo, then, a twelve-hour journey – and what a journey!

Amongst the guests at Santa Margherita I remember my Aunt Giulia Trigona with her daughter Clementina and the girl's nanny, a bony German woman, extremely strict and quite unlike my smiling Annas. Giovanna (now Albanese) was not yet born, and as for Uncle Romualdo, I don't know where he displayed his splendid physique and his impeccable attire.

Clementina was, and still is, a male in skirts. Blunt, resolute, truculent as she was (the very qualities which were later to turn out to her detriment), she proved a quite acceptable playmate for a little boy of six or seven. I well recall those endless pursuits, mounted on tricycles, which took place not only in the garden but indoors as well, between the entrance hall and the 'Leopold drawing-room'; there and back they must have added up to a good four hundred yards.

I've already mentioned the business of our transformation into monkeys in the garden-cage; and I remember the breakfasts eaten round an iron table in the garden. I fear, though, that this latter may be a 'pseudo-recollection': a photograph exists of these breakfasts in the garden, and it could very well be that I am confusing the actual recollection of the photograph with an archaic memory of childhood. This is by no means impossible, and indeed it happens all the time.

I have to say I possess no recollection of my Aunt Giulia, on this occasion; probably Clementina and I were still of an age to take our meals separately.

On the other hand I have the most vivid memory of Giovannino Cannitello. He was the proprietor of the Cannitello mansion already mentioned. Giovanni Gerbino-Xaxa, baron of Cannitello, was his full name, and he belonged to a good local family, feudatories of the Filangeri; for the Filangeri had the right, very rare and much envied, of investing with a barony a total of two of their own vassals in every generation. The Gerbinos (who had been judges of the High Court way back under the Empire) had been granted this privilege, and my grandmother even used to call him 'the very first vassal among my vassals'.

Giovannino Cannitello then gave me the impression of being an old man; actually he could not have been more than forty. He was very tall, very thin, very short-sighted; in spite of his spectacles, which were a *pince-nez* and had extraordinarily thick lenses, squashing down his nose with their weight, he used to walk bent in the hope of recognising at least a vague shadow of his surroundings.

A good, sensitive person, well liked and of no great intelligence, he had dedicated his life (and spent the greater part of his fortune) on trying to be 'a man of fashion'. And from the point of view of dress he had certainly succeeded; never have I seen a man with a wardrobe more sober, better cut, or less showy than his. He had been one of the moths drawn by the glamorous glow of the Florios, and who, after many a dizzy pirouette, dropped on to the tablecloth with burnt wings. He had been more than once to Paris with the Florios and even put up at the Ritz; and of Paris (the Paris of *boîtes*, of luxurious brothels, of high-priced ladies) he had preserved a dazzled memory which made him remarkably like the Doctor Monteleone I have mentioned before; with the difference that the engineer's memories were

based on the Latin quarter and the Ecole de Médecine. They
were not on very good terms, Giovannino Cannitello and Doctor Monteleone, perhaps because of their rivalry in disputing
the favours of the Ville Lumière. There was a long-standing
family joke about Doctor Monteleone being woken in the night
because Cannitello had swallowed a litre of paraffin with a view
to suicide (having been jilted by a pretty chambermaid); and he
had simply turned over on his other side saying: 'Shove a wick
in his stomach and set it alight.'

This because Giovannino Cannitello (who subsequent to the
French period with Mademoiselle Sempell acquired the nickname 'le grand Esco', that is, Spindleshanks) was temperament-
ally inclined to a vigorous pursuit of the ladies. And there is no
counting the times that he made attempts on his life (by means
of a circumspect use of paraffin, or brazier fumes by open window) after suffering rejection at the hands of his beloved, who
generally belonged below stairs.

Poor Cannitello became almost blind and utterly destitute
before he died not so many years ago (about 1932) in his house
on Via Alloro, next door to the Coachmen's church. My
mother, who went to visit him until the end, would return
much affected by his being so bent that, when sitting in his
armchair, his face was eight inches from the floor, and to talk to
him she had to sit on a cushion on the very floor itself.

In the early years Alessio Cerda was also a frequent guest at
Santa Margherita. Then he went blind, and although we always
saw him at Palermo, he made no further appearances at Santa
Margherita. There was a photograph of him dressed in his uniform as lieutenant in the *Guide*, with the soft cap, soft boots, soft
gloves of our unfortunate army of 1866; all this softness was to
find itself asserted at Custozza.[1] But of Alessio Cerda, a most
singular personality, I shall have occasion to speak.

Another person who came once, and came indeed in one of
the first motor-cars, was Paolo Scaletta. I think he arrived on an
off-chance: he was on his way to some Valdina properties at

1 A village near Verona where in June 1866 the Austrians under the Arch-
duke Albert routed an Italian army led by King Victor Emmanuel.

Menfi, not far from Santa Margherita, when his car broke down. And he came to seek our hospitality.

Many of my memories centre on Santa Margherita – agreeable and disagreeable, but all of them crucial.

VIII
The Pink Dining-room

BUT I realise that I have forgotten to mention the dining-room, which was singular for various reasons; singular for existing at all; in an eighteenth-century house it was very rare, I think, to have a room set apart as a dining-room: at that time people dined in any drawing-room, changing continually, as in fact I still do now.

But there was one at Santa Margherita. Not very big, it could only hold about twenty chairs comfortably. It looked out over two balconies on to the second courtyard. Three doors gave access to it: the principal door, which led into the 'picture gallery' (not the one I have already mentioned), a second which led into the 'huntsmen's room', and the third giving on to the 'office', whence the rope-pulley lift communicated with the kitchen below. These doors were white, Louis Seize, and had big panels with decorations in relief, gilt, of a greenish dull gold. From the ceiling hung a Murano chandelier, whose greyish glass showed up the colour of floral designs.

Prince Alessandro, who arranged this room, had thought up the idea of asking a local artist to paint on the walls pictures of himself and his family while actually eating their meals. These were large pictures on canvas, completely covering a wall from floor to ceiling with virtually lifesize figures.

One showed breakfast: the prince and princess, he in green shooting clothes, boots and wearing a hat, she in white *déshabillé* but wearing jewels, sitting at a small table intent on taking chocolate, served by a little negro slave in a turban. She was holding out a biscuit to an impatient hound, he raising towards his mouth a big blue cup decorated with flowers. Another picture represented a picnic: a number of ladies and gentlemen were sitting around a table-cloth spread in a field and covered with splendid looking pasties and grass-plaited bottles; in the background could be seen a fountain, and the trees were young and low. This, I think, must have been the actual garden of Santa Margherita just after it was planted.

A third picture, the biggest, represented a formal dinner-party with the gentlemen in very curly wigs and the ladies in full evening dress. The princess was wearing a delicious robe of silver pink *broché* silk, with a dog-collar round her neck and a great *parure* of rubies on her bosom. Footmen in full livery and cordons were entering bearing high dishes elaborately decorated.

There were another two pictures, but I can only remember the subject of one of them, for it was always facing me; this was the children's afternoon refreshment. Two little girls of ten and twelve years of age, powdered and tightly laced into their pointed bodices, sat facing a boy of about fifteen, dressed in an orange-coloured suit with black facings and carrying a rapier, and an old lady in black (certainly the governess): all were eating large ices of an odd pink colour, maybe of cinnamon, rising in sharp cones from long glass goblets.

Another of the oddities of the house was the table-centre in the dining-room. This was a large fixed silver ornament, surmounted by Neptune who threatened the guests with his trident, while beside him an Amphitrite eyed them with a hint of malice. The whole was set on a rock rising in the middle of a silver basin, surrounded by dolphins and marine monsters squirting water from their mouths through some machinery hidden in a central part of the table. It was all very gay and grand, but had the inconvenience of requiring table-cloths with a large hole cut out of the middle for Neptune. (The holes were hidden by flowers or leaves.) There were no sideboards, but four big console tables covered with pink marble, and the general tone of the room was pink, in the marble, in the princess's pink dress, in the big picture, and also in the chair coverings which were pink too, not old but of delicate hue.

For a small boy at Santa Margherita, though, adventure did not lie concealed only in unexplored apartments or in the labyrinth of the garden, but also in so many singular objects. Just think what a source of wonder that table centrepiece could be! But there was also the music-box discovered in a drawer: a big clockwork contrivance containing a cylinder set with knobs at irregular intervals, which turned on its own axis and lifted minute steel keys, producing delicate, meticulous melodies.

Near the dining-room, in another apartment, were enormous

cupboards of yellow wood, the keys of which had been lost; not even Don Nofrio the administrator knew where they were, and when one said that there was no more to be said. After long hesitation the blacksmith was eventually called and the doors were opened. The cupboards contained bed linen, dozens and dozens of sheets, pillow-cases, enough for an entire hotel (there were already overwhelming quantities of these in the known cupboards); others contained blankets of real wool scattered with pepper and camphor, still others table linen, small, large or out-size damask table-cloths, all with that hole in the middle. And between one layer and another of this homely treasure were placed little tulle sacks of lavender flowers now in dust. But the most interesting cupboard was one containing writing-materials of the eighteenth century; it was a little smaller than the others, and heaped with great sheets of pure rag letter-paper, bundles of quill pens tied neatly in dozens, red and blue sealing wafers and very long sticks of sealing wax.

As can be seen, the house of Santa Margherita was a kind of eighteenth-century Pompeii, all miraculously preserved intact: a rare thing always, but almost unique in Sicily which from poverty and neglect is the most destructive of countries. I do not know what were the exact causes of this phenomenal durability: perhaps the fact that my maternal grandfather spent long years there between 1820 and 1840 in a kind of exile imposed on him by the Bourbon kings as a result of a misdemeanour on the Marine Parade at Palermo,[1] or perhaps the passionate care which my grandmother took of it: certainly the fact of her finding in Onofrio Rotolo a unique administrator, the only one who, to my knowledge, was not a thief.

He was still alive in my time: a kind of dwarf with a long white beard, living together with an incredibly large fat wife in one of the many apartments attached to the house, with a separate entrance.

Marvels were recounted of his care and scrupulosity; how, when the house was empty, he went through it every night with

1 Driving his carriage stark naked.

lantern in hand to check that all the windows were shut and doors bolted; how he allowed only his wife to wash the precious china; how after a reception (in my grandmother's time) he checked the screws under every chair: how during the winter he spent entire days surveying squads of cleaners polishing and ordering every single object, however out-of-the-way, in that vast house. In spite of his age and anything but youthful aspect his wife was very jealous of him; and ever and again news would reach us of terrific scenes which she made due to her suspicion of his paying too much attention to the charms of some young maid-servant. I know for certain that a number of times he protested most vigorously to my mother about her over-spending; he was met, needless to say, with a deaf ear and perhaps some contumely.

His death coincided with the rapid and sudden end of this loveliest of lovely country homes. May these lines which no one will read be a homage to its unblemished memory.

The Siren

A STORY

JANUARY 1957

IN THE late autumn of the year 1938, I had a bad fit of the spleen. I was living in Turin at the time, and my tart No. 1, while groping about in my pockets for an odd fifty-lire note as I slept, had also found a letter from tart No. 2, which, in spite of spelling mistakes, left no doubts about the nature of our relationship.

My awakening had been immediate and stormy. The little flat in Via Peyron echoed with vernacular tantrums; there was even an attempt to scratch my eyes out, which I only evaded by giving a slight twist to the dear girl's left wrist. This fully justified act of self-defence put an end to the scene, but to our idyll too. She flung her clothes on, thrust into her bag powder-puff, lipstick, hanky and the fifty-lire *causa mali tanti*, hissed the Torinese for 'swine!' into my face thrice, and left. Never had she been so attractive as during that quarter of an hour's raging. From my window I watched her go out and move off into the morning mist, tall, slim, wrapped in reconquered poise.

Never again did I set eyes on her, as I never set eyes on a black cashmere pullover of great cost, which had the fatal quality of being styled for either male or female. All she left me, on the bed, were two of those small twisted, so-called 'invisible', hairpins.

That same afternoon I had an appointment with No. 2 at a confectioner's in Piazza Carlo Felice. At the little round table in the western corner of the inner room which was 'ours', I saw, not the chestnut locks of the girl who was now more than ever desirable, but the sly features of Tonino, a young brother of hers aged twelve, who had just finished gobbling down a cup of chocolate with a double portion of whipped cream. As I drew near he got up with the usual Torinese urbanity. '*Monsú*,' he said, 'Pinotta's not coming. She told me to give you this note. *Cerea, monsú.*' And off he went, taking with him two brioches left on the dish. In the ivory-coloured missive I was notified of summary dismissal due to my infamy and 'southern dishonesty'. Obviously No. 1 had traced and incited No. 2, and I was left recumbent between two stools.

In twelve hours I had lost two girls who were usefully

complementary as well as a pullover I liked, and also had to pay
that infernal Tonino's cake bill. My very Sicilian self-respect was
humiliated: I had been made a fool of: and I decided to abandon
the world and its pomps awhile.

For this period of retirement I could have found no place more
suitable than the café in Via Po where I began spending every
free moment alone and always went in the evening after my
work on the paper. It was a kind of Hades peopled by bloodless
shades of lieutenant-colonels, magistrates and professors. These
insubstantial apparitions would play draughts or dominoes,
immersed in a light dimmed, during the day, by arcades and
clouds and at night by huge green shades on the chandeliers;
no voices were ever raised lest too loud a sound disturb their
tenuous woof. A most proper Limbo.

Like the creature of habit that I am, I used always to sit at
the same corner table, carefully designed to offer customers a
maximum of discomfort. On my left a pair of ghostly senior
officers would be playing *tric-trac* with a couple of phantoms
from the Court of Appeal; military and judicial dice slithered
listlessly from the leather cup. On my right always sat an elderly
gentleman muffled in an old overcoat with a mangy Astrakhan
collar. He read foreign magazines ceaselessly, smoked Tuscan
cheroots and spat a great deal: every now and again he shut up
his magazines and seemed to be following some memory in the
volutes of smoke. Then he would begin reading and spitting
again. He had hideous, knobbly, reddish hands, with nails cut
straight and not always too clean; but once when in one of those
magazines his eye fell on a photograph of an archaic Greek
statue, the kind with wide-set eyes and an ambiguous smile, I
was surprised to see his splayed finger-tips stroke the picture
with a delicacy that was almost regal. He noticed I was watching
him, gave a grunt of fury and ordered another coffee.

But for a lucky accident our relations would have remained
on this plane of latent hostility. I used to bring over five or six
newspapers from the office, among them, once, the *Giornale di
Sicilia*. Those were the years when the Ministry of so-called
Popular Culture was at its fiercest, and all newspapers were

identical; that number of the Palermo daily was more banal than ever and only distinguishable from a paper of Rome or Milan by its bad typography; so my reading of it was brief, and I soon dropped the sheet on the table. I had just begun to contemplate yet another incarnation of 'Minculpop', when I was addressed by my neighbour: 'Excuse me, sir, but might I glance at this *Giornale di Sicilia* of yours? I'm Sicilian and it's twenty years since I've seen a newspaper from home.' The voice was cultivated, its accent impeccable; the old man's grey eyes looked at me with utter detachment. 'Please do, of course. You know, I'm Sicilian too, and if you wish could easily bring you the newspaper here every evening.' 'Thank you. I don't think that's necessary; my curiosity is purely physical. If Sicily is still as it was in my day, I imagine nothing good ever happens there, as it hasn't for three thousand years.'

He took a listless glance over the newspaper, refolded it, handed it back to me, and plunged into reading a pamphlet. When leaving he obviously wanted to slip off without a greeting, but I got up and introduced myself; he muttered through his teeth a name which I could not catch, but did not hold out his hand. On the threshold of the café, however, he turned round, raised his hat, and called out, 'Hail, fellow-countryman!' Then he vanished beneath the arcades, leaving me dumbfounded and provoking moans of disapproval among the gambling ghosts.

I wove suitable magic spells to materialise a waiter and asked him, pointing to the empty table, 'Who was that gentleman?' 'That,' he replied, 'is Senator Rosario La Ciura.'

The name meant a lot even to my patchy journalist's culture; it was that of one of the five or six Italians who possess a reputation universal and unassailable, that of the most illustrious Hellenist of our time. Now I understood the bulky reviews and the stroking of that print; the irritability too, and the hidden refinement.

Next day at the office I searched around in that odd card-index of obituaries still 'in suspense'. There was a card for 'La Ciura' there, decently filled in for once. It said how the great man was born at Aci-Castello (Catania) from a lower middle-

class family and, through his amazing aptitude for studying
Greek had, by dint of scholarships and erudite publications,
attained the Chair of Greek Literature at the University of Pavia
at the age of twenty-seven; he had then been called to the Chair
at Turin, where he had stayed until reaching the age-limit; he
had lectured at Oxford and Tübingen, and travelled extensively,
for he was not only a pre-Fascist senator and Academician of the
Lincei, but also doctor 'honoris causa' of Yale, Harvard, New
Delhi and Tokyo, as well, of course, as of the most illustrious
universities in Europe from Uppsala to Salamanca. The list of
his publications was very lengthy, and many of his works, particularly on Ionic dialects, were considered basic; proof of this
was the fact that, though a foreigner, he had been charged with
the Teubner edition of Hesiod, for which he had written an
introduction, in Latin, of unrivalled mastery; final, major glory,
he was *not* a member of the Italian Academy. What had always
distinguished him from colleagues, however erudite, was his
lively, almost carnal sense of classical antiquity; and this was
shown in a collection of essays, in Italian, *Men and Gods*, which
was considered a work not only of high erudition but of true
poetry. In fact, concluded the compiler of the card, he was 'an
honour to the nation and a beacon to all cultures'. He was
seventy-five years old, and lived, not opulently but decently
enough, on his pension and his senatorial emolument. He was
unmarried.

There's no denying it; we Italians, elder sons (or fathers) of
the Renaissance, consider the Great Humanist to be the highest
form of human being. The chance of now finding myself in
daily contact with the major representative of this subtle, almost
magical and unremunerative branch of knowledge, flattered and
perturbed me. I felt the same sensations as a young American
might feel on introduction to Mr Gillette: alarm, respect, and a
form of not ignoble envy.

That evening I went down to Limbo in a very different mood
from that of the days before. The senator was already in his place
and answered my reverential greeting with a scarcely perceptible
mutter. But when he had finished reading an article and

completing some notes on a little pad, he turned towards me and in strangely musical tones said, 'Fellow-countryman, from your way of greeting me I see that one of these phantoms must have told you who I am. Forget it and, if you have not done so already, forget also the Aorists you studied at school. But tell me what your name is, for last night you made the usual gabbled introduction and I cannot fall back, like you, on asking others for your name, which is certainly quite unknown to anyone here.'

He was talking with insolent detachment; obviously to him I was rather less than a cockroach, more like one of those specks of dust that rotate unconstructively in sunbeams. But his calm tone, his precise speech, his use of the familiar '*tu*', radiated the serenity of a Platonic dialogue.

'My name is Paolo Corbera, and I was born at Palermo, where I took a degree in law; now I am working here in the editorial offices of *La Stampa*. To reassure you, senator, I will add that in my school-leaving exam I only got five plus for Greek and have reason to think the plus was added so that I could be given a certificate at all.'

He gave a half-smile. 'Thank you for telling me that; better so. I detest talking to people who think themselves knowledgeable when they are ignorant, like my colleagues at the University; really all they know are the exterior forms of Greek, its oddities and deformities. The live spirit of that language which is so stupidly called "dead" has not been revealed to them. Nothing has been revealed to them, if it comes to that. Poor wretches, anyway; how can they sense that spirit if they have never had occasion to hear real Greek?'

Pride is preferable to false modesty, yes indeed; but I felt the senator was rather over-doing it; it even occurred to me that the years might have softened a bit that exceptional brain. Those poor devils his colleagues had just the same chance of hearing ancient Greek as he had himself; none at all, that is.

He was proceeding, 'Paolo ... You are lucky to be called after the only Apostle with some culture and a smattering of letters. Jerome would have been better though. The other names you Christians carry round are really too squalid; slaves' names.'

I was feeling more and more disappointed; he seemed to be just an ordinary academic priest-baiter with a dash of Nietzschean Fascism added. Surely not?

He was talking on with the seductive modulations and the verve of a man who had perhaps spent a long period in silence. 'Corbera ... Am I mistaken in thinking that to be one of the great Sicilian names? I remember my father used to pay a small annual ground-rent for our house at Aci-Castello to the agent of a family called Corbera di Palina or Salina, I don't remember which. He used to make a joke every time in fact, and say that if there was any sure thing in this world it was that those few lire would not end in the pockets of the "demesne" as he called them. But are you really one of those Corbera or merely a descendant of some peasant who took his master's name?'

I confessed myself to be indeed a Corbera di Salina, in fact the only surviving specimen of that family; all the splendours, all the sins, all the unexacted rents, all the unpaid bills, all the Leopard's ways in fact, were concentrated in me alone. Paradoxically the senator seemed pleased.

'Good, good. I hold old families in high regard. They possess a memory, minute it's true, but anyway greater than that of others. They are the best you people can achieve in the way of physical immortality. Get yourself married soon, Corbera, since you people have found no better way of survival than dispersing your seed in the unlikeliest places.'

Definitely, I was losing patience. 'You people, you people'. Who were 'You people'? All the vile mob who had not the luck to be Senator La Ciura? Had *he* attained physical immortality? One wouldn't say so to look at that wrinkled face, that heavy body ...

'Corbera di Salina,' he was continuing undaunted. 'You won't be offended if I go on calling you "*tu*" as to one of those little students of mine during their few instants of youth?'

I declared myself not only honoured but pleased, as in fact I was. Having disposed of matters of name and protocol, we talked of Sicily. He had not set foot on the island for twenty years, and the last time he was 'down there' (as he said in the Piedmontese mode) he had only stayed five days, at Syracuse, to discuss with

Paolo Orsi[1] certain matters concerning the alteration of semi-choruses in classic drama. 'I remember they wanted to take me by motor-car from Catania to Syracuse; I only accepted on learning that at Augusta the road runs far from the sea, while the railway is along the shore. Tell me about that island of ours; it is a lovely land, though inhabited by donkeys. The Gods have sojourned there, may do still in inexorable Augusts. Let us not, though, mention those four modern temples; anyway you know nothing about them, that I'm sure.'

So we spoke about eternal Sicily, nature's Sicily; about the scent of rosemary on the Nèbrodi hills, the taste of Melilli honey, the waving corn seen from Etna on a windy day in May, of the solitudes around Syracuse, the gusts of scent from orange and lemon groves pouring over Palermo, it's said, during some sunsets in June. We talked of the enchantment of certain summer nights within sight of Castellamare bay, when stars are mirrored in the sleeping sea and the spirit of anyone lying back amid the lentisks is lost in a vortex of sky, while the body is tense and alert, fearing the approach of demons.

After an almost total absence of fifty years the senator still kept an extraordinarily clear memory of a few little facts. 'The sea! The sea of Sicily is the most coloured, the most romantic of all I have ever seen. That will be the only thing you will not manage to ruin, apart from the cities, of course. Do they still serve those prickly sea-urchins split in half in taverns by the sea?' I reassured him, though adding that few ate them nowadays for fear of typhus. 'Yet they're the best thing you have down there, those blood-red cartilages, those images of female organs, tasting of salt and sea-weed. Typhus indeed! They're dangerous as are all gifts of the sea, which grant death together with immortality. At Syracuse I demanded Orsi to produce some. What flavour! What a divine aspect! My finest memory in the last fifty years!'

I was confused and fascinated; a man like this abandoning himself to almost obscene metaphors, showing a childish greed for the, after all, mediocre delights of sea-urchins!

We went on talking for a long time, and on leaving he insisted

1 A famous former Director of the Syracuse Museum of Classical Antiquity.

on paying for my coffee, not without an exhibition of his peculiar boorishness ('Of course, lads of good family never have a
cent in their pockets!'); and we parted friends, if one leaves out
of account the fifty years dividing our ages and the thousands of
light-years separating our cultures.

We went on meeting every evening, and although the smoke
of my rage against humanity was now beginning to disperse I still
made a point of meeting the senator unfailingly in the Infernal
regions of Via Po. Not that we chatted much: he would go on
reading and taking notes and only addressed me now and again,
but when he did it was always a harmonious flow of pride and
insolence, sprinkled with varied allusions, veined with incomprehensible poetry.

He went on spitting too, and eventually I noticed that he did
so only while reading. I think he must have acquired a certain
affection for me too, but I am under no illusions about that; if
he did have any, it was not what one of 'us people' (to use the
senator's term) might feel for a human being, but more like an
old spinster's affection for her pet canary, of whose fatuity and
incomprehension she is aware but whose existence permits her
to express aloud regrets in which the little creature has no part;
on the other hand, if it were not there, she would feel ill-at-ease.
I began noticing, in fact, that whenever I was late the old man's
haughty eyes were fixed on the entrance door.

It took nearly a month for us to move on from his always
highly original but general comments to the indiscretions which
alone make conversations between friends differ from those
between mere acquaintances. I myself took the initiative. That
frequent spitting of his worried me (as it worried the custodians
of the Hades, who had eventually put a dark copper spittoon
beside his chair), and one evening I was bold enough to ask him
why he did not go to a doctor about his chronic catarrh. I asked
the question unthinkingly, at once regretted having risked it,
and waited for the senatorial anger to bring the stucco ceiling
down on my head. Instead of which the well-modulated voice
replied placidly; 'But, my dear Corbera, I have no catarrh. A
keen observer like yourself should have noticed that I never
cough before I spit. My spitting is no sign of illness, but rather

of mental health. I spit from disgust at the nonsense I am reading. If you care to examine that utensil there' (and he pointed at the spittoon) 'you would realise that it contains very little saliva and no trace of mucus. My spits are symbolic and of high cultural content; if you don't like 'em then go back to your native drawing-rooms, where there's no spitting only because no one will ever admit themselves to be nauseated by anything.'

The gross insolence of this was attenuated by a faraway look, yet even so I felt like getting up and leaving him there and then; luckily I had time to reflect that I had only my own rashness to blame. I stayed, and at once the impassive senator counter-attacked; 'Now *you* tell *me* why you frequent this ghost-filled and, as you say, catarrh-ridden Erebus, this geometric site of failed lives? In Turin there's no lack of these creatures whom to you people seem so desirable. A trip to that hotel by the castle, to Rivoli or the baths at Moncalieri, and your prurient urges would soon find an object.' I burst into laughter at hearing from so learned a mouth such exact information on the pleasure haunts of Turin. 'But how d'you come to know these addresses, senator?' 'I know them, Corbera, I know them. That is the one thing, and the one thing only, that one does learn from frequenting senates, both academic and political. But please do me the favour of being convinced that the sordid pleasures of you people have never been Rosario La Ciura's.' That, one felt, was true; the senator's bearing and words bore the unequivocal sign (as we used to say in 1938) of a sexual reserve quite uncon-nected with age.

'The truth, senator, is that I began coming here as a temporary refuge from the world. I've had trouble with two of the sort of girls you so justly stigmatise.'

His reply was sharp and frank. 'Cuckoldry, eh, Corbera? Or pox?'

'Neither: worse, desertion.' And I told him about the ridicu-lous events of two months before. My tone was facetious, for the ulcer on my self-respect had healed. Any man other than this devilish Hellenist would have either jeered at me or, more rarely, sympathised. But the alarming old man did neither: he waxed indignant. 'You see what happens, Corbera, as a result of

coupling with the squalid and the diseased? I would say the same
to those two sluts about you if I ever had the misfortune to meet
them.'

'Diseased, senator? They were both in splendid health; you
should have seen the amount they ate at the *Specchi*; and not in
the least squalid; superb creatures, both of them, and elegant
too.' The senator hissed out one of his contemptuous spits.
'Diseased, I said, diseased: in fifty, sixty years, maybe long before,
they'll crack up; so from now on they're sick. And squalid:
elegant indeed, with their trashy jewellery, stolen pullovers, and
airs and graces taken from the films! Splendour indeed, fishing
about for greasy bank-notes in their lover's pocket instead of
presenting him, as others do, with rose-pink pearls and branches
of coral! That's just what happens to people who go with these
slapped-up sluts. And were you not at all disgusted, they as much
as you, you as much as they, at cuddling yours and their future
carcasses between stinking sheets?' I was stupid enough to reply,
'But the sheets were always perfectly clean, senator!' He became
furious. 'What have sheets to do with it? The inevitable stink of
corpses was your own. I repeat, how can you wallow about with
people of their, of your sort?' I, who had just been eyeing one
of Ventura's delicious *cousettes*, took offence. 'Well, one can't go
to bed only with Serene Highnesses!' 'Who mentioned "Serene
Highnesses"? They're as much charnel-house material as the
others. But these are matters you cannot understand, young
man, and I'm wrong to mention them. You and your little girl-
friends are fated to sink deeper and deeper into the pestilential
mire of your slimy pleasures. Those who really know are so
few.'

He began to smile with eyes turned towards the ceiling: his
face had a rapt expression: then he held out his hand to me
and left.

He did not appear again for three days; on the fourth I had a
telephone-call at the newspaper-office. 'Is that *Monsù* Corbera?
This is Bettina, housekeeper to *Signour* Senator La Ciura. He
says to tell you that he's had a bad cold, that he's better now, and
that he'd like to see you tonight after dinner. Come to 18, Via

Bertola at nine; second floor.' The line was suddenly cut, and I could not ring back.

Number 18 Via Bertola was a dilapidated old building, but the senator's apartment was large and well-kept, due, presumably, to the persistent care of Bettina. The parade of books began from the entrance hall, the sort of modest-looking cheaply bound volumes of every living library. There were thousands in the three rooms I crossed. In the fourth sat the senator wrapped in an ample camel-hair dressing-gown, the finest and softest I had ever seen. Later I learnt this was not camel-hair but rare llama wool, a gift from the Academic Senate of Lima. Though the senator pointedly did not rise on my entry, he greeted me most cordially; he felt better, quite well in fact, and expected to be back in circulation as soon as the wave of cold then over Turin grew milder. He offered me some resinated Cypriot wine, a gift from the Italian Institute of Athens, some foul pink 'lucums' from the Archaeological Mission of Ankara, and sensible Torinese cakes acquired by the provident Bettina. He was in such good humour that he actually smiled twice with his whole mouth and even reached the point of apologising for his own outbursts in our Hades. 'I know, Corbera, I have been excessive in my terms, though believe me, moderate in my concepts. Don't give it another thought.' I was in fact not thinking of it, but feeling full of respect for this old man whom I suspected of being very unhappy in spite of his triumphant career. He was devouring those abominable 'lucums'. 'Sweets, Corbera, should be sweet and no more. If they have any other flavour they're like perverse kisses.'

He was giving big morsels to Aeacus, a large boxer dog which had entered the room. 'This creature, Corbera, in spite of his ugliness is more like the Immortals, to one who can understand such things, than any of your little bitches.'

He refused to show me his library. 'All classics that could have no interest for one like you, who are morally failed in Greek.' But he did take me round the room we were in, which turned out to be his study. It contained few books, among them the plays of Tirso de Molina, Lamotte-Fouqué's *L'Undine*, Giraudoux's play of the same name, and, to my surprise, the works of

H. G. Wells. But in compensation the walls were hung with
huge photographs, life-size, of archaic Greek statues; and not the
usual photographs we can all lay hands on, but superb specimens,
obviously demanded with authority and despatched with devotion from museums all over the world. There they all were, those
magnificent creatures, the 'Rider' in the Louvre, the 'Seated
Goddess' from Taranto now in Berlin, the 'Warrior' of Delphi,
the 'Korè' of the Acropolis, the 'Apollo' of Piombino, the 'Lapi-
thae Woman' and the 'Phoebus' at Olympia, the famous
'Charioteer' ... The room was alight with their ecstatic yet
ironic smiles, exalted by the relaxed arrogance of their bearing.
'You see, Corbera; these, yes; tarts, no.'

On the mantelshelf were ancient amphorae and vases; Odysseus tied to the ship's mast, the Sirens crashing from a high
precipice on to rocks in expiation for letting their prey escape.
'All nonsense that, Corbera, petty bourgeois poets' tales. No one
ever escapes the Sirens, and even if someone did they would
never have died for so little. How could they have died, anyway?'

On a small table, in a modest frame, stood an old faded photograph: a youth of about twenty, almost naked, with unruly curls
and a confident look on features of rare beauty. Perplexed, I
paused an instant, thinking I had understood. Not at all. 'And
this, fellow-countryman, this was and is and shall be' (he accentuated strongly) 'Rosario La Ciura.'

The poor senator in a dressing-gown had been a young god.

Then we spoke of other things, and before I left he showed
me a letter in French from the Rector of the University of
Coimbra inviting him to join the Committee of Honour for a
congress of Greek studies which was to take place in Portugal
that May. 'I'm very pleased about it; I'll embark at Genoa on the
Rex with the French, Swiss and German congress members.
Like Odysseus I shall stop my ears to avoid hearing the nonsense
of those maimed creatures. But there will be lovely days of
navigation: sun, blue, smell of sea.'

On our way out we passed the bookcase holding the works
of Wells, and I dared to express my surprise at finding them
there. 'You're right, Corbera, they're a horror. And among them
there's a short novel that would make me want to spit for a

month on end if I re-read it; and you wouldn't like that, would you, you drawing-room lapdog?'

After this visit of mine our relations became definitely cordial, on my side at least. I made elaborate preparations for some really fresh sea-urchins to be sent up from Genoa. When told they would arrive next day I laid in some Etna wine and peasant bread, then timidly invited the senator to visit my little abode. I went to fetch him in my Fiat *Balilla*, and drove him all the way out to Via Peyron, which is at the back of beyond. In the motor-car he showed some alarm and utter distrust in my driving capacities. 'I know you now, Corbera; if we have the misfortune to meet one of those skirted monstrosities of yours you're quite capable of turning right round, then we'll both go and crack our noses on a kerb.' We met no noteworthy abortions in skirts and arrived intact.

For the first time since I had known him I saw the senator laugh; this was on entering my bedroom. 'So this is the theatre of your grubby ruttings, is it, Corbera!' He examined my few books. 'Good, good. Maybe you're less ignorant than you seem. This man here,' he added, taking up my Shakespeare, 'this man here did understand something. "*A sea change into something rich and strange. What potions have I drunk of Siren tears?*"'

When good Signora Carmagnola entered the sitting-room with a tray of sea-urchins, lemons and the rest, the senator was in ecstasies. 'What? You thought of this, did you? How can you know that these are what I yearn for most?'

'You're quite safe in eating them, senator, they were in the sea on the Riviera only this morning.'

'Yes, of course, always the same, you people, slaves to decay and putrescence, always with ears strained for the shuffling steps of Death. Poor devils! Thank you, Corbera, you've been a good *famulus*. A pity they're not from that sea "down there", these sea-urchins, that they aren't wrapped in our own sea-weed; their prickles have certainly never made any divine blood flow. You've done all you possibly could, of course, but these are almost wild sea-urchins that were dozing in the chilly rocks of Nervi or Arenzano.' Obviously he was one of those Sicilians who consider the Ligurian Riviera (a tropical region to the Milanese) a kind of Iceland. The sea-urchins, split, exhibited their wounded, blood-red, strangely partitioned flesh. I had never noticed before, but now, after the senator's bizarre comparisons, they really did seem to me like a cross-section of some delicate female organ. He was eating them avidly but without gaiety, quiet, almost absorbed. He would squeeze no lemon over them. 'You people are always coupling flavours! A sea-urchin must also taste of lemon, sugar of chocolate, love of paradise!'

When he had finished he took a sip of wine, and closed his eyes. Soon after I noticed two tears slide from under his withered lids. He got up, moved over to the window, surreptitiously wiped his eyes. Then he turned. 'Have you ever been to Augusta, Corbera?'

I had been there three months as a recruit; during time off two or three of us used to take out a boat and meander around the transparent waters of the bays. After my reply he was silent; then said in a tone of irritation; 'And did you milk-sops ever visit that little inner bay beyond Punta Izzo, behind the hill overlooking the salt pans?'

'Indeed we did; it's the loveliest spot in Sicily, fortunately so far undiscovered by the Young Fascists' organisations. A wild bit of coast, isn't it, senator? Utterly deserted, not a house in sight; the sea is peacock-coloured; and right opposite, beyond the iridescent waves, Etna. From nowhere else as from there is it so lovely, so calm, masterful, truly divine. It is one of those places in which one sees an eternal aspect of that island of ours which so idiotically turned its back on its vocation, that of serving as pasturage for the herds of the sun.'

The senator was silent. Then; 'You're a good lad, Corbera; if you were not so ignorant one could have made something of you.'

He came up to me, kissed me on the forehead. 'Now go and fetch that little coffee-grinder of yours. I want to go home.'

During the following weeks we went on meeting as usual. Now we would take nocturnal walks, usually along Via Po and across the martial Piazza Vittorio in order to gaze at the rushing river and the hill, where they introduced a touch of fantasy into the geometric pattern of the city. It was the beginning of spring, that touching season of threatened youth; first lilacs were sprouting on banks, the more eager haven-less couples defying damp grass. 'Down in Sicily the sun is already burning, the sea-weed aflower; fish are surfacing on moonlight nights, their flashing bodies glimpsed amid luminous spray. And here we stand facing this insipid and deserted stream, these great barracks that look like rows of soldiers or friars, and hear the moaning of these couplings of the dying.'

But he cheered at the thought of the sea-journey he would soon be taking to Lisbon; departure was close now. 'It will be pleasant; you should come too; a pity, though, that there's no group for people lacking in Greek; you could talk Italian to me, but if you didn't show Zuckmayer or Van der Voos a knowledge of the optatives of all irregular Greek verbs you'd be out. Though maybe you are more conscious of Greek reality than they; not by culture, of course, but by animal instinct.'

Two days before he left for Genoa he told me he would not be coming to the café next day but be expecting me at his home at nine that night.

The ceremonial was the same as on my other visit: the pictures of the gods of three thousand years ago radiated youth as a stove radiates heat; the faded photograph of the young god of fifty years before seemed dismayed to look at his own metamorphosis, white-haired and slumped in an armchair.

When the Cypriot wine was drunk the senator called for Bettina and told her she could go to bed. 'I will see Signor Corbera out myself when he goes. Now, Corbera, if I've brought you here to-night at the risk of disarranging one of your fornications at Rivoli, it's because I need you. I leave to-morrow, and at my age when one goes away one never knows if it won't be a matter of staying afar for ever; particularly on a journey by sea. You know, really I'm quite fond of you; your simplicity touches me, the obvious machinations of your vital forces amuse me; then I have an idea that you, as happens with a few Sicilians of the better kind, have succeeded in achieving a synthesis between your senses and your reason. So you deserve not to be left dry-mouthed, without my explaining to you the reason for some of my oddities, of some of the phrases I have uttered in front of you and which you must have thought worthy of a madman.'

I protested feebly. 'Much of what you said I've not under-stood; but I've always attributed my incomprehension to the inadequacy of my own mind, never to an aberration of yours.'

'No matter, Corbera, it's all the same to me. All us old men seem mad to you young ones, yet often it's the other way round. To explain myself, though, I shall have to describe my adventure to you, which I seldom do. It happened when I was that young gentleman there,' and he pointed to the photograph of himself. 'We must go back to 1887, a time which must seem prehistoric to you, but is not so to me.'

He moved from his own chair behind the desk and came to sit on the sofa beside me. 'Excuse me, you know, but later on I'll have to speak in a low voice. Important words can't be yelled; the scream of love or hate is only heard in melodrama or among the most uncivilised, which comes to the same thing. Anyway, in 1887 I was twenty-four years old; my aspect was that of the photograph; I already had a degree in classics, and published two small studies on Ionic dialects which had made some stir at my university; and for the last year I'd been preparing to compete for a Chair at Pavia University. To say the truth, never, before that year or since, had I or have I touched a woman.'

I was sure that my face remained marmoreally impassive, but I was deceived. 'That wink of yours is very ill-mannered, Corbera. What I'm saying is the truth; truth and also boast. I know that we males of Catania are generally thought capable of making our very wet nurses pregnant, which may well be true. Not in my case, though. When one spends night and day in the company of gods and demi-gods, as I was doing at the time, one is left with little desire to climb the stairs of San Berillio brothels. Also I was held back by religious scruples at the time. Corbera, you really must learn to control your eyelashes: they betray you again and again. Yes. Religious scruples, I said. I also said "at the time". Now I no longer have them, but that's been no use to me in this matter.

'You, my little Corbera, who probably got your job on the
newspaper due to a note from some Fascist boss, can have no
idea of the preparation needed to compete for a university chair
in Greek literature. It means two years of slogging away to the
verge of madness. The language, luckily, I knew well enough
already, as well as I do now; and I don't wish to boast but . . . The
rest though; the Alexandrian and Byzantine variants of texts,
the quotations, always inaccurate, perpetrated by Latin authors,
the innumerable connections between literature and mythology,
history, philosophy, science! I repeat, it's enough to drive anyone
mad. So there I was studying away and, on top of that, cramming
boys who'd failed their school exams in order to pay my keep in
town. I was living on more or less nothing but black olives and
coffee. Then to crown it all came that appalling summer of 1887,
which was one of the truly hellish ones that happen down there
now and again. At night Etna would vomit the sun's fire that it
had stored during fifteen hours of daylight; touching a balcony-
rail at midday meant a rush to a First Aid post; the lava paving-
stones seemed on the point of returning to their fluid state; and
almost every day the scirocco flapped its slimy bats' wings in
one's face. I was all in. A friend saved me: he met me as I was
wandering deranged through the streets, stuttering Greek verses
which I no longer understood. My appearance alarmed him.
"Listen, Rosario, if you stay on here you'll go off your head and
that will be the end of your chair. I'm off to Switzerland" (the
boy had money) "but I've a three-roomed hut at Augusta twenty
yards from the sea, way out of town. Pack your bag, take your
books and go and spend the whole summer there. Call at my
home in an hour's time and I'll give you the key. You'll see,
it's quite different there. Ask at the station where the Casino
Carobene is, everyone knows it. But do leave, leave to-night."
'I took his advice and left that night; next morning, instead
of being greeted at dawn by lavatory pipes across a courtyard I
woke up facing a pure stretch of sea with, in the background, an
Etna no longer ruthless, wrapped in morning mist. The port was
utterly deserted, as you tell me it still is, and uniquely lovely. All
that the shabby rooms of the little house contained were the
couch on which I spent the night, a table and three chairs; also

a few earthenware pots and an old lamp in the kitchen. Behind
the house was a fig-tree and a well. Paradise. I went into town,
traced the peasant who looked after the Carobene's patch of
land, and arranged for him to bring me bread, spaghetti, a few
vegetables and some petroleum every two or three days. Oil I
had, our own, sent by my poor mother down to Catania. I hired
a small boat which a fisherman brought me over every afternoon
together with a lobster-pot and a few fishing-hooks. There I
made up my mind to stay at least two months.

'Carobene was right: it really was quite different. The heat
was violent at Augusta too, but it no longer reverberated from
every wall, no longer produced utter prostration but a kind of
suppressed euphoria; the sun put off its executioner's scowl and
contented itself with the role of splendid if brutal donor of
energy, as well as of a magic jeweller who set mobile diamonds
in every faintest ripple of sea. Study had ceased to be an effort;
to the gentle rocking of the boat in which I spent long hours
each book became, instead of an obstacle, a key opening up a
world, one of whose most entrancing aspects I already had
beneath my eyes. Often I found myself declaiming verses of
poets aloud, and the names of those forgotten gods, ignored by
most, again skimmed the surface of that sea which once at their
name alone had risen in tumult or relapsed into a lull.

'My isolation was complete, interrupted only by visits from
the peasant who brought me a few provisions every three or
four days. He only stayed five minutes, because the sight of my
elated carefree state must have made him think me on the verge
of dangerous madness. And, in truth, sun, solitude, nights spent
beneath rotating stars, silence, sparse feeding, study of remote
subjects, did weave a kind of spell around me which predisposed
a mood for prodigy.

'This was fulfilled at six o'clock on the morning of the fifth
of August. I had just awoken and got straight into the boat; a
few strokes of the oars had borne me far from the pebbles on
the beach, and I had stopped under a large rock whose shadow
would protect me from the sun, already climbing in swollen
ferment and turning to gold and blue the candour of the dawn
sea. I was declaiming away when I suddenly felt the edge of the

boat lower, to the right, behind me, as if someone had seized it
to climb on board. I turned and saw her: a smooth sixteen-year-
old face emerging from the sea, two small hands gripping the
gunwale. The girl smiled, a slight fold drawing aside her pale
lips and showing a glimpse of sharp little white teeth like a dog's.
But it was not in the least like one of those smiles you people
give, which are always debased by an accessory expression, of
benevolence or irony, pity, cruelty or the like; this expressed
nothing but itself, that is an almost animal joy, an almost divine
delight in existence. This smile was the first of the spells cast
upon me, revealing paradises of forgotten serenity. From
rumpled sun-coloured hair the sea-water flowed over green
widely open eyes down features of childlike purity.

  'Our captious reason, however predisposed, rears up before a
prodigy, and when faced with one falls back on memories of the
obvious; I tried, as anyone else would, to persuade myself I had
met a girl out bathing, and moved carefully over above her,
bent down and held out my hands to help her in. But she with
astounding vigour emerged straight from the sea as far as the
waist and put her arms round my neck, enwrapping me in a
scent I had never smelt before, then let herself slither into the
boat: beneath her groin, beneath her gluteal muscles, her body
was that of a fish, covered in minute scales of blue and mother-
of-pearl and ending in a forked tail which was slowly beating
the bottom of the boat. She was a Siren.

  'She lay on her back with head resting on crossed hands,
showing with serene immodesty a delicate down under her arm-
pits, drawn-apart breasts, perfectly shaped loins; from her arose
what I have wrongly called a scent but was more a magic smell
of sea, of youthful voluptuousness. We were in shade, but twenty
yards away the beach lay abandoned to the sun and quivering
with sensuality. My reaction was ill-hidden by my almost utter
nudity.

  'She spoke: and so after her smile and her smell I was submerged by the third and greatest of charms, that of voice. It was
slightly guttural, veiled, reverberating with innumerable har-
monies; behind the words could be sensed the lazy surf of summer seas, last spray rustling on a beach, winds passing on lunar

waves. The song of the Sirens does not exist, Corbera: the music from which there is no escaping is that of their voices.

'She was speaking in Greek and I had great difficulty in understanding her: "I heard you talking to yourself in a language similar to my own; I like you; take me. I am Lighea, daughter of Calliope. Don't believe in the tales invented about us; we kill none, we only love."

'Bent over her, I rowed, gazing into her laughing eyes. We reached the shore; I took that aromatic body in my arms and we passed from glare to deep shade; she was already bringing to my mouth that flavour of pleasure which compared to your earthly kisses is like wine to tap-water.'

The senator was describing his adventure in a low voice. I, who in my heart had always considered my own varied sexual experiences as far superior to what I had thought of as his mediocre ones and who had stupidly felt that this diminished the distance between us, was humiliated; even in love I found myself submerged in abysmal depths below him. Never for an instant did I suspect him to be telling me lies, and the greatest sceptic, had he been present, would have sensed the utter truth in the old man's tone.

'So those three weeks began. It is not proper, it would anyway not be charitable towards you, to enter into details. Suffice it to say that in those embraces I enjoyed both the highest forms of spiritual pleasure and that elementary one, quite without any social connotations, felt by our lonely shepherds on the hills when they couple with their own goats; if the comparison disgusts you that is because you are incapable of making the necessary transposition from the bestial to the superhuman plane, in my case superimposed on each other.

'Think again of what Balzac dared not express in his *Une passion dans le désert*. Those immortal limbs of hers emanated such a life-force that every loss of energy was at once replenished, in fact increased. During those days, Corbera, I loved as much as a hundred of your Don Juans put together in their whole lives. And what love! Immune from convents or crimes, from Commander's rages and Leporello's trivialities, away from the pretensions of the heart, from the false sighs and sham deliquescence which inevitably blot your wretched kisses. A Leporello did, actually, disturb us that first day; it was the only time: towards ten o'clock I heard the peasant's heavy boots on the path leading to the sea. Scarcely had I time to draw a sheet over Lighea's unusual figure than he was already at the door: her head, neck, and arms which were uncovered, made Leporello think it was some ordinary little romp and this induced a sudden respect in him; he stayed for even less time than usual and as he went off winked his left eye and with thumb and forefinger of his right hand rolled and shut made a gesture of twiddling an imaginary moustache at the corner of his mouth; then he clambered off up the path.

'I have spoken of our spending twenty days together; but I would not like you to think that during those three weeks she and I lived as "man and wife", as the expression goes, sharing bed, food and occupations. Lighea was very often away; without any previous hint she would plunge into the sea and vanish, sometimes for many hours. When she returned, usually early in the morning, she would either meet me in the boat, or, if I was still indoors, slither on her back over the pebbles, half in and half out of the water, pushing herself along by the arms and calling for me to help her up the slope. "Sasà", she used to call me, as I had told her that was the diminutive of my name. In this action, hampered by that very part of her body which made her so agile in the sea, she had the pitiful aspect of a wounded animal, an aspect which the laughter in her eyes cancelled at once.

'She ate only what was alive: often I saw her emerge from the sea, her delicate torso gleaming in the sun, tearing in her teeth a silvery fish that was still quivering; the blood flowed in lines on her chin, and after a few bites the mangled cod-fish or dory would be flung over her shoulder and sink into the water, tainting it with red, while she let out childish cries as she cleaned her teeth with her tongue. Once I gave her some wine; she was incapable of drinking from a glass and I had to pour some into her minute and faintly greenish palm, from which she drank by lapping it up with her tongue like a dog, while surprise spread in her eyes at that unknown flavour. She said it was good, but always refused it afterwards. Occasionally she would come ashore with hands full of oysters and mussels, and while I laboured to open the shells with a knife she would crack them with a stone and suck in the palpitating mollusc together with shreds of shell which did not bother her.

'As I told you, Corbera, she was a beast but at the same instant also an Immortal, and it is a pity that no speech can express this synthesis continually, with such utter simplicity, as she expressed it in her own body. Not only did she show a joyousness and delicacy in the carnal act quite the opposite of dreary animal lust, but her talk had a potent immediacy which I have found since only in a few great poets. Not for nothing is she the daughter of Calliope: ignorant of all culture, unaware of all wisdom, contemptuous of any moral inhibitions, she belonged, even so, to the fountainhead of all culture, of all wisdom, of all ethics, and could express this primitive superiority of hers in terms of rugged beauty. "I am everything because I am simply the current of life, with its detail eliminated; I am immortal because in me every death meets, from that of the fish just now to that of Zeus, and conjoined in me they turn again into a life that is no longer individual and determined but Pan's and so free." Then she would say; "You are young and handsome; follow me now into the sea and you will avoid sorrow and old age; come to my dwelling beneath the high mountains of dark motionless waters where all is silence and quiet, so infused that who possesses it does not even notice it. I have loved you; and remember that when you are tired, when you can drag on no longer, you have only to lean over the sea and call me; I will always be there because I am everywhere, and your thirst for sleep will be assuaged."

'She told me about her existence beneath the sea, about bearded Tritons and translucent caverns, but she said that those too were unreal visions and that the truth lay much deeper, in the blind mute palace of formless waters, eternal, without a gleam, without a whisper.

'Once she told me she would be away a long while, till the evening of the next day. "I must go a long way off, to where I know I shall find a gift for you."

'She returned with a superb branch of lilac coral encrusted

with sea-shells and barnacles. For years I used to keep this in a drawer and kiss every night the places on where I remembered to have rested the fingers of the Indifferent, that is of the Beneficent One. Then one day Maria, a housekeeper of mine before Bettina, stole it to give a ponce. I found it later at a goldsmith's on the Ponte Vecchio, desecrated, cleaned and polished so that it was almost unrecognisable. I bought it back and that night flung it into the Arno: it had passed through too many hands.

'She also spoke of the considerable number of human lovers she had had during that millenial adolescence of hers; fishermen and sailors; Greek, Sicilian, Arab, Capresi; one or two shipwrecked mariners too, adrift on rotting rafts, to whom she had appeared for a second, in the lightning flashes of a storm, to change their death rattle into ecstasy. "All have followed up my invitation and come to me again, some at once, others after the passage of what for them was a long time. There was only one I never saw again; a fine big lad with very white skin and red hair with whom I coupled on a distant beach over where our sea joins the great Ocean; he smelt of something even stronger than that wine you gave me the other day. I think he never appeared not because I did not make him happy but because he was so drunk when we met that he did not understand a thing; probably I seemed like one of his usual fisher-girls."

'Those weeks of high summer sped by as fast as a single morning; when they were over I realised that actually I had lived for centuries. That lascivious girl, that cruel wild beast, had also been a Wise Mother who by her mere presence had uprooted faiths, dissipated metaphysics. With those fragile often blood-covered fingers she had shown me the way towards true eternal repose, and also towards an asceticism derived not from renunciation but from an incapacity to accept other inferior pleasures. Certainly I shall not be the second man to disobey her call, I will not refuse that kind of pagan Grace that has been conceded me.

'Due to its very violence, that summer was short. Just after the 20th of August the first timid clouds began collecting and a few isolated drops of rain fell, tepid as blood. The nights were an enfolding chain of slow, mute lightning flashes, following each other on the distant horizon like the cogitations of a god.

In the mornings the dove-coloured sea would moan like a turtle-dove with arcane restlessness, and in the evenings crinkle without any perceptible breeze in gradations of smoke-grey, steel-grey, pearl-grey, all gentle colours more tender than the former splendour. Faraway wisps of mist grazed the waters: maybe on the coasts of Greece it was already raining. Lighea's mood also changed in colour from splendour to tender grey. She was silent more often, spent hours stretched on a rock gazing at a horizon no longer motionless, seldom went away. "I want to stay on with you; if I leave the shore now my companions of the sea will keep me back. Do you hear them? They're calling me." Sometimes I did seem to hear a different, lower note amid the screech of sea-gulls, to glimpse unruly flashes from rock to rock. "They are sounding their shells, calling Lighea for the storm festival!"

'This hit us at dawn on the 26th. From the rock we saw the wind sweep closer, fling the distant waters into confusion, as near us swelled vast and leaden billows. Soon the broadside reached us, whistled in our ears, bent the dried-up rosemary bushes. The sea below us did not break; along came the first white-crowned wave. "Good-bye, Sasà. You won't forget!" The roller crashed on our rock, the Siren flung herself into iridescent surf; I did not see her drop; she seemed to dissolve into the spray.'

The senator left next morning; I went to the station to see him off. He was grumpy and acid as always, but just when the train began to move his fingers reached out of the little window and grazed my head.

Next day, at dawn, came a telephone-call to the newspaper from Genoa; during the night Senator La Ciura had fallen into the sea from the deck of the *Rex* as it was steaming towards Naples, and although life-boats had been launched at once the body had not been found.

A week later his will was opened; the money in the bank and his furniture went to Bettina; the library was left to the University of Catania; by a codicil of recent date I was left the Greek vase with the Siren figures and a large photograph of the Korè on the Acropolis.

Both objects I sent down to my home in Palermo. Then came the war, and while I was in Marmarica rationed to half a litre of water a day 'Liberators' destroyed my home; on my return I found the photograph had been cut into strips to serve as torches for night-looters; the bowl was smashed; in the largest fragment can be seen the feet of Ulysses tied to his ship's mast. I still keep it. The books were stored in cellars at the University, but as there is no money for shelves they are slowly rotting away.

The Blind Kittens

THE FIRST CHAPTER OF AN
UNCOMPLETED NOVEL

MARCH 1957

THE PLAN of the Ibba property, on a scale of 1 to 5,000, covered a strip of oiled paper six foot long and two and a half feet wide. Not that everything shown on the map belonged to the family: there was, first of all, to the south a narrow strip of sea belonging to no one on a coast line fringed with tunny fisheries; to the north were inhospitable mountains on which the Ibbas had never wanted to lay their hands; and, amid the mass of lemon-yellow indicating various family properties, were a number of fair-sized white blobs: lands that never came on the market because the owners were rich: lands that had been offered but refused because they were of too low a quality, lands desired but in the hands of people who were still, as it were, undercooked, not yet fit for mastication. There were also a very few pieces of land which had been yellow and turned white again when resold to acquire other, better land during bad years when ready money was scarce. In spite of these splodges (all marginal), the main mass of yellow was imposing: from an oval-shaped inner nucleus round Gibilmonte a wide claw extended eastwards, gradually narrowed, then broadening again pushed out two tentacles, one towards the sea, which it reached for a small stretch, the other northwards to the lower slopes of precipitous and sterile hills. Westwards expansion was even bigger: these were ex-church lands in which advance had been as fast as a knife through lard: the hamlets of S. Giacinto and S. Narciso had been occupied and overrun by the flying columns of the Expropriation Acts; a defensive line on the River Favarotta had just collapsed after holding out a long time; and that day, the 14th of September 1901, a bridge-head had been established on the far side of the river by the purchase of Pispisa, a small but succulent estate on the right bank.

The newly bought property had not yet been coloured in yellow on the plan, but Chinese ink and a thin brush were already waiting on a desk for the hand of Calcedonio, the only person in the house who knew how to make proper use of them. Don Batassano Ibba himself, head of the family and near-baron, had tried his hand ten years before when Scíddico had been expropriated, but with distressing results: a yellow tide had spread over the whole map and a heap of money had to be spent on having a new one done. The little bottle of ink, though, was still the same. So this time Don Batassano did not risk trying his hand and merely stared with his brazen peasant's eyes at the place to be coloured, thinking that the Ibba lands would show up now even on a map of all Sicily, flea size in the vastness of the island, of course, but still clearly visible.

Don Batassano was satisfied but also irritated, two states of mind often co-existing in him. That man Ferrara, the Prince of Salina's agent who had arrived this morning to arrange the deed of sale, had quibbled right up to the very moment of signature and even after! And he'd wanted the money paid in eighty of the Bank of Sicily's big pink notes, instead of the letters of credit prepared for him; he, Don Batassano, had had to climb up stairs and draw the cash from a secret drawer in his own desk, a most risky operation because Mariannina and Totò might be around at that hour. True, the agent had let himself be bamboozled about a tithe of eighty lire a year to the Church Fund, for which he had agreed to take off a thousand six hundred lire from the capital value, while Don Batassano (and the notary too) knew that it had already been compounded nine years before by another of the Salina's agents. This had no effect though; any opposition, however slight, to his own will, particularly in regard to money, exasperated him; 'They're forced to sell with the water at their chins, but still fuss about the difference between banknotes and letters of credit!'

It was only four o'clock and there were five hours to go before supper. Don Batassano opened the window on to a narrow yard. The sultry September air, cooked, recooked, resteeped, infused the darkened room. Down below an old man with heavy mous-taches was spreading bird-lime on bamboo rods; he was prepar-ing his young master's pastime. 'Giacomino, saddle the horses, mine and yours. I'm coming down.'

He wanted to go and see the damage to a water trough at Scíddico: some urchins had smashed one side of a basin, so he had been told that morning; the leak had been stopped temporarily with rubble and that mixture of mud and straw always to be found beside horse-troughs; but Tano, the tenant at Scíddico, had asked for proper repairs at once. More bother, more expense; and if he did not go and see in person the workmen would put in an exorbitant bill. He assured himself that his holster with its heavy Smith & Wesson was hanging from his belt (he was so used to having it always on him that he no longer noticed it), and went down some slate steps into the yard. The keeper was just saddling the horses; he mounted his from three brick steps put against a wall for that purpose, took a switch held out by a boy, waited until Giacomino (without help from his master's mounting steps) was in the saddle. The keeper's son flung open fortified gates, summer afternoon light flooded the yard, and Don Batassano Ibba issued with his bodyguard into the main street of Gibilmonte.

The two rode along almost side by side, Giacomino's horse only half a head behind his master's: the keeper's 'two-shooters' exhibited their iron butts, their polished barrels to right and left of the saddle. The animals' hooves clattered irregularly over the cobbles of narrow alleys. Women sitting weaving in front of their doors gave no greeting. 'Life!' cried Giacomino every now and again as some small completely naked urchin was about to roll between the horse' hooves; dangling on a chair, his head against a wall of the church, the archpriest pretended to be asleep: anyway the living was not in the gift of this rich Ibba here but of the poor absentee Santapau. Only the sergeant of Carabinieri, in shirt-sleeves at a balcony of the barracks, leant over with a greeting. They left the village, climbed the track leading to the fork. A great deal of water had been lost during the night, and it had formed a big stagnant pond all around: mixed with mud, chaff, manure, cows' urine, it exhaled a sharp stink of ammonia. But the temporary repairs had done their job; water was no longer flowing between cracks in the stone basin, only trickling, and the thin stream issuing in spurts from a rusty tube was enough to make up the loss. Don Batassano was so pleased at what had been done costing nothing that he overlooked the repair's temporary nature. 'What nonsense Tano

talked! The basin's in fine condition! It doesn't need a thing
done to it. But tell the fool he must pull himself together and
take care not to let my property be damaged by the first little
brute who comes along. Tell 'im to find their fathers and have
'em talk to you if he doesn't do so himself.'

On the way back a frightened rabbit crossed the track, Don
Batassano's horse shied, kicked out, and the magnate, who had
a fine little English saddle but insisted on twisted ropes instead
of stirrups, ended on the ground. He was not hurt and Giacomino, well used to this situation, took the mare by the bridle and
held it firm; from the ground Don Batassano whipped merci-
lessly up at the nose, eyes, flanks of the animal, which was taken
by a continuous quiver and beginning to foam. A kick in its belly
ended the pedagogic operation, Don Batassano remounted, and
the pair returned home just as it was growing dark.

Meanwhile Ferrara, unaware that the master of the house was
out, had gone into the study and, finding it empty, sat down a
moment to wait. The room contained a gun-rack with two
rifles, a shelf with a few boxes ('Taxes', 'Title deeds', 'Cautions',
'Mortgages', said the labels stuck on brown cardboard); on the
desk was the deed-of-sale, signed two hours before; behind, on
the wall, that map.

The accountant got up to look closer: from his professional
knowledge, from the innumerable indiscretions to which he had
listened, he well knew how that vast property had been put
together: it had been an epopee of cunning and perfidy, of ruth-
lessness and defiance of law, of luck too and of daring. Ferrara
thought how interesting it would be to see a map in different
colours showing successive acquisitions, as school text-books do
the expansion of the House of Savoy. Here at Gibilmonte was
the embryo: six measures of corn, half a hectare of vines and a
three-roomed hut, all that had been inherited by Don Batassano's father, Gaspare, analphabetic of genius. In early youth
he had seduced the deaf-and-dumb daughter of a smallholder
scarcely less poor than himself, and doubled his holding with
the dowry obtained by compulsory marriage. His wife, handicapped as she was, entered into her husband's game completely:

by grinding thrift the couple accumulated a hoard which though tiny was precious in a place like Sicily, where hoarding at that period, as in the city-states of antiquity, was based exclusively on usury.

Shrewd loans had been granted, loans of a particular kind which are made to people with property but insufficient income to pay interest. The lowing of Marta, Gaspare's wife, going round the village at dusk to exact her weekly dues became proverbial. 'When Marta's agrunting, homes go atumbling.' In ten years of gesticulating visits, in ten years of extorting crops from the Marchese Santapau whose mezzadro, or share-cropper, Gaspare was, in ten years of cautiously moved boundaries, in ten years of contented starvation, the couple's property had multiplied fivefold: he was only twenty-eight, the present Don Batassano seven. There had been a rough patch when the Bourbon legal authorities took it into their heads to inquire about one of the many corpses found out in the country: Gaspare had to keep away from Gibilmonte, and his wife gave out that he was staying with a cousin at Adernò to learn about mulberry growing; in reality every single night from a nearby hill the doting Gaspare had watched smoke rising from the kitchen of his happy little home. Then came the Thousand, everything was upside down, inconvenient papers vanished from legal offices, and Gaspare Ibba returned home officially.

Everything was better than before. It was then that Gaspare thought up a move which seemed mad, like every stroke of genius; just as Napoleon at Austerlitz dared to divest his centre in order to trap the Austro-Russian boobies between very strong flanks, so Gaspare mortgaged all his hard-fought land up to the hilt, and with the few thousand lire raised by this operation made a loan without interest to the Marchese Santapau, who was in difficulties due to donations to the Bourbon cause. The result was: two years later the Santapau lost their estate of Balate,[1] which they had anyway never seen and from its name took to be sterile, all mortgages were off the Ibba property, Gaspare had become 'Don Gaspare' and goatsmeat was eaten at his home on

1 Sicilian-Calabrian word, from Arabic, meaning 'paving-slab'. (Trs.)

Saturdays and Sundays. On reaching the goal of the first hundred thousand lire all went with the precision of a mechanical instrument; ecclesiastical properties were acquired for a tenth of their value by paying the first two instalments of their wretched assessment; their buildings, the springs nearby, the rights-of-way enclosed, made it much easier to buy up surrounding lay properties that had lost value; the large incomes accruing went to the purchase or expropriation of other more distant land.

So when Don Gaspare died still young his property was already of notable size; but, like the Prussian territories in the middle of the eighteenth century, it consisted of large islands separated by the properties of others. To the son Batassano, as to Frederick the Second, fell the task and the glory, first of unifying all in one single block, then of moving the boundaries of the block itself towards more distant areas. Vineyards, olive and almond-groves, pastures, ground-rents, sowing-land particularly, were annexed and digested, the income flowing into the shabby office at Gibilmonte where they stayed for a very short time and whence they soon issued, almost intact, to be transformed back into more land. A wind of uninterrupted good fortune swelled the sails of the Ibba galleon: the name began to be pronounced with reverence throughout the whole poverty-stricken triangle of the island. Don Batassano meanwhile had married at the age of thirty, and not a handicapped creature like his venerated mother but a buxom girl of eighteen called Laura, daughter of the Gibilmonte notary; as dowry she brought her own health, a considerable sum in ready cash, her father's valuable experience with the Curia, and an utter submission once her own considerable sexual needs were satisfied. Living proof of this submission of hers was eight children; rough sunless happiness reigned in the Ibba household.

The accountant Ferrara was a person of sensitive feelings, a human species very rare in Sicily. His father had been an employee of the Salina administration in the stormy days of old Prince Fabrizio; and he himself, raised in the padded atmosphere of that household, had been accustomed to desiring a life commonplace indeed, but calm; his own little sliver of princely cheese to nibble was enough for him. Those two big square metres of oiled paper evoked harsh and stubborn struggles within his soul, more a rodent's than a carnivore's. An impression came to him that he was re-reading instalments of La Cecilia's *History of the Bourbons of Naples* which his father, an advanced liberal, used to buy him every Saturday. Here at Gibilmonte, of course, were none of the imaginary orgies of Caserta described in that tract: here all was ruggedly, positively, puritanically evil. He took fright and left the room.

That evening at supper the whole family was present except for the eldest son Gaspare, who was in Palermo with the excuse of preparing to retake his school-leaving exams (he was already twenty). The meal was served with rustic simplicity; all the cutlery, heavy and rich, was heaped in the middle of the table and everyone fished about in the pile according to need; the manservant Totò and the maidservant Mariannina insisted on serving from the right. Signora Laura was a picture of health in supreme flowering, that is in major rotundity; her well-shaped chin, her pretty nose, her eyes expert in connubial delights, vanished into an exuberance of still fresh, firm and appetising fat; the enormous bulk of her body was covered in black silk, emblem of mourning perpetually renewed. Her sons Melchiorre, Pietro and Ignazio, her daughters Marta, Franceschina, Assunta and Paolina, showed alternating similarities, peculiar combinations of the rapacious features of their father and the clement ones of their mother. None, male or female, had any taste whatsoever in dress: the girls were in printed cretonnes (grey on white), the boys in sailor suits, even the eldest among those present, Melchiorre, whose budding seventeen-year-old moustache gave him an odd air of some member of a Royal suite. The conversation, or rather the dialogue, between Don Batassano and Ferrara ranged exclusively around two subjects: the price of land in the neighbourhood of Palermo compared to that in the neighbourhood of Gibilmonte, and gossip about aristocratic Palermo society. Don Batassano considered all those nobles as 'starving', even those who after all, if only in collections of antiques apart from incomes, had fortunes equal to his own. Always shut away in his own parts, with rare trips to the local town and very rare journeys to Palermo in order to 'follow' law-cases in the Courts, he did not know even one of these nobles personally, and had created an abstract and monotonic image of them, like that of the public for Harlequin or Captain Fracassa. Prince A. was a spendthrift, Prince B. a womaniser, Duke C. violent, Baron D. a gambler, Don Giuseppe E. a bully, Marchese F. 'aesthetic' (he meant an 'aesthete', a euphemism in its turn for something worse) and so on; each was a contemptible figure cut in cardboard. These opinions of Don Batassano's had a formidable propensity to error, and it might be said that there was no epithet which was not coupled erroneously to a name, and certainly no defect which was not fabulously exaggerated, while the real defects of these persons remained unknown to him: obviously his mind worked in abstractions and took pleasure in contrasting the purity of the Ibbas with the corrupt background of the old nobility.

Ferrara knew rather more about these things, though with lacunae too, so that when he tried to contradict the more fantastic assertions he ran out of arguments; also his words aroused such moralistic indignation in Don Batassano that he soon fell silent. But anyway they had now reached the end of the meal.

This, Ferrara considered, had been excellent; Donna Laura did not abandon herself to Pindaric flights in matters of food: she had Sicilian dishes served, as numerous and highly flavoured as possible and so murderous. Macaroni literally swam in oil of their own sauce and were buried under avalanches of *cacciácavallo* cheese, meat was stuffed with incendiary salami, trifle or '*zuppa in fretta*' contained triple the cochineal, sugar and candied fruit prescribed. But to Ferrara all that, as has been said, seemed exquisite and the apex of a really good table; at his rare luncheons in the Salina household he had always been disappointed by the insipidity of the food. Next day, though, on return to Palermo, after handing over to Prince Fabrizietto the 78,400 lire, he described the meal offered him and as he knew the prince's predilection for '*coulis de volaille*' at the Pré-Catalan and '*timbales d' écrevisses*' at Prunier's, he made sound horrible what he had in fact thought excellent. Thus he gave much pleasure to Salina who, during his 'little game of poker' at the club later on, described every detail to his friends, ever avid for news of the legendary Ibbas; and all laughed till a moment when Peppino San Carlo announced impassively that he had a full-house of queens.

As has been said, there was acute curiosity about the Ibba family in the noble circles of Palermo. Curiosity is, after all, the mother of fables, and from it during those years were born hundreds of fantasies about that sudden fortune. These bore witness not only to the frothy and infantile imaginations of the upper classes, but also to an unconscious unease at seeing that a great fortune could be built up exclusively in land at the beginning of the twentieth century, this being a form of wealth which, in the bitter experience of each of those gentlemen, was demolition material unsuited to the construction of rich buildings. Those same landed proprietors felt that this modern reincarnation, in the Ibbas, of the vast grain-bearing estates of the Chiaramonte and the Ventimiglia families of past centuries was irrational and dangerous for themselves, so they were all secretly against it; and that not only because this imposing edifice was erected largely from material which had once belonged to themselves, but because they took it as a sign of the permanent anachronism which is the brake on the wheels of the Sicilian cart, an anachronism realised by many but which no one, in fact, can evade or avoid collaborating with.

It should be repeated that this unease remained latent in their collective unconscious: it flowered only in the guise of jests and funny stories, as might be expected of a class with a low consumption of general ideas. A first and most elementary form of these was an exaggeration in figures, which with us are always elastic. Batassano Ibba's fortune, though easy to check, was valued at dozens of million lire; one bold spirit even dared once to speak of 'nearly a billion', but the effect was as if he had remained silent, for this sum, to-day so banal, was in such rare use in 1901 that nearly everyone was ignorant of its true meaning, and in those days of gold lire the phrase 'a billion lire' meant really nothing at all. Analogous fantasies were woven about the origins of this fortune: the humbleness of Don Batassano's origins were difficult to exaggerate (old Corrado Finale, whose mother was a Santapau, had hinted without saying so openly that Don Batassano was the son of a brother-in-law of his who had been in residence for some time at Gibilmonte; but the story found little credit because Finale was known to have a habit of attributing to himself or to his relatives the clandestine parentage of any celebrity mentioned, whether victorious general or acclaimed prima donna); that modest corpse, though, which had been such a bother to Don Gaspare, was multiplied tenfold, a hundredfold, and every 'elimination' that had taken place in Sicily over the last thirty years (and there had been quite a number) was put down to the Ibbas, who were, after all, legally unimpeachable. This, surprising though it may seem, was the legend's most benevolent part because deeds of violence when unpunished were at that time a motive for esteem, the halo of Sicilian saints being blood-red.

To these fantasies grown from seed were added others grafted; for instance out came, refurbished, a tale told a hundred years before about Testasecca, who caused a little channel to be scooped, collected his hundreds of cows and thousands of sheep on a hillock above, and had them milked all at the same moment, so presenting King Ferdinand IV with the sight of a small stream of milk flowing warm and frothing at his feet. This fable, which is not without a certain pastoral poetry that should have suggested its origin to be in Theocritus, was now adapted to Don Batassano by the simple substitution of King Umberto I of Italy for King Ferdinand of the Two Sicilies; and though it was quite easy to prove that the former sovereign had never set foot on any Ibba land this persisted, unrefuted.

It was for these reasons of rancour mingled with fear that, when the 'little game of poker' was over, conversation again fell on the subject of the Ibbas. The dozen members present had settled down on the terrace of the club, which overlooked a placid courtyard and was shaded by a tall tree raining petals of lilac down on those gentlemen, most of whom were old. Footmen in red and blue brought round ices and cool soft drinks. From the depths of a wicker armchair came the ever choleric tones of Santa Giulia. 'Well, could someone please tell me how much land these blessed Ibbas really do own?'

'Someone could, and will. Fourteen thousand three hundred and twenty-five hectares,' replied San Carlo coldly.

'Is that all? I thought more.'

'Fourteen thousand, balls! People who have been there say they can't be less than twenty thousand hectares, sure as death and taxes; and all first-class crop-bearing land.'

General Làscari, who seemed immersed in reading *La Tribuna*, brusquely lowered the newspaper and showed his liverish visage embroidered with yellow lines in which very white eyeballs showed up hard and rather sinister, like the eyes of some Greek bronzes. 'Twenty-eight thousand hectares they are, neither less nor more; I was told by my nephew who is a cousin of the local Prefect's wife. That's it, once and for all; there's no need to discuss the matter any longer.'

Pippo Follonica, a visiting guest from Rome, burst out laughing. 'But if you're all so interested why not send someone down to the Land Registry? It's easy to know the truth, this truth anyway.'

This rational suggestion received a cold reception. Follonica did not understand the passionate, non-statistical nature of the discussion; these gentlemen were tossing about among themselves envies, rancours and anxieties, all emotions which no Land Registry certificates could assuage.

The general grew furious. 'When I tell you something there's no need for any registry whatsoever.' Then politeness towards a guest softened him. 'My dear prince, you don't know what our Land Registry office is like! Transfers of property are never recorded and people still figure as owners who've sold up long ago and are now in the Poor House.'

Faced with so detailed a denial, Follonica changed tactics. 'Let's admit that the number of hectares remains unknown; what must be known is the value of property in the hands of this boor who excites you all so much!'

'Perfectly well known; eight million exactly.'

'Balls!' That was the inevitable opening to any phrase from Santa Giulia. 'Balls! Not a cent less than twelve!'

'What a world you live in! You don't know anything! There's twenty-five million in land alone. Then there are ground-rents, capital on loan and not yet transformed into property, the value of cattle. Another five million at least.' The general had put down his newspaper and was getting worked up. His peremptory manner had for years irritated the entire club, each member of which wished to be the only one making incontrovertible affirmations; so that a coalition of reawakened antipathies at once formed against his opinion, and without any reference to major or minor truths the estimate of the Ibba property slumped. 'That's all poetic nonsense; about money and sanctity, believe half a half, as the proverb goes. If Batassano Ibba has ten million all told that's more than enough.' The figure had been distilled from nothing at all, that is from polemical necessity; but when spoken, as it responded to everyone's wishes, it calmed down all except the general, who went on gesticulating from deep in his armchair, impotent against his nine adversaries.

A footman entered carrying a long wooden pole at the end of which was a wick dipped in spirit. The gentle light of dusk changed to the harsh glare of a gas chandelier.

The guest from Rome was much amused: it was his first visit to Sicily, and during the five days of his stay in Palermo he had been invited to a number of houses and had begun to change his opinions about what he had presumed to be the provincialism of Palermo; dinners had been well-served, drawing-rooms splendid, ladies graceful. But now this impassioned discussion about the fortune of an individual whom none of the contestants knew or wanted to know, these patent exaggerations, this convulsive gesticulating about nothing, made him reverse, reminded him a little too closely of conversations heard at Fondi or Palestrina when he had to go out there to see about his estates, or maybe even at the chemist Bésuquet's of which he had preserved a happy memory since his reading of *Tartarin*:[1] and he began laying in a store of tales to regale friends on his return to

[1] *Tartarin de Tarascon* by Alphonse Daudet.

Rome a week later. But he was wrong; too much a man of fashion ever to probe much deeper than the obvious, what appeared to him as a humorous exhibition of provincialism was anything but comic: this was the tragic jerking of a class which was watching the end of its own land-owning supremacy, that is, of its own reason for existence and its own social continuity, and in these wilful exaggerations and artificial diminutions sought outlets for its anger, relief or its fear.

The truth being impossible to establish, the conversation deviated: it was still investigating Batassano Ibba's private affairs but now turned to consider his personal life.

'He lives like a monk; gets up at four in the morning; goes out into the market-place to engage day-labourers, is busy with estate-management the whole day long, eats nothing but pasta and vegetables in oil, and is in bed by eight.'

Salina protested, 'A monk with a wife and eight children, let's remember. One of my employees spent forty-eight hours at his house: it's ugly but it's big and comfortable, decent enough; the wife seems to have been pretty, the children well-dressed; in fact one of them is here in Palermo to study; and the food at his table is heavy but plentiful, as I've already told you.'

The general stuck to his guns: 'You, Salina, believe everything you're told, or rather, they wanted to throw dust in the eyes of your man, who must be an idiot. Bread, cheese and oil-lamps, that's Ibba's daily routine, his real life; when someone comes from Palermo he obviously tries to put up a show, to dazzle us so he deludes himself.'

Santa Giulia, under the impetus of the news he wanted to communicate, was jumping about in his armchair; his well-shod feet banged the floor, his hands trembled, and the ash of his cigarette snowed all over his suit. 'Balls, gentlemen! Gentlemen, balls! You're utterly mistaken. I'm the only one who really knows about this: the wife of one of my keepers comes from Torrebella a few steps from Gibilmonte; every now and again she goes to see her sister who is married there and has told her everything. One can't be more certain than that, I think.' He sought for a confirmation of his own certainty in everyone's eyes and, as all were amused, easily found it. Although there was no bashful ear to be respected he lowered his voice: without this melodramatic preamble the effect of his revelations would never be the same.

'Three miles from Gibilmonte, Don Batassano has had a small house built; the most luxurious little place imaginable, furnished by Salci and all that.' Reminiscences of reading Catulle Mendès, nostalgic memories of Parisian brothels, yearnings unrealised though long nursed, stirred his imagination. 'He had Roche-grosse come from Paris to fresco all the rooms: the great painter was three months at Gibilmonte and demanded a hundred thou-sand lire a month.' (Rochegrosse had in fact been in Sicily two years before: he had remained a week with his wife and three children, and left again after quietly visiting the Capella Palatina, Segesta, and the Latomie of Syracuse.) 'It cost a fortune! But what frescoes he did! Enough to bring a dead man to life! Naked women, quite naked, dancing, drinking and coupling with men and with each other in every position, in every conceivable manner. Masterpieces! An encyclopaedia, I tell you, an encyclo-paedia of pleasures! Just let a Parisian loose with a hundred thousand lire a month! There Ibba receives women by the dozen; Italians, French, German, Spanish. La Otero was there too, I know that for a fact. That fellow Batassano has made his *Parc aux Cerfs* there, like Louis the Fifteenth.'

This time Santa Giulia really had caused a sensation: everyone sat listening to him open-mouthed. Not that he was believed, but they found this fantasy a highly poetic one, and each longed to have Ibba's millions so that others could invent similar splen-did nonsense about himself. The first to shake off the spell was the general: 'And how d'you come to know that? Have you been into the house yourself, pray? As odalisque or eunuch?' They laughed, Santa Giulia laughed too. 'I told you; the wife of my keeper Antonio has seen those paintings.'

'Fine! Then you've a keeper who's a cuckold.'

'Cuckold, balls! She went there to take some sheets which she'd washed. They didn't let her in but a window was open and she saw it all.'

The castle of lies was obviously of extreme fragility; but it was of such beauty, with its female thighs and nameless obscenities, its famous painters and hundred thousand lire notes, that no one had any desire to give it a puff and bring it down.

Salina pulled out his watch. 'Mamma mia! Eight o'clock already! I must go home and dress; there's *Traviata* to-night at the Politeama, and Bellincioni's *Amami Alfredo* is not to be missed. See you in the club-box!'

ABOUT THE INTRODUCER

DAVID GILMOUR has written widely on Sicily and Spain and is the author of seven books, including the award-winning biographies, *Curzon* and *The Last Leopard: A Life of Giuseppe di Lampedusa*.

ABOUT THE TRANSLATOR

The late ARCHIBALD COLQUHOUN was one of the finest translators of Italian literature. His work included the English language edition of *The Viceroys* by Federico De Roberto.

This book is set in BEMBO which was cut
by the punch-cutter Francesco Griffo
for the Venetian printer-publisher
Aldus Manutius in early 1495
and first used in a pamphlet
by a young scholar
named Pietro
Bembo.